DIFFICULTIES
WITH GIRLS

KINGSLEY AMIS

DIFFICULTIES
WITH GIRLS

HUTCHINSON
LONDON   MELBOURNE   AUCKLAND   JOHANNESBURG

© Kingsley Amis 1988

All rights reserved

This edition first published in Great Britain in
1988 by Hutchinson, an imprint of Century Hutchinson
Ltd, Brookmount House, 62–65 Chandos Place, London
WC2N 4NW

Century Hutchinson Australia Pty Ltd
PO Box 496, 16–22 Church Street, Hawthorn,
Victoria 3122, Australia

Century Hutchinson New Zealand Limited
PO Box 40–086, Glenfield, Auckland 10, New Zealand

Century Hutchinson South Africa (Pty) Ltd
PO Box 337, Berglvei, 2012 South Africa

British Library in Cataloguing in Publication Data

Amis, Kingsley, *1922–*
    Difficulties with girls.
    I. Title
    823'.914[F]

ISBN 0–09–173505–X

Set in Linotron Sabon by
Input Typesetting Ltd, London SW19 8DR

Printed and bound in Great Britain by
Mackays of Chatham PLC, Chatham, Kent

To Jessica

One

'Right, on your way, brother. Out. I'm not having you in my house. Go on, hop it.'

'What for? What do you mean? I haven't done anything.'

'I don't know what you've done, darling, and cross my heart I don't want to know. And don't let me guess. Go on. There's nothing says I got to have one of you in here, okay? Not yet there isn't. Any moment now but not yet. So out.'

The last half of this was said to a retreating back. The landlord of the Princess Beatrice, London SE1, turned to Patrick Standish and went on in a tone not much friendlier than before,

'It's getting to be a full-time job, you know, keeping them out of here. They think they can go anywhere they like these days, as if they were entitled to under the law. No good will come. I suppose we ought to think ourselves lucky he didn't go for his lipstick.'

Patrick, standing up at the bar with his midday White Shield, thought among other things that the young man had shown a lot of restraint whatever he was. 'He didn't look all that peculiar to me. These days everybody has their hair in a bloody – '

The landlord, who had pushed up his mouth, closed his eyes and started shaking his head at Patrick's first words, let him go no further. 'It's not the look, my friend. It's the whole je ne sais quoi. You develop a feel for it this side of the counter in sheer self-preservation. No, it's not the look.' He paused and moved his eyes sideways. 'Of course, I don't know, perhaps you, er . . .'

At this interesting juncture he moved away to serve a little old woman hung with crocheted shawls and long ropes of jewellery. Patrick had begun to take to him for his air of total contempt for the world, not only as it was and was becoming

1

but as it had no doubt always been. Ignoring fashion, he had a totally naked skull, its presumably natural baldness filled out by close shaving round the edges. It was rather small in proportion to his broad shoulders and massive arms. Extravagant blue tattoos with some minor touches of pink adorned the lower parts of those arms, made visible by rolled-up sleeves. Over his very white shirt he wore a waistcoat-shaped woollen garment of a tan-and-yellow pattern too awful for the thing not to have been specially knitted by somebody close to him, assuming there to be any such person. He had been heard to answer to the name of Cyril.

Patrick considered he had done well to find the Princess Beatrice so soon after arriving in the district, or rather to have had it there to find: not too large, not too crowded even at night, not noisy but not quiet, bar-billiard table. The provision for darts, cribbage and shove-ha'penny he saw as a token of virtue in the abstract rather than as for his actual use. His eye was caught now by the half-dozen little rectangles of engraved glass attached to the woodwork above the counter.

'Snob screens,' Cyril seemed to say to him.

'What?'

'In days gone by, if you didn't fancy being observed in your carousals by the tout le monde, you just swivelled the . . . ' – he turned the pane nearest Patrick outwards on its pivot – 'and lo and behold you were shielded from their vulgar gaze. Like the partitions there.' These were of some sort of oak, head-high, dividing the drinking-space into three. 'Lot of tommy-rot really.'

'Oh, I don't know.'

'No, you don't, because you haven't got to keep it all clean, have you? Our beer-pipes here, when I took over in '60 I had to shut for three days to wash the goo out. You'd think the brewers could spare a copper to shake the place up.'

Patrick had soon lost interest in this. His glance shifted to the large glass case mounted high on the wall at his side and displaying assorted but uniformly horrible-looking corks and bottle-stoppers fancifully worked. 'Isn't that asking for trouble a bit? I'm sure this is a very nice neighbourhood but it's not exactly Berkeley Square. The sort of chap who enjoys a – '

'Oh, you mean somebody driven to express a well-developed sense of fun. Believe me I'd like nothing better.' Cyril suddenly

2

reached below the counter and laid on it a substantial iron tool that tapered to a point at one end. 'What you see before you is a marlinspike, which is c'est-à-dire an implement useful for separating strands of rope and also for cooling the ardour of those who get carried away by high spirits. Yeah.' He looked affectionately at the spike for a moment before replacing it. 'Well, I'd better be . . .'

He had started to move when he turned his gaze over Patrick's shoulder towards the door. 'Whaw!' he growled, not very quietly. 'God bless your dear old rosy-cheeked mother, sweetheart. Fooh! I could – '

'Before you go any further,' said Patrick, 'that's my wife that's just come in.'

Cyril did a grin that showed no amusement. '*Your . . . wife?*' he asked, putting equal stress on both words.

This brought Patrick definite annoyance. He knew he was quite personable enough and impressive enough and vigorous-and-all-that enough to be married to someone who looked like Jenny, not out of conceit or wishful thinking but as a simple deduction from years of carefully noted experience. And not that much older and hardly going bald at all and anyway only at the temples. And he considered he needed no reminding how lucky he was to have her even so.

Jenny came up and she and Patrick kissed as they always did on meeting. For this lunch today she wore her best suit of cream linen and a navy blouse with the row of cream-coloured pretend-bone beads. She was twenty-eight that year and as slim as ever, with very dark colouring that she was sure had a bearing on the way strangers quite often told her they thought she was French, or sometimes Italian or Spanish, but usually French if it was anything. Patrick himself had made that mistake when he first saw her, or had given that impression.

Evidently the man behind the bar had done the same. At any rate he leaned over it and said, 'Comment allez-vous, mademoiselle – oops, excusez-moi, madame.' He said it without trying to sound French at all, but his manner was genial in the extreme and a bit polite-lecherous too.

'I'm very well, thank you very much,' said Jenny, staring back at him and intensifying her regional accent.

Turning sideways behind his bar to give himself more room, the man swept off an imaginary hat and made her a great bow.

3

'And what is madame's pleasure?' He had rather heavy eyelids and he lowered them in a way that harped on the lecherous end of polite-lecherous.

'I'd like a small medium sherry, please.' This time the important thing was to get it said clearly and quickly. To Jenny the pub was still men's territory, and to shilly-shally over choosing what drink to have in one would have been inconsiderate as well as awkward.

The man did a speedier bow and went off.

'He can't be like that all the time,' said Jenny.

'He's a cockney, you see,' said Patrick. 'Or would claim to be if challenged. He thinks that sort of thing's expected of him. He also thinks he's being funny. I mean amusing. At least I hope to God that's what he thinks he's being.'

'Probably the nudge-nudge stuff is him being amusing too. Or he thinks it's expected of him.'

'Yeah. No, of course not. I mean only partly. Anyway, you know where you are with a bastard like that.'

'Oh, good. A very funny chap came to the door just as I was leaving.'

'Funnier than this chap?'

'No, this was a *very* funny chap. You know, peculiar. Not a nasty piece of work but peculiar.'

Patrick signalled to Cyril for another White Shield. 'Peculiar,' he said, remembering his own use of the word a couple of minutes before. 'What, you mean . . . one of them?'

'What? Oh, you mean a . . . I honestly don't know, I didn't think of it then. He could have been, I imagine. He certainly had a very peculiar manner.'

'What did he want?'

'Well, that was just it, he didn't seem at all clear what he wanted. He said he'd like to ask me a few things if I didn't mind, he was polite enough, because he's just moving into the end flat, the one at the far end. So I asked him in, and then he couldn't seem to think of anything he wanted to know, and he seemed . . .'

Jenny could not express for the moment what else her visitor had seemed. Patrick said, 'Did he mention a wife?'

'No. No, nothing about that, I'd have remembered. Nor a girl-friend.'

'Oh.' There was an odd little silence. 'Did he give his name?'

4

'Yes, but I forgot it straight away, although I remember thinking it couldn't be right. Anyway he said he'd be back. I thought he might be a bit off his head at one point but then he got all right again.'

'Never mind, perhaps he'll take a turn for the worse next time.'

When Cyril brought the drinks he asked Jenny if she had come to live round there, and was told more or less willingly about the flat (the maisonette, actually, said Patrick) in that new block of five over those shops in Lower Ground next to that pretty little square of garden on the corner, and told her in return that the missis was out shopping at the moment but would be only too delighted to give her the benefit of her local knowledge any time, but meanwhile the dry cleaners in the block had tried to get away with losing his topcoat for him last winter, the seven or eight minutes on the 159 down to the old-style butcher's in Kennington Lane was very much vaut le voyage, and the Irish shop two along from the garage stayed open all Sunday for if she ran out of baked beans or fags. In between he asked if she had any children and was told no, or according to Patrick not yet. All this and much more was exchanged while Cyril unremittingly made, handed out and dealt with the money for four rounds of drinks, including three Pimm's complete with slices of cucumber-peel, cocktail cherry and sprig of borage, and served three tasty-looking cold snacks backed up with sauce and pickle. He operated the till without looking at where his fingers were going, like a concert pianist.

When this part was over, Cyril's manner changed. He stared at Patrick and took his time about pointing a finger at him and wagging it rather harrowingly from the knuckle. His words, when they came, seemed inevitable, preordained. 'Right . . . now don't tell me . . . let me guess.'

Patrick hated letting anybody do that where he was concerned, which he was obviously going to be, but he could think of no way of preventing it this time without courting Cyril's marlinspike, so he frowned and muttered to himself as if he was adding up expenses in his head.

After rotating his finger for a space, still from the knuckle, and keeping the opposite eye closed, Cyril eventually said, 'Erm . . . advertising!'

'What about it?' said Patrick, though he knew, and wondered

5

what occupation he might reasonably have hoped his face fitted: test pilot, brain surgeon, tennis seed, major poet – no perhaps not that one. But bugger it anyway.

'All right . . . Public relations.'

'I think if you don't mind – '

'Television then,' said Cyril in a spirit of good-humoured indulgence. 'On the production side. Oh, okay, I give up.'

But he still waited to hear. With Jenny there Patrick had to say, 'Actually I'm in publishing,' and say it sportingly too.

'Publishing.' There was another pause. 'That's books, is it? Or not?'

'It's books. And a quarterly magazine. And now you mustn't let us keep you from your regulars.'

'Thank you,' said Jenny.

'Il n'a pas de quoi, chérie.'

'And don't tell me he was just trying to be pleasant,' said Patrick when he and she had sat down in the little alcove under the window.

'Well, making conversation. Passing the time of day.'

'If you're right I must remember not to get into a serious discussion with him.'

'You said you knew where you were with a bastard like that. And why shouldn't he be interested in what you do for a living?'

'I wouldn't have minded that, but it wasn't that. What he was interested in was joshing me along.'

'What's joshing you along?'

'Pissing on me so I couldn't hit back.'

'Oh, Patrick, people aren't thinking about you the whole time. And what would he want to piss on you for?'

'I don't know. Well, he . . . Come on, do you think I look like somebody in advertising?'

'I hadn't really thought about it. Now you come to mention it I suppose I do, quite. I mean you do. Dynamic. Thrusting. You know, all that. He was paying you a compliment, or trying to.'

'You cheeky little bag. And was he buggery trying to pay me a compliment. He was buttering you up and being charming to you and pissing on me at the same time. Thinking he was being charming. Jesus, perhaps he really was. I've come across that technique before.'

'And used it too, I shouldn't wonder.'

6

Patrick looked amused and irritated in exactly equal parts and said nothing. She saw he had arranged his hair in a slightly new way to disguise his bits of baldness. Given the right approach she was sure she could have convinced him that things like that made no difference to her without at the same time leading him to believe she took no notice of how he looked. It was difficult. She no longer went round saying to herself he was the best-looking man she had ever met, but she could not remember having stopped thinking so. By now it was simply impossible to judge. Rather like the way she went on thinking he was the most wonderful man in the world long after she was quite sure he was not. After years of trying she had never managed to put the matter to herself more satisfactorily than that.

When he spoke again she gave a little start, before realising he had only been quiet for about five seconds. It was amazing how much could go through a person's head in that time.

'Unless you feel like another of those I suggest we move. With Saturday shopping there may be a bit of traffic and I want to be there on the dot.'

Such a simple thing to say, but something cold or bored about the way he said it gave her thoughts a new turn. Their not very long conversation was very much the kind they were always having when nothing of much importance was going on. Jenny kept finding she was in the middle of enjoying it when something one or other of them said, something gone by too fast to be quite taken in, would strike her as not right, out of key, off the track, however you put it. She remembered how Patrick had looked that time when Elsie Carter, one of her colleagues at the school in Hertfordshire, had told them there was one thing at any rate that had to be said about them as a married couple: they were obviously such terrific pals. Well, a possible way of putting *that* was that he looked as if he had suddenly realised just what must have been wrong with those Portuguese oysters he had eaten for lunch, so perhaps he too wondered sometimes about how things really were between them. But then it was fair to say that Elsie had never quite taken to Patrick.

They crossed the wide, bustling street. It was a sunny morning in early May and lots of people, like the landlord's wife from the pub, were out shopping, or anyway out. With nothing on their heads and showing off their bright clothes they strode along the pavements with incredible confidence, altogether different from the eyes-down amble she remembered from home. The ones with small children seemed to be half pulling them along, leaning over to talk to them in a brisk way. Jenny was always being asked how she liked living south of the river, and was usually hearing how that part was going up in the world these days before she had had time to say it was fine with her, and rather like north of the river, and after only a couple of years in the town she still had a great deal to notice and find and compare.

North of the river was where they were going to have lunch, or rather brunch, going to have it more specifically at Simon Giles's new house in Hampstead. Simon was the managing director of Hammond & Sutcliffe Ltd where Patrick worked.

When telling Jenny of the invitation on the Monday, Patrick had not seemed easy in his mind. 'I don't like the sound of it. Apparently there are going to be a lot of bleeding poets there. Where am I supposed to fit in with a shower like that? He must want something. You haven't been there yet, have you?'

'Only to the place in Pimlico.'

'M'm. You see, he's not exactly one for pushing the boat out. And I don't trust this *brunch*.'

'Just breakfast-cum-lunch, isn't it?'

'Well, in theory. But then twelve-thirty. It's supposed to be eleven-thirty or even eleven. That's how they approach it in the States, I gather.'

'Oh. Any news of that trip, by the way?'

'No. I think that trip's going to be what we call a notional benefit, something they tell you when you start off you might get and then phase out before it happens. A con, in other words. I should never have mentioned it to you.'

'Never mind, we'll go one day.'

'Oh, you bet. First things first. Twelve-thirty. It's worrying.'

'Why, what can he do?'

'It's not what he can do, it's what he can't do, I mean what he needn't do. Shit, what he'll think he needn't do. What he won't do.'

'Well, he's got to feed us, hasn't he? And give us drinks?'

'Don't you be too bloody sure, my girl.'

Patrick returned to the subject when Jenny and he got into

the Mini and started to drive up towards Waterloo Bridge. He looked at his watch.

'Yes, we should be able to make it just about on the dot.'

'You told me it was provincial to turn up at somebody's house on the dot.'

'No doubt I did. Circumstances alter cases. This house has got Simon Giles in it, chuckling with anticipatory glee as he makes ready to short-change his guests. I mean to see we get whatever's going.'

'Won't a do like today be on the firm?'

'That's not the point. It's all money that comes under his control and here's a chance to control some out of other people's reach. Not long ago he gave a bottle-party at his place, an antiquated institution anyway these days, you might have thought, but one with a great sentimental attraction for your man Giles. It seems he put away a bottle, put away in a cupboard a bottle of goodish claret brought by some cunt, sorry darling, by some booby he'd decided it was too good for the likes of. Quite openly, apparently.'

'I've heard you say he spends money like mad on authors and publicity and things like that.'

'Oh yes, but according to him that's good, sign of a good publisher to throw money about with three arms and never mind the results.'

'He's thrown a bit of it your way, buster.'

'True. Up to a point. Some of the things he does are all right. Actually I quite like him, but it's no use pretending he isn't very creepy about cash. I suppose he can't help it. Giles. Going a bit far, picking such a resoundingly mangelwurzelly name. Wonder what it used to be. Goldstein, do you think?'

'You know, Patrick, sometimes you sound just like my father.'

'Oh, Christ, No, sorry, little one, sorry, I didn't mean it to sound like that. Yes, he used to see them everywhere, didn't he, lurking under false names. Didn't you tell me he thought I might be Patrick Schtundisch? Mind you I think he was having us on half the time.'

'Well, he didn't mean any harm, that's for sure.'

'Of course he didn't. Any more than I do. Now while I remember, you're to remember, if by any chance you do get offered a drink up there, grab it whether you want it or not.

9

I'll find a use for it, I promise you. I'm going to need all the help I can get to face these bloody poets.'

They were crossing Waterloo Bridge now. The sun was on the water and there was a tremendous amount to see in every direction. Jenny felt her spirits lift at the sheer thought of being driven by her husband to what was at any rate some sort of party in such beautiful weather, then felt them fall again some of the way at the more factual kind of thought of that same husband keeping his eye out for a bit of stuff to pick up there. Whenever he found himself among women in any numbers it was as if something came over him.

On the far side of the bridge Patrick stopped the car at a pedestrian crossing. Only one pedestrian crossed, a pretty blonde girl in an extremely short skirt who turned her head and smiled at him in more than simple gratitude. Jenny felt, or without turning her own head saw, him fail to react in any way to any of it. In the past, and the pretty recent past too, he would have sort of come to attention, more than that, jerked and twitched like a man in a comedy film, and usually half-shouted things to himself as well. Then all of a sudden he had stopped completely. It was none of her doing, because she had not said a word or even done any looks, thinking it was self-centred to complain about that kind of thing, and no use anyway. So perhaps it was actually out of consideration for her that he had stopped. With him you never knew.

Two

Simon Giles's new house was an old house at the same time, one built of stone, not brick, opposite a rather older-looking church near the top of the hill up from Swiss Cottage. It had quite a lot of front garden to which nobody had done anything for many years except keep the grass and weeds down to knee height or so. These varied from straw colour to a rich dark green that brought swampy areas to mind. Just off the path, where some flagstones were almost whole but others in small pieces, there was a collapsed pile of disintegrating mauve-bound books printed in an alphabet unfamiliar to Jenny. Patrick saw her looking about and explained that whenever anyone really important came along, like a successful author on another firm's list or an American publisher, Simon would take the person to a restaurant. Only authors he had already got – sometimes – and colleagues – less often – came here.

Jenny asked herself what anyone really important would have made of the hall of the house. With a coat-cupboard and an umbrella-stand and wellingtons in it this was still a hall, but a sale room job lot of tattered old armchairs made it into a sort of sitting-room as well. She spotted a large painting of grey squares on pale yellow and turned away. In her teens she would have said she was quite keen on pictures, but since then she had completely gone off them. Between this one and the umbrella-stand a dozen youngish and middle-aged people were standing or sitting about with glasses in their hands and looking as if they were waiting for a whistle to blow. One of them was a tall man of about sixty with a pink face, a great cloud of white hair and large blue eyes fixed on a point near the ceiling. 'That must be a poet,' said Jenny.

'I agree it ought to be by rights,' said Patrick. 'I've seen it before but I can't place it. Anyway it isn't one of ours. Don't worry, we'll get to it.'

Simon came up to them with a small girl in huge glasses at his side. He had a brown beaky face and a long mop of dark hair hanging over his forehead that, with his dark-brown velvet jacket, made Jenny think of a Victorian actor. When he had a moment he gave her a big left-right hug-and-kiss like a more modern actor. After that he looked at her intently with one eye, the other being off somewhere in the way it had, and at half speed asked how she was – now she had had both her legs off, he made it sound. Despite the eye it would have been a really good performance if he had dropped it less completely and suddenly and soon. He said in his half-crown voice,

'Vera is one of our new poets.'

The girl with the large glasses, who had a rather wide but quite thin mouth, switched round on Jenny and gave her every scrap of her attention, which cheered her up a lot because she was not used to it except from men.

'How do you do?'

'We're bringing out her first book in October and it's not just an ordinary first book,' said Simon and turned away to ask Patrick a question.

'Which poets do you like best?' asked Jenny, who had been working on this ever since hearing that poets were to be present.

'The name is Ve-ra Se-lig,' said the girl and spelt it. 'I don't really like any poets.'

'Sorry, I meant which poets do you like reading.'

'I don't really like reading anything. I don't think reading is an experience.'

'But what about people reading you? Isn't that an experience?' Jenny felt horrible as she used the word.

'I don't really care about people reading me, I'm a writer,' said Vera Selig, still looking closely at Jenny but now in a slightly different way. 'Excuse me, I missed who you work for.'

'I don't work for anybody, I just – '

'Are you anything to do with books or journalism or broadcasting?'

'I'm afraid not. I'm just Patrick's wife.'

At this news the poetess's attention vanished as suddenly as Simon's, but then was miraculously restored just long enough

12

to last while she asked Jenny if she had a a car here and was told no, it was Patrick who did the –

'So this is the famous Patrick's wife on stage at long last,' said a man who had come up on Jenny's other side. He said it without parting his teeth, the bottom row of which he kept permanently on view although it was not quite complete. He must have been nearly fifty but was got up for a nature ramble. While he just stood smiling and blinking at her and not saying anything more she told him that that was right, that was who she was, and felt absolutely brilliant while she was speaking, as she had felt a great many times since coming to London. Well, and here she was.

After a pause of what seemed some minutes the man jerked his head and said with a laugh, 'I'm terribly sorry, I'm J.L.R. Sebastian. I just didn't realise.'

That anyone in the place could be so thick as not to know who I am, sure. It was already clear to Jenny that this must be another writer, though perhaps not a poet. She said nothing, but J.L.R. Sebastian kept the ball rolling by sticking out his hand to shake hers, or rather to hold on to hers, and saying in a quieter, higher-pitched voice than before and with his eyes shut,

'So you're nothing to do with books or anything like that. May I ask what you are to do with, Mrs Standish?'

'I teach in a hospital, so I suppose I am a bit to do with books.'

'Oh, how splendid. Tell me, what's your, what's your field?'

'I haven't really got one. I just go in in the mornings in the week and teach the long-stay children, some of the younger ones. I used to teach in a proper – '

'Oh, how splendid,' he said again, but this time he meant a different sort of splendid. He had let her have her hand back by now and had opened his eyes, which stayed fixed on her but not necessarily on her face. 'That must be very rewarding. Do tell me, I expect some of the kids are pretty bright, aren't they?'

She went on about one or two of them while J.L.R. Sebastian looked as if he was quite enjoying the sound of her voice, more than she was, anyway.

'How fascinating. And all this happens in the mornings,' he said, giving Jenny the shock of her life by having taken in this

13

detail. 'I gather from Simon that you and Patrick have moved into that new block in Lower Ground.'

'It's called – '

'Perhaps you haven't come across it yet, but there's a marvellous reference library just round the corner from you. It's very useful for me in what I'm trying to lick into shape just now. But you know, it sounds ridiculous but I simply can't seem to find anywhere round about there where I can get a cup of tea, not anywhere decent, simply anywhere at all. And well, after two or three hours on the go, with all that dust there, you sort of feel you could do with a mug of char. So I was just wondering,' said J.L.R. Sebastian, starting to laugh slightly again, 'I mean if you happened to be putting your kettle on about half-past four or quarter to five say Monday I'd be delighted to join you.'

At least it had not been a dish of tay, as she funnily enough remembered a pipe-smoking schoolmaster up home offering her years ago. The way this chap moved his head to and fro as he spoke was good, as if he would have been delighted to tell everybody about the char project only nobody happened to be listening just then. This was like old times for her all right. Since then she had not got any better at a lot of things, but she had at knowing what to say to characters who wanted to come and have tea with her.

'Whenever I'm free in the afternoons . . .'

'Of course this stuff from the 1920s and '30s I'm working on, most of it's never even been looked at since,' he said, piling on the persuasion.

'. . . I go over to the Borough and read to an old lady who's nearly blind. It's only a small thing to me but it means a lot to her.'

'Oh marvellous,' he said disgustedly.

'It's an awkward journey any way you tackle it . . .'.

'Don't you ever – '

'. . . so Patrick comes down on his way from work and picks me up . . .'

'If he should find he can't – '

'. . . regular as clockwork. It's interesting, she likes the old books, Dickens and Jane Austen, does my old lady. She's properly fed up with these modern writers, I can tell you. No real characters to get to know and no story to follow, she says. And then all this sex.'

Not much more was needed after that. Patrick came out of the dining-room, which had a depressing dark-pink-and-green stained-glass panel in its door, carrying two drinks that were most likely Bloody Marys. After holding them up side by side he offered her the smaller, glancing round as he did so in a disgruntled kind of way.

'Make the most of this,' he said. 'It's all you're going to get.'

'Have you seen Barbara about?' Jenny meant Barbara Giles, the hostess, whom she thought she ought to let know she had turned up.

'Somewhere, I don't know. She'll be along. Who are these people, for Christ's sake? They can't all be poets, surely.'

Jenny tried her drink, which she had suspected might be a pretty stiff one but which turned out to be perfectly all right. At once Patrick seized her by the arm.

'Look! Look, over there. Yes, there. No, *there*.'

All her eye fell on was a rather good-looking woman not dressed to annoy anybody and carrying chest-high a plate of food with a fork on it and vapour rising. 'What is it?'

'Mark it well.' He looked at his watch again. 'It's twelve-forty-five and the bloody kedgeree is being doled out. There, there's another one, see? Simplicity itself. Brunch. Brunch minus the first hour, the one with just drinks in it, and minus too no doubt wine, beer, brandy, you name it and we're not going to get it. I told you so. Didn't I tell you so?'

'Have a cigarette, love.'

'I don't want one. Have you got one?'

'I've stopped keeping a packet.'

'It's all right, I've got to learn. But wouldn't you fuffuffuffuffuff, sorry darling, wouldn't you bloody well know, eh? What have we done to deserve it?'

She handed him the rest of her drink. 'Go on, I don't want any more.'

'Are you sure? I don't deserve you. But that shouldn't mean . . .'

His voice went off for a moment when he saw Barbara Giles coming out of the kitchen. Jenny saw her too. She was wearing about the usual number and kinds of clothes, but the only one at all noticeable was a rainbow-striped blouse in some half-shiny material with the top button undone.

Breasts had brought Jenny a peck of trouble over the years. With Patrick it was fair to say that they turned the scale. He seemed able to stand up quite well to things like bottoms and faces, and she had heard him say more than once that he could take legs or leave them alone, which was rather sad, and tactless of him too, because her own were meant to be pretty good, one of her best features. But breasts were in a league of their own, they were not all that counted by any means, but they did sort of upgrade the whole package into the danger area. Knowing as much about them as she did, she might have been expected, after a couple of previous meetings, to have marked down Barbara Giles's. And the rest of her was presumably no more than up to standard, even if you happened to fancy that kind of thin-faced indignant-expression blonde type. And yet, with all her experience, it was as if she had been setting eyes on them, this pair of breasts, for the first time.

Perhaps it had been the same for Patrick, but there was no telling, because he had long ago given up actually letting on how he felt about any breasts whatever. He just smiled and waved and Barbara crossed the hall and joined them. She greeted Jenny without suspicious friendliness or much of any other kind either. After a minute she said in her field-marshal's-daughter accent,

'Tell me, Patrick, while I've got you, about this super new flat of yours, which we thought the other night you'd made look absolutely marvellous, clever old you,' meaning just clever old him and no mistake, 'this, this *block* it's part of, didn't you say, I thought you were saying it wasn't full yet, there were still a couple of, what are they, *flats* I suppose that were still going, or was it Simon got the impression from what you were saying?'

Simon had drifted up during this and stood there agreeing with the general drift of it and giving off a slight hot smell.

'Well yes,' said Patrick reliably, 'I think there are two, aren't there, darling? Next door to us, and . . .'

'The one at the end,' said Jenny. 'The end of that passage. It's a bit bigger than the others, they showed us. It goes the whole width.'

'Oh yes, there's a little extra room at the side you could use as, well, as a study.'

16

The Gileses turned on each other with what looked like utter horror but turned out to be fingers-crossed satisfaction-so-far. 'Sounds just what we . . .' they said. 'Sounds exactly what we . . .'

'But you've only just moved in here,' said Patrick.

'We're not going to be needing here now,' said Simon. 'Too big for us now, here.'

Barbara was shaking her head impatiently. 'We got into here before we'd found this gorgeous little gamekeeper's bothy that we were so incredibly lucky to hear about and *wouldn't* have if our friends in Preston Candover hadn't by the *merest* chance happened to see . . .'

There was one who had never had any aunties, Jenny thought to herself, to lay it down fair and square that you said your say and shut up for the next person's turn and no palaver. She thought several other things to herself while Barbara went on about of course the place was going to need a lot doing to it, though by a stroke of luck the roof had been repaired the previous year, and the others, herself included, listened seriously and nodded and looked thoughtful, and all the time he and she were up to no good, still at the planning stage but up to no good, and if anybody had tried to tell her she was letting her imagination run away with her, well, all she could say was it had run away further than that in the past and still come a poorish second to what actually took place. And if anybody similar had laughed at the idea that a married man of thirty-six would be fool enough to get involved with a married woman in the same block, then they obviously either had a great sense of humour or had never heard about the headmaster's secretary and the prefects' room in the new building at the Hertfordshire school this married man had taught at until 1965, two years before.

'It can be a bit noisy early on but it's surprising how much difference just that one floor up from the street makes,' he was saying now, sounding as if he was being specially normal so as to fool enemy agents listening through hidden microphones. 'But we seem to have got used to it, don't we, darling?'

'Hardly notice it now,' said Jenny.

'The whole thing's unquestionably absolutely exactly what we're looking for,' said Barbara. She for her part sounded just like someone thinking they were lulling someone else into a sense of false security.

'What about communal outgoings?' asked Simon.

This meant nothing precise to Jenny, but she grasped soon enough that it was to do with extra money Simon was guessing he might have to pay, and felt fond of Patrick for being as usual slow on the uptake in this area. 'What?' he said. 'The what?'

'I'm sure that's not going to be a problem,' said Barbara.

'No snags that I can see,' said Patrick.

Even Simon, who had not got the advantage of being able to hear all those massed violins that were so plain to Jenny, started to turn his head at the way they said that, but stopped halfway with one of his eyes on her and the other not, and said to her, 'Oh, have you met Iain Gowrie Guthrie?'

'Is that a poet?' asked Jenny.

'Rather a well-known one, actually,' said Barbara.

'In certain circles,' said Patrick.

Simon put his hand on Jenny's arm. 'Come and meet him,' he said.

Iain Gowrie Guthrie was not the tall white-haired spiritual-looking man but another in the same group. This one was also about sixty with a full head of entirely black hair that hung to his shoulders and a beard that, though carefully trimmed, almost reached his chest. It was hard luck on him that he had been caught up with, so to speak, by everybody starting to have long hair and a beard, but he was still an impressive figure, or would have been with another foot or so of stature. He raised his eyebrows when Jenny was introduced but did not address her.

She felt tongue-tied, especially when Simon immediately went away, but soon saw that was not going to matter.

'As I was saying,' said Iain Gowrie Guthrie, seemingly to everybody within hearing, 'there's only one requirement I make of a poet, and it's a very simple one. Unfortunately it also appears to be an insuperably difficult one. Let's just run through them, shall we?'

He started reciting a list of names of what would have had to be poets, in fact as it went on Jenny was nearly sure she recognised a couple of them. On hearing Iain Gowrie Guthrie's name and taking in his appearance she had immediately resigned herself to not being able to make out a word he said, but his

18

voice was at least an octave higher than she had expected and he spoke in a kind of flattened cockney accent she could cope with. Now and then during the list he looked at her, but not in a way that meant he was going to ask her for her opinion about anything.

When one or two of the names had come round for the second time the spiritual-looking man asked what about so-and-so, and Jenny thought she knew that one too, but Iain Gowrie Guthrie stared at him in heartfelt puzzlement and concern, as if he had mentioned a professional cricketer by mistake, as perhaps he had. An argument developed on whether so-and-so should or should not be mentioned round about now. That suited Jenny quite well as far as it went, but she soon began to be afraid that they would never get to hear what the insuperably difficult requirement was that Iain G-G made of a poet or, worse, that they had somehow heard about it already and like a fool she had managed to miss it. But then suddenly it was all right.

'What none of them is evidently capable of doing,' he said, 'is writing a poem. Not one single poem between the whole boiling. And to my mind that disqualifies them from the title of poet. Every last one.'

'Oh I see,' said a young or fairly young man Jenny had not noticed before.

'I'm glad you do, laddie, and I hope you'll agree with me that when two people are in the same line of work like the profession of letters it's much more suitable for them to suppress any malicious and vindictive feelings they may have in favour of such generous and good-natured impulses as they perhaps possess.'

'If you're talking about that piece I wrote in the – '

'Life's too short for the harbouring of animosity.'

'The thing folded in about 1954, so it must be at least – '

'I can't see that spite serves any useful purpose. Do you agree with me?'

The youngish man looked round the six or seven faces. It was clear that nobody thought that spite served a useful purpose. 'Yes,' he said with a certain amount of gloom, 'I agree with you, yes,' and he snatched at the startled girl next to him and hurried her away.

'Ah, well, nice to have cleared that up,' said the poet genially, accepting without word or look of thanks a plate of food Simon handed him. 'Never does, you know, to let these small fry think they've got away with something.'

'Hallo, Iain, how are you, sport?' said a man of about the same age as he joined the group. He spoke quite warmly and shook hands with both hands. 'Well now . . .'

'Hallo, Bruce, I was a bit disappointed you couldn't manage to find some more favourable things to say about my last collection after all the laudatory notices I've given your novels over the years, starting with that book of short stories before the war. I had rather hoped you could trot out a compliment or two even if it went against the grain, just for old times' sake as you might say.'

'After comparing it favourably with Yeats's *Last Poems* I could hardly have – '

'And by the way, old son, Kendrick's translations of Li Po have no standing at all any more. See you around, Brucie.'

Jenny heard most of this while she started eating from the plate also brought by Simon. At first sight there was nothing on it but small heaps of rice in a pale gravy with green scraps here and there. Very likely risotto, she thought for a moment, but then she turned some of it over with her fork and came across a shred of haddock and something that might have been a piece of egg-white, which made it kedgeree instead. Well, how about that? She looked up in time to see Bruce moving off in a slow zig-zag and Iain Gowrie Guthrie coming closer. He had turned genial again and seemed to think she deserved something for having been part of his audience over the last minutes.

'Very nice fellow, old Bruce,' he said, chewing what was clearly rice, for grains of it were falling from his lips or lodging in his beard as he spoke. 'One of the best. He hasn't changed to speak of since we were lads together at school in Melbourne.'

'Oh yes, Melbourne. And the two of you have kept in touch all along.'

'No, not a bit of it, we haven't laid eyes on each other since we came down from Oxford in 1931.'

'You mean just now was the first time you've met for thirty, thirty-six years?'

'Christ, it does sound a lot, doesn't it? Funny how people come and go. You see, Bruce has been stuck up in Glasgow teaching English for I don't know how long. Beats me what good he thinks he's done himself up there. Of course, he got a pretty lousy degree, old Bruce did.'

From her couple of inches' greater height Jenny had an excellent view of the dandruff on the poet's head, looking whiter than dandruff generally did because of the extreme blackness of his hair, and hence more conspicuous. After picking some fragments of grit out of her mouth, she said, 'Are you based in London?'

'What, with sunny Italy just down the road? I should say not. What would I be doing in London with a flat in Rome and a farmhouse in Tuscany? No, I'm just over for the launch. Know Tuscany, do you?'

'No, I've never been,' said Jenny, who had been wondering unhurriedly about Mrs Gowrie Guthrie, if she existed, for some time and now speeded up.

He helped her out on that straight away by saying, 'I'm on my own there now. It's very beautiful round where I am,' he went on, 'all vineyards and, you know, trees. The garden's full of, full of flowers. Late September and October's really the best time. You've got your own flat there with a separate entrance, come and go as you please. Feel like a trip? Forty minutes taxi-ride from the airport.'

Jenny had been approached in purposely hopeless ways before, though they had usually been more straightforward ways too like asking her if she you-know-what or trying to tear her dress off. So she thanked Iain G-G nicely and explained she had a very full programme and caught the look of relief behind the beard. And people went on about the female mind being hard to understand.

'Perhaps next year,' he said quickly. 'Excuse me a minute,' and he hurried across the room and accosted by the door an old man who had been about to leave and now immediately began to look much keener on the idea.

'Complaining about a bad review he gave him in March 1940,' said the spiritual-looking man, who had listened to everything. Next to him stood a middle-aged female, doubtless his wife, with grizzled plaits and a long upper lip like that of King George VI. The rest of the half-dozen had drifted away.

'He's an Australian, you see,' said the wife.

'True, and small men shouldn't wear beards.'

'Small men shouldn't do anything.'

21

'Yes, I suppose ultimately one has to come round to that.'

'Is he really a famous poet?' asked Jenny.

'Oh yes,' said the man. 'Well, as poets go, that is. Very successful, too. Not quite as successful as he is at getting money off every foundation and committee and university under the sun, but then. Oh, and I should like you to know, just so there's no misunderstanding, my dear, that I'm not a poet myself and neither is my darling wife.'

'Oh.' Jenny realised she had rather set her heart on him being a poet, and a proper one.

'I'm an accountant, which is rather the sort of thing you have to be these days if you actually happen to like poetry. I'll say one good word for the works of . . . Iain Gowrie Guthrie.' He sighed and groaned a little, as if he knew he should comment on this name but for the moment could not face the task. 'They may have nowhere to go but at least they're dressed up. If you've read much contemporary poetry, or tried to, you'll see the force of that. Well, it's been most pleasant talking to you. And now, I think, darling . . . lunch.'

Jenny turned towards where Patrick and Barbara had been standing, but they were not there any more, nor anywhere in the room. Two glasses that had held tomato-juice stood by themselves on a low table next to a chipped blue china bowl of disintegrating daisies. Oh, not in that minute, she thought. Surely not.

22

Three

'Was old Hairy-Phizog as bad as they say?'

'He was pretty bad.'

'You clutched at me as if he'd been coming for you with his didgeridoo in his hand, I was quite worried for a moment.'

'He was rather awful. Have you read any of his poetry? It must be really terribly bad, isn't it?'

'Well actually it isn't as frightful as you might imagine, not quite. I agree it ought to be. At least it doesn't go on about feeling fed up in Islington or Fulham. Of course he's a man, you've got to allow for that.'

'A man like that couldn't write a word that's any good at all.'

'He has got under your skin. The trouble with you, my girl, is you're a romantic. You think you have to be a decent bloke to write well.' Patrick slowed the Mini in front of a changing light to accelerate cleverly through on the green. 'Not so. I should have thought you'd have got used to that principle by now.'

'I have. I just don't like being disappointed by people. In people.'

'Are you all right, love?'

'I'm fine,' said Jenny, turning quickly away from the passenger window. 'Is that girl's poetry any good, you know, the one with the glasses?'

'Vera's. Christ no. It doesn't come any more perseveringly no-good than hers. I don't know how she does it – she must go over it word by bloody word, ready to pounce on any evidence of thought or observation or feeling for words that might have crept in while her back was turned. Do you realise,' he went on, 'can you believe, that when we first met I was teaching schoolboys Latin verse, poems written by Roman men in the Latin language? I sometimes wonder whether any of that's there any more. Well, what would you, the bloody world's moved on without consulting us, as Horace had it.'

There was a minor traffic block ahead of them. Patrick pulled up behind a small inferior-looking van that had halted a couple of yards short of giving him room to turn right. He leant across Jenny, lowered her window and called, 'I say, I wonder if I could just ask you to move forward enough to . . .' Almost as soon as he began speaking the van responded. ' . . . get clear of your ass, you stupid fish-faced twit? Thank you very much.'

As he accelerated a little noisily up the side-street, he said, 'You see, that Latin stuff, even now you can tell the fellow had to know a lot of words and a bit about how to put them together. His idea of giving you a bad time is to send you to sleep. He doesn't make you want to ring him up and ask him who he thinks he is and what the hell he thinks he's playing at, or go round to where he lives and give him a kicking. Well no, I mean you feel, you do feel quite cross with him for taking up your time and especially for *thinking he's a poet*, which after all is still something to be. Get back to your bamboo island, you bloody savage.'

That was a driver trying to pull out in front of them, quite dangerously it had to be said, but only to people going as fast as they were. Patrick had still not completely finished with the poetry. After a false start or two he went on, 'Actually it's more than that. Somebody like Vera isn't just no good herself, she makes everything else in life seem duller and more commonplace and trivial. All right, but we publish her. And others.'

Jenny said, 'Are all the others as bad as that, as Vera?'

'All the Hammond & Sutcliffe new poets are. Mind you, there's nobody who's any better who hasn't already got a publisher.'

'What's special about this lot, then?'

'Well, we've got a black African millionaire Communist politician, and Vera's a female, and you can bet one of them's a queer, and that's three out of the first six, so you can see there's nothing special really. They'll all lose money, but no more than anyone else. Oh yes, everyone knows that, Simon better than anybody.'

'Perhaps he thinks they're good. Worth losing money on.'

'Oh, he doesn't think they're good any more than he thinks they're bad. Poetry's dodgy at the best of times, and here are six new poets with nothing to be said for them commercially or artistically, so whoever publishes them must be a man of vision. Stands to reason.'

'Who's going to think that?'

'Well exactly, love. The answer is other publishers. Are going to think that. Impressing *them*, that's the object of the entire exercise.'

'Just with the poetry, you mean. Not the whole firm, surely.'

'Sometimes I wonder,' said Patrick, very thoughtfully and seriously for a man driving a car. 'Anyway, I've got my own nice little corner and he leaves me alone in it. For the moment.'

'You do still want to go on working there,' Jenny told him.

'Well.' After more thoughtfulness and seriousness he made a great business of managing to put all that on one side. 'Today was a shocker if you like. One bottle of vodka between twenty-three. I think Simon sets aside an hour on Sunday evenings to work out what he won't be spending his money on the following week.'

'His unshopping list. Saturday lunch: enough extra haddock to make a decent kedgeree, say ten shillings round here; enough extra eggs for ditto, three shillings; fresh flowers for sitting-room, three and six. Total unspent, 16/6. Worms from the garden for supper.'

This sort of thing kept them going till they were back in Lower Ground, coming into it through the end where the street market was held on Saturdays. The greengrocers and confectioners, the Polish fishmonger who sold marvellous cheap crabs and mussels, the butcher and poulterer, a cockney with a strange name, who often had game-birds on offer as well as domestic fowl, hares as well as rabbits, at almost suspiciously low prices – these had packed up and left by this time, or were leaving. Others held on perhaps for the after-pub trade, stalls hung with rugs, curtains, tablecloths where only dowdily dressed people stopped to look, places for second-hand books and old books, silver and pewter, stamps, old coins that nobody at all seemed to look at. Two men in dark coats with shovels and long brooms were sweeping up the rubbish and loading it into big rush baskets. Patrick put the Mini away in the handy bulge of a lane

25

to a builder's yard over whose gates, so he had heard in the Princess Beatrice, amorous couples of various ages could be seen climbing after dark at weekends, and not necessarily on warm nights.

He and Jenny mounted the flight of concrete steps beside the off-licence and reached the covered walk along the backs of the maisonettes. Below, limited by a hoarding of some apparent age, ran a strip of unluxuriant greenery on which the tenants could theoretically take the air. So far no refuse was to be seen here, but this happy state of things was not expected to last, once it got about that all there was to stop people throwing any old stuff down was their own sense of responsibility.

Patrick opened the door of 1B and as usual was pleasantly surprised by the amount of light coming through the window that stretched all the way across the front of the sitting-room. To his left a riserless stair ascended, to his right a kitchen held a gas cooker and enough space for two to eat in comfort any time, four with a little management. Out of here a black cat emerged, name of Frankie after some bygone entertainer, so black that at any distance his nose and mouth disappeared. When he saw Jenny start to move in his direction he turned and ran back whence he had come. From the sitting-room Patrick heard something being spooned into Frankie's saucer, followed – not preceded – by the sound of water tumbling into the kettle for the promised cup of coffee.

The light from the window was given back to advantage by the pale blue distemper applied to the walls by Jenny. It was she too who, from markets and auctions, had assembled the round Victorian table, the three Victorian occasional chairs (a fourth was still actively sought), and the small button-back chesterfield and two comfortable armchairs which, being good with her tape-measure, scissors and needle, she had herself covered in rose-patterned chintz. The large nicely done print of 'The Fighting *Téméraire*' over the tiled fireplace had been chosen by her, passed by Patrick as becoming sufficiently trendy to offset any implied patriotism. He had contributed the up-to-the-ceiling bookshelves, installed them anyway under strong pressure to replace the builders'-planks-between-bricks that, it seemed, had been all right in their old Highbury house, even rather bluff and no-nonsensical according to him. But he had not had the least hand in covering the rather scratched table-top with a pretty cotton cloth, nor in putting there a bowl of fruit and, inevitably, a glass vase of fresh flowers.

Patrick spread his forearms along the window-sill and looked down on the stretch of Lower Ground, unlike the other end mostly inactive in the afternoon sun. A deep rustic voice came from Jenny's wireless in the kitchen, followed by music of unabashed amiability. He felt content, or more accurately, a good deal further from either vexation or panic than usual. The quick clinch and largely token feel-up with Barbara on the landing back there had been good for establishing continuity and rousing as a foretaste. It could also be described as the action of a reckless and unattractive halfwit in both the short and the long run, but this time, one more time, he had got away with it, got away clear, as had been shown by Jenny's surge of affection on his reappearance, a positive bloody grab. He had enjoyed their chat on the way home in the car, so much so that for long periods he had forgotten to appreciate its usefulness in promoting marital harmony – Christ, he must have been reading a Hammond & Sutcliffe catalogue. At that thought he pulled himself together and went out to the kitchen to help with the coffee tray.

After all these years, eight to be precise, he could tell from the way Jenny settled herself a couple of minutes later, across the fireplace from him, that something was coming up, some-thing non-sensitive though, he thought. He tried to look generi-cally receptive.

'That Australian chap with the three names,' she said, 'has he got a name for being a terrific womaniser, do you know?'

'I don't think any more than you might expect. What actually happened there, love? He's upset you, hasn't he?'

'It's funny, I carried it off all right at the time, but then I sort of saw myself as he must have seen me.'

'What? Come on, tell me what happened.'

'It was nothing really. He asked me to go and stay with him at his place in Italy, and I said I wouldn't, and that was that, and I thought he didn't really mean it, but then I thought perhaps he did after all, and he wasn't trying to throw a pass in the ordinary way, he didn't make a great thing of it at all and there were other people there who could hear. What he was doing was checking if I was free for the time he said. Last week in September and October.'

'And you told him you weren't.' Patrick was putting everything into this, but he still could not see where it was leading.

'Then he said perhaps I could come next year.'

'So there was the sport being a real sport. What are you getting at, darling?'

'He thought I was a . . . a call-girl. And why should he think that? Tell me why he thought that.' Jenny was sitting bolt upright and blinking fast.

'Oh for Christ's sake, an Aussie spots a sheila at a party, or what he takes to be a sheila, he's flying out on Monday . . .'

'Actually that's not all.'

'Oh for Christ's sake.'

Jenny took a deep breath, in the way Patrick had seen her when she was trying to overcome her stutter, now a thing of the past. She said more calmly, 'Just before that, a chap called Bartholomew or Nathaniel or something . . .'

'Sebastian – what do you think of that for flexibility of intellect? Wait a minute, though, don't tell me he . . .'

'Threw a pass. Yes, as a matter of fact he did.'

'What, that old wreck! Bloody cheek. Sorry, love. Ah, but wait a minute, the last anybody heard, old Sebastian was as queer as a coot. Well, perhaps not as a coot, but certainly assumed to be that way inclined. You know, seen in off-track pubs with unexplained younger men. I suppose you couldn't be mistaken?'

'Oh no.'

'No, you wouldn't be. Well, that's certainly one for the book.'

'Is he a poet?'

'No record as such. Biographical stuff about old literary farts is his line. He's been with the firm for donkey's years. Can't think why he was invited today.'

'Is he any good?'

Patrick shook his head firmly, then gave Jenny a closer look. 'Come on now, come on, let's have it.'

'Do I look like a boy to you?'

'No,' he said, trembling slightly as he sat and trying as hard as he ever had in his life not to laugh. 'No, not a bit. In fact I don't think I've ever set eyes on anyone who looks less like a boy. Feminine to a fault is how I'd put it. One of the ways, at least.'

'Right. Now just think about it. Two crystal-clear passes

within half an hour from two completely different types of chap neither of whom I'd done anything to encourage and both of them, both the passes I mean, the yes-or-no sort, what about it, never mind the opera or can I give you a ring some time. It must be because they thought I'd be easy. Now why?'

'I might have known. Your famous depraved looks. How many times must I – '

'Please let me go through it, Patrick.'

'All right, darling.' He nodded cheerfully.

'I said I didn't encourage them. I don't show myself off, not that it's as if I've a lot to show off anyway. In fact when I saw what was coming I went the opposite, short of glaring like a gorgon. So I must have been encouraging them unconsciously.' Jenny's eyes were on her empty coffee cup. 'Which must mean I look like a tart. A floosie.'

'Yes, I know, a woman of easy virtue. Well, that's not very serious, is it?'

'Oh, so you don't mind your wife looking like a floosie.'

'I don't mind those two clowns thinking she does. One bugger and one cobber. Some panel of experts. So . . . what of it?' He went over to her. 'Stand up, Miss Bunn.' She obeyed instantly and he put his arms round her and his face against hers. 'I don't think our Miss Bunn knows a hell of a lot about floosies, but we'll let that pass. To me, she looks, as well as beautiful, like someone who finds sex entirely natural, and enjoyable, and to do with love. And who looks about as much like a floosie as she looks like a boy. And we've disposed of that one. You silly little bag.'

She clung to him hard for a moment and then broke away and burst into tears, not sniffles or trickles but proper full-scale sobs with the tears jumping from her eyes. Patrick was taken aback and greatly distressed, knowing as he did that she never cried on purpose. What was it about, what had he said to her? He kept asking but she shook her head and very soon was trying to stop, pushing him away, holding her breath, gulping, wiping her cheeks with her fingers and telling him bits at a time that she had no idea what had come over her, the two chaps must have upset her more than she realised, she ought to be able to take that sort of thing in her stride at her time of life, and so on. Presently she carried the coffee cups out to the kitchen and disappeared upstairs to the bathroom.

For the next few minutes Patrick could do nothing but walk to and fro and feel bad. At the end of that time she came down again and he heard her using the telephone in the hall, or rather where the coats were. It was a short call with a pause in it. When she came back into the sitting-room she looked not quite back to normal but a good deal better than might have been expected, and when she spoke her tone was somewhat thin but belonged nowhere in the vast spectrum of female alienation. In her hand were a couple of books with costumed animals portrayed on the covers.

'Sorry,' she said, and hurried on, 'I'm just popping round to the hospital. One of the little girls had a minor op yesterday, just straightening something out, so I thought I'd look in for a few minutes, going for a breath of air really.'

'Fine – do you want me to come with you?'

'No, I'll be there and back in a second.'

He kissed her in a gingerly fashion. 'Let's have a treat tonight. We deserve one after that bloody moistening of the lips midday,' he said, then, putting on the cockney, 'I'll take you somewhere swagger up the other end, ducks.' She already understood that the other end was the West End as seen from the East End, but he always had to remember to lay the accent on extra thick, because if he forgot to she was apt not to realise he was talking any different to usual – just her having come from up North, of course. A treat would be marvellous, she said, and was gone.

Still puzzled and worried, he went back to the window and watched her slender figure moving purposefully across the road and round the far corner where the new bingo hall, lately an old dance hall, unprepossessingly was. He had expected a warm response to his remarks about Miss Bunn, although he had not set out to provoke one, but she had seemed to find something more in what he had said than he knew he had put there. Try it again later. With a great groaning yawn he fished a thick typescript out of his brief-case and ill-temperedly planked himself down with it in his corner of the sitting-room, where dictionary, Hammond & Sutcliffe house-style manual and other reference works stood within reach.

Almost the first to go of his delusions about publishing had been the one that said reading typescripts at home would be rather fun. Or could ever be any fun. The one that said it would or could be usually better than intolerable had gone soon after.

Thinking otherwise was like joining a rugger club in the expectation of making a ninety-yard solo run every Saturday. The trick was to get as much as possible of it done when you were feeling bloody awful on some other grounds, like with a hangover or now.

The production before him at the moment had some ramshackle connection with the history of ancient Babylon and came from the pen of a Welsh madman, an unfrocked minister in Betws-y-coed whose first book, on the aboriginal culture of Australia, had to Patrick's disgust done rather well. He was uncapping his ballpoint to slash at an improper use of the verb 'infer' when the doorbell gave its repulsive chime. He gathered up *Blood in the Tigris* and put it gratefully aside, suffering a reversal of feeling when the bell chimed again while he was still on his way. He flung the door open as abruptly as he could.

The man who stood there was a few years older than he, on the short side, wearing a ginger-brown tweed jacket with a criss-cross pattern and elaborate pockets and leather patches. A peaked cap of similar material was crammed, as if a moment before, on to a large head where there grew a great deal of long brownish hair that curled thickly back over the edge of the cloth.

'Can I help you?' said Patrick, already quite settled in his own mind that here was a return of the very funny chap Jenny had mentioned, perhaps understating matters, in the pub that morning.

'Yes, er . . . Do you live in this, this apartment?' It was a high-pitched top-drawer noise with a hint of wailing in it.

'Yes, as a matter of fact I – '

'Do you mind answering a few questions?'

'That depends. Who might you be?'

'Harold Porter-King,' said the chap with a hanging intonation, as if the name was one on a list of some length, though significant just the same. Then he added grudgingly, 'I'm thinking of taking one of the vacant apartments in this building. 1D?' He peered up at the Standish door-plate. 'Is it 1D?'

'Very possibly. Would you like to come in for a minute?'

'No thank you, no.'

There followed an edited replay of earlier events as reported, with the chap given the go-ahead to ask questions and then showing himself unable to think of any. He might well not turn

31

out to be any great shakes as a neighbour if things went as far as that, thought Patrick, but he was unimprovable now, his face clearing and clouding over again as successive courses suggested themselves and were disallowed in turn. During this he made up for staying outside 1B by seeing all there was to be seen of it from there, and also flourished a latchkey on a striped ribbon which he repeatedly wound and unwound round his extended forefinger. Ultimately he said in the same selection-committee style as before,

'How long have you been living here altogether?'

'Three or four weeks.' You could tell him or punch him. For now, anyway.

'Have you been having any trouble with water?'

'Water?'

'Yes, water. Have you been having any trouble with it?'

'I take it you mean the water supply to this maisonette. No. The whole thing works perfectly.'

'You haven't had to do business with a plumber at all.'

'No.'

Harold Porter-King nodded his hairy head, his curiosity about water allayed for the moment. From the interior of 1B he had shifted his attention to Patrick himself, if those unchanging pale eyes were capable of paying much attention to anything. They wandered away as he stood a moment longer in thought before saying briskly and very kickably, 'Thank you and good afternoon to you' and striding off in the direction of 1D.

Swearing incredulously, Patrick waited inside his own front door till he heard a key trying to get into the keyhole of no doubt 1D. He went and had a pee, combed his hair, looked idly out of the bathroom window and strolled downstairs again to hear the same noises going on along the passage. As he listened there was a pause, about right for the key to be turned the other way up, and the lock at once yielded. A moment later he jumped considerably as the distant door crashed shut.

The confrontation with Harold Porter-King had unsettled him. Or something had. For the moment *Blood in the Tigris* had crossed the threshold into the realm of the fully intolerable. He had a couple of other manuscripts to hand in in his brief-case, but a sanity-preserving regulation forbade the laying-aside of one such for another until the first should be finished and done with. What he needed was a change of scene. A visit to that

32

shop off Charing Cross Road to buy tit-magazines undeniably had its attractions, but to drop in there when passing, or nearly passing, was one thing; to cross the river for no other purpose was not the same, not really. Even so he considered the project long and closely before discarding it. Scrutinising the neighbourhood for a new, more convenient horn-emporium was a pressing need, but he could stave it off a little longer. Going and sitting in the bit of garden on the corner was more suitable and seemly, with the chance of marginally freshening the tan as a bonus. At thirty-six he needed all the help he could get.

The trouble was, as had often enough been remarked in the past, the sun brought them out – well, he might see fit to call it trouble, but nobody would have raised more of a song and dance than Patrick if they had perversely stayed in. One who had followed tradition passed him before he had gone fifty yards from the bottom of the steps of No 1 and gave him a winsome who-do-you-think-you-are look as she did so, one with a greedy mouth, wearing a mostly white dress that buttoned down the front and had its row of buttons seriously pushed out of line from within, walking fast and in a kind of self-centred way on glistening red high-heeled shoes, chafing to track down some other poor bugger and fuck him up. Over to him, thank God.

The female codfish, Patrick reflected, was accustomed to producing ten million eggs at one go, allegedly by way of a copper-bottomed guarantee of the continuance of the species. No doubt that made excellent sense when cod were in question, but there was no reason to infer that the same basic philosophy would do for propagating human beings, not indefinitely, not these days with all the hygiene and drugs and high-protein diet and what-not. For Christ's sake, a pair of normally fertile people – the only ones to be considered – could be relied on to produce, would if left to themselves produce, one healthy offspring in every two or three dozen tries. Round it up to fifty at the outside. Reckon two-and-a-half offspring per set of parents to take care of your continuance situation and you totalled a hundred and twenty-five fucks. Postulate now an optimum child-bearing span of twelve and a half years and you divided out at ten a year, with a couple of supernumeraries thrown in as a potential source of x-factors, wild cards in the genetic deal. Which amounted to twelve in all, or one a month. For twelve and a half years. The question under review was after all purely one of *necessity*, how far Nature could be said to have been overdoing things, nothing more.

M'm. What was more radically at stake was of course the method of propagation rather than anything to do with frequency, necessity, etc. There were strong prima facie grounds there for arguing that Nature had been ill advised to try to refine on the codfish procedure. The female's share of the action there was over when she had succeeded in laying her eggs; that of the male, it seemed, amounted to coming off in the water nearby. If either had happened to have in mind any specific associate prior to the performance, which seemed doubtful, he or she would very likely not care or even notice if a third party nipped in instead. A nice easy-going arrangement. Not readily adaptable to suit the physical conditions of human life, true. And as for . . .

Patrick rather abruptly changed his position on the public bench where he now sat. Only then did it strike him that his train of thought had been fanciful in a special sense, in the unfortunate sense that Jenny and he were not normally fertile people, had not been since her miscarriage nearly seven years before, no great direct grief to him, but he shared in hers. It was something that, perhaps excusably, he tried to forget when he could. All the same, it had surely been unfeeling of him to forget it just then. Well, not really, not in any way that mattered. What was unfeeling, and much else, and what did matter, his reflections ran on without pause, was tolerating for a single instant that demented little bitch Barbara's proposal to come and live on his doorstep, and in no spirit of chummy neighbourliness either.

At the time when she first brought it up as a possibility, having 'dropped in' at his office one afternoon to 'wait for Simon', he had never laid a finger on her, not even verbally, not even optically. Well, not much really. So he had set about her there and then in a very direct way and in what he had told himself was a conscientious, almost statesmanlike spirit, quashing any doubts she might have about what would be required of her at her new address. That had been a day or two before he and Jenny had actually moved into Lower Ground. When he thought about Barbara since then it had been to

34

wonder how barmy she really was and to hope she had not been really serious about her rehousing scheme, until today.

But anyone with half an eye could have seen that the barminess to worry about was not hers but his. Molesting her in the office, not so much as thinking of trying to talk some sense into her, had been no worse than the act of an adolescent psychopath – round about par for him, in fact. Today was quite different. He could not even plead fairly that it had been sprung on him; he had had all the time in the world to decide to do and say all manner of non-insane things, down to and including what was probably the best of the lot: nothing. Instead of which . . . Instead of which he had made it much harder to avert what, again, anyone with half an eye could have seen would be an almost-certain catastrophe for four people. Yet hardly more than a few minutes ago, in cold blood, in the calm of 1B, he had thought it was a bit off but otherwise a fine idea.

Patrick found he was short of breath and something disagreeable was happening to the patch of skin just below the back of his neck. He had been on the point of cheering himself up with the fact that at least Jenny knew nothing. Now, that supposed fact buckled horribly. She had guessed; she had clutched at him, as he had put it, out of relief that he had not been away from the scene of the lunch very long after all, not long enough for anything serious to have happened; she had cried because he had spoken as if he loved her and she had thought he must have stopped.

He had a punishing struggle in the time it took his sense of proportion to come crawling back to him. Jenny was much too bright to attach any but fleeting importance to a mere guess. A guess was a mood, and she would never let a mood influence a decision of hers. Now he came to think of it, it would have been more natural if on their way home he had at least mentioned the Gileses' proposed move – pick that up later. But the vital thing, he now saw, was to block that move, to put a really classy spoke in the madwoman's wheel. He had no idea of what type of spoke it would be, but turn and fit one he would. Madwoman? No madder than he, no madder than he. Ah, folie à deux then, what? Well, un of the bloody deux was pulling out before somebody got killed.

Yes, it was still pleasantly sunny in the patch of garden, an extended square of well-laid turves bounded on two and a half sides by low walls of tiles and shallow bricks, and diversified with transplanted shrubs and trees too stout and well-embedded for local yobs to pull up. Admittedly, at second glance the whole thing began to look a bit too much like a planner's model blown up thirty-six times, but what sent Patrick on his way now was the thought that he might as well close his personal inventory while he was still winning. Even then a finishing touch had time to show: he would confide to Simon on Monday that the owners of the flats were rumoured to be putting in to the rent tribunal for an increase of unknown ratio. A threat like that would fix him up a treat, and that meant darling would be fixed up and all, real nice and tight.

He had started considering happily where he would take Jenny that evening, and was approaching No l, when he noticed a tall round-shouldered man in shabby clothes standing about near the foot of the steps, in fact the look of him was such that lurking or skulking would have been more like it. At the sight of Patrick he hesitated briefly and ran up the steps; again, to say he ran away up them would have been closer. He had no air of actual menace but he aroused no confidence either. There was nowhere for him to go up there except along the walk where the flats were, unless by a gigantic impromptu effort on to the roof of the building, but he might well have had no way of knowing that.

When Patrick, not dawdling but not rushing either, reached the top of the steps and turned the corner he saw the shabbily dressed man standing with his back to him at the far end, in front of the closed door of 1E. Seen there he looked a size larger than down in the street. He seemed to be going through his pockets in an unorganised way. Hearing Patrick's step he threw a glance over his shoulder, threw one if anybody ever did, and a transcendentally furtive and shifty one it was, but peaceable. Out of nosiness Patrick walked up to him, hearing from 1D what sounded like a basin emptying as Harold Porter-King pursued his hydrographical researches.

'Having trouble?'

'Yes. No, not really. It's just . . . I can't seem to . . .' He looked about forty, red and rather shiny in the face, with a kind of serf's haircut starting to go thin at the crown. At these close quarters his clothes could be seen to be not so much shabby as cheap and in need of a clean, a green imitation-suede zip-up jacket and stained denim trousers. Out of an already explored pocket of these he brought a latchkey. 'Ah, I thought it would have to be somewhere.'

Patrick lingered. He was certain by now that this, and not the other unusual creature seen earlier, was in truth the very funny chap of Jenny's description.

'Weren't you here this morning?' he asked.

'As a matter of fact I was. I didn't see you. I talked to a young woman in one of the other flats. She most kindly invited me in for a few minutes.'

'Yes, she told me. She's my wife.'

'Oh. Where do you live, then?'

'I live there too. In that same flat. 1B.'

'Oh. Of course.' Key in hand, the unknown had been looking Patrick over, but with circumspection, and finally with mild and passing disappointment. Straightening himself a little, he unlocked and shoved open the door of 1E in something like a single movement. 'Would you like to see inside?'

'Yes. Thanks,' said Patrick, who had seen the inside on an earlier occasion, but had also seen that if both these aliens decided to take the flats they were respectively interested in, there would be nowhere under this collective roof for Barbara Giles to lay her dainty head whatever else might betide. So he would hang about for a bit.

'After you.'

'Now, let's see, you're, er . . .'

The fellow nodded and smiled encouragingly while he waited to hear whatever Patrick might want to say about him.

'My name's Patrick Standish,' and hands up anyone with a better idea, he thought rather testily to himself.

'Oh sorry, I'm, er, Timothy Valentine.'

How had Jenny put it – 'a name that couldn't be right.' Check. 'I work in publishing. Firm called Hammond & Sutcliffe in Bloomsbury.'

'I see. Do go in. I'm a prison visitor.'

'How interesting. Which prisons do you visit?'

'We're not supposed to talk about it,' the man with the alias said from behind Patrick, who would have liked to hear more on the subject, not least what sort of living you made from visiting prisons. But he kept quiet and looked round without much interest at the perfectly bare room at the front of the apartment where the two of them had halted. On the other hand he paid close attention to the prospective lessee as he produced a sheaf of duplicated papers and seemed to be checking parts of it against the very little to be seen around him. He closely examined in turn a corner of the fireplace, which was a duplicate of the one in 1B, and the left-hand upright of the window-frame. After that he stood in a thoughtful attitude and stroked his chin.

'It's a nice size of room, this, don't you think?' he asked.

'Yes, I do.'

'I mean there's plenty of, er, plenty of room.'

'How many of you will be using it?'

'What? Oh, only one. Just me. Just me for the moment.'

'I should say there was rather a lot of room for one. It's a big apartment.'

This caused some disquiet. 'You mean you think it's too big?'

'Well, that's entirely up to you, obviously.'

Patrick realised he had not spoken like a man trying to press another man into a deal. He wanted to earn the credit of purposely excluding Barbara from No 1 Lower Ground, not to have her forestalled willy-nilly. Nothing daunted, though, Timothy Valentine had started to measure the distance from window to back wall by alternately putting one foot heel-to-toe in front of the other, not caring that his green suede Chelsea boots must stretch half a yard or so, nor reasoning that the information must be among his papers if anything was. After a moment of goggling incredulity Patrick thought he hid his fascination rather well. At what was evidently the close of the measuring session he said, 'I think this is very nice,' with a vague idea of offsetting earlier lukewarmness.

'I think I'll just have a quick look in the kitchen and upstairs. Please don't feel you've got to come too.'

'No, I'd be interested to see.'

It was a very quick look, taking in the sink and what lay underneath it but not the cooker or the cupboard space, and leaving out the main bedroom altogether, though attentive to such items as the cold tap over the bath and, to round things off, the light-switch by the front door.

'Well, I think that's about it.'

'What about the little room there?'

'Oh. Oh yes. No, I've seen that already.'

Outside 1B Patrick duly produced his key. From the bowels of 1D he faintly heard the voice of Harold Porter-King raised in what was very possibly a dialogue with himself. It was no distraction from thoughts of *Blood in the Tigris*, which came plodding back on feet not merely leaden but of actinium, a substance acclaimed in a recent *Times* article as the heaviest known to science.

After some moments' blinking and lip-exercise, Valentine said, 'Would you think it terribly rude and pushing of me if I asked you to let me have a very quick look inside your place? I've seen it before, I know, but there are just a couple of points I'd like to check if I may. Oh, that is sweet of you.'

As soon as he reached the sitting-room, which he pronounced charming twice over, T. Valentine more or less stopped bothering to pretend that his purpose in the last minute or two or longer had been anything other than getting himself invited in here. Asked to sit down, he accepted with a loud sigh of satisfaction, and when asked said he would love a cup of tea. Constraint left his manner. Neither then nor later did he set about checking points.

Waiting in the kitchen for the electric kettle, as Jenny always called it in full, and wondering a little where she had got to, Patrick heard from round the corner a dreadful cry, not really loud but chilling in its utter hopelessness, the sense it gave of profound and irreparable loss. He hurried back whence he had come.

'What on earth was that?'

'I'm sorry, what was what?'

'That, that appalling noise just now. Is anything the – '

'Noise? I didn't hear anything. It must have come from outside. Back there.'

'I suppose it might.'

The conundrum remained troublesomely unsolved while the two drank tea and Patrick tried to answer a question about what he did in publishing, and was put out to find how little there seemed to be to say. He was down to shareholders' meetings when he noticed an expression of childish petulance coming over T. Valentine's face. It swiftly faded, but a few seconds later reformed and intensified, until he seemed on the verge of bawling tears. His breathing became irregular.

'Have you got a cat in here?' he quavered, blinking furiously.

39

'Yes, actually.' At this sort of hour Frankie would have been asleep on the bed upstairs. 'Is anything the – '

Eyes tight shut now, the other gave a couple of brief cries, not the same as the one heard earlier, more like simple pain or need to vomit. Then, after a prodigious intake of breath, there came a succession of what could have been nothing more than sneezes after all. Until now a certain Graham McClintoch, a former colleague and flat-mate, had had primacy in the sneezing domain as witnessed by Patrick, but this chap surpassed him, if not in volume then in wealth of emotional response, the compelling suggestion that here was a gross and unwarranted indignity, and what was more quite out of the blue. They are *sneezes*, Patrick wanted pressingly to point out to him, common-or-garden bloody *sneezes*, not visitations of God. But there was not a great deal anybody could have done.

'There's something in their fur,' explained T. Valentine, blowing his nose inside out in an unexpectedly clean white handkerchief. 'I'll be all right now. You know it's a funny thing, but I once spent a whole afternoon with someone who kept guinea-pigs, dozens of the things, not just one or two, and it didn't affect me at all. Not so much as a snuffle. Which you wouldn't expect, would you?'

'No, you wouldn't, would you? More tea?'

'I say, thank you very much, it's awfully good of you.'

Patrick was on his way out when the call of doom sounded once more. This time he caught the offender in the act, mouth wide open, whites of the eyes showing.

'There! That's what I heard. What the hell was it? What is it?'

'I'm terribly sorry, it was just me yawning. Sometimes I don't notice when I'm doing it. People have mentioned it to me before.'

'Well, for . . . Oh, for . . .' Behind him Patrick heard the door of 1D shut and footsteps pass and die away. For a moment he violently wanted a cigarette.

'I often seem to get drowsy in the afternoons, I don't know whether you find that. Even when I haven't had anything to drink, like today.'

'If you've got any more noises up your sleeve, perhaps you wouldn't mind letting me know in advance.'

'I am sorry, I hope I haven't annoyed you.'

40

'Get away, it's toned me up. I'll get the tea.'

But he had hardly washed out the mugs when T. Valentine joined him in the kitchen. With anyone but Jenny potentially in his way in that small space he was apt to feel crowded, but for some reason not with this chap.

'Your wife's out, I take it.'

'Well yes. She shouldn't be long now.'

'It must be lovely and cosy with the two of you in here. You haven't any children, have you?'

'No.'

'I thought not. When there are children about you know straight away. I've noticed that from my sister's family. There's always stuff lying about. You thought that place I was looking at just now was on the big side for one person, didn't you? I could tell.'

'No, not really,' said Patrick in an open-minded way. 'Lots of people like a bit of space.'

'Of course it is bigger than this. You see, there was a girl I was going to bring, but in the end I decided against it. I could see too many difficulties coming up.'

'What sort of difficulties?'

'No, they're not the sort that would bother someone like you. I ought to have got over them by my time of life. But now, I don't suppose I ever shall.'

Patrick wordlessly but encouragingly passed across a mug of fresh tea.

'As far as I can make out, everything goes back to the time I – '

Provided his trousers were where they should have been, Patrick was always glad when Jenny appeared, but he would have had to confess he would have been even better pleased today to hear her key in the lock five minutes later than he did. Anyway, in she came; she looked fine – fit and cheerful; she had been for a little stroll, she said; T. Valentine was reintroduced and remembered; Jenny drove the men back into the sitting-room to await biscuits she would bring them along with proper fresh tea.

'Mr Valentine – ' began Patrick when the three were settled.

'I wonder,' said the man referred to, sounding as if he really thought it might go either way, 'if I could persuade you to call me Tim.'

41

When that had been cleared up, Patrick said, 'Tim tells me he's a prison visitor.'

'Yes, well I think it is a reasonably useful sort of job.'

'It's a marvellous job,' said Jenny, sounding like her mother.

'I suppose it pays literally nothing at all,' said Patrick craftily.

'No, nothing whatever. Their budget just wouldn't run to it. They have to watch every penny. They're on a very tight, er, budget. They simply . . .'

And try as he might to block this exit by saying a lot of things like 'I quite understand' and going on nodding his head, Patrick was unable for the moment to satisfy his now quite keen curiosity about what Tim did for a living. Even less could there have been a return to those alluring difficulties of which he had barely started to speak. Instead, he told them some incredibly unrevealing things about prisons and visiting them. When about to leave, an event signalled well in advance, he said,   —

'Well, now we're to be neighbours, perhaps you'll let me take you out to dinner to celebrate.'

Not tonight, they said, not even in the jacket and tie he promised, but, Jenny said, when he was that way again he could drop in on them for supper.

'Oh, could I really? When? Tomorrow? What about tomorrow? No, I can't tomorrow. What about Monday?'

Monday was agreed. After prizewinning-type handshakes and dockside-style waves while he moved from just outside the front door to the top of the steps, Tim Valentine was lost to view.

'Oofh!' said Patrick. 'I take it he was your very funny chap?'

'Oh yes. He was funny too, didn't you think?'

'Oh, a bloody scream.'

'No, I mean really funny in himself. The way he pushed his mouth in and out when he was listening. And the way he juddered his leg up and down when he was sitting, as if he was bursting for a pee.'

'Was it really necessary to invite him to supper like that? Not a moment to be lost?'

'Well I think it was in a way. Well, not necessary, but he was so disappointed when we said we couldn't make it tonight. I think he's lonely, don't you?'

'You want to be on your bloody guard against lonely buggers, you know. You tend to start finding out why they're lonely when it's too late. There was a new bloke at the Grammar one year like that. Wouldn't talk at first. Would later, though.'

'He's all right, is Tim.' Jenny was clearing away in the sitting-room. 'More tea?'

'No thanks. He's off his head too. Is Tim.'

'You don't mean really?'

'I don't know. No, not really, I suppose. I'll tell you over dinner.'

'Ooh lovely,' she said, no doubt thinking more about the promised restaurant meal than having Tim's derangement explained to her. 'He seemed quite set on taking that flat, I thought.'

'Sounded like it, didn't he?'

'The one at the end, you said. Wasn't that the one Simon and, er, Barbara seemed to like the sound of?'

'That's right, yes.'

'Well, I dare say they might still like the one two doors along, 1D it'd be.'

'I was going to tell you,' said Patrick, trying and failing to remember a time when he had felt more like a robot – 'there was a bloke looking over that earlier on.' When she said nothing he added, doing his best not to babble, 'He was in there for a hell of a long time.'

'So what with one thing and another it's on the cards the building's going to be all full up.'

'Yes.'

'Oh well, there we are.' Jenny paused by the door and giggled slightly. 'I'm sorry, I can't help thinking of that Tim sat there juddering his leg up and down. Of course legs are apt to be funny anyway when you can see them. Men's legs.'

'So I remember you saying before.'

Four

By Monday morning the fine weather had gone. Gusts of rain dashed irregularly across the windows of 1B Lower Ground as if propelled by a trainee effects man. A uniform charcoal-coloured sky hung over the low-price department store opposite. All its lights were on, illuminating abominations of three-piece suite and Turkey carpet, panelled bath and plastic tile. The traffic had passed its rush-hour peak, but still stretched back from the corner where vehicles waited to turn up left for Waterloo Bridge.

Patrick was well on the go, had to be with a board meeting at 10 o'clock. He was taking a final pee when the cat Frankie jumped up on the nearby stool and stuck out his nose towards the lever of the cistern. This was standard practice, designed to show how starved of affection he was. If he strained to put his head as close as he could to where his stony-hearted master's hand was going to be, the poor lonely creature might just cop a quick stroke or so to cheer him through the morning. Well anyway, he had never been seen to try that kind of thing with Jenny.

'Get down, you bugger,' said Patrick, having fallen for it as always, and gone all the way from forehead to tail-tip for good measure. He might have merely jogged the stool while so doing, nowhere near enough to send any normal cat hurtling from the room like that, head again outstretched, now indicating dread. This was Frankie's other role, the refugee from casual torture. In face of all this Patrick managed to quite like him, and generously forbore from ever reminding Jenny of his liberality in giving Frankie a home when he married her. It was sometimes said

44

that he was not ideally suited for life in a flat but no remedy was ever proposed.

By the front door Patrick picked up his brief-case. *Blood in the Tigris* was not in it; he had suspended as an emergency measure his interdiction on passing in mid-read from one manuscript to another. His happiness, his wife's happiness, had depended on it.

His wife was there now and he kissed her. 'Good-bye darling. See you tonight.'

'Don't forget we've got that Tim chap coming.'

'Oh Christ, so we have. Anything you want me to bring back?'

'Some of that nice bread.'

When Patrick emerged he found his neighbour at 1A, an Admiralty civil servant named Eric Davidson, standing outside its door and ringing its bell. He turned his neat dark head towards Patrick, still a short-back-and-sides man, Eric, even in this shaggy age, with businesslike glasses and a pointed nose.

'Lost your key?'

'I'd need a hatchet, Patrick. Silly cow's bolted it.'

'Some sort of row, I presume?'

'I presume too.' Eric rang the bell again and pounded with his fist. 'She fancied a *News* with her coffee, see, so I go out and get it, all the way to the corner in this, and when I get back, no entry.' He pounded again. 'Stevie! Stupid bag! What's the matter? Come on, bird-brain, open up!'

'It must be something you said.'

'Oh it *must*, must it? When did it ever need to be something? Nothing's just as good as something, you know that as well as I do. You're married,' said Eric, with a glance heavenwards. 'I've got to get to the office.'

'So have I. If you – '

'Look, Patrick, you give her a yell. You never know, she might come for you. Half-witted tart.'

'Stevie, it's Patrick!' He thumped. 'Stevie!'

There was silence inside for a moment, then a substantial crash of glass or china.

'Oh God, we've got to there, have we? Of course, it's all her not being in work any more, you know, the whole thing. Well, thanks for trying, Patrick. Bring me a hot Cornish pasty when you get back tonight. I'll be needing it by that time.'

45

Struggling to reach the Mini through the thick rain, Patrick thought about Eric and Stevie, whom he and Jenny had run into on their first evening and had exchanged drinks with a couple of times since. Eric, a few years the younger at, he said, forty-three, seemed a straightforward sort of person compared with Stevie, who was more generally known under his professional name of Steve Bairstow. Until a few years ago he had been in some demand in films and broadcasting for hard-bitten masculine parts that also called for a touch of puzzled integrity. But since then, as Eric had indicated just now, Stevie's public appeal seemed to have dwindled, and he had had to confine the rendering of his special qualities to household sulks and rages like this morning's. Patrick found them an entertaining-enough couple, but he would have put up with a much lower standard so as not to miss the way Jenny looked and behaved in their company, like someone in a cage of very reliable wild animals.

The rain had let up marginally, but the light was still miserable when Patrick drove across the bridge. Barges and tugs moved slowly up and down the channel in what had to be an intrepid way, making dismal noises audible through the swish of tyres. He was a Londoner now, had better be one to put up with such filthy weather. Of course you were born in this city, Mr Standish, in fact not five miles south of this very bridge, but tell me, what brought you back? Well, as it happened he could be quite specific on that one.

He remembered it like yesterday, the dinner-party at the house of his headmaster, one Torkington, in Abbots Langley, the excellent and abundant claret, Simon Giles, the go-ahead young publisher from London, and his wife, who was almost as go-ahead in a different way, even the reflections of the candle-flames in the polished oak. He remembered how some combination of these forces had induced him to answer in detail, and at some length, when challenged to say what he thought an uncontrollably go-ahead publisher should be publishing in the later '60s and the '70s. And he remembered no less clearly waking up the next morning without the faintest idea of anything he had told them, which was all right in a way.

Or would have been. What was in his head was a fantasy about somebody saying something about a contract being sent up. This he tried to shake off until the moment he also remem-

46

bered well, when the school porter limped into his *Aeneid*
X-XII class and haled him off to the lodge. Here or in the adjacent echoing hall, under the porter's malevolent gaze, he was
confronted by a helmeted, gaitered figure in black. Film-fed
images of conspiracy and madness, boosted by his hangover,
swirled about him. They were not much abated when he found
the person before him was a motor-cycle messenger; in those
days you were as likely to be brought a message by light aircraft
as by motor-bike. The contract, which was what the message
had indeed turned out to consist of, sent him rebounding into
euphoria, a title to the promised land, a ticket to the good life.

It had even looked all right later. 'I think you ought to
consider it quite carefully,' said Torkington, a youngish man
for his post and father of a girl whose roving eye had caught
Patrick's in the insufficiently distant past. 'Taking into account
the end of the school year.'

'Are you trying to get rid of me?'

'If I were, you wouldn't have to ask. No, I'm thinking of
your future if you stay. Latin's on the skids. When do you
retire? '94 is it?'

''96.'

'Good God. Even if there's any of it left at all by that time,
you'll have been fighting a losing battle for ages before then.
You're decreasingly relevant, Patrick. Civics or whatever they
call it, that's the trend these days. I seriously think you could
do as much good in publishing as where you are now. Or where
you will be in a few years. I mean with your qualifications.'

'Something in that, I suppose.'

Torkington said earnestly, 'I thought young Simon was very
interesting on the importance of a strong classical list. So were
you, if I may say so.'

'Oh well, you know, one can't help running over these matters
in one's mind from time to time. How long have you known
Simon?'

'I agree he's not quite the sort of fellow you might expect me
to know at all, but despite the age difference our fathers were
at Cambridge together. Believe it or not. Do, er, do have a good
think about what I've said. Go into it with Jenny, of course.
And Graham.'

Patrick had certainly had a good think about what
Torkington had said and what he had not said, though without

47

being able to decide, then or ever, how far this caper had been fixed up or discussed beforehand, if at all. Of course he had indeed gone into the thing with Jenny, asked her to weigh up moving to London, leaving her friends in the neighbourhood, changing her job, all that, and she had been surprised to be consulted rather than told. Graham McClintoch, noted for sneezes, also incidentally chemistry master, had been less encouraging.

'I'm fully aware I'll get no thanks for saying so, Standish, but let me just remind you you'll be subject to temptations and pressures in London you can barely guess at here.'

'I think I can completely guess at some of them. London is on the same planet, after all.'

'To hell, there's more than one kind of temptation, even for depraved fellows like you. Remember too, once you leave the profession there's no way back in.'

'I'm just jumping before I'm pushed, mate.'

'I learnt at my mother's knee, if you sell yourself make sure you get a good price. Don't forget it just because I've said it before – the money won't go so far up there as it would here.'

He could actually have said it again and no harm, thought Patrick as he trotted to his office, in fact he had, but not loudly enough. That princely emolument had shrunk, when he started living on it, to about all right, to needing to be taken in here if it was to be let out there, and most memorably to his giving up smoking. Even his room on the second floor had come to seem less grandly spacious than in his first weeks, its rare moulded ceiling a foot or so lower than the optimum. But the panelling, the carpeting, the leather-covered chairs, the leather-topped desk called for no complaint, and it was a fine Georgian building that looked out on to a fine Georgian square, where the tops of the big horse-chestnuts in the garden were looking greener as the skies began to lighten. In fact, Patrick at the moment was feeling about as good as a man could have felt who had no workshop-run-in 1968 Tedeschi-Pratt with the twin Brownings scheduled for delivery outside at 12.30 and no lunch date thereafter at the Caprice with Elizabeth Taylor, or even one at the Golden Egg in Leicester Square with the sulky girl who doled out the green stamps at the garage by Euston tube.

Patrick assured himself that nothing disagreeable had arrived in his absence to claim his attention. In a sense nothing could, disagreeable or not, since his departure on Friday evening, unless paranormally. His secretary, lately redesignated his assistant, was not due to turn up for over half an hour, and over the weekend the place was shut up like a bullion vault. But somehow Simon, the bugger's very presence in the metropolitan area, had a way of throwing doubt on that.

It was seven minutes to ten. Before the bugger could summon him Patrick was off downstairs. Actually the summons, over the posh and bizarre-looking American intercom installed that January, would by routine have come from Simon's assistant. Unlike the other assistants, she could be coerced into appearing at the office before ten, but then she was called not Simon's assistant but his deputy.

Of course he was not to be found in his first-floor sanctum. No: with a good five minutes still in hand he was sitting, his deputy at his side, in the new board-room in the basement. The ceiling here was much lower than the one in Patrick's office, and instead of being moulded it had strip lighting attached to it. Simon had explained that touches like that, taken in conjunction with the long plastic-covered tables and tube-frame chairs, gave the right practical, hardheaded impression, the feel of a place where decisions were taken, costs counted, merchandise sold. It got clean away, he had further elucidated, from the stuffy sherry-decanter, sporting-print image of publishing. The old board-room across the landing from his own office was closed pending redecoration, nobody said in what style or for what destined purpose.

Patrick sat down opposite Simon and poured himself a paper cup of ice-water, a beverage always in generous supply at Hammond & Sutcliffe. Another man sat at right angles to them, a frowning bespectacled man in a dark suit and striped tie who was writing steadily on a large lined pad with an old-fashioned fountain-pen. He too was attended by an assistant or deputy; at least a younger man, lumberjacketed and bearded like a Russian mystic, in all likelihood no assistant but a simple packer in search of a minute's sit-down, straddled a nearby chair. For the packing department and such branches of the firm were all over the lower floors, in fact had made good use of this very room until ousted for ideological reasons.

Simon leant compellingly forward. 'Patrick, have you met Gary? Gary is our sales manager.'

'Of course,' said Patrick, who of course had inescapably met and had to do with Gary half a dozen times.

'And Gary, you know Patrick.'

And Gary did, and inclined his head, though cleverly without having to look up or interrupting the flow of his pen.

'I've asked Gary to come along today because I think we on the board need to be reminded from time to time that we don't live in an ivory tower. That's to say we're not working in a vacuum. There has to be somebody there to *translate* our ideas into action, to get everything that can be got out of the passable ones and pick up the pieces of the stinkers. And that means we've access to feedback.' Simon's dark eyes, in accord for once, seemed to gleam with the pure love of his profession. 'You see, Gary's down there on the shop floor, where things actually get made.'

More followed. For the first time, and with a lot of ground to be made up, Patrick began to feel there might be something to be said for Gary. It was not only that he wrote on through it all as fluently as a chef setting down a favourite recipe, considerable as that was. He also carried the concept of ignoring something or somebody much further than usual, to the point of obliterating them from all levels of consciousness. What was he writing on that big lined pad? Patrick hoped very much it was pornography, of a sadistic or scatological tendency for choice. He tried to edge round to see.

'A book is a commodity like any other,' Simon was affirming, 'and like any other it has to be sold. Which means the traditional approach must go. Ah – morning, Jack.'

Grey-flannelled, with close-clipped grey moustache, Old Something tie and polished brogues, R. Elliot 'Jack' Sutcliffe nodded silently and separately to all present, including after some hesitation the bloke with the face-fungus. Jack's complexion and the state of his eyes linked him securely with the sherry-decanter rather than the sporting-print aspect of the old image of publishing. He was then sixty-four years old. People were always pointing out, perhaps more emphatically than was needed, that he was not the great Robert Sutcliffe who had co-founded the firm in 1923, but the much younger brother of that long-departed pioneer.

'I was just running over a few points with Patrick,' said

Simon, decently not looking at his watch at Jack's arrival. 'So very briefly . . .'

It was fairly briefly considering. At the end, Simon leant forward even more vitally than before and just then Gary decided he had written enough for now. The board-meeting was in session. In the interests of flexibility and spontaneity, no minutes or agenda had been circulated at these gatherings for some months past. Patrick had learnt how to deal with such do's from years of staff-meetings at the Grammar. The trick was to disengage, to think about sex and other matters in that general area of interest, but be ready to leap to full alertness, or what might have passed for that, at any one of a number of triggers or stimuli. He had got so good at it that he sometimes came round without knowing why. That happened this morning, when the group were only a couple of minutes into their deliberations, quite long enough though for him to have been well away in his brown study.

'Now the new Mabuse,' Simon was saying. On the table in front of him was what was most likely an agenda, one restricted to that single copy so as not to interfere with anyone else's flexibility, etc. 'It's done brilliantly in the States and I think we should go for October, alongside the update of *The Mode is the Meaning*. We agreed last time we should strengthen the Media Monitors, and to me this feels right for that.'

It was sociology, either the word itself or a synonym, that must have rung the bell for him, thought Patrick. That being the subject he had in a sense left teaching to get away from. More to hinder Simon from scoring another felt-tipped tick than anything else, he said, 'How did we do with the previous one? *Sexuality and Culture*, was it?'

The words were hardly out of his mouth when the unnamed youngster, who had pulled his chair up beside Gary's on the call to order, pressed a button at the side of a kind of shallow box. This move, as it seemed, caused the thing to fly open with a resounding click and present to his hand an oblong of light-red paper which he passed to Gary. The operations had taken perhaps four seconds.

'Eight-four-three-eight as at thirty-first-third,' said Gary in his no-bones-about-it cockney accent.

'You can't assess the impact from that,' said Simon.

'Maybe not, but if it means eight-thousand-odd copies by the end of March it doesn't seem like much, however you look at it. Not after what it's cost us. How did it do in America?'

Gary glanced at Simon, who said rather sharply, 'The contexts aren't comparable, Patrick.'

'Ah, well that answers that. What's the new one called?'

'Er, *The Ethics of Insurgency.*'

'Alternative title,' said Jack Sutcliffe, speaking for the first time, 'Communist propaganda pamphlet number two hundred and two.'

'Some pamphlet, if it's anything like the last one,' said Patrick.

'We have to face the fact,' said Simon, 'that serious works on the media are apt to be written from a Marxist or neo-Marxist point of view. It's simply the trend.'

'Isn't there something called,' – Jack breathed noisily in and out – er, er, bucking the trend? So my grand-daughter appears to think.'

'When and if something of sufficient standing comes along taking a negative view, then, naturally, Jack, I need hardly say, I hope, well, we'll obviously consider it very carefully.'

'I can't see why we started bothering with the damned things in the first place. We've just heard we can't even give them away. Not surprising if you've ever tried to read one.'

'We felt these were books we as a serious house ought to be publishing and would benefit from having on our list. That was what we decided.'

Jack looked down at the table in front of him as if to turn up the record, but of course there was nothing there to be turned up. Then he looked at Patrick as if for support or sympathy, but caught on that it was Patrick he was looking at and looked away again.

After an unexpected polite pause, Simon started talking about something to do with what he called the developing countries.

Patrick realised with a sudden glow of elation that the shop where he would be getting the nice bread for Jenny and the second-best horn shop known to him could be no more than two minutes' walk apart. If he dropped in at the one after the other he could legitimately be said to have been passing. It further occurred to him that a new number of *Titter* ought to be coming out about now, perhaps even a new *Twosome*. If the latter, it was much to be hoped that the promising central idea should not be diluted by attempts at puckish humour, by

52

frivolity. There was no point in putting the fair one and the dark one into a boxing ring if all they did when they got there was fall through the ropes or count each other out. He might offer himself as editorial adviser. Series consultant. Planning groups. Conferences. A happy vision was opening up when he heard Simon say,

'. . . Jerry Sebastian. I'm sorry but I'm afraid he'll have to go.'

'Which is he?' asked Jack. 'I've forgotten him.'

'Did the book on Lord Alfred Douglas and his circle.'

'*Circle* is right. I've got him now. Urhh! I know all I need to know about him, thank you very much.'

Patrick felt he could hardly cite Sebastian's reputed pass at Jenny in mitigation. So he said, 'I saw him at your party on Saturday, Simon.'

Jack said nothing, but his eyes swelled and stood out more conspicuously from the rest of his face.

'Just a small do,' said Simon. 'Poets mainly. Not Jack's kind of thing, was it, Patrick?'

'No, not at all his kind of thing,' said Patrick with some feeling. 'Anyway, as I say, Sebastian was among those whose kind of thing it was. He didn't do anything while I was there to get him thrown off our list.'

'Yes, well you see the point is it's not a good idea to let a dropped author feel he's being let go because he's been passed over or forgotten or his face doesn't fit. It's only fair to him to show him he's still very much a person as far as we're concerned and a fully conscious decision has been taken about him on the merits of the case.'

'So having him to that – having him to brunch was to show him he was still a person?'

'Yes,' said Simon, with a pleased smile that this had got across.

'A person who hasn't got a publisher any more. I see. And what about the merits of the case?'

'He's spending without delivering. Gary?'

'Provisional title *The Yellow Book and After*, contract signed one-eight-sixty-four, for delivery one-one-sixty-six, £500 advanced, delivered twenty-twelve-sixty-five, £350 advanced, returned for rewriting two-four-sixty-six, £200 advanced twenty-four-four-sixty-six, £150 advanced two-eleven-sixty-six. Ends.'

This could not have taken more than fifteen seconds to deliver, and Patrick was quite charged up by having taken parts of it in. 'What was wrong with what he delivered at the end of '65?'

'There was just nothing in it. Lance said it was unpublishable and I agreed with him. Simply not enough relevant material.'

'But we had commissioned it.'

'Yes. That's to say Lance had.'

Patrick had joined the firm just too late to have met Lance, who had gone to a job in New York two years before, since when follies and misdemeanours attributable to him had never ceased to come to light.

'And that's to say we had. And presumably we asked him to rewrite it.'

'He brought in a couple of chapters last September. Still impossible. Damn-all there.'

'It sounds to me a bit as if there never was a book there and we were wrong to commission it.'

Simon stared at Patrick, still unifocally, and gave one of his rare but famous loud silly laughs. 'So what's this great attack of scruples? What do you care about a no-hoper like that?'

'Yes, can't we get on, chaps?' pleaded Jack. 'Good riddance to bad rubbish if you ask me. Actually I glanced at the Alfred Douglas book. Not particularly clever. Rather filthy. Not very funny.'

'Say the word and I'll give Sebastian to you to look after, Patrick. Would that be a good idea?'

'No no, a bloody awful idea, forget it. Just idle curiosity. Sorry, I don't know what got into me.'

At the time he thought it was the memory of that nefarious brunch, then a concern to get back at Simon for being married to Barbara. But he would settle it later, because now Simon was saying, perhaps to underline who was in charge,

'The Centuries' Heritage. Patrick.'

This series of books about ancient civilisations, both words interpreted pretty freely, was what he had been hired to organise, or so it had turned out. He had quite quickly found that its purpose was not educational or of course commercial but political: anybody who accused Hammond & Sutcliffe of

54

opportunism or greed could be refuted by pointing to the relentless austerity of The Centuries' Heritage. But even after that discovery, and working here, it was fair to say that he was still interested in the series, and he answered up about it satisfactorily today.

Or he did until Simon put a finger on his bit of paper and said, 'You haven't mentioned *Blood in the Tigris*.'

Patrick had been ready for that one, but he muffed things rather with his first line, which went, 'Ah – now *Blood in the Tigris* I'm taking very seriously indeed.'

He had forgotten for a moment too long that the phrase was not far from a house formula pleading idleness and asking for a postponement. They all got it; even Jack lifted his head like an old buck wondering if he had heard a twig snap. Try again.

'Yes. I have to say bluntly at the outset that I found this book something of a disappointment after *Dreamtime Children of Ayers Rock*' (outdid even that hotchpotch of illiterate fabrication).

'Which has now sold . . . Gary?'

Click. 'Three-one-oh-two-two as at thirty-one-three.'

'Thank you. Carry on, Patrick.'

'Right. Now nobody's asking for strict historical truth' (more than a faint concern for probability) 'but here and there' (throughout) 'the author seems to be writing pure fantasy' (at a level to defeat comparison).

'Really. Can you give me an example?'

'Oh yes.' Patrick could always do that in situations like this. He read aloud a passage selected, with old-examinee's finesse, from a late page of the work.

As the fine summer night sank over Sippara and his hosts sank to rest in their tents, the king was wakeful. The illuminance of the young moon smote his face and Nabonidos sank down. 'Great One,' he supplicated, 'hast thee forgotten the sanction of Belshazzar and I, of we who renovated thy temple at Harran and watered it with the blood of many internees?' For a reply there came naught but the mysterious cry of a nightbird.

'Well I ask you, honestly!'

He was going to have to do better than that. Simon and Jack

looked at him in mild expectation and concern, anxious not to let him down and spoil the joke. The others just hung about.

Simon said tentatively, 'Is that very . . . bad?'

'Christ, I don't know where to begin. Nabonidos's place at Sippara was a fortified encampment, so it's most unlikely anybody would – '

'I didn't know you were an expert on this bit of ancientry.'

'I just glanced at the encyclopedia, which is the most old Pedrain-Williams can ever have done. If only he'd stuck to it. There's no evidence the Babylonians – '

'What you read out seemed to me by way of being a rattling good yarn,' said Jack. 'At least the fellow wasn't supplicating for his boy-friend. Or singing the praises of Comrade Lenin.'

'But look at the *writing*, he can't even – '

'As Jack would agree, you couldn't call it trendy. Mark my words, they'll soon not be making them like that any more.'

'But the way he simply – '

'You remember we agreed from the start that these were to be books aimed at the general public.'

'That hasn't got to mean morons, has it?'

'Calm *down*, Patrick. You must always keep trying to remember, dear boy, you're not publishing for the benefit of the Latin Sixth. That's it in a nutshell.'

Patrick asked himself whether he had expected them all to jump up in spontaneous indignation, shaking their fists and begging him to let them hear no more, at about the point when Nabonidos started supplicating. After that had failed to happen he might as well have thrown in the towel straight away. But that came later too, and in the meantime he agreed to select no more than say twelve passages, preferably not too long, and tell the author, ask the author if he would care to put more work into them.

Finally they arrived at Jack's weed-infested domain, an inheritance from pre-1939 days and now a diminishing area that held a bare half-dozen elderly novelists, all but one of them women, all steadily producing and selling and including among their number the second and fifth biggest earners on the Hammond & Sutcliffe list. Jack gave what energy he could summon to trying out recruits, but none had really taken so far.

'How's the new Deirdre?' asked Simon when that part was over.

Jack sighed and brushed scurf off his eyebrows. 'To be quite frank with you I don't know. You may remember just after Christmas she had a chapter and a bit to do – well, that's the last I heard. Of the new novel, I mean. I've now written to her four times but I can't get a word out of her. Not about that.'

'Have you tried the phone?'

'She won't talk over the telephone. Well, she is seventy-seven. And Irish.'

When Simon said nothing Patrick put the obvious one. 'What words can you get out of her?'

'Ho! Complaints. Accusations. Justify if we can the scurvy publicity we gave her last. Why haven't we put the three early novels and the short stories back in print. I know, she didn't really find her length until 1933 but I shouldn't like to have to be the one to tell the old girl that. And we wouldn't lose money on the early stuff, even today. As I believe I've told you before.'

'Difficult,' said Simon.

'Difficult! I should have thought it was positively – '

'Have you thought of going over there?'

'No. Anyway she won't see visitors.'

'Shall I write to her?'

'I don't think I should if I were you, old boy.'

Simon seemed to find difficulty in concentrating. 'What does her agent say? It's er . . .'

'Trevor. He says he's sure she'll deliver soon. That's what he was saying in January. I don't like the sound of that somehow.'

'Difficult. Let me have a think about it. I'll let you know.'

Patrick decided that in Jack's place he would not have cared much for the sound of that either. When the meeting started to break up Jack looked at him and away again rather as he had done earlier. It was clear the old fart fancied a drink with somebody, only it was a bit early for a drink and in any case there was no somebody in sight.

In rising from the table Jack managed, half on purpose perhaps, to knock the sales-register box of tricks on to the floor. While Gary and his aide set about picking it up and retrieving the pieces that had fallen out of or off it, Patrick took a quick couple of paces to one side and squinted at the few lines of neat handwriting across the top of Gary's pad. They ran:

to bed in a cosy hollow under the river-bank. Herbert took the outside place because he was the biggest and strongest of the brood, though he would have been no match for a four-legged antagonist. But Mr and Mrs Webtoes between them reckoned they could beat off Humphrey Otter, Alan Water-Rat or any other foraging intruder. So they thought . . .

Well, it just went to show, thought Patrick, feeling somehow threatened by his discovery.

The board and its assistants straggled out of the board-room, or wartime-type ops room as Simon could have thought of it in some part of his mind. For a moment or two he laid his arm along Patrick's shoulders in the completely non-queer but still creepy way he had.

'Are you happy in your work?' he asked, using a faded catchphrase.

'Eh? Oh yes.'

'I thought you sounded a wee bit . . . er, restive once or twice back there. If, you know, if you feel unsettled about your life here it would be silly not to say, wouldn't it? I mean just plain silly, yes?'

'Yes, but I don't at all. I feel absolutely . . .'

Feel absolutely what on earth? Simon halted on the metallic staircase, forcing Gary and his lad to do the same lower down. He fixed Patrick with his direct eye while the other voyaged none knew where. 'You don't feel like having a think about it and then a chat?'

'No, not a bit. No, no.'

After a definite pause, Simon moved on up. 'Fine,' he said, climbing. 'Fine.'

At intervals through the rest of the day, Patrick thought over the reasons why Simon had hired him. Or rather he did that for the thousandth time since it had happened. His account of the reasons had changed in emphasis with the passing of time. He himself could not have been safely ruled incapable of making such an offer out of drunkenness pure and simple, but even he would have come round long before reaching for that motor-bike. A fit of vainglory, brought on not by alcohol but by egotism, was all too possible in Simon's case as a clincher, a topper-up. A reason that had always been part of the field but had gradually moved up among the front-runners, not to his comfort, was a more or less considered desire on Simon's part to cut such a figure as never was seen before in the publishing trade, to be spoken of in awed tones from Henrietta Street to Queen Square as the fellow who *on a couple of hours' acquaintance* went and hired *a schoolmaster* who taught *Latin*. Then there was securing what certainly ought to have been a rock-solid pro-Simon vote on the board, and, last and least, the bloody old Centuries' Heritage. Field-marshals had been appointed on shakier grounds. Oh, and just as a long shot, a really daft reason that at the same time was not so far from one or two of the others, what about the eruption of an unfocused but strong feeling of impatience with the world? Patrick could understand that.

At the end of the afternoon he read through the typed-up letter to the author of *Blood in the Tigris* he had dictated earlier, and enjoyed the experience so much he sagaciously put the thing aside for rereading the next day. Then he went and got some of the nice bread, and then he went on and got, yes, *Titter 7* (new series) and, yes, *Twosome 3*, with four pages showing details of a wrestling-bout approached in a reasonably responsible manner, without levity.

Five

The new nurse, the pretty little Scottish one, had of course meant no harm, just spoken without thinking, and Sister, blessedly on hand at that very moment, had come to the rescue straight away. It had been nothing – over and done with in a flash. All the same, even these seven years after her miscarriage, Jenny had still not got quite used to being asked out of the blue if she had children. And obviously being in the ward at the time, with actual children all around, including a little girl only a year or so older than her own would have been, had made it that much more difficult.

She forgot about it over lunch with two or three nurses she knew in the very good canteen, but going home in the bus she found her thoughts drifting back. No one knew what had caused her to miscarry after five months of normal pregnancy; no one knew why she had been unable to become pregnant since. At least, it was known that she was failing to ovulate, but not why or what to do about it.

'I'm afraid it's exactly the sort of thing we'll be able to put right like an ingrowing toenail in twenty years, but for now, well, we're stuck.' The nice serious young doctor had been the most recent of several. 'I wish I could say something more cheerful.'

'In twenty years I'll be forty-eight. Do you mean there's no hope?'

'Not at all, you might conceive next week. But I'd be misleading you if I told you it was at all likely.'

'What are the chances? No, you can't say, I understand.'

Everyone agreed it was not her fault, nothing she had done or failed to do, and she was as convinced of that herself as she

60

could be. And yet she could not help feeling she had let Patrick down. He had never said or shown he thought so, and nobody would have picked him out as the husband most eager to become a father, but after all he had married her because she was going to have a baby, and to put it crudely the least she could have done was give him his money's worth. And then she felt pretty useless, not having a baby to look after at her time of life and the way she was fixed. In her opinion, no wife could have a full-time job and expect to look after her husband properly, hence her reluctant switch from proper infant-school teaching to mornings-only at the hospital, though that had turned out reasonably well – anyway, there was still no denying she seemed to have too much free time. She remembered putting the point, well wrapped up, naturally, to one of her Highbury neighbours, and being told it sounded like about time she started looking round for a boy-friend. To that she had replied as humbly as she knew how without crawling on the floor that she was afraid she was not cut out for that sort of thing, and got for her pains a very shirty look and a hurried change of subject.

Back in the flat she sat down at the telephone and talked successively to two mothers of children in the ward where she taught. Both wanted to be assured that their offspring were not missing their mums too much, secretly fretting, etc. Jenny did her stuff as several times before, not telling them they must know the answer better than she and so must the hospital staff. Nor did she go into the extraordinary idea of secret fretting. But it was right amazing how two women who ought to have been so different, one an estate-agent's wife in Hampstead, the other perhaps nobody in particular's wife somewhere in the East End, should be such similar pests, even to ringing her up in the same grade of tizzy if they reckoned she was late with her call. She just had to stick to believing she was helping.

She went out into the kitchen, where Frankie swore blind she was quite mistaken if she really thought she had given him a sardine as soon as she came in, and took the Taskmaster off its hook. This was a whitish oblong of some composition material with a special pencil to write things on it which you could rub off again. The first thing there now was *Birthdays*, as every Monday, but that could wait, and she went straight on to item 2, *Feed plants*. So the Fosfagro was duly prepared and scattered over the daffs in the bedroom and the maidenhair fern and the spider-plant in the sitting-room. The spider-plant, on a fluted wooden pillar she had stained and varnished herself, was doing really well and starting to grow baby spider-plants on itself. A shower blew up just then and she quickly put everything outside to catch a few drops of real rain.

Some drops, unexpectedly cold, fell on the back of her hand and straight away she felt as she had not felt for years, not since her marriage, longer ago than that. She would have had a hard time describing it, saying more than that she felt physically detached from where she was, emotionally or mentally as well, as if all her feelings the next second would have changed. What was around her seemed thin, unreal, about to disappear and she would be somewhere she knew nothing of and almost a different person too. But then very soon those emotions or imaginings had faded. Her surroundings, the flat, the world she could see outside, held that weird fragile quality a moment longer, but she was always going to be the same and always here in the life she knew, not that it was so bad, not that it was bad at all, but whatever happened it would never change in that big sudden way. She had finished growing up now. A moment later she was simply looking vaguely out at the rainy street.

The telephone rang and she let it ring some moments before walking slowly to it.

'Jenny Standish here.'

After a papery rustling sound, a voice said very cautiously, 'Is that . . . Jenny?'

'Jenny speaking.'

'Jenny, good afternoon, it's Tim, er, Tim Valentine here.'

'Yes, Tim, aren't we – '

'Jenny, are you, you are expecting me for supper tonight, you and Patrick, aren't you?' It was a posh voice too, not overdone but there.

'Yes, we thought if you came round about –'

After three or four more remarks on each side it was agreed that he should come round any time he liked. He was funny all right, some of it in ways she had yet to take in properly, let alone describe to herself. She had realised she had not had much idea of what he was going to do or say next right from the start, before he had had a fair chance of doing or saying anything. Yes, and why did he want to get her on her own? Nevertheless her instinct had told her he was not a nasty piece of work and her instinct had a way of being right.

She took Frankie on her lap and gave him a routine check for tangles, which his longish coat was liable to, and not forgetting fleas, though he had always been a very clean cat. Naturally he had no idea of what was going on and just thought she was making a fuss of him, though he would have turned quite difficult enough if she had started dragging out a tuft. Luckily for him he was clear, but again he could not understand when she went to move him off. It was that sort of thing about him that irritated Patrick and set him muttering about that bloody cat taking up too much of her life.

Write to Mum. That was every Monday too, but putting it down made the list on the Taskmaster longer. Actually it was timed for later, when she was having her cup of tea. *Library books* was now, straight away in fact. The shower had passed at just the right time and she took the plants in before setting off. She made a bit of a walk of it, but there was no real place to walk to, no real park, none with a pond, in other words, and therefore no ducks to feed.

A nasty moment came up at the library when she thought she caught sight of J.L.R. Sebastian working on some of his stuff from the 1920s and '30s in the reference section, but it turned out to be only an old man with something terrible wrong with one side of his face. Jenny looked round the lending shelves. She reckoned that one way or another she knew the names of plenty of authors, but she came across comparatively few of them in here, and was positive without looking that none of the works of J.L.R. Sebastian or that Vera Thing, or even Iain Gowrie Guthric, would be present. There were authors you met, and authors whose books were in libraries. A great many of the latter who were not already dead seemed to live somewhere else anyway, like Graham Greene and the man who wrote *Waiting for Godot* and Lawrence Durrell, and of course the Americans. According to Patrick quite a few English authors had had to live in places like France and Greece at one time because of being queer, but these days they were not bothering to so much.

Jenny finally came away with books by Elizabeth Taylor, Daphne du Maurier and Pearl S. Buck. She had tried lots of novels by men in her time, and had found some very good things here and there, but had never managed to feel really at home with any of them. They never seemed to give you a feeling of what it was like to be a person, to be inside yourself and experience things happening; they just went round noticing things all the time. And the way they wrote about women, though admittedly that was only half the picture, tended to make them out to be either maddening or funny. For some reason the Americans were particularly prone to that, she had noticed, and rather artificial with it.

Going up the steps at No 1 Lower Ground she nearly walked into somebody coming down who she thought at first was Tim Valentine, but then she saw it was a manager or an executive in a very smart subdued tweed suit with a collar and tie and gold cuff-links and an umbrella with a bamboo handle. After that she realised it was Tim Valentine in tweed suit and the rest of it. On recognising her he ran partly sideways back up the steps saying only the beginnings of words until they faced each other at the top, with him still in the way.

'There you are, Jenny,' he said not very compellingly, but he said it with a smile of pleasure.

'I'm sorry, I wasn't expecting you quite so soon.'

'I'm sorry, you did say I could come round any time I liked.'

'Yes of course.'

He had spoken in an entirely apologetic way and she hoped she had too. They went into the flat and Tim made for the front window, which was sunny now, and Jenny thought to herself very, very slightly that absent-minded people often ended up getting their own way better than ordinary ones.

'What a charming room,' he said with his back to it.

'Would you like a cup of tea?'

She quite easily beat down his protests and went and put the electric kettle on. Patrick had explained to her about the sneezing, but she was a little bit thrown when she heard what sounded like a long up-and-down wail of fright from Tim's direction, making you think of someone losing control on skis or roller-skates. The presumable sneezes that followed were more like people being stabbed in films. Could he really not know?

Frankie shot past her and up the stairs as she went back in

with the tea-tray. Tim heaved himself massively up and moved his hands here and there without actually helping.

'It's something in cats' fur,' he said. 'It's an awful nuisance because it means I can't keep one myself. And I'm very fond of them, you know. Are you an animal-lover?'

'Yes.' Jenny could not say any different, though she considered it a silly expression.

'I thought so when I saw the horse in the kitchen.'

That made her blink for a moment, until she remembered the one looking over the stable door on the calendar there. 'Oh, yes.'

'I saw it when I was here on Saturday. I do notice things, you know. What made you such an animal-lover?'

'I don't know. Well, my uncle was a farmer. I used to go there quite a lot.'

'My father used to make me ride. On horses. I hated it but he kept on at me. Just like him. Oh, the horses were sweet but I didn't like riding them. All the nonsense about breeches and putting your stirrups up and trotting round that awful barn place.'

Jenny was interested. 'Have you ridden is it to hounds? Gone fox-hunting?'

'Well I have, yes, but it's not the sort of thing one's particularly proud of.'

'Oh, but it must be marvellous fun, isn't it? Exhilarating and that?'

'I suppose it is if you enjoy chasing an animal to death.'

'I wasn't really thinking of that side of it.'

'No, that's the whole . . .' He stopped and smiled and gave a half wink. 'Actually it can be quite exciting. Terrifying too, though. Galloping at a hedge with no idea what's on the other side?'

'Galloping anywhere.'

'The mad things one does.' Then his manner changed again. 'Would you credit it, that father of mine, in these supposedly enlightened days he *still* . . . goes *hunting.*' Tim made it sound as if his father regularly hunted men as a matter of course, like the Czars and Polish peasants.

'Oh well, I think that's rather – '

'He's a judge. That's right. They don't retire, judges don't, did you know that, Jenny? Go on till they drop. I wish to God

65

he'd drop, the old swine. I tell you, Jenny, it makes me feel quite awful to think of that old monster sending poor devils to gaol. With his barbaric attitude to life. At seventy-one. Well, perhaps he won't last much longer.'

'Drink your tea up before it gets cold.'

'Sorry. It's silly, I know, but I can't help feeling sort of responsible in a way. As if I ought to do something.'

'Is that why you visit people in prison?'

'What? Oh yes. Yes, I suppose it is, really. Partly, anyway. To make it up to them a tiny bit. Of course I don't tell them my father's a judge. The prisoners I mean.'

'No. You've been visiting some of them today, have you?'

This turned out to be in some hidden respect an unwelcome question. Tim reached over to the tray and carefully selected one of two identical biscuits.

'I just thought, with you being all nicely turned out and everything.'

'Oh no. That's on Thursdays – Wednesdays, Thursdays and Fridays. No, when I go visiting I dress pretty rough, you know, on purpose. So as there won't be a painful contrast with what they're wearing,' said Tim, evidently well satisfied to be giving this explanation. 'It's important to bridge the gap as far as one can.'

'I can see that.'

'Do you mind if I tell you something?'

She would have given a lot even to hint at how much she minded, but she just shook her head.

Even after getting this permission he seemed to feel some further squaring-up was advisable, frowning at her and pushing his mouth in and out. 'I hate my father,' he said briskly then. 'I absolutely hate him. Does it shock you, my saying that?'

'Well yes it does actually, since you ask me.'

'I'm sorry, I'm sorry but it's true. He was brutal to me. And he neglected me in the most shameful fashion. When he wasn't off on circuit he was studying his briefs. Never any time for me. He left my upbringing entirely to my mother. Which was actually the most marvellous thing he could have done, because I happen to adore my mother. No other woman could ever touch her.'

Having said this he smiled, but it was not a very happy smile, not as nice as the one she had got from him on the steps just now. His face looked shinier than last time, too. And surely no one *happened* to love their mother. Her own parents would have said that that was typical of how they talked down south, purely for effect. All for effect and to seem clever.

When Tim went on about his family she started hoping in a rather nasty way to be told about childhood thrashings and lockings-up in cupboards, but what she got about his father was more a matter of his meanness over money and not even anything to do with his wigs, and when his mother came in again he revealed how he had hardly ever helped her with her passe-partout, treasures like that. There was a sister, older than Tim, living in Weybridge. Married to a solicitor. Two children. Both girls. Big deal.

She gave up wondering if this was the sort of stuff he had got her on her own to confide to her, put the blue photograph-album on his lap, the pre-Patrick one, and went out to the kitchen, where at least she could afford to let her attention dwell on the way he had been juddering his leg up and down in his chair. Or so she had intended, but there seemed nothing funny there now. She shook herself, lit the oven and got out the plates. Frankie had heard her and walked in, not hurrying, just happening to drop by. With his barely visible eyes more than half shut and his body tilted over, he rubbed himself in passing against the corner of the cupboard, a table-leg, her carton of ginger beers under the table. This habit was another that irritated Patrick. 'They're not people's legs, you bloody fool,' he would say. 'You won't get anything out of them.' But there was no distraction for her there either, not for the moment.

When she told Patrick she thought Tim was lonely she had spoken almost without thinking. But if there had ever been any doubt of that it had been seen off in the last half-hour. But then what had he said? With a couple of short breaks, during which he had actually been *talking* to her in an ordinary sort of way, he had been – not showing off exactly, but talking about something different from what he had been saying, in a way not really talking at all. More like reciting, while his feelings were fixed on what she could only think of as some sad and awful thing. Loneliness was not just a matter of being short of people to see; she knew enough about it herself to know that much. What more there was to it in Tim's case would come out when he was ready, if ever, and of course that could be

67

never. None of which meant that there were no other questions about him to be asked meanwhile.

Anyway it was a good job Patrick had let her know about Tim's yawns as well as his sneezes. Even as it was she went quite still for a moment when the first wail of despair rang out from the next room. Eccentric, that was the word for him. She cheered up, suspecting she had read too much into Tim's tales of his father's meanness and his mother's passe-partout. One reason for his loneliness she could rule out now – though not her cup of tea exactly he was fanciable enough, she considered, in spite of the shiny face and the leg. Leaving the kitchen she carelessly let a scrap of cold chicken fall on the floor where it was obviously going to get golloped up by any passing cat.

Tim had finished with the album and was looking over Patrick's books on the shelves in an uncommitted way. That suit of his must have cost a bomb. She would have to find out what he did for a living before it got too rude to ask.

Turning away at once from the books, he said, 'I'm sorry I shocked you with what I said about my father. I dare say you're pretty attached to your own father.'

'My father's dead.'

'Oh I am so sorry.' He was really distressed.

'That's all right, it's years ago now.' Only three, but the best thing to say. 'When are you moving in, along there?'

'Oh. Oh yes. Er, in a week or two I should think. Soon.'

'What stage have you got to?' When he looked at her in silence she went on, 'I was thinking of carpets and curtains and things. I mean you must have someone coming in to measure up before you can do anything.'

'Oh yes, someone's coming in and, measure up. On Wednesday.' The way he said the last word strongly suggested to Jenny that he had said it chiefly because it was a well-known day of the week. Added on to what Patrick had told her about the behaviour in 1E on the Saturday, it made her think that actually Tim had no intention of moving into the building at any time. In a flash of intuition she thought she saw that he had not turned up in these parts to try and find something but to get away from something, perhaps the law. But very soon, as had happened before, the intuition flashed away again. If this chap had enemies, they would not have been the sort that anyone else would feel threatened by.

'May I be terribly rude and ask if I could possibly have a drink? No, anything at all will do, honestly.'

A drunk, she could not help thinking at once. That might explain a lot of it. 'I don't think there is anything, I'm sorry.'

'Oh. Well it really and truly doesn't matter.'

She went just the same to the cupboard next to the telephone, selected by Patrick as more secure than anywhere in kitchen or sitting-room against furtive nosing by the thirsty, but often holding nothing bar gloves and scarves and stuff. He tried to let stocks of booze run down, seeing that as a way to spend less, and drink less, and get drunk less, though he would sometimes absent-mindedly bring home a drop of something ahead of need. Today there was a small leftover in a half-bottle of Scotch, to Jenny's eye about two very stiff drinks for a man in the pink of condition.

'Ah,' said Tim, looking over her shoulder.

'Would you like ice?'

'No thank you. Just plain.'

'Help yourself,' she said, bringing him a glass.

'Aren't you having any?'

'No, I don't usually at this time.'

'Right.' He emptied the bottle into the glass, looked at the result, drank the lot in one in what looked like a practised movement, and handed the glass back with a nod of acknowledgement and his lips pressed tightly together.

His face seemed to turn redder for a moment. 'Tha –' he had time to say before plunging headlong into a coughing-fit that led without a break into another sneezing-fit with full eye-bulging effects. About the fourth in the series sounded as if something serious inside him had gone. Anyway, it went to show he was probably not a drunk after all. Jenny made for the kitchen with the empty glass and it was there that Patrick found her, not a moment too soon, she thought quite seriously.

'Christ, how long's he been here? Has he been like this all the time?'

'Not all the time, no.' She turned the cold tap on hard.

'What's he been saying?'

That took a very short time to answer.

'M'm. How early do you think we can chuck him out?'

'Oh, I don't think it'll be dull.'

'I can always take him to the pub.'

'I should leave that to another night.'

'Another night? How many of the buggers are we in for?'

'Quite a few.'

'You want some histamine for those sneezes,' said Patrick when they had gathered in the sitting-room. 'Or do I mean anti-histamine?'

'Yes, I'm sorry about them. I know I make rather the most of them. The thing is, they're so boring I sort of throw myself into them.'

'Yes, you certainly do that.'

'I'm sorry. I realise I do make an awful row with them. It's as if I'm trying to get all the benefit I can from them.'

'I think I've probably got it now. Oh, would you like, er, a drop more whisky?'

'Ooh, yes please. Super. Just plain.'

'Say when.'

Patrick started pouring from the full bottle he had brought home, quite gently. After what seemed like ages, Jenny reckoned Tim's thoughts must have drifted off, and it came as quite a surprise to see him still watching in attentive silence. 'Oh! – when,' he said as soon as he noticed her.

'Better take it a bit easy this time,' she said. It was school-marmish of her to say it, but in his case she felt it was both necessary and all right.

'Oh, of course I will after that,' he said seriously. 'Hey, I thought you said you weren't drinking, Jenny.'

'I've changed my mind.' Perhaps she had become a drunk in the last five minutes, considering the way she had plunged at the sherry Patrick had brought.

'Well, what have you been doing with yourself today, Tim? And incidentally why have you dressed yourself up in those fine clothes?'

'Oh, the clothes are nothing, just to show you and Jenny I have got one or two decent rags to my back. If you're wondering what I do for a living I'm afraid the answer is not very much. I've a sufficient private income, I do my prison stuff because we've always done that sort of thing in my family. And the rest of the time I try to be a writer.'

'Oh really? I see.'

Jenny told herself that Patrick had not really got an unbeliev-able amount of hatred and disgust into four words, it was just that she knew better than anyone what working for a publisher for two years had done for his feelings about writers. But she spoke up quickly in case. 'What do you write about?'

Looking very directly at her, Tim said, 'Well, shall I tell you what I was writing about today?'

'Yes, do.' Now she felt like somebody's jolly sporty auntie.

But he hesitated, and when he spoke he told her nothing in so many words. 'Have novels always got to be about things going wrong? After all, some people are happy. Even people who've never done any harm to anyone and are quite innocent and defenceless. Some people like that must come off best somewhere. After all – '

'That's right,' said Patrick, but not very horribly, 'and why have books got to be full of sex and filth when there are so many baa-lambs and kittens and babies and lovely gardens and little old cottages to write about? Well, if you ever do write a novel about all that, or anything about anything, I'm sure you won't come to me to get it published for you, Tim, and I mean sure because if I wasn't sure you'd never have been invited to share our bread and salt. I hope you like bread and salt, by the way. And till then you know what I think? I think we should go to the pub.'

Jenny could have put up with that, but when Tim found it meant leaving her behind he refused to go. When the time came he ate more than enough of her beef casserole and apple pie to make her worry slightly about what and how he had eaten earlier that day and even, when he asked for bread and butter, that week. Back in the sitting-room she put out a packet of chocolate mints and he ate them all. Perhaps he was greedy, or had the babyish tastes that would have gone with his looks, never mind the shiny cheeks.

She kicked her shoes off, tucked her feet up under her and forgot about Tim's worryingnesses, of which not the least had been that odd stuff about innocent and defenceless people. At last she was beginning to feel really settled in London. She was in her own home, Patrick was with her and there was nothing going on.

71

Six

'I regard you as someone whose life has gone pretty smoothly.'
'Well, it has and it hasn't.'
'I envy a fellow like you,' said Tim, presumably referring to only the first half of what he had just heard. 'Because mine hasn't. In fact you might say it hasn't *gone* at all.'

It was very clear that the next thing was supposed to be waiting three seconds and then asking him how he meant, but Patrick hated being expected to prompt people like that. Birds were great ones for it. 'Oh, what bad luck,' he said.

Pause. 'Here you are, obviously attractive to women, with a beautiful wife whom you're obviously nuts about, aren't you?'
'Am I? I mean all right, why shouldn't I be?'
'Well, she's obviously devoted to you. Even I can see that.'

And it was obviously unbosoming time. Patrick had seen it coming almost since first exchanging words with Tim, and the bottle of Teacher's was on the table half full and with its top off, and Jenny was in bed, but the moment would not arrive. Well, almost from the start, too, Patrick had registered the presence of one of those blokes who instinctively resisted the flow of events, who when they must see the way things were going tried to go the other way, contrary of spirit however affable – awkward buggers, in fact. Throughout the evening Tim had displayed a strong negative sense of stage-craft, you could call it, never letting the Standishes alone for a minute to confer. With wonderful automatic-pilot vigilance he had insisted on helping to clear away, followed Patrick out to the kitchen to go on asking him about his school, uncannily waited till he was answering a telephone-call from a drunken friend before going for a pee, taken the chance of a breath of fresh air and helped escort Frankie down for his late-night stroll in the pitch-dark bit of garden below the flats.

Perhaps a token disclosure or two would ease things, even if it meant compromising one's own sense of style. 'Actually Jenny and I have had our ups and downs,' said Patrick, pouring whisky. 'More or less from the start. I haven't behaved too well, I'm afraid.' That was going to have to be enough and to spare for that part, to this chap.

'But things have settled down now, I take it.'

'Not a bit of it, I'm sorry to say. All my fault, of course. Though there's no trouble going on at the moment. No actual difficulties.'

'Difficulties?' Tim seemed to find the word unexpected in some way. 'What sort of difficulties?'

'Well, what would you? Difficulties ... arising out of females.'

'Oh. Could you be a little clearer?'

'Christ, I get interested in other women and that upsets Jenny, right?'

'Oh I see. Of course. Do go on.'

'What are you talking about, go on? You're the one who's supposed to be going on. You know that. Otherwise what are we doing here?'

'Yes. All right, Patrick. Just one thing – I hope I haven't bothered Jenny or annoyed her or anything.'

'No. Absolutely not. You can rule that out. Why, how might you have done?'

'Well, you know, turning up early, someone she hardly knew from Adam, nobody else around, coming out with what she must have thought was some rather odd sort of stuff.'

'That sort of thing doesn't bother Jenny.'

'I must say you sound very certain.'

'I am certain, sod it. I ought to be after all these years.'

'I just think Jenny's a marvellous girl and I hope you – '

'If you're going to start telling me you hope I appreciate her I'm going to get very ... bored. *Christ*, Tim, this is supposed to be about *you*, not me.'

'Oh, all right.'

'Oh all *right*!' But Patrick had to admire the way he had been manoeuvred into being the one to whom the favour was being done, too much so to go on being cross. 'In your own time, then.'

'Thanks. First of all I want to say I'm sorry but I'm not a writer.'

'Don't apologise for that to me, old boy, I won't hear of it.'

'I bet you guessed I wasn't really one, didn't you, with all your experience?'

'To be honest I didn't give it a thought. Get on with it.'

'And I'm sorry I spouted all that guff about – '

'Forget it. And I mean that literally.'

'Thanks.' After gazing round for a time, apparently at random, Tim fastened his eye on the glass in front of him and drank most of its contents at a swallow. His cheeks became convex and an extra flush passed up his face, but both soon subsided. His intake over the evening had been patchy and his outward show of drunkenness changeable, though not in any corresponding way. All in all he could not have been sober, though there was that thing about chaps with a bigger frame to spread it over being able to take more. 'You asked me what I'd been doing today, well as usual I spent a lot of it with a psychiatrist and a lot more mulling over being with a psychiatrist. I'm not mad – it's not a question of that.'

'Oh, good.'

'I know what you're thinking, Patrick, and I used to think it too till a couple of weeks ago. Then I was recommended to somebody called Mr Perlmutter and I started to see the point of it all. Most of these fellows, you know, all they do is tell you everything's just an example of something else. Mr Perlmutter went to the root of my trouble straight away. Difficulties with girls.'

Tim pronounced the last three words in such a special clinical way, mouthing them energetically as if the only hope of under-standing them would have been to visualise their look on the page, that for an instant Patrick thought they could not be English. Then he appreciated Tim's mild consternation just now on hearing of what must be a very different difficulty, and sniggered to himself. His curiosity was undimmed: the unbosoming had always been going to involve that very inter-esting side of life, and it was certain that no mere tale of sexual woe was on the way.

A solitary car hummed gently along Lower Ground, which

was always quiet by this time of night. Tim looked at Patrick with a new expression, one cautiously signalling trust. 'They don't, the difficulties don't include lack of success with girls in the ordinary way. I've never had the slightest trouble there, right from a schoolboy. In fact Mr Perlmutter seems to think I may actually have suffered from too much easy sexual experience.'

Patrick tried to give some suitable hint of the sympathy he felt for one in this predicament.

'And then it's not a matter of being so to speak unable to perform altogether, which I'm told is quite common, in fact actually getting commoner for some reason. No, the exact opposite – not a problem in sight, not a cloud in the sky, everything bowling along beautifully and everybody as happy as a sandboy for about ten seconds, and then after that there's nothing happening at all and never will be. You, er, you do follow what I'm saying?'

'Oh yes.'

'I mean it's absolutely fine until – you know.'

'Yes.'

'Because after that I see things in a completely different light. I always think I'm not going to, but then I always suddenly seem to find I somehow do. Every time without fail. Like clockwork.'

'I know what you mean.'

'And the trouble is,' pursued Tim, who had forgotten he was supposed to be drunk as he warmed to his theme, 'she's still there, and she hasn't changed her outlook one bit. Far from it. She's unsatisfied, in fact. Frustrated. And girls object strongly to being frustrated.' He said this on a note of personal warning to Patrick. 'They hate it. They start – '

'Don't let's go into that, eh?'

'No. All right. Of course you can see their point in a way. It was rather well put by an American I got talking to once. Oh, I know they're very brash and crude, Americans, but just occasionally they do go right to the heart or the crux of something in a rough sort of style that wouldn't really be possible for an Englishman, don't you agree?'

'Yes, yes.' When he knew Tim better, Patrick was to find it to be characteristic of Tim to put forward confident over-simplifications of subtly discerning points which then became impossible to advance on one's own account. 'Often been said.'

75

'I don't know how we got on to it, this Yank and I, but there we were, and he said, when that happens, you know, what we've just been talking about, it's as if you're saying to the girl, "Linda Kowalski, this is your fuck." ' This came in semi-plausible American. 'Rather crude, as I said. He was quite a bit younger than me.'

'Very trenchant, though.'

'Well anyway I thought it was quite funny. Where was I? Oh yes. Er, of course I've been given all sorts of advice about pretending I'm doing something else entirely, like riding a bicycle or being a snowflake. That's what they tell you in Harley Street but you'd probably do just as well for free in the saloon bar of the Dog and Duck. So Mr Perlmutter says, anyway. Actually he just said in the pub, but my impression is he doesn't know much about pubs. But the thing is it doesn't work, not with me. I keep stopping the pretending, you see. It's not so much I can't go on pretending any longer, it's more I get fed up with pretending. I'm sorry, Patrick, all this must be complete Greek to you.'

'Oh, I wouldn't say that exactly. What does Mr Perlmutter advise?'

'Well, that's just it, he sort of doesn't advise anything in that way. Not his field, he says.'

'Really? What does he say is his field?'

'Well, that's the next bit, so to speak. I say, are you sure you really want to hear all the – '

'You're not going till I've heard the lot. No, not the lot. Enough.'

'All right, fine. Well . . . there's a whole nother kind of difficulty with girls that may be just as important. Mr Perlmutter thinks it's more important. It's . . . I don't think I necessarily like girls much. Not enough. Oh, I like their, their shape and so on but I'm not sure about the other side of it. I'm not interested in what they think and do and say. What they say is all about them, have you noticed that? Of course I'm not getting at – '

'No, we don't mean Jenny. But what about you? Haven't you ever been married?'

'That's got nothing to do with it,' said Tim, who clearly found this an improper question. 'It was years ago and it was a disaster. I'm not talking about that, I'm talking about *girls*.'

'Oh I get it, you're talking about girls.'

'Yes. Er, what happens, the sort of thing that happens typically is I turn up at one of them's flat and she gives me a drink and tells me about her flat and her, and then we get a taxi and she tells me about her family and her, and then we get to the restaurant and I spend twenty pounds and she tells me about the people at work and her, and then we get another taxi and she tells me about her boy-friends and her, and then we come to the part I was describing to you earlier, all of it, including her objecting to being frustrated, all of that, and after that I come home or she goes home, or if it's a hotel we both go home.

'Well. One of the things I start thinking to myself at that stage is that I can stop myself being frustrated on my own without upsetting anybody. Also for free, though that part of it doesn't actually bother me because I can afford it and I'm a pretty generous sort of fellow anyhow. But more than either of those, it's over in a couple of minutes and I can go to the pub. Oh dear, there I go talking more nonsense from your point of view.'

Patrick made no reply.

'So you can forget all that but, this is the point, I strongly suspect that even if I were the most perfect sexual technician in the free world, hundred per cent success guaranteed every day of the year, I'd still prefer the company of my own sex except when actually . . . Because they don't talk about themselves all the time, or *go on* about themselves whatever they're talking about. It may sound like a small thing to you but I don't think it is. Yes, I know I've just been talking about myself a lot but you encouraged me and I don't do it *all the time*.'

'How does Mr Perlmutter see it? By the way, I suppose he is a . . .' Patrick hesitated. 'I mean he is in Harley Street?'

'Old Harley Street to be precise. No, Mr Perlmutter doesn't seem to care one way or the other about what I talk about. What he does say, he's convinced I have all these difficulties with girls for one reason only. I don't like them, not really, and wanting to go to bed with them's just, you know, subservience to custom and family pressure and things like that. Basically they don't interest me. Deep down I'm a . . . well, what do you prefer to call it, a homosexual, a queer, a poof, one of those. Deep down.'

Of course anybody could have seen it coming, but not from all that far off, and in any case a hundred miles away would have been too close for it to have arrived without some kind of shock. In the last half-minute Tim's manner had lost the vivacity, almost the enthusiasm, that had carried him along earlier and he had spoken with a harrowing pretence of jauntiness. Patrick tried to rouse himself. It could not be true that he had been here countless times before or even once that he remembered; it just felt like it. He reached for a non-existent cigarette and then for his glass instead.

'What are you, forty?'

'Thirty-six.'

'Same as me. Have you ever had a, a homosexual experience?'

'No.'

'Ever fancied one? Wanted one? Been interested in one?'

'No.'

'And can't you bloody well tell simply by the sheer terribleness of those sentences and the words in them and how they sound that you never could have? I mean you were never anywhere near, were you?'

'No.'

'Well, I mean, Christ, Tim, you know, really, for . . .'

'It's all buried, all that. Deep down, as I said. I'm going to have to drag it to light. What did you say?'

'I didn't say anything, I just made a noise with my mouth.'

'Have you any other suggestions?'

'How deep down is deep down? What? How do you mean?'

'For instance whips, leather, handcuffs? Harnessing up to little carts? There was a chap in our village who was supposed to have gone in for that.'

'I don't know what you're talking about.'

'Only joking. What I'm trying to say, I've got to be queer, there's no other way. Good God, I must be something, mustn't I? It stands to reason.'

As he spoke, and half obliterating his last words, two cars, the second one using a police siren, came rushing down Lower Ground in the direction of the river, with such a din that for a moment it was as if they were about to burst into the room. The pitch fell off almost sickeningly as they swung past the window and the noise they made seemed hollow in comparison as they made for the traffic lights on the corner. Round they

78

went with sounds of tyres and accelerating engines and were soon lost to hearing. The siren called briefly once more, perhaps from as far away as the bridge.

Now at last Tim did go for a pee. Patrick got up and searched for cigarettes in drawers and along shelves in sitting-room and kitchen, although he was perfectly certain there were none to be found. His thoughts fastened on Mr Perlmutter sitting in his lead-lined bunker in Old Harley Street, deciding that Tim might as well try boys instead of girls over a probationary period and have difficulties with them for a change, and reflecting that should the difficulties extend to beatings, arrests, extortions, murders, imprisonments or suicides, that would be most regrettable. More soberly and coarsely, Patrick considered that Tim's least debatable difficulty with girls, his estimated ten-second attention-span, might be transformed into a noteworthy asset in the new career he had chosen.

In the lavatory now his distinctive howl of anguish started up, to be cut off abruptly as he perhaps remembered the bedded-down Jenny near him. If this was so he soon offset matters with a tumultuous teenager-type plunge downstairs. Then he was quiet, dithering on the threshold of the sitting-room.

'You haven't got to go yet,' said Patrick impatiently.

'Are you sure? I've been a most awful – '

'Sit down while I tell you exactly what balls you were talking just now. You're no more queer than I am.'

'Ah, but that's just it. You can't say that, you see.' Youthfully again, Tim fell backwards into his chair. 'You're straight, as you say. You couldn't tell.'

'Rubbish, I know a queer when I see one.'

'Ah, but you only know he's a queer when you know he's a queer. You don't know about the ones you don't know about. Only other queers know about them.'

'You are quite sure you're not mad, are you?'

'Now women are a different matter – *they* can tell all right, however straight they are. The straighter the better, so to speak. You know, Patrick, it's marvellous, I can't tell you how marvellous it is after all these months of listening to jargon and fantasy, what a relief to find someone like Mr Perlmutter who talks plain English and actually gives you practical advice, tells you what to do. Oh yes, thanks, can I help myself?'

'What's he been telling you to do?'

79

'Well, for instance he said it would help me if I could get some independent evidence of, you know, my homosexuality. To back up his diagnosis – actually he calls it his tag. That was why I turned up early tonight, to get Jenny's undivided attention.'

'Oh I see, she was being the straight woman who was going to be able to tell whether you were queer or not. Brilliant.'

'If you'd let me know what she thought I'd be most grateful. Of course I wasn't going to give the show away by behaving the way queers behave when they don't mind whether you know they're queer or not. There wouldn't have been any point in that, would there?'

'What sort of behaviour are you talking about?'

'Well, you know the kind of thing.'

'Maybe I do, but I'd like to see a sample of the way you think queers behave when they don't mind whether you know they're queer or not. Go on, just a snippet.'

'Okay, if you think there's any point in it.'

For the first few seconds Patrick quite thought it might be going to be all right, no worse than any publisher's party might throw up, sticking to a slight widening of the eyes, a slightly faster blink-rate, slight swaying about with neck and shoulders, a bit of wrist-play, but then Tim shoved himself forward to the edge of his chair and, while still in the strict sense sitting on it, began moving his arms and legs to and fro in a style that might have gone down well enough as part of a turn at a men's club in the north of England, Patrick considered, though it was true that he had never actually visited one.

'What are you doing?' he asked.

'What you asked me to do, behaving the way – '

'No, I mean which bit – are you trying to get picked up or are you just passing the time? All right, but I take it you don't propose to start behaving like that in public.'

'Well, not yet, anyway.'

'Not *yet!* Bloody – '

'There'll have to be a developmental period of reorientation.'

'Is that the sort of plain English Mr Perlmutter talks?'

'I think he means time to get used to the idea.'

'No, really? Now listen, Tim – you don't know what you're taking on. Don't think that because there are lots of jokes about it that it's a joke itself. That world is incredibly nasty and

80

incredibly dangerous. It's full of blackmail and, well, rather nasty physical things, one can't help hearing. Violent too. If you go blundering in there you're liable to get your bloody head kicked off.'

'I think I can probably cope with that side of it,' said Tim, straightening up for once and revealing a really quite powerful pair of shoulders and looking altogether different from a minute before. He spoilt the effect to some degree by adding, 'I used to box a bit at school.'

'Oh? Where was that?'

'Rugby, though I don't see what it – '

'Rugby, now – surely you must have gone in for a spot of the old one-two there.'

'If you mean homosexuality, no, as a matter of fact I didn't.' Tim spoke rather coldly, no doubt without thinking. Then he went on in a different tone, 'It may be all you think it is, that world, as you call it, though you don't know anything about it at first hand, do you? Anyway, it can't be much worse than the *world* I'll be leaving behind, where you have to spend half your time sucking up to them – you know, conciliating them, soft-soaping them. Finding ways of making it up to them for you being there in the first place. Persuading them not to hold it against you being a man. At least queers aren't going to need any winning round there. It's quite funny actually, realising I don't really like them much – it can't have reminded me exactly, it's opened my eyes to them not liking us much. I don't know, perhaps they do deep down, they must I suppose, some of them at least, but good God you'd never think so to hear the way some of them go on. So what, I'm tired, see if I care, you give your orders, be like that then, I said I'm sorry, you and who else, I can't help that, look who's talking, that's your problem, if you don't want me to come out with you that's okay by me, I can assure you I've other things to do with my time. You can't help feeling a lot of them would be a jolly sight better off with each other.'

Well, the silly sod might have been talking at random half the time, but there could be no doubt that he felt strongly about that part. Patrick said, 'Perhaps Mrs Perlmutter has patients who suffer from difficulties with men.'

'Oh, I shouldn't think so. They don't mind, you see.'

'Where do you live?'

81

Tim was not ready for this question. He cleared his throat and said, 'Enfield.'

'Look, Tim, it's nothing to me where you live, but I might as well know in case I have to take you there some time with your back broken.'

'Hadley Wood, actually. I'd better go there, hadn't I? I've brought my car.'

'What have you got?'

'Just an old Jag.'

'I'll ask you about it another time. Do you think you can drive it all right?'

'Sure, no problem,' said Tim brightly, then remembered he was drunk, snatched up the sizeable remains of his last drink and downed the lot. Yet again he came through relatively unscathed, though his chin receded far back into his throat as he screwed the muscles there into a convulsive act of swallowing. 'I can manage,' he said finally in a thick but entirely unstudied voice.

'I hope so.'

Tim had nothing to wear or carry. He did a lot of thanking on the way out.

'You are in fact intending to come and live in that flat, are you?'

'Well, of course I am. What do you mean?'

'Because you haven't done anything about it at all, have you?'

'No.'

'You just got the key off the agents for a scout-around, didn't you? What have you got lined up for the rest of the week for a once-over? Mansion in Golders Green? Penthouse in Mayfair?'

'That's not how it is,' said Tim, meeting Patrick's eye. 'I'm just lazy. I've signed up and I've paid for the first six months in advance.'

'How much was it?'

Without benefit of slide-rule it seemed right. But Patrick had started to believe Tim before he started to answer, having already recognised him as one unwilling to tell a proper lie, though quite eager to evade, misdirect, falsify details he considered immaterial. He rather reverted to that level now in proffering a bogus draft time-table for his occupancy of 1E before departing.

Patrick took the glasses out to the kitchen. It was quite

touching, though at least as boring and menacing too, that Tim had shown himself so prompt to make friends and unload confidences. Well, he should make a tolerable neighbour, and could hardly be blamed in the circumstances for not being about to give any parties swarming with beautiful unattached nymphomaniacs. That was as much as he was going to do on Tim Valentine tonight.

He went and unlocked his brief-case and settled down for a short session with *Titter 7* and *Twosome 3*. Good taste, self-respect and fear kept Patrick away from the hard-stuff joints in Soho, and the magazines in front of him stayed on the inner edge of the law in leaving some features unshown. He felt no constraint, finding plenty in what was visible to arouse his delight and wonder. So what, he tried to imagine the dark one saying, who do you think you are, from the one in the straw hat on the swing. No, they stayed as they were, wise, compassionate, silent and with enormous breasts.

Seven

Over the next few days Tim seemed to set about moving into
1E Lower Ground. Funnily enough it was on the Wednesday,
as advertised, that the first activities were noticed. Jenny peeped
out in time to see two men at the door of 1E, one of them
looking very useful in tipped-back felt hat and brown overall
coat with lots of pens in the top pocket, and carrying a wooden
drum of the sort that held serious tape-measures. There would
be no trifling with anything he and his mate set their hands to.

She reported to Patrick as he sat finishing breakfast in the
kitchen. 'He means to come all right,' she said.

'Quite likely. It did occur to me he might be rich enough and
barmy enough to go in for a bit of this just so as to be able to
go on coming round here.'

'He's not short of hot dinners, that lad.'

'No, not at all. He can't be, really, can he?'

'What's the joke, then?'

'Sorry, darling, it's not very good really, but there is this
saying about blokes who've had a lot of girls, another bloke
might say, old so-and-so, well he's had more, you know . . .'

'Yes, I know.'

'Er, than I've had hot dinners. I told you it wasn't very funny.
I just couldn't help thinking of it.'

'But you said Tim had had plenty of, well, experience.'

'I wasn't being logical about it, I just thought of it.'

'Have some more coffee.'

Jenny knew she should have kept her mouth shut. Whenever
anything like that came up and she said anything at all about
it, she sounded disapproving however hard she tried. She knew
she did; she could hear herself. Patrick had said he thought it

was mostly to do just with her accent. Anyway he took the coffee, bless him, and then started sighing and clicking his tongue behind the spread pages of the *Guardian*.

'Bloody idiot! No to all immigration restrictions, eh? They haven't got to live with 'em.'

'You used to think the world of that paper.'

'I know. They just go on as if nothing had happened. You wouldn't think it was possible, would you?'

'Why don't you change? One of the nurses was saying the *Telegraph*'s very good for foreign news.'

'Oh for Christ's sake, there are limits. And what do I want to know about what's going on in all those places?'

He held the paper up at the part where the pages folded and started trying to get them to double over the other way round, but instead of doing so cleanly they kept buckling along the middle. After pulling repeatedly away at top and bottom, hard enough to start a horizontal tear, he delivered several savage backhand chops at the inside of the fold with the edge of his hand, asking as many times what was the matter with the bloody thing. When he had it more or less straight he laid it on the table and hammered and punched it flat, using the bottom of his fist for this part. More of the same got it folded into four.

'If you're like this now,' said Jenny, and stopped before he said anything. She had not kept her mouth shut again.

There could be no more talk of Tim for the present, but he turned up in person a couple of afternoons later, dropping in, he said, to see what the decorators were up to in that new flat of his, but not asking Jenny to have a look-see herself. When she asked him for supper later or another night, he said fine but he must look at his diary, making out he had quite a lot going on in his life and being sad and soft. Once or twice he eyed her in a way that made her hope he was not shaping up to ask her whether she had taken him for a queer or not at the now-famous test-exposure the previous Saturday.

'But he didn't actually,' said Patrick. 'Ask you, I mean.'

'No.'

'Did he look any different to you today?'

'No.'

'I was thinking, that line he shot you about his father and mother, that goes with one pissy Perlmutter-style theory of how queers are made. But why bother? It doesn't cut any ice with him, you know, what you or I think. I can't tell whether he's one because I'm not queer myself, and you can't tell because anyway he's burying it too deep, and probably a bit because you're not a queer either as well. Hey, I tell you what, what about exposing him to Eric and Stevie? Christ, I only mean let them have a look at him, have them all round at the same time. We owe them a drink anyway, don't we?'

'And I suppose we ought to help him to meet the neighbours.'

'Oh yes, what about the other neighbours, at which is it, 1D?'

'Well, there were more men there today, but I've not had more than the one squint at the people, just the chap, really.'

'Describe him again.'

'Quite little, looked as if he was fed up about something but couldn't think what, with a big bowler hat sort of crushed down over his hair, a suit nobody could have – '

'That's him, Harold Porter-Twatface Esquire. What kind of wife could a bloke like that have? Still nothing going on in 1C. I suppose it is actually taken, do you think?'

'I'm still trying Mr Bigger.'

Mr Bigger, who must have been called something else as well, like a supervisor or a caretaker, had appeared in the flesh on the Standishes' first day in residence and had been very free with information on how to turn taps on and off and open and shut doors. He had also said that apartment 1C had been taken by a couple living abroad, that and no more. Since then Jenny had telephoned him a few dozen times, intending to ask him not so much to find out more about 1C as to do some supervising or caretaking on the bedroom ceiling of 1B, where an orange-coloured patch of damp had started to spread. Mostly no one answered, though once a cross man had said he had never heard of any Mr Bigger, and she had had an anxious couple of days before somebody put her mind at rest by saying Mr Bigger was out of the office that week.

It would have been very late to try Mr Bigger now, and the telephone rang anyway before Jenny could have picked it up. After his usual silence Tim spoke, with the news that what he called his dinner engagement had fallen through and he could come after all.

'I call that a bit bloody cool,' said Patrick.

'I thought you liked him.'

'Yeah, well I do quite but I could do with him more spaced out. I suppose he's sweet, is he?'

'He's fairly sweet.'

'Only *fairly* sweet?' Patrick opened a tin of Long Life. 'Where does he fall short?'

'You've got to stay switched on all the time when you're with somebody, when you're talking to somebody, if you're going to be completely sweet, you can't go wandering off on your own, not while you're still talking to them. You're not to make them wonder what you're thinking. They needn't know but they mustn't wonder.'

'Christ, I never knew there was so much to it. To being really sweet. But I can see Tim wouldn't quite qualify. What the hell does he do for a living?'

'Nothing much, rest assured of that, or we'd know.'

'M'm. But then of course he's pathetic, which must stand him in good stead.'

'He's not that pathetic, you know, in that suit, and it only goes so far, does being pathetic. But sometimes you've got to do things for people.'

'Is he attractive?' asked Patrick after a pause and in a very nonchalant way.

'Oh yes. Yes, he's not bad at all.'

'What about that shiny red face?'

'That sort of thing doesn't matter in the least.' Like bits of baldness, she thought of adding, but not for long. 'You must have heard me say.'

She could see Patrick trying quite hard, as hard as he ever tried, not to show his annoyance at this information. Although he never came near admitting it, he would really have liked her not to find any other man attractive, even, say, a Kurdish goat-minder in a magazine photograph. If she ever wanted to get back at him, as it might be for going on more than was reasonable about another girl's breasts, she could always do it in two seconds by reminding herself aloud not to miss gorgeous Gary Cooper or dreamy Clark Gable in the old film coming up on the telly. Now he said, with what she had to admit was really not bad grace, 'What about him being funny, with his mouth, wasn't it, and juddering his leg?'

'Well, I mean yes, he does do that, but it doesn't make him any less attractive. Quite the contrary. Anybody who hasn't got

87

something like that, that's funny without them realising it, they're not going to be attractive at all, not to me. Just good-looking if they're lucky.'

Well, he had brought it up, so it was no more than fair in a way that he should have to sit there for a bit turning over in his mind whether to ask her how he fitted into this scheme himself. And for a moment things looked none too good, but then he said, pouring out the last of his beer, 'I suppose some people do need that kind of thing, yes, juddering legs and that. Others are irreproachable with legs, perhaps a touch on the long side, though. Personally I'd advise you to go for them,' which showed he remembered a conversation of years ago in which she had been rather forthright about his undeniably stumpy legs, and he had been quite huffed at the time, no question.

'I love you,' she said, and was honestly surprised when he came round the kitchen table and took her in his arms, and even more surprised (well, in a way) at what followed, which went on until a very short time before Tim came. In fact she brought up the question of what they would do if he turned up early like last time, and was glad she was the only one there to hear some of the things Patrick said to that. But there was no problem, and everything got eaten up and nobody quarrelled or went quiet.

Soon afterwards Jenny got back from a hospital morning and lunch to find the door of 1D wedged open and a man in a grey boiler-suit and woolly hat coming out with an unmistakable look of having dumped one piece of furniture inside and being about to fetch another. When he had passed her with a rather rude once-over she went to peep through the open doorway, but her nerve failed and she retreated into 1B. She stood inside her own closed front door for some minutes going over the fact that curiosity about new neighbours was a perfectly normal human reaction, and the even surer fact that at a time like this her mother and any of her aunts would have been stood out there in the open watching events, as everyone would have expected. But Jenny lost that argument hands down: up home was up home, and down here you were meant to keep yourself to yourself. But then later, when she was in the kitchen boiling the electric kettle for a cup of tea, she heard approaching her kitchen window a high-pitched male voice that could only have gone with a hat crammed down on somebody's head over a lot of hair. She drew back so as not to be seen gawping, waited till it pulled up a few yards further on and went outside, telling herself more persuasively now that if it was bad to pry it was bad not to be friendly too.

She had correctly identified the man who stood on the walk apparently watching something in the strip of garden below and finding it incomprehensible. When he heard her approaching he reluctantly abandoned this.

'Good afternoon.' He got a lot of freeze into it.

Nevertheless she told him who she was, keeping it short, reciting what she had prepared over the last minute. She plugged away; he looked her up and down in a different spirit from the removal man, more detached and social. All that in ten seconds.

He heard her out and then suddenly, with his eyes still on her, shouted out 'Darling!' But it was all right in another moment or two, because a woman appeared in the doorway, about the same age or a couple of years younger, late thirties, a couple of inches taller, well dressed. Jenny took in not much more because the woman was treating her to her third inspection of the afternoon. This one concentrated on her clothes, shoes, hair, make-up, her general standing as an object of attention. (No man ever looked at another man like that, Patrick had said once.) In the meantime the chap told her their name was Porter-King and he was Harold and she was Wendy, though he seemed far from sure on these points and turned with some relief to the idea that they were moving in, you know, though they had a lot of stuff to find room for, an awful lot of stuff.

'Would you like to pop round for a drink later?' asked Jenny, by now quite willing to see the two of them disappear into their flat and never come out again. 'About half-past six?'

'That is most kind,' said the chap. 'That really is extremely kind. Isn't that kind, darling? Most kind of you.'

With this established, though without actually saying the invitation was accepted, he nodded a good deal, throwing in a couple of two-second smiles, and took his wife off inside.

'I don't think he's being rude,' said Jenny to Patrick while she got the glasses out. 'I think it's just his manner.'

'Just is underdoing it rather. His manner was a tremendous amount of him when I saw him. He came as near being all manner as anybody could. What did you make of the wife?'

'I didn't really get a look at her. Quite smart.'

'M'm. Well, they probably won't come with any luck.'

But they did, at least he did. He had put away the narrow-brimmed green soft hat he was wearing before and looked noticeably shorter, and of course hairier. Round his neck he had knotted a mauve-and-yellow scarf to show this or that about himself. 'Wendy will be along in a few minutes,' he said after some thought.

Before that, in fact more or less straight away, he made it clear enough that having decently agreed to turn up he was prepared to bend a strong rule of his and allow some selected facts about himself to become known. When Jenny mentioned children, early on to get the subject out of the way, he quite frankly admitted he had two by his first wife, aged twelve and nine; not very satisfactory, he went on more vaguely, but there it was. He seemed to understand what Patrick meant by saying he was in publishing and said he himself was with a unit trust in the City, perhaps even mentioning a name, and Patrick seemed to understand that. Next he started talking about the troubles he had had and was still having, first of all the ones to do with fitting his great amount of stuff into that new flat of his, then the ones that had come before that, like getting the flat decorated as he wanted it, and then a much broader set featuring unsatisfactory supply of goods, inferior quality of goods and other things. Of course Jenny's father would have asked him if his bowels were playing him up too after a very short time.

'Life's becoming very difficult,' he said once or twice.

'It never was a picnic,' said Patrick, staring at him a little.

'Quite soon it'll be impossible to carry on.' The way he spoke ruled out any feeling that he was just putting his side or getting ready to compare notes, implying instead that he would probably have been all right if he had not been a lord with this old castle to keep up in the proper style. Part of it was never mentioning what anything cost. He sipped his Scotch with little eyebrow-raising nods of appreciation, pleasantly surprised to find the native brew really quite drinkable.

'I suppose you must think this is a reasonably good area,' said Patrick with just a touch of astonishment.

'What's a good area?' asked the man they might have to get used to calling Harold. 'Are there such things any more, with

90

all these funny-looking people coming over from wherever they live and seeming to think it's all right for them to settle down in any place of ours that happens to take their fancy? To my mind there are no good areas left, merely bad areas and even worse areas, and you and I are lucky enough to live in a no-worse-than-bad one.'

Jenny had her back to the men at that moment, picking a couple of babies off the spider-plant with the idea of starting them off on their own in a jam-jar. It could only have been her fancy, but she would have sworn she could hear the silence that had fallen. Although she could never let him see she knew, Patrick actually liked to hear things like that said because of the come-back he could make. It had nothing to do with how he felt personally about the point in question. Or rather it had: the amount of umbrage he took seemed to correspond pretty well to how close the other fellow had come to saying something terrible he would probably be saying himself in half an hour. Now, feeling rather like the heroine in a film as well as on pins, she turned round. Patrick had gone a little red in the face, not a thing he went in for as a rule.

'Do you think it's wise to go round blurting out things like that?' he was asking.

'No, not a bit, uh-boy.' Old boy was what the Porter-King chap must have been trying to say, not for the first time. He lit a cigarette with a very ordinary lighter. 'Not at all wise. Very unwise indeed.'

'Aren't you afraid of finding yourself up against a lot of opposition?'

'Now there with respect I think you're on the wrong tack, I think an awful lot of people would go along with me. Deplorable if you like but there it is.'

'Maybe, but they wouldn't be very nice people.'

'I couldn't agree with you more, uh-boy. That's the whole trouble. People aren't very nice about that sort of thing. I do see it would be a much better world if they were different.'

While he spoke, Porter-King had been moving his lighter up and down in the general area of his right hip, perhaps polishing it against the ginger-coloured dog-tooth check, more likely because he fancied there was a little pocket in his jacket round about there. As for Patrick, she had never known him to hit

91

anyone, but as they said there was a first time for everything. Like her falling down in a faint.

There was a chime from the doorbell that Patrick swore every day to get changed. Jenny was there very quickly and then more gradually the company was joined by was it Wendy. Something happened when Patrick saw her, but no more than most times he saw a non-hideous female in the right age-group, especially one rather showily dressed and over-made-up. Any chance of an upset between the men went straight away, because this was obviously one of those women who made everything stop and start again just by turning up.

'It's good in here,' she said, looking to and fro. 'This is a good room.'

Jenny mentioned the window and the afternoon sun.

'And there's air too, plenty of air, the feeling of being able to breathe.'

Jenny said you could get more air still if you opened the front door.

'Everything seems to give an impression of life growing.'

'What can I get you to drink?' asked Patrick.

'It's unmistakable because it's so rare,' said Mrs Porter-King. 'And so when it does come along it must be seized with both hands. I'm so sorry, did you say something?'

'Yes, I did. I asked you what I could get you to drink.'

'Oh . . . Do you have tequila?'

'I'm afraid not. No.'

'Bacardi?'

'I think I know what you mean, but no, I don't seem to have any of that either.'

'Oh. Oh, anything, then.'

'Right,' said her husband briskly. 'Vodka and tonic, which I see here, vodka and tonic falls within the said category if I mistake not. Ha, huh, do forgive me, uh-boy, I just thought I might save us all a little bit of time, do you see. I'm afraid the old girl's getting a wee bit choosy with her drinks. Eh? I said you're getting a bit choosy. Got to make up your mind for you, darling.'

'This is a new place and summer will be here soon,' said the wife.

Jenny said the evenings were really drawing out.

'Life seems to have begun at last in a strange way.'

92

The four of them jogged along for a surprising time. Wendy Porter-King reminded Jenny slightly of Harold Porter-King by the way she let you know it got lonely up there at the top where she was. Perhaps she never came down, or perhaps she was shy. Jenny told herself it was early days. She could listen. But when she did it was to hear them saying,

'So much time goes by when nothing seems possible.'

'As I see it you don't move on a thing like that till you have to and then you go for the kill. Simple as that.'

'Can I top that up for you?'

But then again after a few more minutes she suddenly blinked and looked about in a new way, like a person in a drama class doing a sleepwalker coming round. The voice was different too.

'What's the time? Harold? What's the time?'

Having nothing else to do, Jenny watched him put his glass down and carefully push back the tweed cuff on his right wrist. Very soon he noticed that there was no watch on that wrist and lost no time in looking at the other one instead. 'Ten past, er, seven, darling. Why?'

'My silk jacket'll be ready at half past.'

'Are you sure?'

'If we leave now we can just make it.'

'But there's no need to be there on the dot, after all. She'll keep it there for you as long as you like,' said Harold Porter-King, reluctantly taking his eyes off his watch. 'I mean she'll keep it there for you as long as you like,' he added on thinking again.

'Good-bye. So sweet of you. So lovely to have met you.'

After that the two were gone very soon, but not too soon for Jenny. First of all there was the woman's looks, not so classy as to scare him off, in fact one of those come-on mouths, quite good eyes you had to grant, and breasts went without saying. Then there was her attitude, on her perch and sort of daring anybody including him to try and knock her off it. Then the husband, enough on his own to set quite a few men thinking, having fantasies at least about doing him down. But the real crunch had come with the wristwatch section. She had seen Patrick's little eyes gleaming at the sight and him reckoning that if a chap like that found his wife in bed with the bloody milkman he would wonder whether that was her out on her roller-skates or picking daisies. And of course they were next door but one, which ought to have been the biggest turn-off, but was actually the biggest attraction, no, that was not really fair – just the good old stand-by excuse. Getting fixed up with a regular girl-friend in Primrose Hill that no one ever saw or thought of, that was cold-blooded adultery; having it off with the neighbour now and again or a bit oftener was a string of lapses, slips, failures and you being your own worst enemy every time it happened. Quicker, too. More exciting. And nastiest of all, cheaper, easier to face than cutting down the Scotch.

'Right, outside in two minutes, everyone,' said Patrick the moment the front door was shut. 'Or not much longer. I'm not having you cooking after that lot. Fuck me wept. Sorry, love.'

'There's an oxtail in.'

'Well take it out again. Feed the bloody cat while I call up a couple of human beings if there are any left in this horrible town. I'll book Gioberti's at eight.'

By what Patrick invariably said was sheer coincidence Frankie turned up smartly, flopping down the stairs in an exaggerated way. He had actually had the whole of the last of the boiled beef that afternoon and could not have forgotten it.

'You've got vibrissae on your upper lip,' Patrick told him.

'He can't help that,' said Jenny on her way to the kitchen.

'They're his whiskers, you bloody fool. Related to the hairs in your nose.'

'Oh, charming.'

'Hey, do you realise that rotten Porter-King sod got through nearly a quarter of a bottle of Scotch? In that minute. Mind you, it's fair to say he needs every drop he can get.'

Of the wife halves of the two couples they were meeting for dinner, one was an ex-girl-friend of Patrick's of ten years before who even Jenny believed was now just a family friend, and the other one had a nose that went much too far down her face and then turned up at the end, so that you could see straight into her nostrils. Jenny felt slightly bad about thinking of this at all, let alone with satisfaction. The ex-girl-friend's husband was in television and knew David Frost slightly.

'What are we going to do about those perishing Porter-Kings?' asked Patrick when he and Jenny were on their way. 'He'll be programmed to return drink for drink. Never know when a feller may be able to do you a good turn, uh-boy. But I reckon you needn't worry about her coffee-mornings.'

'They might get better.'

'Nah, they've got too far to come, love. Left it too late to start, too. Actually, him I can see myself learning to put up with after a fashion. But her, ooh, no thank *you* very much I'm sure, and my best respects to Mrs Brown. Now I know you saw me looking her over . . .'

'Well, I sort of couldn't help . . .'

'Of course not. So Mrs Porter-King was duly looked over and the answer's . . . no. Just . . . not . . . worth it.'

Jenny said, 'Am I meant to feel flattered or something?' She said it glaring out of the car window into a kind of strip-lighted corridor where frightening dirty men crouched over pin-tables.

'Hang on.' Patrick moved them over to the left and up a narrow street. 'I've got to park.'

They found a place on a corner by a shop full of typewriters and very spindly tables and chairs. He joined her on the pavement and stood, looking quite tall and also serious, with his hand resting on the roof of the car. Couples of hairy youngsters passed to and fro and a taxi drove up the street with its rattling engine. Not much else. It was still early enough for the daylight not to have faded at all.

'It wasn't only you noticing me when I was looking her over.' He spoke hesitantly. 'After that, it was almost when they were leaving, I happened to catch an absolutely terrible expression on your face. Here we go again, that was what you were thinking. Another one of those. I'll never forget it. Well, it isn't going to happen this time. Right?'

She reached up and put her hand on top of his but said nothing.

'I have no intentions towards Mrs Porter-Christ-King. Do you believe me?'

'Yes.'

'Good for you, little love.' When they were nearly at the restaurant he said, 'I do realise it would be much better if none of this was ever necessary.'

Eight

'Eric rang. He wants us to go along for a drink at half-past six or so.'

'Isn't it our turn?'

'I know, I said, but evidently he's having some people in he particularly wants us to meet.'

'You'd have thought he'd particularly want to prevent us meeting the sort of people he has in.'

'It's probably somebody he knows at work,' said Jenny.

'Oh yes, that'll be it. I mean after all it could hardly be, er, somebody he knows not at work. No. Somebody he knows at work. Of course.'

Jenny could not quite look forward to going along to Eric and Stevie's, though up to now she had found them perfectly friendly and reasonable. If two men decided they wanted to live together then that was obviously up to them. Everybody said the law about all that side of life was out of date and what a good thing it was just coming up to being changed, they said. And in the same way what happened when they lived together was entirely up to them. Well no, not really. If it was *entirely* up to them, why did she go on feeling that what they did (she disliked getting even as far as that way of putting it) was unpleasant every time she thought of it, and just as unpleasant, absolutely as unpleasant, when she thought of it now as whenever she had thought of it the first time? More so, in fact, which was the other way round from how it was meant to be. To be quite truthful, she was still not sure about a lot of what they did because of the way the conversation had gone the time she asked Patrick to explain it to her.

'Now you are quite set in your mind you want to know.'

'Of course, why not? I'm a married woman now. You can't shock me.'

'Don't you be too bloody sure of that, my girl. All right then, but you're not going to like it.'

'I'm not expecting to like it.'

'Very wise. Now: I'm going to have to mention parts of the body, okay with you?'

She had said it was, and thought she had meant it, but then after hearing some things that made her say, 'Oh, they don't, do they?' a couple of times she said quite sharply she had had enough.

'There's only a bit more. We've been through the worst.'

'I told you I'd had enough, Patrick.'

'All right, for Christ's sake, it wasn't my idea. I didn't invent it, you know.'

'How do you know about it?'

'Well . . . one gets to hear.'

'If I found you'd done that last one to someone I'd never forgive you.'

'What? Look, don't start blaming it on me if you'd be so bloody kind. Let me tell you I don't like it either. Jesus.'

Later she had apologised completely, and quite right too, and it was absurd to sort of hold it against Patrick, any of it, and yet she would have had to admit that in her heart of hearts, though not once in a month of Sundays, she did very slightly hold it against men. They had thought it up and it was they who did it, along with other things of theirs like shooting birds and caning schoolchildren. Of course there were lesbians, but she had never asked Patrick or anybody else to explain about them.

Jenny's mind played round the edges of this while she got into the powder-blue job with the white collar – only its second time out. She was putting on the light-blue eye-shadow when it occurred to her that from one point of view it could not matter less what she looked like, but she must not fail to pay her hosts the basic compliment, and apart from self-respect there was always Patrick to look nice for. She also had the fleeting thought that the whole thing about what queers did was untrue, all romancing and gossip, that it stood to reason that nobody really behaved like that, much as she had thought when her sister Trixie first told her what their father must have done to their mother to produce the two of them and Robbie, though before she could develop this analogy the doorbell chimed.

It was Tim, announcing with true good-boy smugness that he had come in to check on the laying of his carpets. Today he was wearing a fresh outfit that included a button-down check shirt and oyster-coloured corduroy trousers. To replenish the store-cupboard, he said, he had brought a bottle of Scotch, a classy item in a historical-looking cardboard box. Jenny recognised the name as that of a brand or grade Patrick had once vulgarly described as tasting of french letter, but he thanked Tim and offered him a drink on the spot, explaining why it could only literally be one. Tim evidently thought that was a fine idea and was just settling down with his glass when the doorbell chimed again.

This time it was Stevie, in no sort of fresh outfit, actually as ever in one of the dark navy typhoon-proof jerseys, looking as though it had been knitted with walking-sticks and was steeped in tar, that he must have had a stock of. With a nod and a quick word to Patrick he strode up to Jenny, a bulky figure with arms held slightly away from sides like a wary wrestler's.

'Sorry to come barging in, Jenny my love,' he growled in his dependable West Country accent, 'but I've been sent along to beg some ice. Seems we've tumbled down somehow and we just haven't got enough.' He sounded rather disaffected about the last part.

Tim had politely got up. His face had taken on the querulous look that merely heralded one of his sneezes, but Stevie was not to know that. While Jenny introduced them his own face began to go narrow-eyed and sidelong in a puzzled way, as it once had on the screen, at least, to herald a punch-up. Tim began breathing heavily as his sneeze gathered. Patrick was pouring himself a drink. Jenny squeezed her hands together. But then Tim's expression changed into something like incredulous joy. Blinking in quick tempo, he held out a forefinger.

'You're Steve Bairstow,' he said, still trying to come to terms with it. 'Steve . . . *Bairstow*. Good God. *Fear on the Waterfront. Boats Away!* Er . . . hang on a minute . . . *The Hard Man*. The fight with Stewart Granger in the lorry-park. Correct?'

Stevie had hung his head and now nodded it once or twice. Those who had followed his career would have had no difficulty just then in recalling those inquests and courts of inquiry at which the Steve Bairstow character had been commended for carrying the gang chief through the forest fire on his back or staying at his post in the engine-room after the second torpedo had hit. Blindly he grasped Tim's hand and wordlessly threw his other arm round his shoulders. 'How marvellous,' Tim kept saying, though not by a miracle going on to say that he seldom saw anything of the Steve Bairstow character these days. Steve had a hand free by the time Patrick had a drink ready to go into it.

After that, nobody could have prevented Stevie from insisting that Tim should join the party and come and have a drink with his old mate Eric, as he described him – no, no messing, Timmy lad, come along straight away. Patrick looked at Jenny and sent her messages or asked her questions about Tim and Stevie and Eric, but in vain. Even if Tim could have been prised away from Stevie for a moment, he was by nature about as receptive to winks and nudges as an elephant, one of the African sort with the big ears and the low IQ. He and Stevie were still intertwined when the four of them reached the door of 1A.

Since her first visit, Jenny had assumed that somebody's sister or sister-in-law had seen to the furniture and stuff here. Only a woman, she felt, would have put in all those lamps, none of them at a handy level for reading, all those long-fringed rugs, all those triangular and muffin-shaped and roly-poly cushions. Not so easy to explain the three pictures, the tall narrow black-and-white one of a horse in mid-air, the squarish one of an Asiatic girl with a green face, and the long narrow one of a deserted beach with palm-trees, which she had thought were meant only for shops. Perhaps an auntie. The place was cosy in a way, but a way that helped to explain why some sons turned out drunken wastrels and a few daughters went on the streets.

Jenny delivered her pudding-basin of ice to Eric. He greeted her warmly and introduced a couple in their fifties as Mr and Mrs Armitage. The Mr and Mrs, by not being Brian and Norma, say, told you something about them, and perhaps the Armitage did too. Eric, who seemed a little strained, went off with the ice. Mr and Mrs Armitage, but especially Mrs Armitage, looked closely at Jenny. She recognised the look from the time the mother of one of the children at her school had mistaken her for a prostitute and accessory in several recent sweet-shop robberies whose picture had been in the local paper. 'Come from round about, do you?' Mrs Armitage asked Jenny after a time.

'I live next door actually.'

'Oh. Nice and handy for here I expect you find.' Mrs Armitage had piled-up grey hair and a grey suit like a girls'-reformatory officer.

'Er, with my husband. That's him over there.'

'Which? Which one?'

'The . . . slim one standing on the left.'

'You mean the one who hadn't got his arms round the other one a minute ago. I see. What does he do for a living, your husband?'

'He's a company director.' Jenny had felt it sounded respectable and sort of all there, but remembered too late that company directors had taken over from scoutmasters in court reports in the Sunday papers. 'He's a publisher,' she added quickly, and saw Mrs Armitage thinking of nude magazines. 'He publishes books.' Dirty books.

Mr Armitage had begun to twist about slightly where he stood. 'Very interesting,' he said.

Just as Jenny was trying to tell herself that this was all in her mind, Mrs Armitage said, 'Who's that other one you came in with? The one between your, your husband and what's he called, is it Stevie?'

'Oh, that's another neighbour. Tim Valentine.'

'Oh. That's an unusual name if I may say so. And what does he do? For a living, I mean?'

Jenny could not see how not to tell her Tim was a prison visitor. She tried to make it sound as if it was very hard to get into.

'Oh.' Mrs Armitage did wonders with that word. Only an English person could have appreciated it completely. Well, perhaps an American if he had lived in London ever since the war.

'My wife likes to get people fitted together in her mind,' explained Mr Armitage. 'Sort of all fitted in.'

Still looking at Jenny, Mrs Armitage said, 'I've always believed in knowing who I was dealing with. I've tried to make that a rule.'

Jenny said, 'Have you known Eric long?'

'Precisely ten minutes in my case,' said Mrs Armitage, but Mr Armitage answered straight enough, 'It's coming up to four months since I took over the section of which Eric is an important part.'

'To do with the Royal Navy, isn't it?'

'Yes, but we don't exactly weigh anchor and sail the seven seas, you know, my dear. Just pensions is what we look after. Sailormen's pensions.'

'Money in other words,' said Mrs Armitage. 'Taxpayers' money, and lots of it,' but then for some baffling reason changed her tone to Jenny and went on almost confidentially, 'That Stevie is it, you'd think he was a sort of tough guy just at first glance, wouldn't you, but then you begin to wonder. You notice the way he moves his hands about, never still for a moment, not like any sort of tough guy I've ever had to do with. Look, look there now, the way he's going on, up and down and sideways, look, and the other one, there now, see? How does a fellow like that earn his living if he does?'

'I told you he's a film actor,' said Mr Armitage. 'Twice, once this morning and then again on the way over.'

'Oh well,' said his wife, 'we know what we're dealing with there, don't we, eh, right off. We know we're dealing with an abnormal psychological type, just like that, never mind what else may or may not be, er, in question. It's a well-known outlet for exhibitionistic tendencies. We've got that on our hands before we even start, as you might say.'

'That's grossly unfair to a profession that gives pleasure to millions every year. What do you say to that?'

Mrs Armitage's reply was going to be very definite, but just then Eric came up and handed out drinks off a tray painted with the Union Jack. His own looked like neat whisky except there was so much of it. Across the room Stevie had Tim more or less penned into a corner and Patrick looked as if he felt like a good read.

With expert timing Mr Armitage got off an absolute tranquillising-dart of a question about what kind of agreement Eric had with the apartment owners and Eric was back to him in a flash. There he stood, reasonable and responsible in his well-pressed dark suit and clean biscuit shirt, too clean in this London air not to have been put on within the last hour. Although she could not at the moment remember meeting anybody through whose eyes she less wanted to see anybody else, Jenny could not help seeing him a bit through Mrs Armitage's. Go on about deposits and penalty agreements as he might, there was no knowing what he was thinking about. Or rather there was plenty of knowing what he could easily have been thinking about, all too much. She wished that none of these suspicions and guesses had ever entered her head, but in one way or another they had, and there was no driving them out again. Among other things, Patrick had said that quite a few of the kind of men under discussion never did anything, or did very little, or only did it to begin with, on the honeymoon so to speak. Eric had to be one of those.

Eric now started shifting the three of them over to the other three. Jenny thought uneasily that Stevie's face was turning puzzled again.

Tim was saying, 'I've been going on about how attractively this room has been got up in how long is it, Stevie? – a few weeks, really,' and if he meant it then God help the inside of 1E. 'But there's been a woman's hand at work in it, no doubt of that, and I was just wondering who the clever lady was.'

A mysterious silence fell and Stevie shook his head slowly. 'Well, how it could have come about that young Tim here should have fallen into that way of thinking, it fairly beats me hollow,' he said, and sounded as if it did too. 'You've properly got hold of the wrong end of the stick there, my boy, and no ifs or buts. Seeing as I designed and ordered the whole lot myself, wall to wall, floor to ceiling, every mortal thing my own choice or creation.'

'Really. In that case all I can say is you must have an amazingly feminine side to your nature hidden away somewhere behind that manly exterior, ridiculous as it sounds.'

Eric said, 'I think what, what our friend is actually trying to say . . .'

Any real expert on how the Steve Bairstow character behaved in a crisis could have told you that the moment for his adversaries to look out was when his brow cleared as his course of action became unmistakable at last. So it was now with Stevie. He swept Eric's words aside and spoke at slightly reduced volume, another famous danger-sign. 'I'm very disappointed, I am. I thought we were all settling down to a nice friendly chat and much to my surprise I find somebody trying to be funny in what I can only take to be an uncalled-for way. Now I don't mind telling you that really upsets me. It upsets me good and proper. So much so – '

'There's no question of anyone trying to be funny, Stevie,' interrupted Patrick – 'Tim was making a perfectly serious point about artistic creativity. Not a new one, incidentally. Far from it – the ancient Greeks saw the human soul as divided into a masculine principle and a feminine principle and the marriage of the two was what produced art. The Romans . . .'

Jenny remembered him saying that the one thing teachers really had at their back was boredom: better than any amount of tear-gas. In less than a minute now he had Stevie's arm round Tim's shoulders again and his head hanging in apology and self-reproach. And after that everything went swimmingly, with even Mrs Armitage saying ordinary things, until Tim called for their attention and said it was a shame to break up the party and would they please let him take them all out for dinner.

At once the unthinking smile vanished from Mrs Armitage's expression and she said she was afraid she and her husband would have to be getting back to Mill Hill. 'Won't we?' she asked him, and he agreed that they would.

Eric and Stevie were in no such instant accord. After trying without success to catch Stevie's eye, Eric said hesitantly, 'What a smashing idea, Tim, of course we'd love to . . .'

'But,' said Stevie.

'Well,' said Eric, and took a long shaky breath, '*but* you said you had a new sort of veal concoction you were keen for us to try, *and* you said you particularly wanted to see this old pal of yours in the play on the BBC. Now obviously we can always –'

'You don't care about any of that more than sixpenn'orth. Anyone can see with half an eye that jealousy's made a big meal of you. You've seen me enjoying myself yarning with a new friend and you want to put paid to that, don't you?' To Jenny it was very funny and dreadful to hear this coming out in Stevie's deep yo-ho-ho voice.

'Look, all right, all right, Stevie, we'll forget all about the –'

'I don't like you at all, you know. I think you're a mean killjoy sort of a fellow, that I do.'

Staring gloomily at Eric, Stevie poured the contents of his glass, only an inch or so of liquid, slowly on to the carpet and walked with his rolling tread into the kitchen, whose door he shut behind him firmly but not noisily. Jenny went over and stood beside Eric, who said in a controlled way that he owed them all an apology and Stevie had recently had some depressing news from home. After looking to and fro and making some grumbling, muttering noises with little breathy snorts, Mrs Armitage left, followed by Mr Armitage, but then before any of the rest of them had had time to say anything he was back.

'I left my cigarettes,' he said, though he picked up none in the very short time he stayed. 'It's regrettable that there was this slight cloud over the closing moments of an exceedingly pleasant party. Thank you very much, Eric, and I'd like you to know that I quite realise and accept the fact that in this life we all have our difficulties. All of us. I'll be seeing you in the morning as usual. Good night all.'

When he had gone Patrick said in an American accent, 'Mr Armitage stands up to be counted.'

'That's right, Patrick,' said Eric from where he was dabbing at the carpet, 'and believe me I'm quite glad of it myself. Because he could make my life a misery if he felt like it. The other half of it, I mean.'

'Yeah. Sorry.'

Something large and breakable fell to the kitchen floor.

'That's just in case we start patching things up amongst ourselves,' said Eric. 'Bye-bye Tim, you run along, not your fault, see you again, sorry about this.' That part came out almost singsong but when he got to Jenny he squeezed her arm and gave her a very friendly look. 'Thank you, my dear, I'll let you have your basin back tomorrow. Don't worry about me, any of you, I can handle this just as easily as any poor bleeder with a jammed rifle in the jungle with a wounded tiger. Tigress I should say. Patrick, if you could hang on for about five seconds.'

Back in 1B, Tim said to Jenny, 'I think there was something funny going on between those two fellows.'

'Oh really? Wherever did you get that impression from?'

'What's the matter, Jenny? Are you cross with me about something?'

'Those two fellows that you refer to are a pair of queers.'

'What?' He sounded quite cross himself, and mystified too. 'Nobody said anything like that to me.'

Jenny thought of telling him that she or Patrick must have

104

said something at some time but he was too wrapped up in himself to have taken it in, but to go on like that when you were not absolutely sure of your ground was giving way to emotion, so instead she asked him if he would like a drink. That was what this generation said where their grandfathers would have suggested joining in a short prayer.

'No thanks,' said Tim. 'I mean yes please.'

'Help yourself. Anyway you shouldn't have needed anyone to say anything to you, a man of your experience. You only had to use your eyes and ears in there. Two men of that sort of age living together, not two young lads starting off, and not two old boys whose wives have died. And how can you not realise it could be dodgy telling, telling Tarzan he had a terrific feminine side. In fact come to think of it . . .'

Jenny let it go. She realised she was indeed fairly cross, or had been. Frankie was passing and she picked him up, spread him on her lap and began stroking him partly for the calming effect on her. As he always did when he knew he was needed he immediately turned on his great snoring purr and made himself weigh more than usual.

Opposite her, Tim reflectively let himself drop from a standing posture on to one of her armchairs without quite spilling the glass of whisky he held. From next door there came a faint regular thumping and Eric's voice calling Stevie's name.

'So Stevie got fed up with me because he thought I was making fun of him for . . . All right, but I should have thought he'd be used to that by now. No, just a minute, Jenny. Then why did he get so cross with Eric?'

'That's what Eric's there for. That part of it's easy enough to understand. That part of their lives.'

'What?'

Not a moment too soon Patrick turned up just then and took the door off the latch and shut it. 'Bloody hell,' he said, his choice of words coming as no surprise. 'Firing has died down. It's just a matter of time. Stevie's time.'

'Tim wishes someone had tipped him off about them,' said Jenny.

'Well, of course,' said Patrick. 'Like Tim, these two friends of ours are a pair of queers. Most natural thing in the world.'

'All right, you might have put it differently, but there's no shame attached to it, is there, not these days, and the law's going to be changed any minute.'

'Write this down and take it home and look at it morning and evening. There'll always be shame attached to it whatever the law says.'

'Only while there's prejudice and ignorance. Especially ignorance. And listen, Patrick, if those two are a pair of queers – '

'Listen, Tim, *they're a pair of queers*. But then you never do fucking listen, do you? Sorry, love.'

'If I can just go on – which is the pretty one? I mean they're both so masculine. That's what I could never have – '

'You mean you really don't know? The one who went on about being hard done by and got annoyed and attracted all the attention and broke up the party and generally behaved badly is the pretty one. You've had quite enough to do with women to be able to take that in. All right, love.'

'No, of course anybody can see the sense of that,' said Jenny sturdily, but when she went on she just paid special attention to not sounding as if she was hard done by or annoyed or any of the others. 'There's some cold beef in the larder and I can do a salad in a minute.'

'Nonsense, I'm taking you out to dinner,' said Tim.

'Lovely but we'll have another quickie here before we shift,' said Patrick. 'Er, hey, what did you think of that female? I thought all that lot had died out.'

'What I don't see,' said Tim, then glared for a moment. 'Among other things, I grant. *One* thing I don't see is why Eric invited those people there in the first place, Mr and Mrs Armitage. Or didn't he realise how it might go?'

'Oh, he realised that all right. In fact he was fully expecting it but there was nothing he could do. Stevie insisted on him inviting his boss round for a drink complete with wife. Or was he ashamed of him or something? Who did he think he was? Look who was talking.'

'Why didn't he invite more people? With more of a crowd he could have spread it out better, couldn't he?'

'A bigger audience would only have egged Stevie on. And he wasn't going to ask his queer friends, Eric wasn't, was he, and there were none of his straight friends he reckoned he could ask except us.'

106

'I think you and Jenny should take that as a great compliment,' said Tim. 'No, seriously.'

'Oh, for fuck,' said Patrick. 'Oh, I didn't see you there, love.'

Jenny put out some crisps and nuts. 'Did Eric tell you all this just in that minute?' she asked.

'No. Some of it I, which is it, I inferred. Deduced.'

'You do know a lot about it, don't you?' Jenny could not resist saying.

'I've had a bit of experience,' said Patrick. 'And I don't mean of queers.'

'I suppose I *really* put my foot in it by asking everyone out to dinner,' said Tim resignedly, 'and Eric didn't want to go and Stevie did. Oh dear. People are so incredibly – '

Patrick shook his head. 'You're reading too little into it,' he said. 'It was doomed from the start. Stevie set the whole thing up just so as to humiliate Eric and score off him. Whatever had been said, whoever had been there besides the Armitages, didn't really make any difference. There's always something. Well no, actually they don't need there to be anything, as Eric remarked to me just the other day, as I recall.'

'I can't believe it of Stevie. A nice chap like that.'

'He is not a nice chap like that. If you want to understand his lot, the pretty ones, imagine the most hysterical, egomaniacal, solipsistic bloody female in more or less male biological shape. I'm sorry, darling.' Patrick stroked Jenny's arm. 'You know I know you're not one of that sort.'

As a little later she got into the back of Tim's Jaguar, which smelt of peppermint humbugs, she said, 'Mightn't Eric get the sack for being queer?'

'He's a civil servant,' said Patrick from the front. 'They don't get the sack for anything, not even treason. Especially not treason. Stevie knows that, of course. Very nice for him. Just what the doctor ordered, in fact.'

The resounding moan of anguish that was Tim's yawn fell across the last words. He was the one driving not because he was or was thought to be soberer than Patrick but because the Jag was incontestably bigger than the Mini.

Patrick said to him, but making sure Jenny could hear, 'I'm going to get you for this. You do it on purpose, for effect, because you think it's wild and free and interesting. Carry on by all means but kindly take note that we know that.'

107

'I don't do it *for* anything, Patrick, I just – '

'And don't try telling me you can't help it. You wouldn't do it in church or anywhere like that.'

'No, I wouldn't, because I'd be remembering all the time not to. You've put your finger on it. I do it when I'm not thinking, when I'm enjoying myself or when I'm on my own. I spend quite a lot of time on my own and you get into bad habits that way, I'm afraid.'

'Now you're trying to make me cry. What about letting me drive this cookie up the M1 one evening next week? Taking you along too, I mean.'

'We'll see,' said Tim, apparently quite naturally using a phrase Jenny had supposed confined to parents and sounding very odd coming from him.

'Steady on,' said Patrick, who must have felt the same. 'Think about it before you commit yourself any further.'

'You may have noticed I haven't yawned since we came in here,' said Tim while they were sitting at the restaurant table. 'I've been remembering not to even though I am enjoying myself.'

'Don't let all that hard work spoil your dinner,' said Patrick. 'Well done, old bean,' he added when a second bottle of Burgundy arrived without having been visibly asked for. 'I'd have betted you wouldn't be much good at taking somebody out, but bugger me it's gone like a bloody film. And in a place like this, crawling with things to go wrong.'

'It's been absolutely wonderful, Tim.' Jenny thought that was more the right tone to take, but as so often she found herself feeling completely the same as him. The place was just as he had said, without actual fountains playing or animals in cages, and the cooking got done in the kitchen rather than under your nose, but everything was in French, a kind of French that was entirely different from her own French from school, and the cutlery was laid out like an operating theatre, and the wine-list looked from outside like a church Bible. But Tim went straight to the page he wanted, the chapter anyway, and what he ordered was positively pleasant instead of being so acid that the saliva came spurting out from all over the inside of your mouth (white), or having the sort of taste that made you tell yourself that at least it was doing your digestion good (red). He was even fine with the waiters.

He was explaining now how he had learnt to manage. 'Then there's all the practice I've had with those birds. You know, the look who's talking and see if I care brigade, the ones I used to – '

'Yes, I remember you telling me,' said Patrick emphatically.

'Yes, the Linda Kowalskis of this world who got so cross when I – '

'Not the sort of person you want to have to do with at all.'

'Absolutely not. Oh well. You know, I can't tell you how marvellous it is to be here like this with the two of you.'

Jenny reached over and gave Tim's hand a squeeze.

'Not only because of the present moment but because of afterwards, not having to take one of them back and pretend I'm riding a bicycle to stop me – '

'Tell me, Tim, have you always yawned like that or is it something you've only found yourself doing recently?' asked Patrick.

'Oh, I think it goes back a long way,' said Tim, clearly ready to discuss this point and disappointing Jenny by being side-tracked from the much more promising topic of a moment before, whatever it might have been. 'I realised the other day that lots of things about me haven't changed since I was a child. I realised that in lots of ways I simply haven't grown up. Oh I know I'm pretty intelligent and all that, I was thinking of psychologically. Emotionally. I think people take growing up too much for granted, you know. I think it's the most difficult thing people ever have to do. And they have to do it themselves, on their own, if they're going to do it at all. They don't need help. Or rather the only help you can give them is not give them any, just give them the chance to do it alone. Oh Lord, here comes Asdrubale. Every decent place has got a snag somewhere.'

Jenny had been watching the gradual approach of the man later described by Patrick as the old fart who ran the restaurant. He looked like at least an ambassador with his full tail-coat, crimson silk sash over the shoulder and long almost-white hair, too distinguished to be borne. In one hand he held a bunch of red and pink carnations, from which at every successive table he chose one and fixed it to the dress of each female eating at it. All conversation and possibility of interest in anything else closed down there for the three-quarters of an hour or so it took him to get through the performance, which he played like the non-dancing part of a ballet. Now that he had reached the next party the silent zone stretched out to include Jenny and the others.

Not for long. 'Do you want him to do that to you?' asked Tim.

'Well I'd sooner he didn't.' Jenny could feel a huge blush like an attack of measles already starting up somewhere round the back of her neck.

'I'll stop him then.'

'Oh don't bother, it'll be too embarrassing.'

'Leave it to me.'

Jenny never knew what were the few words Tim muttered to the man with the sash, but they were enough to make him not only leave her alone but stare at her for a second with something like awe, or possibly dismay at his own unworthiness. He faded away, and the sweet-trolley came, and she started on some beautiful strawberries tasting of distilled water.

'Before I so much as catch sight of the brandy-bottle,' said Patrick, 'let me just impress this upon your attention, old stick. Eric and Stevie, right? – Eric and Stevie are not typical or representative or average queers. They're from the show-piece end of the spectrum, the top ten per cent, models of respectability and domestic harmony and maturity and restraint and general right-thinkingness and God-fearingness in a sadly depraved world. Whereabouts on that scale do you want to come? But I mean thanks anyway for a marvellous evening.'

'It's not a question of wanting in that sense or choosing, it's a matter of one's own basic nature. Oh it's been great fun and would you like some more coffee? What about a cigar?'

'You're trying to choose away like mad, you bloody fool, and fuck Mr Perlmutter and all his tribe. Yeah, tell you later, love. No, but I would really rather fancy another drink. Then off.'

In the hall place on the way out Tim simply happened to step aside politely for a female in her thirties very poshly dressed but not overdone, smashing-looking in a lush blonde way, altogether anybody's idea of a really serious woman. She gave Tim a look that would have made Jenny thoroughly indignant if it had been going Patrick's way instead. And Tim might miss a lot but he got that one all right. There was nothing wrong with him if only he could be made to see it.

110

Nine

Patrick was in first-class shape one morning the following week as he walked across the square to his office. There had been more days of rain, but the trees in the central garden, far from being discouraged, had responded with a rather showy outburst of foliage, both in quantity and in concentration of greenness. He liked trees. They reminded him of sex in a way, or at any rate were a distinguished form of life, and he made a point of being on the side of life, though he would have done so with an easier mind had it not been for all the terrible craps who volunteered the information that that was what they were. More straightforwardly, the sun was shining. Among those it shone on were two remarkably pretty girls, dark-haired, upright of carriage, secretaries perhaps, assistants rather.

In the ordinary way this was not the kind of thing Patrick cared to see: the passing of two such without his having laid even a finger on them would have made him unhappy for most of a minute. But feeling as he did today he threw the two charmers a warm, indulgent smile, unfortunately without being seen throwing it.

In the hall of Hammond & Sutcliffe, or the lobby as he had heard Simon call it, he ran into Jack Sutcliffe coming out of his room behind the stairs. This had been said at one time to be Jack's temporary room, while his real or proper room held an equally temporary display of the firm's new publications, but nowadays it seemed to be just his room. He was wearing a grey suit with a bluish tinge to it and his Old Something-Else tie, the purple-and-white stripe. He greeted Patrick with a cordiality that was a notch or two down from being actually glad to see him, but an approach to cordiality for all that. His reasoning

111

seemed to be that because he, Patrick, disagreed with Simon now and then he could well harbour other reactionary traits which might in time be coaxed into the open.

'Coming up to morning prayers?' he asked. This was his term for the directorial conferences Simon had instituted to start the working day, often lasting only a couple of minutes and said to be informal, not really worth the saying now that all transactions within the firm were meant to be that.

They started on the first flight of green-carpeted stairs. 'When you come to think of it,' said Patrick, 'that's not a very appropriate phrase considering who conducts the prayers.'

'No, readings from the gospel according to St Marx would be more in character, I agree.'

'Well, I meant rather that Simon's fraternity would have left after the announcements and before the actual prayers, with the RCs and those of other faiths.'

Jack had paused on the half-landing. Mouthwash fumes came wafting across from him. 'I'm sorry, I don't follow you. Getting awfully dense, I'm afraid.'

Patrick said, not loudly, 'Oh, just he's one of a certain . . . persuasion . . .'

'Oh, you mean a Jew. No no, you've got it wrong, quite wrong. I happen to know his uncle was Bishop of where was it, Bath and Wells, Exeter, I've forgotten, one of the West Country sees. Family comes from round there.' Jack started up the second flight. 'Might as well be one of the chosen from how he goes on, if that's the point you're making.'

The noise Patrick offered in reply could have meant anything. Actually all his euphoria had fallen away in the last few seconds. He was so far from being anti-semitic that a couple of his best friends really were Jews, and if he lived to be a hundred he would never forget the marvellous piece of luck he had once had at a barmitzvah in Two Waters. And now, trying to do no more than raise a not very creditable laugh, he had ended up one down from an old shag on whose real anti-semitism any punter would have plunged. Not possible in a just world.

'Yes,' said Jack with vague approval, looking not much more alertly round the unremarkable walls and ceiling of the stairhead outside Simon's room. 'Lovely, isn't it, all this. Not likely to last, I fear. It'll be steel and glass and what-not if the young master has his way.' But it was he who now seemed in unusually good spirits.

Simon had taken his jacket off to suggest industry and dedication. His floral braces and matching sleeve-bands weakened this effect but the position of his desk, pushed back for no obvious reason against the wall, gave a useful cleared-for-action look. He was sitting on the edge of it turning through some pasteboard sheets, attended by someone in worn jeans Patrick took at first for a house-painter or window-cleaner. He looked up when the other two came in but when Jack wished him good morning returned wordlessly to his inspection.

'I hope we haven't come at a bad time,' said Jack.

Simon still said nothing, merely handing him the bundle of material, which Patrick saw had coloured shapes of some sort on it. Jack glanced briefly at the first two or three. 'Are you asking my opinion of these, or just showing me them as a fair sample of what you have to put up with?'

'They're the first draft of the cover designs for H & S Poets in Progress.'

'Assuming that means you are asking my opinion, I'm afraid there'd be no point in my giving it. Try me on nuclear physics instead.'

Patrick took the sheets when Jack passed them. The composition on the top one seemed to be the work of two persons, creators respectively of the lettering and what had to be called the illustration. The lettering, which spelt out a title and a name, that of Vera Selig as it happened, was evidently the result of a quick test session with some new and severely imperfect type of pen or marker, the other stuff was coloured whorls and patches calling for talent of a much lower order. Patrick spent a token couple of moments on the next of the batch. 'I think they're ideally suited to the series,' he said, speaking in a flat tone. He was still enraged at being scored off by Jack, not so much the fact as the manner of it.

'We seem to be in agreement,' said Simon, trying and failing to tear the sheets across, indeed making not the slightest impression on them. 'Take these away,' he said to the fellow in jeans, 'and forget they ever happened. We're not marketing toiletries here.'

'We're not?' said Patrick, and regretted it temporarily.

113

'I take it that is the, er, the artist,' said Jack when the door had shut. 'I'd have kicked his backside for him if I'd known.'

'Chris is the new art editor. I assumed you'd recognised him from last week.'

'So he's not the actual perpetrator of the atrocity. I see.'

'Nice of you both to have come up,' said Simon. 'I'm afraid I've really nothing for you. Oh, just the reps' party has been brought forward to the fourth of next month to allow for their conference.' He drove home this information visually by tapping at the relevant place on the stadium-size wall-chart by which he now stood. 'Do bring your wives if you can. You need only stay an hour or so. Remember – the reps are the people who actually have to go out there and do it. We sign papers. They sell books.'

'It's Berlin tonight, boys,' Jack muttered to Patrick.

'What?'

'Well . . . Oh yes, I knew there was something.' Simon was already back beside his desk. 'Deirdre. Any new ideas?'

Jack had obviously been waiting his chance. His perkiness of manner was about to be explained. 'Ideas, regrettably, no,' he said. 'News yes. Deirdre is coming over for a couple of weeks from Monday, staying at the Bridgwater, and expresses herself eager for chat over a nice lunch. Her letter arrived yesterday but you were off to Manchester and I wanted to report to you in person, Mr Managing Director.' He smiled uncaptivatingly.

'What does she say about the book?'

'Not much. Well, you'll see. A few finishing touches required.'

'Did you get hold of her agent? Isn't she with . . .'

'Trevor. He was out of the office yesterday too. I left a message.'

'Let me know what he says. Well, that's encouraging as far as it goes. Good. Right, that's all I've got. Any other points? Super. Good to see you.'

'At least he forgot to tell us not to get our hair cut,' Jack murmured to Patrick as they reached the doorway, but there was no more of that because Simon called,

'Oh, Patrick, just a quick word if I may. While you're here.'

Jack looked straight at Patrick for a second or so and went out.

'*Blood in the Tigris,*' said Simon. 'To cut a long story short I've come round to your way of thinking, I know it's bad of

114

me to have taken all this time. I think you should write to Pedrain-Williams and just tell him, okay, he shortens it by half, he rewrites every sentence, or we don't want to know. We're not a benefit society for Welsh loonies.'

'No. No, we're not.'

'Or Irish loonies, come to that. Well, that's a bit unfair, I suppose. You have met Deirdre, haven't you?'

'Just. A party here a couple of years ago.'

'She's quite an interesting old creature in her way. According to legend she had it off with H.G. Wells in about 1899.'

'Lloyd George too, no doubt.'

'Oh, absolutely. I think you'd find her quite good value. You might like to have a drink with her while she's over. Get to know her a bit. Take her out to lunch if she's not all booked up.'

'Won't that make Jack feel his back's being gone behind a bit?'

'Would it mean all that much to you if he does?'

'Not really,' said Patrick. Bugger the Bishop of Bath and Wells, he thought.

'You see, dear boy, I can't help wondering whether Deirdre's with the right publisher. When people think of us and of her they think of two very different things. Or they should.'

'She manages to do quite well for us even so.'

'Oh yes, for the moment. Anyway, we'll have a chat about it nearer the time. I'll be fascinated to hear what you make of her.'

Halfway through that, Simon's telephone had made its expensive trickling sound, but he affably finished his closing words to Patrick before picking up the handset.

Jack did not reappear: he was usually gone by midday. Patrick was off by 2.40, having waited around for some minutes for his assistant to get back from her lunch. When asked if there was going to be a number where he could be reached, he had replied evasively that he would be back in his office about five.

'There's a call just coming through for you now,' she told him an instant later.

He missed the name but got the voice. 'Graham,' he said. 'Are you in London?'

'I am not, but I will be.'

They exchanged the necessary banalities. With Graham

115

McClintoch it was almost as necessary to stick to specially banal banalities at this stage, or he was liable to suspect that something was being concealed from him. While saying he was fine and hoped he was fine too, Patrick was feeling the tiniest bit put out that Graham showed no surprise at finding him apparently at his desk at such an hour instead of gorging and swilling at the Savoy Grill like any other publishing executive. Well, being in touch had never been Graham's thing.

'And how's Jenny?' he asked now in a tone that showed no great confidence in her husband.

'Oh, never better.' Patrick took a long time answering this and a few supplementaries, surprisingly long for a man who had been pacing and groaning with frustration while he waited for his assistant and had sworn ardently if briefly when told a call was coming through. He even put in pauses while he thought of more to say about how Jenny was.

Finally Graham mentioned an interview in Surrey the following week and some things he needed to get in London, asked for and was granted a bed for the night, and took his leave. But Patrick sat on for a few minutes yet, going over memories pleasant enough in themselves, disagreeable when forced back to mind at this moment. Of all the people he kept up with, Graham had known Jenny the longest, as long as he had himself, all but a few days.

But then again, by the time he was behind the wheel of the trusty little Mini he had forgotten all about Graham and all about Jenny too. His morale returned to the height it had reached as soon as he awoke that morning. From here he was able to take a balanced view of that minor contretemps with Jack over the matter of Simon's doctrinal orientation. It was right, it was salutary, to be dealt a rebuke for any kind of anti-semitism, even when it was just words and no feeling. Jolly good, actually. But not bloody good. No, it was bloody annoying to be upstaged by a fellow like that on any issue, a fellow whose lightest reference to Lenin or any American Marxist pundit set you desperately searching your mind for any shreds of mitigation. He drank too much, too. Jack must be fetched some smart return thump, and with the Deirdre business on the horizon . . . No, that showed the wrong spirit. He would use Jack with wonderful clemency, spare him with a flick of the

116

hand from the imperial throne, at least if the mood of the moment held.

Up through Camden Town bowled the Mini in the bright sunshine, past Hampstead Pond where children's toy yachts scudded cheerfully, round by Golders Green tube station and to within a couple of hundred yards of the North Circular Road. Here Patrick pulled over to the side and took out his pocket diary. On the second page of its list of principal monetary units of the world there was the purposely garbled address of a house in a neighbouring street. He drove round there and left the car directly outside, on the theory that if anyone spotted it he was done for anyway. The house, which was semi-detached, had a red-tiled rooflike structure over a bow window and more tiles arranged in patterns round the front door. He rang the bell, waited and let himself in with a latchkey.

Inside it was supposed to be better, but it was just as awful in a different way, full of unshaped bits of wood mounted or left lying about on shelves, vases holding prickly twigs that had been plunged into lime-green, gold or scarlet paint and tiered cubes in glass and ebony that might have been puzzles or works of art or neither. Larger constructions passed him by for the time being. He explored the kitchen, where he unloaded two wrapped bottles, and the upstairs. Back down again he unwrapped the bottles and put them on a tray with writing on it in some language unknown to him. The only possible glasses were chunky tumblers whose bases were half as thick again as the useful part. Paper napkins. With their simulated linen texture and scalloped edges they subtracted plenty of tone, but they did hide large parts of the tray.

Thanks to Graham and consequences, Patrick had cut it fine but, now that he was here and ready, not fine enough. He looked at the bottles, left them and went and stood for some seconds in what he supposed was the sitting-room. Then he went and got himself a drink, returned and stood as before. This time he spied a skeletal rack holding long-playing records. These proved to reflect two tastes, or inclinations, one for fashionable trivia, the other, less venial, for what he had heard grown men call modern jazz. At one time, not so far distant, nearly all jazz had been two-beat bullshit, all smearing trombones and out-of-tune clarinets playing the scale. Then very soon afterwards, just over the weekend in retrospect, it had shifted to squeals and thrashes, with an occasional hymn to suicide or a – well, this was not the time. The books were not much better, but at least the fraudulent acorn symbol of Hammond & Sutcliffe was nowhere to be seen. Patrick settled down with a prize-winning novel of yesteryear, giving it the only chance it would ever get from him, his back to the window. He felt nothing either way, good or bad.

He felt something, good and bad, when the doorbell rang tremendously, many times louder than it had sounded from outside, like an alarm at a jeweller's, or so he thought. At an unvarying three miles an hour he went into the nasty little hall and opened the door. No, it was not the gas-man. In she came, into the sitting-room. Rather late in the day he contemplated the amount of talk, and the kind of talk, that might lie between him and his objective. But for the moment there was no trouble of that sort. Would she like a drink? Yes. Would tequila and lime be all right? Yes. To some men the appreciable pauses before these two replies might have carried a hint of menace. But Patrick's eye was firmly on his objective, or what could be seen of it.

'Here we are,' he said cheerily, delivering her glass. 'Hope that's how you like it.'

She took it looking not at it but at him. When she had gone on doing so for a few more seconds she said, 'What shall we drink to?'

Afterwards, not very long afterwards in fact, he saw with crystal clarity that he should have said forthwith, right then, that he thought he heard a noise, gone through to the kitchen and sprinted out of the back door, vaulting over fences till he could double back and find some sort of outlet to the road. It was his last chance. No, if he had ever had a chance at all it had gone long before, probably when he first saw her in the street without ever expecting to see her again, certainly when she came to live next door, double-certainly when she had popped along to ask to use their telephone because Harold was expecting a call from New York, and Jenny had been out with one of her Highbury mates, and, well. Anyway, Patrick stepped forward now and made to take the glass out of Wendy's hand, intending to let his actions speak much louder, but she was up to that and twisted aside. With a sense of the ghosts of millions of men shaking their heads at him and droning in unison, 'You

118

poor son of a bitch,' he told her in vivacious tones that of course she must be the one to settle what they should drink to.

'Then let it be to the moment,' she cried. 'The one and only unrepeatable moment.'

'To the moment,' he said, feeling that with any luck he could safely leave the rest of it.

'They're so few, aren't they? So pitifully few.'

'What are?'

'Oh, the moments in our sad little lives that make us real. Frighteningly few, those golden moments. I expect you think that's a silly word.'

'Which one?' He spoke before he could stop himself.

'Golden,' she said, her eager wide-eyed look dimming slightly.

'No, never. Thank you for not being afraid to use it. That's where men so often fail. When the occasion comes it scares them into silence. Women are braver.'

'Then, Patrick, you do feel it too? You do feel . . . something? It would be so bleak if you felt nothing. That's what scares women, you know.'

'I do know, and you needn't be scared. I feel something all right.'

'Promise me you'll always treat me as a person.'

'I promise.'

'Promises are so easily given.'

'I'll fulfil this one. Let me show you.'

After a shaky start he was comfortably into the swing of it, having recognised he was on familiar ground after all. Experience had brought him to see that this kind of thing was nothing more than the levying of cock-tax, was reasonable and normal, in fact, even though some other parts of experience strongly suggested that what he had shelled out so far was only a down payment. There was also a touch of your cosmetic element at work, representing this afternoon's doings as something more than a short-notice bash with the next-door neighbour. He had come across that kind of thing before too, and had likened it in the past to the proclamations of a dictator, full of talk about ethnic integrity and his historic mission, when all he wanted was to seize the industry and mineral wealth of some helpless, peaceable neighbouring state. It would not go on for ever. Meanwhile the most he could do was put up a decent show of taking it seriously, though not so seriously as to encourage her

119

into more of the same, and stay tuned for the next instalment. Ask not who it was supposed to fool. As well ask why some women ever opened their mouths.

This one's was shut at last. What lay under the clothes Mrs Porter-King turned out to have been wearing emerged as thoroughly satisfactory, and her behaviour when that stage was reached was even more so, outstanding in fact. Neither discovery could have been predicted, especially not the behavioural factor. It was impossible, Patrick reasoned, that he was the only man to have run into more amenable, much down-to-earthier characters who were hopeless when it came to the crunch, almost making you wonder what you were doing wrong. None of that today, bless her heart.

Although beyond reproach hygienically and so on, the bedroom was nevertheless of appalling aesthetic and moral squalor. At the same time it had to be remembered that that curious little thing with the fringe, wife of the radio-critic mate he had borrowed the house off, had presumably done her best with it. And whatever dreadful material the curtains were made of, they were drawn back far enough to let in the sun, which shone agreeably on to the bed. Wendy Porter-King had evidently noticed this too. With her arms clasped round her drawn-up knees, she said,

'The sky is blue and I feel gay.'

She never knew how close she came to losing her front teeth for that. Taken off guard again, Patrick again spoke too quickly. 'Are you an American?'

'What a strange question, darling.'

'I know, I'm sorry. Anyway, are you?'

He had headed her off from the sector of crap she had been making for, but at least he was asking her about her. 'Boringly English. Well, a touch of Irish on my mother's side.'

'I thought there must be something. I'm all Irish on my mother's side.' No reaction whatever to that, and serve him right. 'You'll have to forgive me, but I know so little about you . . . in some ways,' ha ha ha. 'For instance, have you been married a long time?'

She wriggled about a bit then, to get him to look at her more closely. 'A long time?' He could see her reluctantly deciding not to ask him what he meant by a long time. 'Not long by the calendar, but long enough.'

120

'I see.'

'I dare say in his way Harold loves me. It just doesn't happen to be a way that leaves me much room to breathe.'

'Oh.'

'I sometimes wonder whether I exist for him at all as a person. He never looks at me. It was different years ago, when we were first married. But now, as far as he's concerned, I have no identity any more.'

Patrick nodded understandingly.

'Do you know he never kisses me? Can you credit that?'

'It's not easy to, darling, here and now. But it does explain why, now and then perhaps, you feel you need a little air.'

'How beautifully you put it. A little air. He stifles me. He never leaves me alone for a moment.'

'He what?'

'He's at me all the hours God sends. Every night as a matter of course. Half Sunday morning, regular as clockwork. Saturday afternoon unless he's at the football. When he gets home from the office in the week as often as not, especially if he's been in a lot of traffic. There's never a minute. Do you know at a party the other evening . . . I think he's trying to set up some sort of record.'

'You said he never kisses you.'

'He hasn't got time.' She was glaring at him, transformed with a comprehensiveness no mere outside pressure could have wrought. 'And why should he bother, from his point of view? He wants it. I'm his wife. I'm there. What else is there, for Christ's sake?'

After that she had to cry in order to regroup, but not only for that, Patrick saw. Rather late in the day, comforting her gave him a chance to hide his chagrin. He had never before set out to cheer up the neglected wife of a satyromaniac, as far as he knew.

By and by she lay back vulnerably on the pillows while he hung protectively above her. If Harold really never looked at her he was without doubt missing something. Patrick would not make that mistake. He recognised that her face might not be commended in all quarters, with the faint buck-toothed effect that gave her in repose a look of self-satisfaction or pomposity as well as a kind of greed, as he had noticed even in the couple of seconds of first seeing her. But from the chin downwards, as

121

far down as he could see without craning his neck, she was beyond reproach. He set about putting this view to her.

If he had imagined that, inadvertently and through no merit of his own, he had nevertheless made some sort of breakthrough, penetrated to her inner self, he was very much mistaken. After an interval during which he would have said he had behaved as attentively to her needs as any man could have done, within reason at least, she broke away and gave him a look of bitter reproach.

'What is it?' she asked him.

'I'm sorry, I don't quite . . .'

'I don't understand. You drove at me so remorselessly, so . . . implacably. You seemed tormented by some kind of hatred, for me, for yourself, whatever, I don't know, I'm just baffled. What is it with you, darling? Won't you tell me, for the love of God?'

If he had not felt slightly indignant at the thought of all that good work going for nothing, he might not have said, as he did, 'I know I've asked you this already, old thing, but are you absolutely *sure* you're not an American?'

'What's that supposed to mean?'

He moved his head to and fro for a time in a tortured way. 'Oh, what could I have meant, why does one say these things, something or somebody I remembered, who knows what lingers in the memory?'

He had fallen shamefully into her idiom, this time without premeditation, and of course it did the trick, it cooled her off. 'We're both overwrought and no wonder . . . so much has happened so fast . . . emotions in a whirl . . . human beings aren't attuned to so many of the things of which they're capable . . .'

'We owe it to ourselves to give each other time . . .'

Everything went smoothly after that, until the moment when without preamble she looked him in the eyes and said, 'I love you.'

Patrick heard that with definite satisfaction and approval. It had been said to him before in very much the same circumstances, and on each occasion it had led to something special on the lady's part. Like the cosmetic stuff earlier, it meant that what was to follow came from outside her routine. Only a select few, perhaps just this select one, rated it. Without hesitation he said a great deal back, though not that he loved her, a scruple

122

he wondered at for a moment, considering what he had said already, let alone done. But that soon slid out of mind. Now he remembered, the others had had mouths rather like hers, too. Later, he thought perhaps Mrs Porter-King's difficulties with her husband ran deeper than she had said.

But that was after they had parted. For the moment he found distaste for her falling off when she helped to change the sheets and tidied up unasked in the bedroom and downstairs. He looked at her almost with tolerance when, newly self-contained as they all were once back in their clothes and ready for the outside world, she told him she would be off to the tube station just round the corner.

At the front door she stopped and faced him ominously, but all she said was, 'I'm taking more of a chance than you are, you know.'

'I do know.' He worked at that one.

'Don't worry, I'm not going to go and spoil it.'

She reached up and kissed him on the cheek with something he might perhaps have taken for affection or thanks if he had not been such a downy old bird, and was gone.

When he came to leave in his turn he felt as if he had spent in that frightful little shack many times more hours than a standard afternoon contained, and as he drove away the place seemed at the ends of the earth from where he had come from, but by the time he was back in his office it was like coming back from holiday: he might just have nipped round the corner for a packet of cigarettes. Doing so in reality, by the way, would have had a bit of point an hour or two earlier. He had often said, though not aloud, that the post-coital drag was the one you missed most.

Patrick let himself into 1B giving every sign of ill-concealed rage. Barely acknowledging Jenny and sending a token kick in Frankie's direction he strode to the whisky-bottle and poured himself a stiff shot, swearing viciously when a splash fell outside the glass, or nearly did. He squinted at Jenny again, this time as if it could have been her he was cross with.

'Oh, it's nothing really. Bloody Simon again. Honestly I don't know how much longer I can stand it there. Urhh.' He gulped whisky, jerking his head at the same time. 'I told you a bit about Collier Sampson, didn't I?'

'I don't think so.'

'Oh. Well, old Sampson is really the last of the great Homeric scholars,' and after much persuasion Patrick had finally got him to agree to do a book on the daily life of that period for The Centuries' Heritage, and last week a synopsis had arrived, and today Simon had turned it down. Quite casually, as if it had been a book on bloody gardening. Too old-fashioned. Not the image. Dated outlook. As if he knew. Awhh!

Patrick decided it was really quite good, especially considering he had thrown it together since putting his key in the door. Up to that moment he had thought he could get away with just seeming ordinary, back after a day's work, but then he had been attacked not only by remorse and dismay at his own folly but also by remembering telling Jenny he had no designs on Mrs P-K. That he had meant it at the time only made it worse. After that he had had to be something else but ordinary to stand any chance of appearing normal. He had been drunk too often before.

Jenny listened carefully to what he had said, or to the first part of it. Then she seemed to lose interest, nodding mechanically and fiddling with her watch-strap.

'I know it's a bit boring, love, but it's sort of what I do these days.'

'Oh, of course it must be very annoying. But you won't do anything like all of a sudden, will you?'

'No, no,' he said, remembering to sound impatient again at renewed thoughts of the affront to the distinction and eminence of Collier who? Collier Sampson, and see it gets written down for next time. More to keep the show going than in any hope of entertaining himself he started to look through his gramophone records, but the figures to be seen on their sleeves, whether got up as truck-drivers or old-style college professors, seemed to augur nothing but ennui and dejection.

The flat was completely silent. Where was Jenny? She had disappeared even more quietly than usual. Now he came to think of it she had been looking a little tired or something, a little peaky. He went up and found her in front of the bathroom window. There was not much to be seen from there. She turned her head and smiled at him.

'Are you all right, love?'

'Yes, fine.'

'I thought you seemed a bit . . .'

Heavy-eyed would have been one way of putting it. She blinked and said, 'I have had a rather depressing letter from my mother. By the second post. She hasn't been well. She's got to go into hospital for observation.'

'Oh. Have they any idea what it is?'

'Just observation, she said. And tests.'

He went to give her a commiserating hug, but before he could start she had moved aside to the bath-tub. All he could do was hang about while she fitted in the plug, set the tap gushing and took the yellow tin of scourer off the window-shelf, very intent on her work.

He watched her incuriously. 'You know, ten to one it's nothing at all. These days they haul you in if you sneeze. Means bugger-all in itself.'

'She didn't say what was the matter.'

Well, at least he would not have to go on being fed up with Simon now.

Ten

Later that week Patrick was again looking for an address, this time on foot and in a district he knew after a fashion, in the very next street to the place that sold him *Titter*, *Twosome* and their contemporaries. A few minutes before, he had looked into an obviously more advanced place where magazines were displayed singly on shelves like items in an exhibition of ceramics. Each was so securely wrapped in transparent plastic that no ordinary mortal, even left to himself, could have got inside without technology. Noticing his dissatisfaction, a heavily moustached man in what looked like Observer Corps uniform had asked him, 'Was it bondage, sir?' Patrick had left without verbal reply, and not cared to go inside the next establishment along, but as he started to look in its window a strangely similar man had come out of it and asked him, 'Care for a film, sir?' Maybe, and maybe not, but not at the price of telling you so, my good fellow.

On his way again, Patrick spotted a number of females in ones and twos sauntering, loitering, standing about on the pavement. Not many, really. Were they prostitutes? All of them? The newspapers carried little else nowadays but news stories, feature articles, leaders, even letters encouraging every such belief. At this moment he was walking, he knew, through the most notorious quarter of the population centre that foreigners were said, in their quaint parlance, to call the shocking city. All of them? Nothing remotely shocking ever came his way. No nubile girls, many of good family, ever offered themselves to him for the price of a 'reefer' (a cigarette made from hashish or cannabis, also known as a 'joint'). He was never there when an apparently respectable dinner-party degenerated into an orgy

126

of promiscuous lust. He never even caught any filth on TV. Was it bondage? Fancy a film? Maybe, right, but in all such cases it was hard work to believe that anybody would still feel like it by the time he got to it.

Patrick looked quite closely and long at three girls grouped, presumably for effect, round a smart silvery dustbin overflowing with avocado rinds and other restaurant debris. The three, who effortlessly failed to see him, were widely varied in size and to some extent in colour but united in their difference from girls he was used to coming across, indeed in a kind of family resemblance among themselves, like drawings by the same artist, even cartoonist. Yes, but were they prostitutes? Apart from the context, what persuaded him to say they were, or might have done so, was exactly what would have made any auntie of his say the same thing, their short skirts, their eye make-up, no more than that. Very well, but *were* they? (A good job Tim was not with him.) If he had been any writer on the Hammond & Sutcliffe list, now, he would have been able to tell for sure at fifty paces. 'Three prostitutes giggled round a rubbish-bin,' such a one might have written. That was the way to do it.

Not that it mattered, just a fellow liked to know. He was not at all the sort of man who used prostitutes, though it was true that he had once or twice found himself, after the event, in the unmistakable position of a little-present donor. Anyway, there would be no such problems where he was going.

But perhaps there would be problems of another kind. At the address he had been given there was an open doorway, a flight of stairs ascending out of sight and a shallow cubby-hole apparently excavated from the wall. In it sat a big ugly girl in an old ball-gown who was doing absolutely nothing but sit there, no transistor, no newspaper, not even mucking about with her nails. Nor was she paying any attention to the well-dressed youngster, short-haired for that era and clean shaven, tall and square-shouldered, who stood just inside the threshold.

'Now this is what I call a really beautiful evening,' he said to Patrick in a better accent than his. So far he was from the same mould as some of the prefects at the Hertfordshire school.

'I don't know what we've done to earn it.'

'We shall probably find ourselves paying for it in the end, I'm afraid.'

'You may well be right.' Oh, pox vobiscum. 'Erm . . .'

'Yes?'

'I wonder if you can help me: I'm looking for – '

'Excuse me, but are you a member here?'

'No, actually I'm a guest of – '

'I'm sorry, but there are no guests here, we find it leads to misunderstandings. You can't come in, if that's what you want to do, unless you're a member. Now we can offer you a life membership at ten pounds or a visiting membership at one pound. A visiting membership entitles you to one visit.'

'A pound for coming in this once? Very reasonable.'

'We think so. Cash only. We seem to run into endless trouble with cheques.'

That was communicated in a way that put Patrick off being funny about anything. He said quite humbly, 'I don't need a sponsor, do I?'

'Oh no. No, we waive that in the furtherance of cutting out the red tape wherever we can. For the same reason you don't get a receipt. It saves us paperwork, you see. Have you nothing smaller?' asked the young shit, taking Patrick's five-pound note just the same. 'Oh dear. And I can't change your note. That lands us in a difficulty.' There was a long pause for thought, or at any rate a long pause. At the end of it the fiver changed hands in the reverse direction. 'You seem like an educated, responsible kind of man. I'm going to put you on your honour to give the barman upstairs a pound when you have change. Tell him Mr Colin said it would be all right. If you'd just sign the book.'

This the girl had produced unseen and unheard. Patrick wrote in it.

'That's fine. Now remember, you're entitled to use all the facilities of the club while you're here. Enjoy your visit, Mr Giles.'

The stairs were edged with metal strips but were otherwise covered by battleship-grey linoleum. At the top of the first flight Patrick found a door painted roughly the same colour, with dents and scuffs at shoe height and a chipped panel of bathroom glass reinforced with wire. It said it was for members only, but nothing else. He felt quite intrepid, and much further than a few yards from Corsica Street W1.

The room beyond suggested a seaside landlady's sitting-room of the pre-war period. Under-exposed photographs of forgotten or never-known people, elaborately inscribed, covered the walls. There were more in stand-up frames on the baby grand piano, once no doubt a chic off-white, now nearer the colours of a nicotine-stained finger. Of the dozen or so people, mostly men, sitting here and there, mostly in ones rather than twos, all looked older than Patrick. The counter was topped with some early plastic material and had behind it a nearly bald middle-aged man in a crumpled navy-blue suit peering up and down, an untrained helper of some sort, perhaps, or a customer in search of ice. He seemed unaware of Patrick's presence.

'Excuse me, how do I get a drink around here?'

'How do you think? You ask me.' The alleged barman turned away and spoke to a fat old wreck with brushed-back brillian-tined hair, tie like one of Jack Sutcliffe's and heavily braided mess-jacket who was propped between the counter and the wall. 'Needs to be told how he gets a drink round here.'

The other man got out some syllables in an unknown tongue. Their tone was remorseful or self-pitying.

'All right, what do you want?'

Patrick's Scotch cost him less than twice the pub rate. The barman sighed heavily when he saw the fiver but gave change, pressing the coins down hard in Patrick's palm. 'What's this?' he asked at the offer of one of the pound notes back.

'Mr Colin put me on my honour to give it you when I had change. He told me to tell you he said it would be all right. Exactly that and no more.'

The barman gave a trumpeting laugh. 'On your honour, no less. Been put on his honour,' he said to the fellow in the fancy jacket. '*Colin* put him on his honour.'

This time the response seemed to acknowledge a heavy share of blame.

With a return to his fussy, resentful manner, the barman took out a ten-shilling note from his clothing, slapped it into Patrick's hand and pocketed the pound. 'This comes to us by the inadver-tent courtesy of Mr Colin Zurrico. I'm very fond of these old West of England names, aren't you?'

'Where does he actually come from?'

'West Ham. If you mean his ancestors, the answer is South Africa. Did you form any opinion of him during your conversation?'

'Oh yes. I thought he was about the . . .'

'Go on, let it come out. It'll do you good.'

' . . . bounciest most offensive young bastard I've ever met.'

'That's the idea. This place is supposed to be for people to let their hair down in. Any more? Take your time.'

'And a patronising la-di-da cunt who's asking for a bloody good ram up the duff.' Saying this made Patrick feel better but, Christ, was this the right club?

When he was sure there was nothing further, the barman said, 'Well, that's one more for the consensus. Yes, at college in Oxford he is now. Well, home for the hols at the moment, don't you know. He's studying the law up there. Now if you ask me that's very far-sighted on his part, studying something that's going to be of great use to him in later life. You were lucky to catch him, sir. It's not often we see the young master up this way. He'll be off down the track soon. Yes, my love.'

A small fair-haired woman had approached. From far enough away she would perhaps have resembled a Hollywood actress of the period between the wars, and was about the age to have been one in fact. With horrifying speed and agility she climbed on to a tall, chiefly metallic stool by the bar. First smiling sweetly at Patrick, she ordered a gin and ginger ale.

'You're a new boy,' she told him.

'I was just saying to the major, Florrie, Colin put this one on his honour to pay his way in.'

'Well, he could tell straight away you was a good boy, couldn't he?' asked Florrie, taking out a tipped cigarette and examining it intently.

'That must have been it,' said Patrick. Truth is stranger than fiction, he said to himself. By now he was hoping this was the wrong club.

At that moment Eric came in.

'I'm sorry, there's nothing for you here,' said the barman. 'You can push a man just so far.'

Florrie cried out and lifted her stumpy arms, the cigarette fallen to the floor unregarded. Making noises in a lower key, Eric embraced her. The barman almost smiled, the major screwed up his eyes and pushed his head forward. Eric got away from Florrie in the end and looked round with an expression of studied gloom before taking out his wallet.

'I suppose we might as well. What else is left? Let 'em have what they want, Perce. It's little enough to do for 'em, God knows.'

Moving appreciably faster than earlier, the barman began to serve the drinks. 'And how's the ever-accommodating Stevie?' he asked.

Patrick tried not to look too quickly at Eric, who said, 'Nobody knows, Perce. Everything's guesswork. As soon as you start reckoning you've got some idea of where you stand, you find the rules have been changed. I was thinking, it must be rather the same living in one of these tinpot South American republics. Never mind the statute-book or the official proclamations, it's how the Top Person's feeling at any given moment decides whether you're in for a medal or running for your life. And the police have taken your passport so you *can't leave.*'

Not a lot more than the general theme and tone got across to the group as a whole, Patrick suspected, but Perce laughed, and Florrie laughed, and even the major voiced a loud groan or two of heartfelt recognition. Others barely in earshot also laughed, not so much out of amusement as good will and habit.

'Yes, I've carved out a nice little niche for myself in here, Patrick,' said Eric as they moved off to seats in a corner. 'It's like another life. I've been coming in here for nearly two years now, just an hour once or twice a week after work, and I've got to look forward to it. There's nothing to beat a place where you can really relax and not be yourself.'

'How did you manage to get into it?'

'Oh, now that was a bleeding miracle, that was. A straight mate from work brought me in for a quick one, but what he didn't know, I'd had a rough night at home, ructions till three am, and I'd tanked up lunch-time, see, and I start sounding off in here, and my mate's absolutely terrified. But – it's dead funny looking back – you know how I do, I always refer to her as her, well, there we are, that was it, I just went on about her as usual and of course they all thought I was talking about my wife. Which I was, wasn't I, but not quite in the sense they assumed. Anyway, I was the hit of the evening.' Eric smiled affectionately at the memory. 'And I've never looked back.'

'I suppose these things are basically very much the same.'

'What, you mean for your sort and my sort?'

'Yes, in the way we – '

'Oh no they're not, Patrick,' said Eric, shaking his head in

131

slow motion. 'Oh no they're not.' This time he varied the stresses. 'Superficially I grant. Basically – no, no. Never mind how I know but I do. But that's another story. They're a nice crowd here. Florrie, well. Perce, he's all right.' Eric paused and went on less positively, 'Yes, he's all right. And the major – of course he's not really an actual major.'

'I thought he might not be.'

'No, he's a commander RN, or was, but nobody bar me knows what that means. Look, Patrick, I'm going to buzz out for a crafty pee. I was in too much of a hurry getting away before.'

In the middle of the room he was clawed at and checked by a female in mauve with a governessy centre parting in her hair. She was sitting next to a tall man in a heather-mixture suit who looked rather silly because about a third of his height was between his shoulders and the top of his head. Otherwise he seemed fine, and he and the woman exchanged some words and a couple of chortles with Eric before letting him proceed. Patrick was peacefully considering how it took all sorts to make a world when he saw with disgust that the same centre-parted female, grinning and looking behind her every couple of seconds at the tall twit, was diffidently approaching him.

'Excuse me,' she said from a distance, and then when she was nearer, 'Excuse me, do you mind if I ask you a question?'

'Oh not a bit,' he said as inhospitably as he knew how.

'I expect you're a great friend of Eric's, aren't you? Do tell me, is Stevie as,' another backward glance, 'as awful as he says? You know.'

At that Patrick found himself calculating almost as fast and furiously as in a sexual emergency of his own. Frowning in his earnestness, he said, 'In a way of course she *is*, no getting away from it. But then he does rather pile it on, there's that side of it too. It's not what you'd call a fair picture. Because . . .' He leant forward a little and crinkled his eyes. 'Well, because in his funny old way, there's no doubt he thinks she's the most special, amazing . . .'

'You mean he's devoted to her, don't you?'

Not quite trusting himself to speak, Patrick nodded and moved his lips about.

'Of course he is,' she said stoutly, with a scornful backward glance. 'Well . . . thank you for telling me that, I do appreciate it.' And she stretched out her hand to him.

Caught without his meat-cleaver he gripped her hand for a moment, then switched to a look of conditional consternation. 'Now don't you *dare* let on I've dropped the slightest whisper of any of that – it'd be more than my life's worth. Eric'd kick me all over the place.'

'Oh, not a word, don't you fret,' she said, falling back into the local lingo, 'say no more, safe with me, cross my heart. Now I mustn't take up any more of your time.'

She retreated, or rather advanced on the lanky shag, who flinched perceptibly at her coming to tell him she had told him so. Patrick went back to reflecting how there was nowt as queer as folk until Eric reappeared and, pausing to greet another fan, a horsy-looking fellow a bit on the flash side for a place like this, returned whence he had set out. He asked Patrick if he was all right with a solicitude that vanished as soon as he realised it was only old Patrick he was having to deal with.

'Yes, it'll be two years in August I started coming in here,' he said. 'Mind you, I reckon I'm living on borrowed time these days.'

'How is it he hasn't, I mean she hasn't found out about it already?'

'That's the other half of the miracle, Patrick. In the shape of the British worker, modern-day style. Every Friday, see, like now, the switchboard at work shuts down early so the ops can get out to their country estates for the weekend. Five o'clock prompt, which means they've all gone by twenty or quarter to. And there's usually one or other evening in the week they just happen to have buggered off out of it by about then. Well. Even that cow's not too thick to realise you can't get a bloke on the blower when there's no one there to put you through.'

'But if she finds that happening regularly, isn't she going to come to track you down in your office? You know, find she simply has to see you, just can't wait another moment?'

'Now *there* of course we have an excellent example of a similar situation for your sort and my sort. She couldn't stand it. How do we know? Well, she didn't stand it, did she? Right?'

'Right.'

'While I think of it I'm sorry if I sounded niggly just now about, what was it, things being basically the same for us both.

133

I can see you were just being sort of ecumenical and chummy about it. Anyway, ten out of ten for psychology *so far*. But: in this case there's more to it. When she does ring me at work she likes doing it at a busy time like mid-morning when there's plenty of people about. More to embarrass me then.'

'Has she ever actually come walking in on you there?'

Eric turned his face away and held up his hands palms outwards. 'Perish the thought, and I'm serious. Answer, no, not so far, but God knows why not, and there's a first time, et cetera. But when we come to threats it runs at about number two, as you can probably guess.'

'What's number one? No, sorry, Eric, I can probably guess that as well. Still, she doesn't go in for following you, I hope?'

'Will you kindly shut up, Patrick?' said Eric in a much higher voice than usual. 'I was going to apologise for being late. I was – '

'Oh, don't worry about that, forget it.'

'No, please, I'm not going to, I want to explain, I hate turning up late. No, there's a sort of glassed-in passage affair leading off from my front door at work, rather nice really, they're all old Regency houses along there, the point being you can see out from it on to the triangular part with the Barraclough statue, and I was just . . . Sorry, Patrick.' There was a short pause while Eric swallowed and drew a deep breath or two. 'I simply spotted a taxi parked the far side and I thought I saw the bag in it. I sat on in the hall I don't know how long and it didn't move, so in the end I made myself stroll across, and do you know it wasn't at all like her, not in the *least*. Fat little bloke with a tash holding his brief-case on his lap and half asleep. So that's why I was late. Silly, isn't it?'

'Quite understandable, I should have thought.'

'Oh, would you really? You poor bugger. No, it's just how you get. Guilty conscience, except you haven't done anything. You said there was something in particular you wanted to see me about.'

'Yes, but I didn't know it would entail an operation on this scale.'

'No, well there's no way you could know, is there? But don't worry, it's par for the course, any time there's something you don't want the bloody old trout to get her nose into. No, hold it, Patrick, I'll get these. This is me having a friend along for a drink.'

Patrick watched him at the bar, aiming a very thoroughly simulated mock punch at the major, whispering histrionically in Florrie's ear, halting in mid-stride on his return to mouth feigned abuse over his shoulder. You lived and learned, there was no question. At least where other people were concerned you did. When it came to yourself there was a strong case for saying you just lived.

'It's this Tim character,' said Patrick when the drinks were in position.

'Oh.' Eric got a lot into or out of the syllable. 'What about him?'

'I realise he didn't make too good an impression that time . . .'

'The impression he made that time was trouble, Patrick. Not the worst trouble, i.e. Stevie-type trouble, but still trouble. And though he may not *be* Stevie-type trouble, he bleeding well *triggers* it, or he did on that occasion.'

'Unwittingly. Innocently.'

'Unwittingly, innocently or on a mystery tour in the chara, he's still that very sweet man she was getting on so well with till I put a stop to it. Yeah, it's blown over now, not that anything ever does quite with her. Apart from that, what seems to be the problem?'

'If I say anything you find offensive, Eric, please remember I didn't mean – '

'My dear Patrick, you can say *anything you bleeding well like* with her out of hearing.'

'Fine. Here goes, then. Do you reckon Tim is queer?'

'Queer.' Eric seemed to savour the word for a moment, perhaps morphologically, in its relation to Germanic cognates or its inferred Primitive-Indo-European root. With similar detachment he went on, 'I could be much more colourful about it, but plain no. No, I don't reckon he is. And in so far as you can be certain about it, and at my time of life I'm pretty bleeding certain, I'm certain he's not, childhood, one per cent, not anywhere. I'll go further – he's unusually un-. Any normal straight would have cottoned on to the 1A set-up in two minutes, wouldn't he?'

'Yes, I thought that myself.'

'Course you did, Patrick.' Some of the affability left Eric's manner. 'Well, is that all you want me for? Or am I breaking him in for a bet?'

'Sorry – I just want you to tell him, I want *you* to tell him he's not queer. He thinks he is, you see. It sounds ridiculous now I've said it, I do realise.'

'Yes, it does, doesn't it? Anyway, granted he's not, why on earth should he think he is? He must *know*, surely to God.'

Patrick explained some of this and other matters.

'I see, someone's told him he is. Well, this Perlmutter wants locking up for a start, but I dare say you'd got that far on your own. Er, it's none of my business, Patrick, but what do you care what this bloke says he thinks he is?'

'You've got to understand he's a bloody fool. It's not only queer he's unusually un-, it's a lot of more important things too. Sorry, Eric. I mean like worldly, realistic, able to take care of himself in general. And if something isn't done soon . . . Put it this way: I told you he goes in for this prison visiting. Well, he turned up the other day with a black eye after a spell of that. As a result of visiting a chap who was doing five years for an act of gross indecency with a minor. Any comment?'

'What? Yes, I'd say very reasonable. When the beak's been at the port the night before you can go down for eight for AGIM – I wouldn't really know, it's not my end of the field. No, sorry, Patrick, I'm being flippant. Irresponsible in the well-known propensity of my ilk.'

'I have offended you. Shit. Let's talk about something else.'

'No, it's all right, it's just I'm not used to discussing these matters in this particular way. Any light thrown on the build-up to the black eye?'

'Not a lot, I'm sorry to say. That's another of his troubles. When he must know he could tell you anything and everything you can't get out of him what he had for breakfast.'

'Ah, now that does strike a chord, I must say.'

'But it doesn't matter what happened that time. He's playing with fire and not realising it. Isn't he? I mean, well, when it comes to the world we're talking about, there's nowhere you can get your block knocked off quicker if you don't know your way around. Agreed?'

'Oh, most certainly, Patrick.' Eric spoke as warmly and reliably as when he had earlier denied the overall likeness of sexual afflictions. 'Oh, you want a block knocked off or even if you don't want it knocked off, we knock it off. No problem. Any time you're passing. No, you're absolutely right as far as that goes.'

Patrick grunted. He had had nearly enough of this, but forced himself to go on, 'You haven't seen the sort of draft performance of how he proposes to swing his hips and the rest of it when he decides to come out in his true colours.'

Eric shuddered theatrically. 'I'm trying not to picture it,' he said. 'But tell me why I care whether this bloke gets his block knocked off by whoever you please or not.' He looked at his watch. 'I'm all right for the moment but I am expected home soon.'

'Tim Valentine is about to become a neighbour of ours. Yours and mine that is. Do you want an unreconstructed bloody fool – who knows about you and Stevie – on the rampage a couple of yards from your front door? Yours and Stevie's?'

'Urhh, you got a point there, Patrick, there's no question about that. So I take this nit aside and tell him he's not one of nature's ladies after all, *and* just how lucky he is not to be. I must be the best-qualified bloke in the eastern hemisphere on that. Not but it'd be a bizarre bleeding enterprise, though there again you'd think I'd be used to that by now. It wouldn't be an easy one for me either. It'd mean a big, big mental turn-around. My guns are all pointing the wrong way, see. You know, like Singapore. This Tim, can he keep his mouth shut?'

'If I explain to him it's important, yes.'

'Funny sort of life he must lead, having to have everything explained to him. It wouldn't do for me, I don't mind telling you. But we're going to need all the security we can get on this one. Don't say anything to him yet. M'm, I'm thinking it might be best to let the slag know something about it from the off, if I can work out what and how. You still haven't actually let on why you're going to all this trouble for a bloody fool.'

'Well, partly because he is a bloody fool. If he did get his block knocked off I'd feel responsible. I know it's a laugh.'

'Come on, Patrick, you must know dozens of bloody fools whose blocks you're dying to see knocked off. You like him, don't you? It can happen, you know. I can remember it myself. Don't ever ring me up at home again.'

'I'd just seen him go out. Her go out.'

'Next time she'll see you seeing her go out. At work only.'

Eric passed Patrick a visiting-card with an inscription that made him appear quite grand in a modest way. 'Not here. Nobody gets in touch with me here. You don't know you're born, sunshine, being able to be just rung up anywhere any time. Extraordinary.'

'But not by anybody.'

'Sorry, Patrick, I wasn't thinking.' Eric sounded a little prim. 'Throw that back. It's a relief there are some things that come easy.'

All the way home Patrick was looking forward to telling Jenny everything that had taken place at the Arcadia Club, as he had delightedly found it was called, but as usual he opened by kissing her and asking if there were any bits.

'Just the one,' she said. 'Tim looked in about twenty minutes ago. He said he felt like a pint of beer, so perhaps you'd like to join him in the pub. Oh, the Princess Beatrice.'

'What? Oh, bugger it, I'd better get over there straight away. Before Cyril sets about him with his marlinspike. Tell you later.'

One of the survivors of the old London that was fast passing away, though not fast enough to suit all tastes, accosted Patrick in the street in the shape of a decaying female wearing a bonnet and a flowered toga that brushed the pavement. Round her neck there hung a cloth bag brimming with copies of some almanac or racing calendar printed comically small on dingy paper. She held out a handful of them in his path, but he shook his head and pointed to his mouth and ear and back several times as he swept by. While still elated by this he found himself breaking into a half-trot when he came in sight of the pub. Anyone would think, he said to himself rather sourly, that he was hurrying to establish an alibi or head off a meddling husband.

Half the interior of the Princess Beatrice was hidden by a billowing dust-sheet hung from the ceiling. Whacking and drilling noises came from behind it. Cyril was bowed over a table near the door, his fingers ready crooked to pick up two clusters of dirty glasses. He gave Patrick his usual belligerent stare by way of greeting.

'Bonsoir, mon cher monsieur,' he said, and grabbed convulsively at the glasses.

'Bit late in the day for this bloody row, isn't it?'

'It's time and a quarter, my poor friend. Who'll be satisfied with four doubloons when he can get five? Nothing I can do. It hasn't kept the thirsty proles away as you can well see.'

Too many people filled the reduced space for Tim to be in sight at once, if indeed he had not already been taken out the back and beaten to death. Patrick followed Cyril to the bar. While ordering a whisky, only his fifth that evening, he looked round again. Still no Tim, though boozers standing or sitting by the windows were mostly cut off from plain view. As if to relieve this difficulty an agonised yell resounded now from that direction, of a kind all too familiar to Patrick's ears and, as expected, the first of several. By the third or so of the series, more clearly to be heard in the comparative hush, a note of grisly triumph could be detected. A couple of seconds later a shift of bodies revealed Tim at last, frozen in that instant prior to the next outburst.

'Quel dommage,' said Cyril. 'What have we here?'

Before Patrick, his whisky deferred, had managed to push as far as halfway across the room, Tim had finished his sneezing fit and was well into a horrific routine with a lime-green silk handkerchief that demonstrated exhaustively how he thought queers behaved when they were past minding whether you knew they were queer or not. In an instant of time there flitted through Patrick's memory a procession of jessies and nancies as mimicked by contemporaries in school playground, college hall and saloon bar, all of them, it seemed to him, with more subtlety and restraint if anything. When, late on, Tim caught sight of him he whinnied, 'Why, hallo there,' gruesomely working it into his act.

Cyril, a little delayed by the business of emerging from behind his counter, was still some yards off. Trying unskilfully to mask Tim from him, and feeling like the US Cavalry, Patrick said, 'Why you silly old sod fancy seeing you here what the hell do you think you're going on about a fine bloody performance that'll do for now joke over,' and more of similar consequence.

'Hallo hallo hallo, I very much hope we're not going to quarrel, anyone fancy a breath of fresh air, let's have a proper look at you, s'il vous plaît très bien.' When he had had his proper look Cyril said, 'Oh dear. Oh dear oh dear oh dear,' rather vaguely, Patrick thought.

Tim had politely got to his feet. 'I'm sorry, do you want to speak to me?'

139

'Well, I had thought of doing so, yes,' said Cyril, who was now revealed as half a size smaller.

Tim frowned with what Patrick knew was pure puzzlement. 'Because if I'm behaving in a way that doesn't meet with your approval, I wish you'd tell me, and then we'll understand each other, won't we?'

In that toff's accent, and with real diffidence coming out as pretended detachment, it undoubtedly did sound quite nasty. As he spoke Tim put his handkerchief away and out of sheer physical awkwardness half folded his arms.

'I can assure you, mon bon ami, that I don't want to spoil anybody's enjoyment – if you're happy I'm happy and if I'm happy everybody's happy,' said Cyril amiably. His eye fell on a couple of used glasses and a gorged ashtray on a table near him, and as if they had been his real objectives all along he scooped them up and retreated.

'What was all that about?' asked Tim, while those standing nearby gave up hope of trouble and turned away with mutters of disappointment.

'If you really don't know,' said Patrick eagerly, 'you're in even more appalling trouble than I thought. And what was *that* about, what you were up to? What came over you?'

'Oh, I can explain that. I sneezed because of all the dust from the hammering.'

'Oh, balls to you. The pansy-boy act – what was that in aid of?'

'I just thought I'd better start trying to get used to it.'

'Oh, for . . . If you were related to me I'd half kill you, do you hear? Now you sit down there and don't you dare even look at anybody till I get back. Try it and I'll never speak to you again.'

'I really have annoyed you,' said Tim when Patrick had brought them drinks from the bar. 'I didn't mean to.'

'Annoying me makes no odds, you raving lunatic. That landlord has a thing about queers, and you escaped by a miracle this time and next time it could be real bad stuff. The boot in. Broken bottles. You don't realise, do you? Oh God.'

'Patrick, I am most terribly – '

'And *stop apologising*. Idiots like you are always apologising to the wrong person for the wrong thing. What had you said to the guy who thumped you in the nick?'

'I told you, just would he like to talk about it.'
'Your trouble is you're irresponsible to a fault.'

Eleven

'No, you go,' said Patrick. 'You know you're dying to see the inside of their place.'

'Not dying exactly. Just naturally curious after all this time.'

'All what time? You're not in the outgoing North now, you know. Down here they let you cool your heels for a couple of weeks before they give you a chance to run your neighbourly eye over their curtains and wallpaper and china and think shit to them.'

'I expect I'll get used to it.' Jenny had unpinned the invitation card from the new cork notice-board on the kitchen wall and brought it to the breakfast table. 'I realise already it's normal to say At Home like that, but why does it say Harold Porter-King Esquire OBE and Mrs Harold Porter-King like that?'

'Well, because she's not the one with the OBE, that's him, and because he can't leave it out because then he'd be missing impressing some people, and because he's a pompous buffoon.'

'No, or rather yes, but why does it say Mrs *Harold* Porter-King like that? Because he's worried some people might think he means his mother?'

'No, that's because he's a pompous buffoon, you see. Have you accepted?'

'Yes. In the third person.'

'Actually,' said Patrick, picking up the card, 'this does evoke him quite powerfully. Especially his voice. When I wash I use soap, uh-boy, which you must have heard of, surely. I'd like to see him up against Simon. Which I've got to be myself in – Christ – slightly over four minutes' time.' He threw the card down again. 'I don't think I can resist a refresher course of our

Harold after all. Don't hang about for me, I'll probably be a bit late, but I'll do my best to get there.'

'Oh, can't we go along together? First time.'

'No. It'll do you good to brave it on your own. Tank up on the vodka first.'

He was looking at his best that morning, really lovely, Jenny thought, tall and handsome with almost nothing left of the slight sissy look she had noticed the first time she saw him, quite dashing too in the light-green man-made-fibre suit, which though off the peg fitted perfectly after minor surgery to cuffs and trouser-bottoms. They kissed warmly and with a lot of fondness. Stepping brief-case in hand and without much fuss over the stretched-out form of Frankie, who looked up at him in wonderment, he departed.

Anybody could have told that that day he was not going anywhere he ought not to be going. As long as Jenny had known him, he had been a bad actor and a terrible liar. People usually said such things in a kind of admiring way or at least with a touch of respect, to be fair, you had to grant him this much, and so on. She sometimes wondered how many women admired their men for that. If a husband decided he was only going to behave himself as long as it suited him, the least he could do was be a fabulous actor and a fantastic liar to go with it. And be them *all the time:* one fair cop and Mr Wonderful was going to be under surveillance for the next hundred years. And that happened whether anyone liked it or not, because no one could decide what to forget and what to remember. What's done cannot be undone. For years she had thought that was meant to cheer you up after something bad had happened, to encourage you to get on with your life, the same as saying there was no use crying over spilt milk. But since then she had come to the conclusion that it was actually about as sad as anything you could say.

She had no business to be going on in that strain on such a fine sunny morning. The first thing to do was to get the place fit to be seen by the charwoman. From films and books and such Jenny had formed some idea of London charwomen before she ever set eyes on one. It said they were sharp and often sarcastic in their talk, but humorous, honest and hard-working. The succession of dailies she had had in Highbury, which after all had been part of London for many years, had borne this

143

inventory out fairly well up to about half way, after which its accuracy dropped off sharply. One of her neighbours, whose husband was a councillor somewhere, had explained to her that household help, as it was now called, had stopped being the servile employment it had been historically and become a skilled occupation like any other, and Jenny had done her best to take this in. But nothing could have prepared her for the peevish little short-haired thing in T-shirt and blue jeans who turned up about three times out of four, never rang to say she was not going to, spent her first twenty minutes getting her mops and cloths out and her last twenty putting them away again and was always calling for new scientific formulas and appliances based on up-to-the-minute research. If she really was skilled except in ways you could be funny about, it must have been in some sphere of household helping far above and beyond what was called for at 1B Lower Ground. Jenny had worked out that, allowing for the time she had to put in herself getting things straight, Linda was about forty per cent cost-effective, not counting the stuff she nicked, of course.

But she was far from ready to tell Linda not to come any more, greatly as she longed to do so. You might have thought that anyone who so obviously disliked doing a particular job would be pleased to be stopped from doing it, but not this one, you could tell, and there was no knowing what a badly brought-up creature like that might not chop to bits or set fire to in retaliation. Worse really, there was the question of Mr Bigger, the truant superintendent-person who had sent Linda along in the first place. One of the things it was impossible to get hold of him about was whether he had sent her along out of the goodness of his heart or had some sort of legal control over recruiting the building's charwomen. Either way he might be angry if one he had sent along was told, just like that, not to come any more. Unfortunately this fell into the category of what Patrick hated to be bothered with.

Jenny thought she might as well try Mr Bigger now. At this time she might just catch him, in his office perhaps for the few seconds it took to seize his mail and hare for the door again. But the telephone rang before she reached it. She half-fancied it might be Mr Bigger himself on the line, telepathically spurred to call and ask if there was anything he could do for her. But as once before when she had been thinking of that great absentee, it was Tim who spoke. When she had told him who she was and he had asked her if she was Jenny and she had told him she was, he said,

'Oh. Is Patrick there?'

'He's left for work. You should be able to get him there in a few minutes.'

Tim wondered about that for a time. Then he said, 'Can I leave a message?'

'Yes, of course,' she said, and hastily added after a few seconds, 'What do you want me to say?' She was not yet quite used to this blood-out-of-a-stone style of conversation.

'Just say . . . I'll meet the people as arranged.'

'You'll meet the people as arranged. Right.'

'Yes,' he said, going on in a burst of fluency, 'He'll know what that means.'

'Oh, oh right. Er, is there anything else? About anything else, I mean?'

'Not really. Just . . . Well – has anybody been asking about me?'

'No. What sort of person?'

'Any sort of person.'

'No. No one at all.'

After another silence he said in quite a hurry, 'Thank you, my dear, I'll be popping in to see you soon,' and rang off before it was her turn to recite.

The doorbell chimed. To Jenny's surprise it was Linda, hardly ten minutes after the time she was supposed to turn up, the equivalent for her of having spent the night outside the front door in a sleeping-bag. Perhaps she was going to have turned over a new leaf, and certainly she had had all her hair cut off, but once inside she looked round the place with all the baleful curiosity or incredulity she always showed in these first seconds and yet brought out as good as new every time. As usual too, Jenny felt uneasy about leaving her, but there was nothing for it but put her make-up and pricey tights under lock and key and let it happen.

'Will you be all right, Linda?' That was what she usually and ridiculously said.

'Shouldn't be surprised.'

Jenny's morning at the hospital included a lecture from a child-psychologist. This proved to be a staring, straight-haired

145

woman in her forties who somehow reminded Jenny of the mothers she used to see each day waiting for their children outside the school in Hertfordshire. She had not been able to help noticing that quite a high proportion looked much too horrible to be the mother of anything, certainly not of a child of four or five, and she could remember thinking unwillingly that that said something worse still about the fathers. But, barring the odd auntie or stand-in, mothers was what they had undoubtedly been, and a mother was what this one would surely have had to be before she started laying down the law about what children were like, or even about what they were really like. Then – hey, not so fast, she said to herself; that was an out-of-date reaction, belonging to the time before she came to London and began to learn how the world was organised. On that reckoning Dr Thing could quite well have been a virgin, which at least put your mind at rest a bit about the men in her life.

The lecture opened with some pieces of information that would not have surprised anyone who had ever seen a child and went on with some seeming to show that children were all the same to start with, and might all have been all right still if they had not had parents to cope with or been brought up in some other way. As it was, children's problems were either so well understood by now that they could be seen to have no prospect of solution, or when stripped of out-of-date phraseology and properly described turned out not to exist. On the other hand, electro-convulsive therapy was thoroughly discredited. Well, that line of talk could only help to keep the population down, and everybody agreed that was a good thing. Jenny came out of the theatre place feeling not only more ignorant than when she went in but also stupider. The thought made her wish Patrick had been with her. He had the gift of being able to rise above things. She hurried off to the canteen before she could start glooming about not having any children's problems in her life.

Back home again, she found a note on the kitchen table in Linda's astonishing handwriting that said Mr Something had phoned and gave a number. The something was no recognisable name or word, but then the number had too few figures to be on the dial, so she was no worse off. While checking the cupboard for pilferings she heard a woman's footsteps passing down the walk outside and stopping at the door of 1E. The bell there now rang a couple of times – somebody asking about Tim, or trying to. The inquirer soon moved via 1D and 1C to 1B.

She was revealed as middle-aged but quite good-looking, dressed in an unfashionable shade of light blue. Everything about her from her nose to her waistline seemed higher than usual. Her manner was cool, though not unfriendly.

'Ah,' she said when she saw Jenny. 'Who am I speaking to?'

'My name's Standish,' said Jenny, stuttering slightly as she had not done for ages. 'That's Mrs. Mrs Standish.'

'Ann Wolstenholme. Do you happen to know somebody called Tim Vatcher?'

'No. Well, not Vatcher.'

'But Tim.' The woman laughed quite heartily, showing long narrow teeth. 'There's old Tim for you. What's he calling himself round here?'

'The man who's coming, who seems to be coming to live down the end there, he told my husband and me his name was Tim Valentine.'

'Much nicer than Vatcher, I agree. Not all that appropriate, perhaps. I'm his sister.'

Jenny's first thought was that a true sister of Tim's would have been more likely to say she was the Shah of Persia, only the Shah of Persia would not have been claiming to be Tim's sister. Or something. In other words she was confused. But she successfully said, 'How nice to see you,' blocking off the dreaded pleased-to-meet-you formula without turning a hair.

'Is he all *right*, old Tim?'

Jenny mentioned his telephone call that morning, and reminded herself he had not asked her not to say anything or anything.

'He is a worry, the silly old chump.' Mrs Wolstenholme, as she would have had to be, screwed up her nose, lifting it a fraction higher still, and took the latest of several close looks at Jenny. 'Always has been.'

'Would you like to come in for a minute?'

She was quite tall enough to be Tim's sister, and the accent was right, but oddly enough it was the waft of liquor-fumes as she crossed the threshold that seemed to clinch her credentials. In the sitting-room she took in the spider-plant and said with

147

a touch of real approval, 'Well this is nice,' without breaking stride on her way to the best chair. She lowered to the floor there the orange-and-black carpet-bag she had been carrying.

'Can I get you something?'

'Well do you know my dear to tell you the truth you rather *can*. Er, there wouldn't by any chance happen to be a tiny drop of sort of gin tucked away anywhere, I suppose?'

'I'll just see.'

And by an outside chance there was nearly half of a half-bottle of a brand Jenny had never seen before, but it was acceptable pretty much as it stood, never mind about tonic or ice, just a wee bit of tap-water. According to Jenny's father, whisky and water meant a whisky-drinker, but gin and water meant a serious drinker. Drunk for a penny, dead drunk for tuppence, clean straw on the house, he used to add cryptically but impressively.

'Do I gather you see a bit of old Tim? *Is* he all right? Does he truly mean to move into that flat, do you know? Do you know where he's staying at the moment? He's good at covering his tracks which is the last thing you'd expect. I do so want to see the old fathead, it's most frustrating.'

'I could see he gets a message. I'm afraid that's about all I could do.'

'Oh, is it really? Oh dear. I mean of course thank you for offering, but what, I suppose you've just had drinks with him a couple of times, you and your husband, in a neighbourly kind of way, nothing more than that, m'm?'

'Well . . . not really, no.' But in a way of course it was yes. 'But then we have talked to one another.'

'Oh.' This unsurprising piece of information stopped Mrs Wolstenholme in her tracks for a moment. Then she continued as before, 'He's not such a bad old thing in his awful way. But he is extraordinarily tiresome, you see. He's very clever, but he's also extremely impressionable and extremely obstinate at the same time. He gets some preposterous idea into his head and *nothing* will drive it out again.' She pushed back her pale-blue cuff to see her watch. 'Did he tell you he'd got a wife, for instance?'

'No he didn't.'

'Not a hint? You didn't pick it up?'

'It's a complete surprise to me.'

'Well, there you are.' No laughter this time. 'Anyway, he has. She's called Augusta, if you please. They've been married nearly twelve years now. No children, thank God, though that's part of the story too in a way. They got along, well, they got along somehow until just a couple of months ago when he didn't exactly walk out, no drama, he just said he thought they should live apart for a bit and he'd be getting in touch. Well, he hasn't got in touch. I've been trying to get him to get in touch, do you see. He's left her plenty of cash, it wouldn't be that with him. I shouldn't fancy being married to him myself but apparently Gussie quite likes it. Likes it better than not having him round the place at all, at least. Some women, they're like that. I suppose he's got a girl, old Tim.'

'I don't think so, no.'

'Oh surely. That was how all the trouble started. Or rather how it went on. He'd been a devoted husband for years and then suddenly there he was attacking every female in sight. He'd had a, well what could one say, an eventful youth but Gussie's quite firm there was nothing going on at all until recently, though it beats me how you can be sure about a thing like that. Gussie says she found she could adjust to the new situation. Well, I dare say there too we're not all made the same. Anyway, there was comparative peace and quiet for a time, until Gussie had a heart-to-heart with a horrible old school-chum whose absolute bugger of a husband has always been rather thick with Tim, and it emerged that Tim had told this simply ghastly swine about his problem. To be quite frank with you I'm not completely sure of the best way of putting this. Would you very much mind telling me how old you are?'

'I'm twenty-eight,' said Jenny, and while Mrs Wolstenholme showed she considered that a very serious age for someone to be, took her time over going on in a grown-up voice, 'I rather gather Tim mentioned something of the sort to my husband.'

'Oh, jolly good. Well now, going on with the story. Er, before I do, I wonder if I could possibly . . .'

'Oh, please help yourself. Have you got enough water there?'

'Bless you. Perfect. So: Tim poured out his troubles to this vile creature, who told him not to be content to just go on suffering in silence but do something about himself. Bring the whole business out in the open, he said, or words to that effect. Isn't that the most half-witted, irresponsible advice you can

149

imagine? In my experience if a thing's been hidden away for a long time and kept quiet about, then there's a jolly good reason and a jolly good case for leaving it there. Of course, I realise people think they know better these days.

'Well: Tim doing something about himself meant Tim going off with one popsy after another and, what, trying his luck. Nothing loth either, let it be said. Tim may have had his difficulties with the ladies but he's always fancied them. And now I suppose he's found one that . . . can . . . as it were . . . No, I see it isn't that. If there's anything you can tell me, Mrs . . .'

'Standish. Of course. You did know Tim's been going to these psychiatrist men in Harley Street?'

'In my view that entire fraternity should be lined up against a wall and machine-gunned. Like the SS. Yes, my dear, I did know.'

'Well, there's one that's told him his troubles with girls are because it's not girls he really likes.'

Jenny had been expecting a sister of Tim's, or at any rate this one, to put on something of a show at such news, but she merely slumped her high shoulders and looked at the floor for a time as if an old friend had died. She gave a few feeble nods. Then she shoved herself upright again and seized her glass.

'You said yourself he gets hold of ridiculous ideas and won't let go of them.'

More nods, less feeble.

'But from what I've seen of him he's very bright.'

'He's clever, you see, that's his trouble. Or one of his troubles. I imagine I can take it for granted you see nothing in that idea yourself? No, of course not. Nor your husband? Of course not.'

'Can I ask you something now? What is Tim's profession?'

'I'll tell you right enough, but first you tell me what he says it is. I could do with a good laugh.'

'Well, all he says he does is be a prison visitor.'

'Oh, sucks. Oh, what a sell. Oh, I was hoping for something like a gigolo or a professional escort.'

'Why them?'

'I don't know, aren't they supposed to be terrifically good in bed? No, I don't really know why I said that. It is so easy to make fun of the poor old boy. You know I think we tend to forget that idiots have just as rough a time as the rest of us. Perhaps rougher. Old Tim never said much but I know he felt awful about his life. When that stinking mate of his told him he owed it to himself to hammer the womanhood it must have seemed like the fire from heaven. I think he was actually off his rocker for a bit. I suppose one shouldn't be too hard on the stinking mate. In this day and age someone would have been bound to have said something like that to him sooner or later.'

'You haven't actually said. . .'

'Oh dear, nor I have. He's a barrister. Not the kind that appears in court, clearly, but he makes a jolly good living out of advising on charities and wills and what-not. No revelation, is it? An old-fashioned respectable job like that. In a way I think that's part of the trouble. He's led this very conventional life and then he suddenly finds he doesn't fit into it any more, or so he believes. If he were a stick-in-the-mud all through he might have been all right, but he's half stick-in-the-mud and half romantic or child or bloody fool, whichever you prefer. The prison visiting's another bit of that. But as I say he really does like the law. Well, it's in the blood, do you see, our aged pop now being a distinguished judge.'

'How does Tim get on with his father?'

'Oh, like a house on fire, my dear. Thick as thieves until this last excitement. Upon which aged pop turned extremely starchy and I don't blame him. For one thing he's very fond of Gussie.'

'And Tim said your husband's a solicitor.'

'Oh he did, did he?' Mrs Wolstenholme glared indignantly at Jenny. 'I ask you, the sheer stunning cheek of the bloody man. Was he trying to be funny or something? Sammy was called to the bar as soon as he could walk and he's been a circuit judge since 1960. Solicitor, indeed. Specialising in legal aid, no doubt he said. I know someone with a big smack-bottom warming up for him. Don't breathe a word to Sammy should he ever come your way.'

'No, of course not. So that's all Tim is.'

Mrs Wolstenholme again looked at the time, made a pleased noise and face and poured the remains of the gin into her glass. 'Of course, Sammy's starting to get on a bit himself now, you know. He'll be sixty in the autumn. Not that it seems to be slowing him down at all.' This clearly meant more than just in moving round the house, but nothing was said for the moment about what, indeed there was another small hesitation. 'I can't help feeling there are some sides of life that tend to be overrated,

151

well, given more than their fair share of importance, especially in things like marriage, these last few years particularly. People ought to leave things alone more and learn to get along with what they've got. I think they're better off like that.'

She paused again and looked at Jenny and laughed in anticipation of what she was about to tell her. 'When our chauffeur goes on his holidays,' she said, turning extra serious, 'the agency people send a temporary chap along, do you see. Now these chaps are often quite talkative and chummy with one. I suppose the way they look at it, they're going to see a fair bit of one for a couple of weeks and then not any more. Well, the chap last year was quite young, youngish anyway, and rather good-looking. He talked about his wife in the kind of half-comical, complaining way some men do, giving the general impression that they have their ups and downs but by and large they hit it off not too badly. You know. Then one morning coming back from Peter Jones, he'd been grousing about how he always had to remind her they were going out exactly when she needed to start getting ready, however many times he might have warned her earlier, all that, amusing enough but just routine and I was almost nodding off, but then . . .'

This pause was for dramatic effect and putting down the last swallow of the gin. '*Then* he suddenly said, "Mind you, madam," he said, he'd a funny plummy sort of voice like a butler in a play, "Mind you, madam, that isn't the most deep-seated of our differences," he said. "Oh no, I remember very well the time we woke up after our wedding-night, and she said to me, my wife said to me, 'Fred, don't you ever do that to me again,' she said. And do you know, madam," he said, "do you know, I never have." So I asked him how long they'd been married. "Sixteen years, madam," he said. After that he went on to what it was like getting her off the telephone when he was expecting a booking. But don't you think, Mrs . . . Standish, don't you honestly think that's an example to us all?

'So if you could perhaps just have a word with Tim – '

The actual telephone, the one twenty feet away, rang. When Jenny answered it a female jabbering began, all too recognisably coming from the worst of her current mothers. This one's child, a nasty peevish little thing of seven with only a pair of sticky-out ears to make up for the rest of her, had recently had her appendix out in one of the smoothest operations ever performed

152

in that hospital. She was also meant to have an iron constitution. But her mother, who spent most of the day at her bedside anyhow, seemed to think she was being sneakily allowed to die. On she went; there was never anything for it but to let it blow itself out, like a hurricane in the Caribbean. If Patrick had been there he would have mouthed 'Woman?' at her, shaken his head in a fit-to-drop way and signalled to her to hang up, but she never could.

By the time this instalment had blown itself out, Mrs Wolstenholme had got her stuff together, smilingly tapped the face of her watch, mimed a kiss and departed. Jenny saw she had very good legs. She had left a visiting-card with 'Ann Wolstenholme JP' engraved on it and 'Many many thanks' and 'If you could . . .' dashingly written, and had taken her glass and the empty gin-bottle out to the kitchen and emptied her ashtray into the rubbish-bin.

With her visitor gone Jenny felt a little flat, but she soon brightened up again as always at the thought of telling Patrick. She went through bits in her mind, feeling that for a start she understood something now about why Tim dressed as he did, while she got ready to go to the party.

That was not a straightforward proposition. Since coming to London Jenny had found out that parties, that could only be one of two or three different things at home, could be any one or more of an uncountable number here. In her memory, invitation cards went with old buildings, ladies in long skirts, waiters and waitresses with trays, sometimes a chap calling out names. That could hardly be going to help with 1D Lower Ground. Or could it? Some of it might. Who could know what might not? Supposing everybody except her . . . She sat firmly on that one, thinking to herself she would do well to remember the time at home when she had gone to call for her friend Shirley Brick before the school dance, and Shirley had been worried about the bows on her frock, and Mr Brick had made her feel all right about that by telling her without fear of contradiction that she might as well go in a sack for all the notice anybody would be taking of her.

When it came to it Jenny settled for the cream linen suit and navy blouse without, this time, the string of pretend-bone beads, on the argument that from any point of view, not wearing them could not possibly be as wrong as wearing them. It was only a silly old party, after all, and she could just walk out of it whenever she felt so inclined and Patrick would not exactly faint, but still her fancy was bothered with visions of dukes and footmen, eyeglasses and cigarette-holders, bowing and curt-seying and her falling over full length without having swallowed a drop. The last bit made her gaze wistfully towards the drinks cupboard for a moment before she went on her way. Nobody would ever know how much at times like this she longed to take Patrick at his word and throw down a couple of tumblers of neat vodka. She considered that as regards what you were born with she had had a better deal than most, but she had definitely been behind the door when they were doling out the knack of getting on with booze. Those who could go through life half cut were just not aware of how lucky they were.

For some minutes or more Jenny had been aware now and then of a vague continuous roaring in the distance, like Abbey Park on a Saturday afternoon. It turned a lot louder when she opened the door of 1B, and louder still by an unbelievable amount as she approached that of 1D. As always at this stage she felt she only liked parties with about two and a half people there, and one of them somebody she had been at school with and another one a witness at her wedding. When the door opened to her ring there was another surge of sound, which had seemed impossible, but then she saw that about a thousand times too many people to suit her had packed themselves in. There were so many that it seemed no more than reasonable to have the door opened by a butler, whom fortunately she tagged well before she could have told him how nice it was to see him.

She had never dreamed she would find Harold Porter-King hard to pick out of a crowd, but every man in sight looked like an old-fashioned businessman or City gent with very long hair but not usually a moustache or whiskers. But luck was with her again, and in a few seconds one of the smallest of them separ-ated himself from the others and came over with his hand stuck out. Although he made more or less straight for her there was a moment quite late on when she thought he might be going to miss her altogether.

'So sweet of you to be able to come,' he said, perhaps running two expressions together. Something seemed to be preventing him from looking her in the eye or anywhere else.

'Thank you for asking me.' That was one prepared phrase gone in a second.

'Nigel isn't with you.'

'No,' she agreed.

'He'll be along later, no doubt.'

'Oh, I should think so, yes.'

'Now who don't you know?'

'A glass of champagne, madam?'

That was a much easier question to answer. By the time Jenny had taken a glass off the proffered tray, which was really quite soon, the man who must surely have been Harold Porter-King had gone. He had probably registered the fact that he had spent a quarter of a minute with a new arrival and that was it. Jenny had seen enough of the world to understand that he would not have had to be drunk, or dazed by recently hitting his head, to be like that. Apart from being very thick, he could have been affected by the excitement of giving such a huge party or just the wear and tear of having been at it for some time.

For it was a pretty huge party, with seriously eighty people in a space all right for twenty, with the butler and two aproned maidservants squirming in and out of the thickest parts with their trays still brilliantly held aloft. Jenny went in the wake of one of the maids along by the wall to the fireplace. Above this a large and terrible picture hung, if not an ugly painting of a woman then a painting of an ugly woman. Even so it was the only thing in the room that someone had chosen to put there; no flowers, no plants, no knick-knacks, no little touches.

Guiltily, remembering Patrick's words, Jenny hung on long enough to glance at the row of cards on the mantelpiece. There was no colour to be seen there, not even a photograph, mainly invitations like today's. The most noticeable was about a yard thick and said that the Master of St Philip's and Mrs Percival invited the Porter-Kings to something or other. Did that mean that even in Oxford and Cambridge things had turned so free and easy that a top person could get his lady-friend along to act as his hostess at an official function? But surely . . .

'Ah my dear, you look completely lawst.'

Jenny jumped round and saw a tall man smiling down on her in an incredibly friendly way. His tallness meant he was not Harold Porter-King, though he was doing a very clever imitation of him. 'Lawst? Oh, lost. Oh, sorry. Oh, do I?'

'I said to myself, there's a nice little gel who looks completely lawst. If – '

'Come along, Cedric.' This was said by a short and far from striking woman who had emerged from behind a fat one in the last ten seconds. It was not much to say, not much at all, and it had been said in a perfectly ordinary, quite genial tone, but it immediately turned out to be enough for Cedric. He gave Jenny a quick, cheerful nod, to show he had enjoyed the talk they had had, stepped aside and was hidden from view in a moment. The short woman gave her a look, but not for long enough to settle whether it was a proper old-fashioned one or more a woman-to-woman, aren't-they-impossible one, because she too was soon gone for good.

That short conversation, perhaps one of the shortest on record, impressed Jenny. Its end particularly filled her with envy and respect. What an eye that woman had, what resolve, what command of words. What a flair for timing. If only she herself had been able to manage a fraction of that long ago, there might have been such a different tale to tell, one that took a lot less out of everyone. Come along, Patrick. Hopeless. When she said it to herself it had a kind of artificial, stagey feel to it, no authority at all. She supposed differences of upbringing might have had a bearing somewhere.

She was reluctant to leave the cards along the mantelpiece or whatever you were supposed to call it. For a moment she wondered if they were to really remind the Porter-Kings of where they were due to go and when, or to make some of the other people who looked at them jealous and upset at not being asked themselves. Except she knew she was not really wondering. If she had put the point to Patrick and he had happened to be in a bad mood, he would have been capable of accusing her of doing her wide-eyed little-girl act, being an innocent abroad and suchlike. Well yes, a bit, but he quite liked it at other times, and actually it was not so tremendously different from the way he sometimes went on himself, except it came in a different accent. He had always been rather one for things being all right when he did them, as she could tell him when he was in a better frame of mind.

Her hostess was obviously not going to come looking high and low for her, so it was up to her to do the looking. Mrs P-K was nowhere in sight, but then hardly anybody was. Jenny decided to go through the middle. It was very like moving about in a pub on a Saturday night, especially in the way they all took an amazingly long time realising she was trying to push past them when she was trying to push past them. Which was worse, the noise or the heat? When she had about reached the opposite corner she almost bumped against her hostess, noticeable in guardsman's red and, to be fair, not looking at all bad.

'Hel*lo*,' she said with a ready broad-spectrum smile. 'Do you belong to a group?'

Jenny had only just started to think about that when a man with whiskers growing down to his collar, like an old-fashioned composer, said, 'Of course I have to keep my head down and my trap shut at our do's. Afterwards too. I'm let in but only on that condition.'

'You don't hear me holding forth either,' said a younger man.

'I don't know what I'd do without ours,' said the chubby freckled girl next to him.

'It really is possible to help people,' said Wendy Porter-King. 'One had given up hope of that light-years ago. Like bringing rain to thirsty plants.'

'What do you actually do?' asked Jenny, trying not to sound high and mighty and also not to notice the way the younger man was looking her over and the chubby girl was minding.

'Well, in our case,' said the whiskered man, 'it consists very largely of a brown gentleman telling us what the world and the universe are about in general and then the rest of us, the benighted peasantry, take him up on various details. I'm not allowed to, as I said. If I did I'd be inclined to ask him why he doesn't . . . Well, never mind what I'd ask him.'

'Ours is English,' said the chubby girl. 'Or at least he was.'

'Really?' asked the whiskered man. Burst veins showed above the hair on his cheeks. 'Taken out a Hindu passport, has he?'

'Well, I mean he's called Krishna Ram Das now.'

'Oh ah, one of the Somerset Ram Dases. What ho.'

'He's marvellous,' said the chubby girl enthusiastically. 'He's so uplifting. You go along there, it's just an ordinary house in Eaton Terrace, and you're full of your silly troubles and fears when you arrive, and after he's talked for just fifteen or twenty minutes about the greatness and goodness of the world spirit, and how he wants us all to be happy, that's the world spirit does, and all the pain and grief is just an illusion, well, every-

157

thing seems different. Because Krishna Ram Das has made you see the world is good.' She appealed to the younger man. 'Am I right?'

'Oh, you're right. That that's just about what he tells us.'

'Much the same with our lot,' said the whiskered man. 'Give or take a mantra or two. Tell me, what does your fellow wear?'

'Oh, just a simple suit that cost a hundred guineas if it cost a tanner.'

'Ours is mostly in a white sheet – spotlessly clean, of course. But then his place is in Kilburn Lane. Seems to satisfy the customers all right.'

'Oh, I see,' said Jenny. 'But you're just getting these men to help you all feel better. I thought when you talked about helping people you meant other people. You know, like the blind.'

'Isn't everybody blind, in one way or another?' asked Wendy.

'Well . . .' said the whiskered man, and stopped abruptly and drew in his breath.

Jenny was used to hearing Patrick say that something somebody had said had made him want to hit them, though of course he was much too nice and cowardly to mean it anywhere near literally. But there were times like this when she reckoned she could see what he meant. Of course she would describe it to him to the best of her ability, but she wished he had been on the spot to hear. Then perhaps he would have asked Mrs P-K if she was an American, his favourite insult, a very handy one too because unless you were in the know it sounded like just a polite question. He always said he had nothing against real Americans, most of them anyway.

The moment passed. The butler wriggled through with a tray of drinks and Jenny took a glass of champagne to be sociable. A maid followed through the same gap with a tray of snacks and Jenny took a damp bright-yellow biscuit with a triangle of glossy purplish meat and half a stuffed olive on it. A new man, one not seen before, asked her if she had been away and without waiting for her answer said he had just come back from Spain, where, she understood him to say, they had had a lot of trouble with the Reds.

'Oh, I thought they'd taken care of them,' said Jenny. 'Since that war they had there.'

'They haven't, believe me. Well, not up anything you could call a mountain.'

158

'No, I suppose that's where they would tend to hole up.'

'Not only that, they're twisty and treacherous too, I tell you for a fact.'

'Funny, you never see anything about it in the papers in this country.'

'Rather not,' said the man, who had thought of that objection a long time ago, 'nobody would go there if they knew the facts.'

'But surely it can't be like that all over Spain.'

'Oh no. No, no, that wouldn't be fair at all. No, er, round Madrid and the other main population centres they seem to have hammered 'em out all right. Put rubble and concrete and metal down on top of 'em the same as in any civilised country, my sweet. Of course, even there I'm only talking about the major Reds. The minor ones are dirt and dung to this day, I promise you. Some things never change, you know. Now that's quite enough travelogue for one evening. There must be something I can get you. You've only to say.'

So there was not after all to be a comparison between the Spanish Reds and closer-to-home characters like the King's Red or Tottenham Court Red. Jenny excused herself. Just about then, the crush, the heat and the noise quite suddenly became too much for her. A headache had started over her eye, not helped by the champagne, which had definitely been on the sour side. Oh, where was Patrick? She had decided in advance not to leave before he arrived, but come to think of it he had not sounded sure he was going to make it at all. If he did he was bound to look in at 1B first; she would catch him there and explain she had had enough. While she was thinking this the doorbell sounded and it was Patrick who was let in. She almost ran to him.

'Hey, hey, what's all this then?' he said, beaming at her.

'Nothing, darling, it's just such a terrible crowd in there I don't think I can stand it any more.'

'Oh, bloody awful, love, as is all too apparent from here. Sorry I got held up. Are you all right?'

'Oh absolutely, I just want a bit of peace and quiet.'

'You go and put your feet up. I'll be with you in twenty minutes. Oh, Christ,' he added at something he had just seen or heard. 'More like ten.'

Feeling all floppy just in that moment, she went out and stood in the walk for a moment or two, gazing dully at the bit of garden, and enjoying not being in the thick of it any more and feeling about ninety-five. She had pulled herself together and was rootling for her key when it occurred to her that she had not thanked either of the awful Porter-Kings for their terrible party, which at the same time was something you were meant to do however much you might have disenjoyed yourself. What about writing instead? No. Ringing? Good Lord no. On your way, Miss Bunn.

Finding the door of 1D unlatched she slipped inside. In her head was the nice prospect of going over with Patrick what Mrs Wolstenholme had told her. She could not have been gone for literally more than a minute, but that had been long enough for Patrick to have run down that Wendy P-K and separated her off from the crowd, and for the pair of them to be gawping at each other in a way she instantly recognised and hated, a way that could only have meant one thing. It was really very bad luck: but for the red dress she might never have seen them, or not just then, and they could not have been in sight from where she was for literally more than a second before someone else moved across and masked them, but it was enough. Jenny forgot about thanking her hostess. She went on standing where she was for another few seconds before the fear of being seen sent her hurrying out.

Was this the one he had started with that day, the day he had come in pretending to be cross about some publishing thing Simon had done or not done, and she had shamefully made up a story about her mother being ill to account for her being upset, or had that been another one? It made no difference. This was the nearest he had come so far to having a bit of stuff next door. And it was one he despised – she had believed him about that, just as she had believed him when he told her he had no intentions towards Mrs Porter-Christ-King. Then. What had happened to make him change? Anything: five seconds' temptation and ten seconds' opportunity had always been more than enough for him. Where had he taken her? Not here in 1B, she hoped.

But none of that made any difference either. The only important thing for now was to get out before he came back. In two minutes flat she had got through to Elsie Carter and everything was fixed up and absolutely straightforward: a couple of hundred yards' walk to Waterloo tube station and all the way up the Northern Line to High Barnet, where Elsie would collect her in the car as before. A note mentioning Elsie in unspecified trouble, nasty but nothing awful, took no longer. The little satchel affair she took her books to the hospital in held quite easily all the things she would need. Frankie scored by getting two whole sardines in his plate. That was the lot. She was off and away down the walk, making herself as small, as nearly invisible as possible. Behind her the door of 1D opened and closed, but no one came running and calling after her.

Twelve

Patrick stayed longer at the Porter-Kings' party than he had intended. He had turned up purposely late, with the vague idea of limiting the time he could have spent with Wendy trying not to listen to what she said. To that end he had stopped off for a quick one and then a slower one or two at the Princess Beatrice, where magically the workmen were nowhere to be seen or heard and Cyril smiled at him. The stated number of drinks Patrick considered most reasonable; after all, he told himself, he had been on the wagon ever since finishing lunch at Simpson's. Then when Jenny had more or less passed him at the front door of 1D his own departure seemed to become less urgent. In fact it was no more than considerate of him to stay out of the picture till she had had the chance of a doze. After a severely restricted exchange with Wendy, no more than was needed to keep the ball rolling, he had found himself chatting lightly to a charming girl whose visible assets rather exceeded Wendy's, chatting without intent, too, as it turned out when her husband, one of the biggest men in the room, came over and joined them. He had taken a last drink, a large Scotch wrested from Harold himself out of a sense of natural justice, before quite thankfully leaving.

So by the time Patrick got back to 1B and found Jenny had gone, he had no reason to suppose there had been anything very hurried or at all disquieting about her departure. Not really. Elsie had been in sudden and forgettable trouble before. He had been left to fend for himself before, and as before the cupboard held easily enough tinned junk for that. He felt a little flat, but he also felt more than a little pissed. He came through quite satisfactorily on corned beef, Russian salad, artichoke

162

hearts from the treat corner, most of a quarter-bottle of Bell's, *Gun Law* on the BBC and *Titter 8*. A telephone-call at half-past nine drew no reply, and then he found he had left it too late to try last thing.

By the next morning his mood had changed, but then so had his physical state, meaning he felt bloody awful. As the morning wore on, however, his hangover wore off while leaving intact a certain disquiet about Jenny. Two goes at Elsie's number brought the engaged signal. Other matters filled his attention, of which the most important, or the least mortifyingly unimportant, was Deirdre. The Milesian spinner of yarns had arrived in London earlier that week and, as expected by all, lunched with Jack Sutcliffe. Nobody seemed to know much about what had taken place at this encounter. According to Simon's version, Deirdre had been affable enough but cagey, freely admitting the new novel was ready for the press, disclosing that it might be thought something of a new departure, confessing that Trevor, her agent, had various ideas about it while shrinking from saying what they were. Patrick had happened to glimpse Jack returning from that lunch and thought he had looked distinctly unhappy as well as fit to be drained on a paper napkin, which was how he often looked after a lunch.

Morning prayers that morning, the one after Jenny's excursion to Elsie's place, were deferred to allow Simon to consult with three Japanese, one of whom, but not all, were stated to be publishers. His manner of referring to the event afterwards suggested that his fellow directors should not be unduly surprised if next Monday they found their offices infested with baffling apparatus, or even (loud silly laugh) their chairs occupied by smiling Orientals. He brought up the Deirdre question again.

'She didn't go into what sort of new departure at all?'

'I pressed her, but that was as far as she'd go,' said Jack.

'And she said nothing about delivery?'

'There I didn't press her. In fact I didn't ask her.'

'Very wise. Well, let's hope Patrick manages to get a bit more out of her than you did.'

'What?'

'It is today you're giving her lunch, isn't it, Patrick?'

'Yes, I wondered whether to try that new place in Frith Street.'

163

This development came as news to Jack and it clearly disconcerted him. 'I don't, I mean Deirdre has always been my responsibility.'

'Exactly, I thought she might be interested to meet another of our number.'

'She didn't say anything to me about it.'

'Really. I can't imagine why not.'

Jack could be seen coming to the conclusion that there was nothing he could say for now about any of that. He fingered a razor-cut, or rather slash, at the side of his jaw. Then he said abruptly, 'You saw the news about Sebastian, did you? Yes, J.L.R. Sebastian, erstwhile chronicler of Lord Alfred Douglas and his circle. Picked up dead in the street just the other day. Not entirely sober when he laid him down, I dare say. Did you see that?' he demanded of Simon.

'No, I missed it.'

'Oh. Well, he's certainly an ex-author of ours now, isn't he?'

Simon upset this decent exit-line by saying, 'Just before you rush off, Jack – I hope you can both make the board-meeting tomorrow? Oh, good. One point you might like to think about in the meantime. I'm going to suggest we take Gary on to the board. In ten years' time every publisher will have the sales manager on the board as a matter of course. You see, Gary's out there on the ground, where it's actually happening.'

Jack said, 'I presume you don't intend to take a vote at this moment?'

'Oh no, no. So what's this vote anyway? We'll throw it around tomorrow.'

'Have you any more points?'

'No, that's all for now. Oh and of course thank you very much for coming.'

Now Jack did go, but not before looking directly at Patrick for the first time since hearing of his lunch with Deirdre, probably since entering the room. It was reminiscent of a look he had given him once before at a similar juncture, only this was rather less affectionate. When he had left, Simon held out an opened packet of Celtique.

'I've given them up, thanks.'

'I'm not sure that's wise. I think people ought to have their vices. It makes them nicer.' In his turn Simon looked straight at Patrick, seeming for once to be using both eyes to do so. 'I always try and remember that. Well now, somehow I don't think Jack likes living in the 1960s very much.'

'Any more than J.L.R. Sebastian. Well, a bit more perhaps.'

'The poor old thing doesn't have that problem, does he? You know, it beats me where these people find the money. He certainly wasn't getting any from us. Oh, you can afford to give Deirdre a bit of a spread at lunch-time. Let her choose a nice bottle. You'll find her quite an interesting old thing in her fashion. It's a crying shame she doesn't really fit in here any more.'

The one-eyed look that went with this prompted Patrick to say, 'That's what you want me to break to her, I suppose.'

'I don't know about *break* to her, I haven't been keeping any secrets from her exactly. In fact that's rather where you come in. Now: either she wants to be off, which is fine, or she's trying to force up the ante. I'd just like to know how the land lies. I seem to have failed to impress her with my charm, so . . . you are sure you won't have a cigarette? . . . So she won't tell me, and she won't tell Jack so as not to upset him or whatever. But she might tell you. The other thing is just Jack. The more he can be made to feel uncomfortable, unwanted, irrelevant the better all round. You and I between us have done quite a good job there already this morning, I feel.'

Patrick watched Simon inhale his Celtique and thought of that descending ball of the second strongest cigarette-smoke in London. 'That's a bit brutal, isn't it?'

'Brutal?' This was surely another and a suitable occasion for the loud silly laugh, but it did not come. 'Brutal! Brutal would be asking for his resignation. I do hope it'll never come to that. You could let Deirdre have a tiny leak along those lines, merely predicting that Jack will shortly be finding something else to do. But of course you handle it any way you like, you're a free agent.'

There was a goggle-eyed fixed grin of Jenny's that would have made a brilliant answer, but Patrick just nodded.

'Enjoy your lunch. Oh, I knew there was something else. *Blood in the Tigris*.'

'Oh, Christ, that Taffy charlatan, what's he called, Pedrain-Williams. He's not dead too by any lucky chance?'

'He sounded as though he soon might be. He was on the telephone yesterday, demanding to speak to the managing

165

director.' The stage-Cambrian was not too bad really. 'We were to publish his masterpiece as it stands or not at all, so I told him not at all. I wish half our problems were as easy as that one. Mind you, I doubt if we've heard the last of him.'

'Well, thanks anyway.'

'You were right about him all along. I'll be guided by you next time. Oh, are you going to be in later?'

Patrick said he was. From back in his room he checked Deirdre's sales figures. Their trend was firmly and immemorially and acceleratingly downwards, and the last two books had never made a great deal of money, the last one less than the one before over their respective first years of publication. All the same, to pass up their successor, even allowing for an increased further drop, seemed if not the act of a fool then not the act, or intention, of a brilliant newcomer to the very heights of the trade, never mind any talk of the firm's image or identity. But who was going to say that Simon was a fool? Often, more than once indeed through their last conversation, he had seemed to Patrick to be shrewd enough, perhaps more than enough. But nothing anyone said ever could be safely taken as intended or even understood. Sooner or later a fool was bound to say what only a wise man could have been reasonably expected to say. Or words to that effect.

His secretary, or rather his assistant, assured him that she had booked a table as instructed, or rather requested, which at least meant she thought she had. He had time to give Elsie Carter's number another ring. He was on the point of hanging up when Elsie answered.

'Jenny's not here, Patrick.'

'Will she be there later? Can I speak to her later?'

'I'm just going to pick her up and then we're going out together. I'll say you rang.'

'Would you tell her – '

That was it. She had said enough to remind him in full of her unpleasant accent, which differed so radically from his own. But she had not said enough to let him decide whether she was somebody who had never liked or approved of him and now had sensational cause to do even less of either, or somebody who had never liked or approved of him. She had sounded exactly like both. He had had no chance to ask her what trouble she was in, had it occurred to him to do so, nor did it bother him that even if he had she would just have disliked him more.

The questions of what Jenny knew or specifically knew or thought she knew, and which it was and whether it was any, circulated in his head for a couple of minutes. Then he put them out of it and headed for the restaurant. He had always been good at that type of thing and was getting better at it all the time. In the taxi he wondered about Deirdre's new departure. Irish folk-lore? Everyone dead? On the moon? In verse? And nobody had better try to tell him she was too old for such.

He sat himself down in a kind of ground-level balcony among wrought iron and creepers, the whole intended to remind him of Spain, assuming him to have some acquaintance with that country in the first place. Nothing else about the concern, down to its name, seemed so intended. From a marbled-paper list he chose something called a Vodkatini, stipulating after pretended reflection that it should be a large one of its kind.

He had taken no more than one life-enhancing sip when Deirdre arrived, right on time. He well remembered from their previous meeting that she had struck him as not only rather horrible, but horrible in a way he soon recognised from visits to his mother's side of the water, a practice now long discontinued. Which precise way it was he had forgotten. It had had something to do with talking, or with words. Well, it would have. He had to admit now that there was nothing immediately horrible about her appearance for a female of seventy-something: tallish or at least not dwarfish, wearing suitably old-ladylike clothes, remarkably unchanged from her usual publicity photograph of twenty years or more earlier. Nor was there anything, it quickly turned out, that she had to have before she could do anything, like the exact time, a cushion, directions to the nearest fire exit, a glass of water, though she called for a large glass of John Jameson without much delay. And whatever might betide, a certain interest was guaranteed.

Was she having a pleasant trip? Not really, it seemed: so many of the people she had known were dead. She mentioned some. He tried to conceal the fact that in most cases he had been unaware of their having been alive, and was resigned to it, and skilfully turned the subject to his own activities within Hammond & Sutcliffe. He emphasised here the depth of what he more than once called his involvement with The Centuries'

167

Heritage, trying to give an impression of boring sedateness. In part of this at least he was probably successful, because after a couple of minutes of it she interrupted him.

'Of course you'll know my old friend Jack Sutcliffe quite well.'

'Well, I don't see a great deal of him because we're concerned with quite different parts of the list.'

'To be sure, but it's impossible you should know nothing of each other at all. It's a little early to be asking you, but I'd be fascinated to know your impression of the old fellow.'

After feigned consideration, he said, 'It's only fair to say to begin with that we respect each other, which among other things is a – '

'Do you know, I think that might do very well to finish with too. Thank you for being so frank, Mr Standish, and with somebody you've only met this moment.'

In Patrick's experience restaurants were not noted for their timely fetching of menus or of anything else, but today was paranormally different. He clutched with real enthusiasm at the poster-sized pasteboard sheet with its elegant, barely legible script, not indeed doing his damnedest to read it straight through. Hesitantly but inexorably, he was putting together the way in which Deirdre had struck him as rather horrible when he saw her previously. Her questions to the waiter about the dishes on offer revealed either an obsessive curiosity about random detail or a genuine ignorance about what things like baking and onions were. Or such would have been the case with an otherwise normal person. He could not afford to under-value the fact that Deirdre was not merely an Irishwoman and an old Irishwoman but a bloody woman as well; only with Jenny had it ever been safe to disregard that for more than a couple of minutes on end and even possible to forget it. Never-theless the Emerald-Isle convergence of T- and TH-sounds, which no one on earth could have made sound unaffected with a general upper-Brit accent, the on-off smile with eyes-shut supplement and earlier hints combined to tag his luncheon guest as the kind that enjoyed insulting your intelligence by pretending to be genuine. *That* was the way she was rather horrible.

Rather horrible or not, she too had evidently been thinking and noticing. She must have chosen the moment when their first courses were being delivered to say reflectively, 'Patrick, now.

I couldn't help noticing the name, and wondering. And the colouring. Would I be right . . . in thinking . . . perhaps . . .'

If you want a straightforward uppercut to the point of the jaw, thought Patrick, one Jesus, Mary and Joseph will get you it by special delivery. He took time to look round the room, where he took in more greenery and some iron grilles over non-existent windows, and also down at his plate, where there lay a number of pale shrimps and similar stuff. Neither view persuaded him that he must stay here at all costs. 'Assuming that means am I Irish, the answer is no. My mother was born in what has since become the Republic of Ireland but she's lived here since she was twenty and I never go there.'

'You do sound quite English when you say that.'

'I feel quite English all the time. Actually.'

'Of course you do. Well, full marks to you for being so honest. Again.'

'Oh, it's only as it came out.'

'That's often the way, I find.'

They inspected each other, more openly than at their first moments in the restaurant. He decided that, although in her way she looked her full seventy-something, it was an old woman, bloody or not, that she fully was even so. She came right in the opposite category to the pathetic and dreadful but still hale androgynous great-aunt of his, also Irish, who had once memorably come visiting. He also made up his mind to do what he had not done before and glance at one of this one's books.

'I think it would pay you,' she said now – 'I've had to say this to men before – it might pay you to remember that other people can feel shy as well as yourself, or when you're not feeling shy, as the case may be, and they don't need reasons. Oh well that was very nice, though I confess I could have done with a touch more salt in the dressing. Jack Sutcliffe gave me to understand you do and say what your man Simon Giles wants. Is that fair?'

'Oh,' said Patrick. 'Er, I'm sure it was what he intended you to understand.'

'I hadn't the heart to tell him you and I were fixed to have lunch today. It would have ruined the time he spent with me entirely. But I dare say he knows by now.'

'Yes.'

'I'm very fond of young Jack, you know, which is what he was when I first began to be published. Maybe you're wondering what I think I'm doing, accepting your notwithstanding very kind invitation at all. Now you didn't deny that you're very responsive to Mr Giles's wishes. But I suppose even if you weren't you still couldn't do anything to stop him throwing Jack out of the firm.'

'Not really, no.'

'Making it worth his while to retire, that is. Spiritually as well as materially, of course. And while we're about it Mr Giles would greatly like to see the back of me too.'

'Yes,' said Patrick, being unable to think of anything else to say just then, and trying to win back a mark or two for stoutly coming clean. 'Though – '

'And Mr Giles has sent you here to tell me so. Not that it's exactly red-hot news, is it?'

Patrick was quite surprised at how much he disliked the role he found himself occupying, or rather unfairly depicted in. 'No. I mean there's a lot more to it than that. Er, he, he wanted me to ask you about how you felt yourself, whether you were still happy with us. And just what sort of new novel you have in store for, for the public.'

'Believe me I do appreciate your frankness, Mr Standish, and you're entitled to answers to your questions. Ah, now that looks perfectly delightful, doesn't it? One thing I have very much noticed on this visit of mine is how greatly the restaurants seem to have improved. I've always found London in the past a city rather turned in on itself, if you know what I mean, but I suppose that may be changing.'

For the next few minutes Deirdre developed this theme, or at least stuck to it, while Patrick contemplated his record as a teller of the truth. Once, he had judged himself above average in this field; now, it was rather that he kept blurting things out for want of a handy lie. He was too frivolous and impatient to put in the mental reconnaissance necessary for effective deceit. Rather than dwell on this shortcoming he went off into half-baked musings about the way the Saxon part of his heritage might have shattered the valuably dishonest Celtic strain. At the same time he felt sure he would hear about the new novel when the moment came.

That was not forthwith. 'It's interesting,' said Deirdre, 'to notice the wine-buyers here cottoning on to the notion that there are other Graves of merit besides Chevalier and Haut-Brion. I think I can say we've known that in Dublin for many years, certainly in my father's time. He was renowned for his excellent table, which attracted all the Dublin wits in those closing years of Ireland's first and last regnant queen.'

Oh Christ, thought Patrick in the moment it took him to realise she was enjoying herself at his expense again. And not just at his moral expense either, he further reflected, pouring her out more wine from the bottle he had chosen for its position three down from the top of the price-range. If he looked he would no doubt find the word Graves somewhere on its label. As he generously topped up his own glass he asked himself what he could have expected after putting a couple of drinks into an old mick.

'I've always found Dublin wits of any era full of laughs but woefully wanting in bearability. They're like Irish charm, an acquired taste you have to be born with. My loss, I'm sure. Unfortunately I haven't had the same experience with what shall we call it? – Celtic whimsy. Yeats and Jimmy Stephens and them. My old father was right about those people all along, but I took a long time to get the thing out of my system. I picked up one of my early books the other day – I call it early but I was nearly out of my forties when I wrote it, and I was perfectly appalled by the shallow would-be clever would-be poetical way it went on. It was quite unreal. But by that time I'd not only put the finishing touches to the new one, I'd also had my agent's verdict on it.

'Maybe Mr Giles has made known to you, Mr Standish, that in my distant youth I was well acquainted with the merry lads of my time and others that weren't lads at all except by courtesy. To be sure, no decent Catholic girl of the time could say any different. I'd guess you yourself have no little acquaintance with these matters in general.'

Patrick rotated his head modestly. He took the last remark as a genuine attempt to flatter him.

'Yes, among others of no possible interest to any rational person I was friendly with Willie Yeats and Paddy Laoghaire and one or two songsters of lesser note than Paddy if such a thing can be imagined. And a couple of Englishmen besides, not just the compulsory one, meaning Herbert Wells. So much is generally known, I think. But not quite as generally as it'll be known in a little while, nor in the detail I'll be telling it. In realistic detail too, you understand, no Celtic twilight this time. No doubt you'll be acquainted with Mr Fowler.'

'Your agent. Yes, I know him.' Know him for a nasty thrusting little shit who could not be bothered to hide his low opinion of publishers he sensed were better-educated and more fastidious than himself. Patrick thought of saying that Trevor Fowler was very well spoken of, but decided he might not be able to manage the requisite sincerity.

'I have the greatest confidence in his professional judgement.' After some prattling in that strain, Deirdre said, 'Mr Fowler has secured me an advance on royalties from Grimmett Bradman, whom he described as an excellent firm, of twenty thousand pounds.'

Patrick had no sincerity problem this time. 'That's a lot of money.' He did his best to conceal the simple irritation he felt towards Trevor, who along with everything else was about seventeen.

'I'm glad to hear you say so, Mr Standish. I thought as much myself, but then Mr Fowler took the view that there would be widespread interest in the rather curious episode involving George Bernard Shaw, though of course he appears under a somewhat different name in my novel. Some of the living also have their place, and that'll raise its own problems I shouldn't wonder. For example I'm afraid Rebecca West won't be best pleased at some of the particulars in the episode involving Herbert Wells, or rather the character that closely resembles him. And not only there.

'I think I've probably told you enough, Mr Standish. I've certainly told you far more than enough to make Mr Fowler fall down in a fit. Anyhow it looks as though I'll be having a couple of pennies to rub together in my dotage. My only regret is that after all these years of service, no, devoted loyalty, poor Jack is to have no share in the enterprise. Or so it seems settled at the moment. But it did just occur to me: from your unrivalled knowledge of Mr Giles's outlook on the world on top of what you've been hearing from me, would you say he could be persuaded to let Jack stay in his post in return for publishing the novel I've described? He would of course have to match

172

Grimmett Bradman's offer, as I believe the phrase goes. Perhaps I needn't assure you that this is not Mr Fowler's idea.'

'No indeed,' said Patrick, but the next moment something that looked like a large part of the rood-screen of a Spanish cathedral was wheeled into his view. Along the shelves carved into it stood a very large number of assorted bottles. Deirdre after some inquiry called for a glass of Tokay Aszu, Patrick for one of a cognac he had never heard of but was attested to be the most expensive in sight. He put in further simulated pondering before opting for a large glass. At the mere sight of it in front of him he knew what he was going to say to Deirdre. As he contemplated it, he wondered briefly if Jack had perhaps told Deirdre more about him than that he was very responsive to Mr Giles's wishes. He was also held up for a moment by the fear that someone, somewhere, might think he was doing this for J.L.R. Sebastian, but decided he could afford to charge ahead regardless.

'If you put that proposal,' he said finally, 'Simon Giles would really have no choice but accept it. He'd hate doing it, and I must say I couldn't blame him – just think of what Jack would be like round the office after that, and I couldn't blame him either, and that wouldn't be all, but Simon would have to be a very big fool to let you go now. But then of course he might have to.'

Patrick could not resist taking a sip of brandy at this point, nor was it solely for dramatic effect. Any such effect was a little tattered anyway when Deirdre, far from obliging with a prompt, began very slowly to look past him. So he said quite soon.

'If you went to Grimmett Bradman as planned but made it a condition that Jack should go along, be given a job by them that is, there's nothing Simon could do. He has an option on you, naturally, but Trevor obviously knows how to get you out of that.'

Deirdre said with all the alacrity that could be wished, 'Grimmett Bradman would never entertain such a notion.'

'Have you asked them?'

'Mr Fowler was most emphatic when I started to make the suggestion.'

'Well, he would be, wouldn't he, as, er, as they say these days. I doubt if he cares much for Jack either, I'm afraid. My strong feeling is that a deal could be fixed up along those lines.

There's nothing to be lost by trying. You haven't by any chance thought about a successor to this new one, I suppose?'

'I'm on page thirty-three,' said Deirdre.

'Who knows that?'

'So far only you.'

'Well . . .' Patrick spread his hands.

'Tell me: Jack would have thought of some such arrangement as you propose, would he?'

'Oh yes. Impossible not.'

'Then why the devil didn't the silly little bugger put it to me?'

Patrick hoped the question would prove rhetorical, but it was not to be. Forcing the words out, he said, 'I presume he thought it would be improper or something.'

'Oh, the silly little bugger.' She held her hand over her mouth for a moment or two. Then she said, 'Will you let me be the one to tell him about this if it goes forward?'

'Of course. And he can be the one to tell Simon.'

Deirdre gave a shout of laughter and clapped her hand over her mouth again. 'Oh dear. I'm afraid your Mr Giles will dislike this even more than the other arrangement.'

'Yes, I'm afraid he will.'

'But you're . . .' She looked at him and changed her mind. 'Well now. Would it be possible, please say it would be possible, for me to buy you a drink?'

'Yes,' said Patrick, and signalled for the ecclesiastical grog-cart. But the waiter, a smallish youngster with sham-RAF moustache, trooped up without it.

'Bar's closed,' he said when he understood what was wanted. 'Three o'clock.'

A strange sensation filled Patrick. He felt as if some alien being had come to possess him and speak through his mouth. 'Look at it this way, sonny,' he heard it say – 'either you fetch us a drink nice and respectful, or I rip you to bits, all right?' The being had exerted itself to thicken his own south-of-the-river tones to dispose of any residual affability.

The waiter looked at him with great weariness. 'Tell me what you want and I'll get it. I'm not hauling that contraption over with His bleeding Nibs watching.'

When they had been comfortably settled for a few minutes, Deirdre with a shot of John Jameson and Patrick with some more of the terrifyingly priced cognac, he gave her a careful look and said,

'What was H.G., you know, actually *like*?'

She laughed silently this time. 'Oh, he was on and off like a little sparrow, my dear. It may sound odd to the present generation, but I don't think any of us minded at all, or even noticed. You didn't then. Rebecca did, of course. She was always the girl for noticing and minding. The voice of the future, they called her, and they were right. My grandnephews and -nieces tell me that's the general way of it in this day and age, noticing and minding everything. I suppose the the truth is there's never been many as much fun as H.G.'

Ah to be sure now, thought Patrick to himself, acushla masodding-chree. But he quite enjoyed the rest of it, though he got nothing further from her that was as specific. Well, not till right at the end, when they were outside and looking for a taxi.

'I think what I was talking about just now,' said Deirdre, who carried a venerable umbrella in purple silk that might have had its first outing at the golden jubilee of the monarch she had referred to, 'I think a lot of it started with David Lawrence. He invented having to get it right when you went to bed with somebody. To be sure, I can see as well as anyone how it was he came by the idea. Oh yes, he gave his women plenty to, how did I put it, plenty to mind and notice. Ah, here comes one now. Thank you for a very pleasant lunch, my dear.'

'Well, I thoroughly enjoyed it. Would you like me to have a word with, with Mr Fowler?'

'I would. But with young Jack not a word at all.'

'Have no fear. Understood.'

'And I'll have no word of any kind with a soul till I've spoken to you again.'

She gave him a smile that induced him to, much against his better judgement, indeed against all of his judgement, before he could cry out, like a bloody fool, lean forward and – aagh! no, don't! Oh no, not that! Patrick, for Christ's sake, whatever you do! *please* NO – kiss her on the cheek ... oh ... *God* ... It was done, it was over. There was nothing to be said. At least she had the common decency not to hang about but smiled again and was borne away. Well, it was clear enough that the old thing had had no trouble, even across the dividing decades,

175

in spotting him as a king of shaft, effortlessly outclassing any hero of her Dublin girlhood. Simple as that.

What was done was done, and he would keep his promise to say nothing to Jack of what was afoot. That proved easy enough; what exercised him more was not dropping some vile hint that the situation was even worse than the old turd feared and also irreversible. In the end he wondered quite how he seemed to Jack, who must have been watching for his return to the offices and who certainly nipped out into the hall smartly enough to bar his path to the staircase.

'Good lunch?'

Patrick pretended to take this for a gastronomic inquiry. 'Pretty fair,' he said with a considering nod. 'Mind you I'm damn sure the French beans were frozen.'

'How was Deirdre?'

'Oh, I thought she was looking very well. Didn't you? Of course you know her much better than I do. Yes, for an old lady of seventy-whatever-it-is . . .' Well, he could keep this up all night, but it seemed a shame to take the money. 'I'm afraid I didn't get any more out of her than you did about the new novel.'

'Oh really?'

'No really. She went on about her early experiences in the realm of Brian Boru instead.'

'I expect you mean Ireland, don't you?'

'Willie Yeats, do you know. Bernie Shaw. Fellows of that kidney, would you believe. Ah, a great time they did be having of it one way and another.'

'Yes, well I can see one fellow has been having a great time of it,' said Jack without transmitting any camaraderie at all. 'One way and another. Thank you for your wealth of information.'

'Ah, think nothing of it. I'm to say she'll be in touch with you shortly.'

Something in how that came out fetched a quick glance from Jack, but without further inquiry he turned and marched off towards his lair at the back of the building. Patrick climbed to his own room and approached his desk with uneasiness, wondering as often before what appalling omission or fit of impetuosity on his part might have emerged in the past couple of hours, but there was no sign that anybody had so much as remembered his existence during that time. Perhaps Simon had marked him down too for dislodgement from the firm. He blotted out that idea by ringing Trevor and arranging a drink with him the following day, then forgot about it altogether as Simon appeared in the flesh, having informally bounded up the stairs to chat to him in preference to informally summoning him down.

Now that he had put himself into a good position to do his managing director a disservice, Patrick realised at once how much he had always disliked him. He gave him an extravagant smile of welcome and esteem that drew no response beyond a parking of the arse on the edge of the desk and the lighting of a Celtique.

'Well, does she want to go or stay?'

'She wants more money.'

'Did she mention any reason why we should give it to her?'

'It's sexier, the new one.'

'Oh God, I'm not sure I like the sound of that, Deirdre's idea of sexier. Just sexier?'

'Sexier or possibly more sexy was all she'd say.'

'Did she say anything else? About the book, that is?'

'Not a lot, no. Oh, it's more realistic too, which may or may not be part of its being sexier. Yes, and it's set, er, in the earlier years of the century.'

'What, not the troubles and all that? When the British butchered the Irish revolutionaries?'

'That sort of time, I understood.'

'We did a book on the question a couple of years ago, the IRA and the Black and Tans and so on. The sort of book one's quite glad to have published. *The Cruel Cross of England*, that's right. Yes, who was it? Some American, of course. Anyway, it didn't do frightfully well, as I rather predicted – the whole thing's a dead issue now.'

'Perhaps Deirdre has a different approach.'

Simon nodded and gave off smoke. 'I gather Jack accosted you on your return.'

'Christ, you do, do you? Also what of it? I mean if you gathered that I'd have thought you'd gather everything else.' When Simon just looked at him with his usual eye, Patrick went on, 'Well, he seemed very anxious to know what had taken place at the lunch.'

'But you didn't enlighten him.'

'No, I didn't. There wasn't much I could have enlightened him with. But I told him nothing at all if that's what you want to know.'

Simon nodded again, got off the desk and paced to and fro a time or two. Patrick was grateful for the past half-minute, a helpful qualm-quasher, assuming one to be needed. For a short time it looked as though Simon might pace out of the room without more words, but then he blew out his breath like a fellow cooling his porridge and said, 'You and Jenny like living in that place of yours in Waterloo, do you?'

'Yes, thanks. It's fine. Why?'

'Is it a, you know, a reasonable neighbourhood?'

'Well, it's good enough for us to live in. So?'

'Because Barbara was passing by there the other day and thought she'd just drop in on the off-chance. You weren't there, either of you, and she was on her way out again when a chap came out of one of the other flats and very decently asked if he could do anything. A sort of he-man type, apparently, but quite nicely spoken, she said. Thought she'd seen him in a couple of films and TV things.'

'Ah, that would be Stevie, that's Steve Bairstow. He's very nicely spoken.'

'Now you, Patrick, you said all the flats in that block were taken, but according to this Bah, Bare, did you say Bairstow character there are two still standing empty.'

'Yeah, but they're both *taken*.' Patrick passed on what little he knew of the couple destined for 1C, and did all that most people could have done to explain about Tim. As a performance aimed at generally turning aside interest and further inquiry it was not up to much, and hopeless in the present circumstances.

After a good bit but not all of it Simon said, 'You see young Barbara does seem rather to have set her heart on one of those little nooks if it's halfway possible, she was very taken with yours if you remember, and apparently seeing this Bagstock character's place sort of stirred it all up again.'

'Ah, he asked her in, did he?'

'Offered her a drink. Couldn't have been more charming.'

'Good old Steve. Er, what did she think of the way things were set up there?'

'Rather unimaginative approach was how she put it if I

178

remember rightly. But nice enough. The basic structure's the main thing, I suppose.'

'M'm.' It could not be that Simon was fully informed of what kind of household existed at 1A Lower Ground and yet judged the subject unmentionable within these walls. But to acquaint him now with the truth would have been to guarantee his enthusiastic support for his wife's scheme to move into 1C or 1E. He was what Patrick saw as odd about queers, fanatically tolerant of them in both talk and fact, courting their society, bending over backwards to please them to an extent that seemed to go beyond mere pissy progressivism. Indeed it would have been rash to rule out the possibility that once upon a time he had bent over the other way to please some few of them.

He interrupted Patrick's thoughts at this stage by asking, 'Are you going to be in this evening?'

'Well yes, yes I think so, unless I – '

'Barbara was thinking of dropping in on you if you're not doing anything, just to ask a question or two.'

'But . . .'

'I can't make it myself, I've got the Mabuse lecture at the Laski Institute, but she's going for drinks at the Old Vic anyway, on your doorstep. That's if you're free.'

Patrick was nearly sure he stipulated a telephone call in advance. He was even closer to being sure that there had been some unbearable theatrical or dramaturgical thing in Barbara's earlier life that he was supposed to know about. He had still not finished trying to make up his mind to bother to try to remember what it was when Simon left. Following him down-stairs for a pee shortly afterwards, Patrick detected the redolence he had left in his wake, not strong but easily perceptible, like a large zoo passed at a distance.

Thirteen

'Can I speak to Jenny, please? It's Patrick.' He wondered if he had been heard or what, because he got no answer, but then Jenny came on.

'Hallo.' She always said that and no more. When he asked her, she said things were all right and nothing much was going on at the moment. She sounded quite friendly, not very friendly. Why should she, how could she? She never really liked the telephone. Elsie would have been in the room.

'When are you coming back?'

'I thought the morning now.'

'You're very faint.'

'Is that better?'

'Yes, that's fine. How are you? Are you all right?'

'Yes, I'm all right. How's Frankie?'

'Oh, he's, he's okay.'

But Frankie was not okay, or if he was, then Patrick had no way of knowing it, for Frankie had not reappeared after his late-night constitutional. That was not very uncommon, especially in the warmer weather, but he had always been there in the morning. Not this morning. Patrick had gone out to the back and called him several times, the last time five minutes ago on getting home from the office. Nothing. He could not tell Jenny that now. What he did go into with her was the next day, when she was to take her time, get a taxi from the station, ring him at work as soon as she arrived. All that. It was done in twenty seconds and he had put the receiver back without being able to think of any of the bits he knew he had wanted to bring up. He went out and again called Frankie without result, even beating his plate with a spoon as he had seen and heard Jenny do.

His feelings of anxiety and unearned guilt over the cat got in the way of those of anxiety and earned guilt over Jenny, rather handily for him because he knew it was no good trying to shift the getting in the way. Finding nothing to do at the office he had come home early and, now he had finally got hold of Jenny, found nothing to do here either. Or rather there were only two things he felt like doing, and the other one was having a drink, which there were objections to. The chief of them was that it would have been not a drink but yet another drink. Although what he had had at lunch-time was only a memory now, it was not at all a pleasant one. That cognac had produced in him a tiny refined concentrate of a hangover, mundane stuff like headache and dry mouth hardly there at all, his attention fixed on whether or not a giant fist would fall on him from heaven before his heart blew up. With the scientific part of his mind he could see that a couple of brisk stiffies would pull him round in fine style, but at the end of that road there lay a fearful morning, one with Jenny also in it, and the directness of the proposal, the lack of shame affronted his puritanism, unfortunately for him. He often recalled the horror and admiration he had felt on coming upon his American overnight visitor, one morning of the sort in question, standing by the open refrigerator with the vodka-bottle upended at his lips.

Seeing somebody and incidentally perhaps in due course having a drink with them would be more like it. Cyril would not do; he was no longer sure he liked Cyril, or that Cyril had much time for him. And Cyril was not open yet anyway. What about Eric and Stevie? — he had heard movements next door. Ah, but at this hour they would be Stevie's only, with Eric not yet returned from the Ministry, and Stevie on his own was no great draw at the best of times, less still when spoiling for a discussion of Barbara — another day for that, and another again for a discussion of Stevie with Barbara, winningly grotesque as that encounter would have been to observe. And just imagine her not realising . . .

Sternly he pulled himself back to the practical. Before he looked further afield, what about Tim for a drink, or rather a chat? He had been in and out of 1E a couple of times lately, and could conceivably be there now. Or that might very well be he at this moment, causing the doorbell to chime.

Wendy Porter-King stood on the threshold wearing a pink-and-light-green something. It took Patrick a little while, like nearly a second, to remember the thing he felt like doing that was not having a drink. 'Can I come in?' she asked him.

How could he have prevented her? When she was in she wanted to know where Jenny was, and he said she was away. What else could he have said? Well, as he recognised even at the time, there was an immense array of what else he could have said, starting with Jenny having just popped round to the shops for a minute, but he ignored it all. But after more seconds, with only a few to go before he reached critical mass, he managed to get out a question about where what-was-his-name, where Harold was. She muttered that he was out. Out where? *Out.* Something about her show of being too far gone to say any more, and proud of it, irritated or otherwise distracted him. He let go of her and found her glaring at him, or perhaps simply glaring.

'What's the matter with you?' Her top row of teeth seemed to have advanced a small distance since their last meeting, though this seemed hardly possible in less than twenty-four hours.

'Nothing's the matter with me. I just want to know where Harold is, that's all.'

'Well . . . he's . . .' Now she elaborately came round, blinking, shaking her head half an inch each way, swallowing. 'He's changing at his office and going on to a do in the City.' By now evidently quite recovered, she added, 'If you want to know where I've got it written down in the flat.'

'What were you going to do if Jenny had been here?'

'I was going to ask you both in for a drink. What's the point of – '

'I'm not usually home at this time.'

'I heard you calling the cat.'

'You haven't asked where Jenny is. She might have been going to come back any moment.'

'But she's not. All right. Where's Jenny?'

'Staying with a friend for once in a blue moon. She's very much round the place as a rule.'

More blinking set in, with eyes staying shut for short irregular periods and eyebrows raised, and mouth open. Then she said, with rests between the words, 'Darling, what's happened to us? What's become of us?'

'What? I don't know. Nothing as far as I know.'

'How can you say that? Look at us. Look at me. Look at you, frowning at me like an enemy. Asking me questions. You had no questions . . . before.'

It was that last caesura that settled it. 'That was different. You know very well.'

'If I didn't then, I'm learning now. Fast. I remember our first time together, in that place at the end of the world, under a blue sky, and when we made love you drove at me with such fury, such hatred, and I asked you what it was with you, and you turned me aside, I forget with what, and no more was said of it. But now . . . I have the answer.'

'Really? And what would it be?' he asked with boyish eagerness.

'It's me you hate. For being a woman, for challenging your masculinity, for being somebody other – whatever. Maybe you hate yourself, who can tell? But you certainly hate me.'

She had a point there, he considered, but anyway she altogether misinterpreted his expression now. In slow motion she raised her chin, half shut her eyes again, undid one-handed and with near-comic difficulty the top button of the pink-and-light-green outfit and pulled her shoulders back. Things would probably have gone differently even so if she had done that immediately after assuring him that Harold was indeed out, or even if she had smiled.

As it was, he said with ludicrous sternness, 'Not here, if you don't mind. Not in her bed. That would be too much.' Get it said somehow, never mind how.

'Since when have you insisted on a bed?' This was an unladylike allusion to something that had gone on in his car the previous week. 'There's enough floor, isn't there, and carpet on it too, or is it her floor as well as her bed? A bit late, I'd call it, to start fretting about where. You shit.'

'There are some things . . .'

'Yeah, too true, and one of them is it's easier work turning moral on someone when you've fucked them a bit. My Christ. Married men. Thank you very much. Well, in future you won't have to get into a state about where you do it with me.'

183

'We just got off on the wrong foot.'

'Don't you try that with me, you *shit*. Aren't you afraid I might go blabbing to my lord and master about you and everything?'

'Yes, I am rather, to tell you the truth.'

'He'd smash you to pieces. He's little but he's bloody rough. He's been in court twice about it. Bound over. He'd be through you like a battering-ram. The snag is he'd trample me to smithereens too. One time I got it because he imagined he'd seen some guy at the golf club leering at me. At the Carshalton golf club. So you can stop shaking in your shoes. And you needn't worry about your own end of it either. She'd be better off without you like any woman would but I'm not going to chance it, having that on my conscience. I've been in on one marriage breaking up already and that's enough.'

Patrick muttered something successfully designed to be inaudible.

After a moment she said more quietly, 'Will you look at me? Please? You know, you're a fool, We could have had something worth remembering. Something a little bit special. And no harm done.'

'Do you mind if I ask you a question?'

'Now? Hardly.'

'Will you lay your hand on your heart and *swear* to me that you're not an American?'

Silence. Very much against his expectation he found himself wishing she would say something, or at least not run her eyes over his face in the way she was doing or have that disrespectful but resigned expression on her own face. After another moment she did her top button up again in matter-of-fact style and made for the door, within ten feet of which they had been standing throughout, neither slamming it behind her nor closing it over-quietly. He heard her key go into the lock of 1D, that door close and then final silence.

Well, he had had his chat all right, now he was presumably eligible for a drink. While he put it together he thought to himself that the whole thing had been like a political argument. In a way not just *like* either. Oh, there was a hell of a lot of politics in sex, and again not just in the struggle-for-power sense. Founding fathers, historic texts going back to the last century, manifestos and ritual formulas nobody acted on or even

184

understood, believing your own propaganda, party adherences being not empirical but entirely down to temperament, and above all of course the struggle for power. No, bugger it, that was where he had started. All right then, so why then had she not overridden his not-Jenny's-bed objection by offering a bed or something comparable at her own place? Because that would have been to sacrifice a principle for tactical advantage. Why not hold off that fearful blue-sky style, or at least tone it down, when surely she could see how far from well it was being received? What, and betray what she had always stood for and lived by? Renounce socialism, abandon free enterprise? Better to lose the election.

Such ruminations were still lasting him quite well when the telephone rang. Now this absolutely might be Tim.

'Hilloo,' cooed or trilled or carolled a feminine voice. 'Patrick?'

He grunted a sort of affirmative.

'Barbara. Listen, is Jenny there?'

'No, she's away.'

'Out somewhere, you mean? Will she be in this evening?'

'Staying with a friend.'

'Oh *dear*. Oh I was hoping to look in on her later to discuss the situation about these flats in your thingummytight, your block. I'm coming down your way to have drinks with some ghastly Thespians I've got tied up with at that hell-hole just round the corner from you. Why one agrees to these bloody chores I simply can't imagine. Will you be there yourself for a bit? Actually I'm about to leave this very minute.'

Patrick had remembered on recognising her voice the very same thing he had remembered not half an hour before at the sight of Mrs Porter-King, the thing he felt like doing that was not having a drink. He had also had time to remember less vividly Simon's mention of the proposed visit and to recover from the torpor which had allowed him to blurt out the truth about where Jenny was. Now, the instant Barbara stopped speaking, he took up smoothly, 'Well, I'll be here for about the next . . .' – pause for pretended look at watch – . . . twenty minutes, when one of our neighbours is collecting me and carting me along to some frightfully boring do in the City. Somehow got sucked into it. Actually I'd just started to get into my black tie when you rang.'

185

'Oh *poor* you.'

By the time Patrick had played a couple of tracks of his scratched, worn old copy of *Two Degrees East, Three Degrees West* (featuring Bill Perkins and John Lewis) it was clear to him that he had dodged getting a bit twice in quick succession as some sort of amends to Jenny. Unfortunately it was also clear that, while Wendy was gone past recall, Barbara was very much not. He found it hard to say quite how he felt about that. He was not used to not eating his cake.

Soon he fell asleep in the armchair, coming up from it at the sound of the bell like a champion hell-bent on a knock-out and almost as alert in a moment. So much so that walking to the door gave him time to remember from some time ago who his visitor must be, and to wish powerfully that it was some other evening.

Graham McClintoch, looking as much like a schoolmaster as anybody could look without going as far as wearing a gown and mortar-board and carrying a pointer, gave his shy smile. It was better than his other ones because while it was on it distracted you from the considerable ugliness of the rest of his face. As a whole, however, the face had not got any worse in the couple of years since Patrick had last seen it, perhaps a shade paler. They shook hands warmly. Graham did not spontaneously step across the threshold but, by a well-remembered but still pissy quirk, waited for some sign that it was all right to do so. No doubt if challenged he would have maintained that that had been how they handled these things in Dundee or wherever it was.

Indoors, the formalities met, he yielded up his cream-coloured pork-pie hat and raincoat covered with straps and flaps, but perforce hung on to his slightly too-blue suit, hairy tie and shiny square-toed grey shoes. He had always been strong in unwise clothes, as often observed by Jenny in the past. His haircut made no concession to prevailing taste, nor had he grown whiskers of any description, which was a disappointment in a way.

'No, no drink, thank you,' he said. 'I seem to have developed something of an acid stomach.'

'An ulcer?'

'No no, an acid stomach.'

'Oh, I'm sorry to hear that, Graham. Well now, we've plenty of soda-water.'

After thorough consideration this was approved, though no ice must enter the glass. Was Jenny perhaps on her way home? Mentally gritting his teeth a little, Patrick explained, leaning heavily on fact. Graham listened as attentively, accepting, asking no questions, being very good about it, in fact a degree or two better than needed, in his old manner.

As soon as it was done Patrick tried to break for the open. 'So tonight I'm afraid it's going to be just – '

'How is the dear wee girl after these many long years?'

'She's *fine*,' said her husband, narrowing his eyes and nodding his head slowly to give some idea of the comprehensiveness and intensity of her well-being. 'Ab-so-lute-ly *fine*.'

'I'm glad to hear it.' Graham's tone indicated he would be back on that. 'Does she still retain that charming trace of a stutter?'

'Thing of the past now.'

'As you no doubt recall I'm a married man myself these days.'

'Yes, I – '

'I invited you to the wedding of course, but you had to attend an important conference.'

'Yes, it was a damn shame, I just couldn't get out of it.'

'Is it still fun being a publisher?'

While he was pretending it was, Patrick thought to himself that if they were going to keep getting on to topics and off them again at the present rate, they would be through Vietnam and the Middle East before you could say Jack Robinson. Indeed after no more than a few minutes they had reached an area he had hoped would remain inviolate until feet-up time, news of old acquaintances from darkest Hertfordshire.

'Do you remember Dick Thompson?'

'What? I'll remember that laugh of his to my dying day.'

'That's the laddie. He's in gaol.'

'Oh no, really, bloody marvellous. So they got him at last, eh?'

'Six months for various misappropriations, including Spanish holidays for sanitation contractors. It's quite a story.'

'Before you embark on it I'd better just check the restaurant.'

Needless to say, when Patrick got Gioberti's on the line it was to book, not check, but he certainly thought it was needless to say so, not that Graham was even physically capable of listening to another's telephone conversation. The report of

Dick Thompson's confinement was pure joy, not solely as a rare case of a shit landing in the shit but because to have known, to have courted (and later married) a girl lodging with a gaolbird made him feel vaguely colourful, a cut above the common herd. It would be a jolly evening after all.

As he hung up, smiling rather complacently, he caught sight of a small cheap suitcase standing by the wall. Oh fart, of course buggerlugs was going to stay the night in the flat as well as not be given dinner in it. A quick recce established that as usual the bed in the little spare room was freshly made up and aired, a facility put to grateful use one night the previous week when a made-redundant art editor had come lurching in from the pub. Keeping that sort of thing in top-line order, Patrick knew, helped Jenny to fill up her day as well as being what she considered necessary. But there was no sense in pursuing that thought.

When he got back to the sitting-room he found Graham frowning through his glasses at a thin book he had evidently taken from the shelves.

'Walking the bone street in the blood and hair town,' he said, 'your eyes of time and ash make me rubble. Would you hold that those are two lines of verse?'

'Well no, not really. But you see . . .'

'They're set out as verse, though admittedly the first words in each *line* in most cases lack an initial capital. The title-page characterises the contents as poems. And . . . the book as a whole or its author is one of what is described here as Hammond & Sutcliffe Poets in Progress.' Staring at Patrick he lowered the volume to arm's length, then at once raised it again. 'Those, we'll agree to call them lines also contain a solecism. Grammatically it must be the eyes of time that are walking the bone street, while reason and mother wit surely insist that the walking must be performed by whoever is made rubble. But then no doubt the laws of reason, as of so much else, have lately been suspended.'

If the teaching of chemistry was stopped or ceased to appeal, Graham could undoubtedly have made a very passable living as an actor in plays on the Home Service. You could have drawn a picture of him doing that bit just from the sound of him, thought Patrick, but he only said, 'Yes, but it's nothing to do with me.'

188

'Excuse me, Standish, but you must see it's very much to do with you. I understand you're a director of the firm concerned, which if it means anything at all must – '

'I think that one probably comes from the time before I – '

'The date on the verso of the title-page is 1965, which to my knowledge lies within your period of, eh, employment there, does it not?'

'Yes, well there again if we only published books I thought were some good, or had a chance of being some good, any good at all, we'd probably publish about eleven a year. Not including carpentry and accounting but including histories of the Indian Mutiny. There we are. I think it's probably much the same everywhere.'

'That's as may be,' said Graham, but his tone had softened. 'I'm afraid I let myself be carried away. It won't be the first time by a long chalk. You're a good-natured fellow, Patrick. There's many a man would have fired up at the kind of inquisition I've been subjecting you to. I admire such tolerance.'

'Just conceit really.'

'There you go disparaging your best qualities. That seems to have become modish too I'm sorry to say.'

Graham mostly kept quiet while they drove to dinner, uttering no more than a grunt of disapproval or a click of the tongue as he craned out of the passenger window of the Mini, often at buildings and bits of bridge and suchlike that had been there since something like 1900, or so Patrick would have said. But then when they had settled down in the back room at Gioberti's there came a momentary return to the theme of reconciliation.

'Nobody who works in our education system has the right to point the finger of scorn at anyone,' said Graham after he had accepted provisionally that what were in front of him were indeed mussels as advertised. 'The lads are no less bright and willing than ever but they go out knowing less every year. Less chemistry, that is. A little more biology or physics and such comparatively respectable subjects and a lot more art, if you please. But less chemistry. Tell me, is that wine what might be called tart or sharp or sour to any degree?'

'No, these wop whites are perfectly innocuous.'

'These . . . They must still be of substantial acidity.'

'I think they get most of that cooked out of them when they're pasteurised.'

189

'Pasteurisation merely halts change.' Graham spoke mechanically, his eyes on the bottle. 'Apart from its sterilising effects. I think perhaps with a little water . . . I'd be a poor companion if I let you drink on your own. No doubt you remember something called premature specialisation.'

'Quite well enough, thanks.'

'Well, soon you'll be able safely to forget it. It's in process of being eradicated. Specialisation itself will be the next target. Already one can see . . .'

Graham went on about what one could already see until more food arrived and he explored his portion of it with the unaffected interest he had always shown at the advent of a loaded plate. Patrick held his peace. He was sure there was more and different to come and betted on its coming the quicker from this fellow for not being prodded for.

It started off like more of the same. 'This new post I'm going for in Surrey. A pleasant enough part of the world. The place is a thoroughly respectable institution in so far as the term still has meaning. It's a step up and it's more money. Rather more money. But the position is called Head of Chemistry Studies.' When this failed to draw the gasp of horror or whatever it was Graham had been counting on, he said indulgently, 'In other words not chemistry as such or not only chemistry. Like any other *subject*, chemistry is quite hard. Not everybody can expect to do well at it. That can only happen with non-subjects.'

'Like Lives of the Great Chemists.'

Graham turned less indulgent for a moment. 'Not quite that, I trust. Or not yet. But you grasp the general drift. In fact, *drift* is an excellent description of . . . I'm sorry. The point is, nobody at that school will come clean and tell me just what I should be expected to *provide*. If left to myself I wouldn't touch it with a *barge-pole*,' he said, making it really sting. 'But the further point is, I'm not left to myself any more. That red you're drinking, would you describe it as harsh or pungent or anything of that sort?'

'No, not a bit. Bland as, as your hat. Harmless. Not even very strong.'

'Not rough?'

'Absolutely not. Smooth.'

'Maybe with a drop of water . . .'

Not for the first time, Patrick was reminded of Tim. But

perhaps Graham really did want a drink, not a mask or a dispensation. The question remained in the air while he produced his wallet and took out a postcard-sized photograph which he dealt himself face down on the tablecloth. There it lay while he recounted an irreproachably academic, unvulgarised history of his association with his wife, whom he referred to consistently as his wife. That, her couple of years' seniority and her former job as a receptionist at a health-farm were all that stayed in Patrick's mind. He would have welcomed some unrounding and varnishing of the tale when that point was reached, for the health-farm in question was not just any old health-farm but one famed throughout the county and far beyond for the illustrious fatties and drunks, more particularly drunks, who came back time after time to fork out their hundred quid a day for not being given anything to eat or drink. But it was there and gone in a sentence.

Soon afterwards, with fateful deliberation, Graham slid the photograph, still face down, across to Patrick. 'This is my wife,' he elucidated. 'Not only need you make no comment but I positively require you to make none.' His eyes stayed on Patrick's face for a first-to-last view of his expression.

Of course it was not as bad as Patrick had imagined. It was not even as bad as he had reasonably imagined. The smiling glossy-hatted lady in the remorselessly well-produced photograph was not especially old or ugly or evil-looking, just very hard to take in as married to anyone you knew, though as a rabies victim's estranged wife, say, glimpsed while turning through the newspaper – no problem. Well aware that he lied better with his words than his looks, forbidden to speak, and feeling a bit of a shit, he screwed up his nose dementedly and pulled at it with finger and thumb.

But the whole thing was over in a few seconds, but then there came a turn for the worse, because when Graham had taken back and stowed away the photograph he said, without lowering his naturally strong, clear voice at all,

'Do you remember telling me that in your view the most attractive part of a naked woman was her face?'

'No,' said Patrick, looking more intently than he had ever expected to at the bottle of Valpolicella from which Graham was now pouring his second half-glass. 'No, I can't honestly say I do.'

'Well believe me you did, it doesn't matter when or where. I won't dispute with you the truth of that observation, but I'll advance another, on which again your comments are not called for. My suggestion is that the most important part, under-standing that word in a broad sense to include voice, manner-isms and so on, the most important part of a clothed woman is her face. And since most men in Western society see women much more often and for much longer at a time clothed than naked, the importance of the female face when the rest of her is clothed is of a distinctly higher order of, eh, importance than when the – '

'Ah, but it's only the prospect of getting her to – '

'Please, this really will be much easier, believe me, if you can manage to withhold your comments whenever possible – I've very nearly finished. Now where was I? Oh yes, I'll just ask you if you will to imagine that particular face with you for large parts of every day. No more than that. Well, take into account that my wife is talkative by nature. Very talkative, so that the periods when I can concentrate on a book or a newspaper or even the television screen are comparatively few and also brief. In addition to which, it must be an almost universal human instinct that makes us look another person in the face when he or she is addressing us, and even in the eye from time to time. I find it difficult and most unnatural to behave otherwise, not to speak of its being soon noticed and taken amiss. Someone once said the eyes are the windows of the soul, though I've been unable to trace the quotation. But in any case it's true, and most unfortunate. In what must be a large number of cases, that is. Of course no photograph will show that. Not that one, anyway.'

Patrick dealt with a mouthful of veal scaloppina from first to last before saying, 'Is it all right if I say something now?'

'Certainly, but before you do, perhaps I could trouble you to ask the waitress to bring me some dressing for my salad. I heard you ask her earlier but she seems to have forgotten.'

Here was the bloody old codger invoking Dundee bullshit again in petitioning his host to act as his intermediary with the servitors. It was not a matter of Graham's ideas so much as his whole style, though perhaps Mrs McClintoch saw it differently. No conversation was possible while the waitress came, went, came again, supplied dressing under intense scrutiny, finally went, apparently without affront to protocol.

Feeling about ninety after all this, but still a good forty years younger than Graham, Patrick said, 'I was going to say, there must be compensations to be got from being married, I mean in your case. Well of course there are in all cases but naturally I'm thinking of your case.'

'Compensations for what?'

'I was thinking of companionship and, er, you know, having somebody at your side to face things with, and no doubt she – '

'I was meaning compensations *for* having *done* what, not compensations *consisting of* this or that.'

'Compensations for . . . Well, Christ, you married her, didn't you, and after all . . .'

'I'll not embarrass you further. Yes, I married her when it was clear to most people that nobody else was going to do so. I can still remember most vividly the way her colleagues at that quite disgraceful establishment looked at me when I was produced as her fiancé. What manner of man could it be that was said to be resolved to marry their friend? As one might look at a missionary to some immeasurably wild region of South America.'

'Oh really.'

'If anything it was intensified at the wedding reception, the bill for which I incidentally footed myself, there being no appropriate kin of the bride to be seen. Yes, it had really happened, what they had all agreed never could.'

Patrick thought of telling Graham he must be imagining things, or at least exaggerating a great deal, but then he remembered the photograph, so he just nodded thoughtfully instead.

'In my wife's eyes however I had done nothing out of the ordinary, certainly nothing then or later to be *compensated* for. She had remained a spinster merely because no man of sufficient merit had yet presented himself.'

'But now she's clear that one has. Did.'

'Away, she's clear about no such thing. No no, she's received not more than her due but less than it. If you've anything as ignoble as gratitude in mind you can unhesitatingly discard it. She entered upon marriage with me through being over-optimistic, as she would put it, meaning she expected too much.

193

Why I married her is very likely mysterious, but I can't remember well enough to say. When I try, which I do less and less often, my thoughts keep drifting to other things. I think I must have had a notion that marriage held some value or satisfaction only appreciable from within it. As may be the case. Is that brandy you have there? Not raw in any way or fiery, is it? Of course it is after all a distillate.'

Just as they were about to leave, a middle-aged man three tables away from them on the side nearer the door, who had probably looked quite ordinary a moment before, rose from his chair with a lot of noise and at once fell back into it with even more noise, taking some of the tablecloth down with him and scattering plates and glasses. There was shocked, excited hubbub. Two waitresses hurried over and then the assistant manager.

Graham, turned right round in his chair, took careful note of this. When he had seen enough he turned back and said, 'Have you settled the bill, et cetera? I think we might as well leave quietly now, don't you? There's nothing much to be done for that poor fellow by the look of him, though needless to say I'm no judge. In any event, you and I can do him no good by gazing and gawking here.' After a pause during which he refreshed his memory of the scene and noted any new developments, he went on with an air of solicitude, 'Though maybe – forgive me, I didn't think – maybe you know him?'

'No, I don't know him.' Patrick not merely thought they might as well leave, he wanted to leave so urgently, so violently that it seemed to him that if he had been anybody else he would have run out of the restaurant in the first few seconds and gone on running.

'If we keep to the other side of this partition we can avoid passing directly by, can we not? Unless of course you'd like to call at the toilet, which I see is close by the – '

'No. No, I can wait.'

They went out into the street where, because of the time of year, it was still not quite dark. The rain that had been falling earlier had stopped, but there was enough of it left on the roadway for vehicles' tyres to make a continuous sizzling sound as they passed to and fro. Just when it seemed Graham must have decided to keep his mouth shut he spoke up again.

'It's a trite enough reflection, but an event of that kind forces one's own petty concerns back into perspective with something of a jolt.'

Patrick had to fight down a second impulse to run. 'Yes,' he said. 'Yes.'

After that Graham did keep quiet, but only until they were approaching Waterloo Bridge, when after a great many preludial glances he said, 'I should have remembered we were touching on a subject particularly abhorrent to you. I'm sorry.'

'That's all right,' said Patrick, reflecting that it was one of Graham's great virtues that when he said he was sorry he sounded sorry, not huffy. But then of course he was a bloke.

'You told me once it was not so much the event you found disagreeable to consider as the subsequent state. As I no doubt said at the time, you must see that that's . . .'

With some difficulty Patrick refrained from looking at the river as he drove over it. 'Illogical. Yes, you did say. And I do see it is. If you could just – '

'If you'll cast your mind back to the time before you were born, you'll agree with me that it was perfectly tolerable.'

'But that was going to end. Tell me more about your marriage.'

Graham answered up readily enough, making it clear that his remarks since that subject lapsed had been made out of various senses of duty. 'There's no more in particular. In general, well, let me just suggest that as the years have passed I've come to know a certain amount about women as a sex, though obviously not in your sense.'

'Oh, fuck my sense. Sorry, Graham, I mean . . . forget my view of that or of anything else.'

'I have upset you with my stupid blundering talk. Do please forgive me.'

He still sounded sorry. Patrick told him there was no offence with as much as he could manage in the way of sounding sincere back, but neither spoke for the rest of the journey and when they got out of the car by the builder's yard a horrible feeling of indifference hung between them. Left to himself Graham would mutter a few formalities, slide off to his bed and in the morning mutter some more and be away. Patrick found he could not face that outcome, but again when he tried to think of something to say he could not concentrate, nor by then even

195

remember anything they had talked about since leaving the restaurant.

There were still plenty of cars hurrying up and down, though no pedestrians but themselves. No daylight at all was left now and the moon was hidden or not up. Side by side they moved over to the flight of steps. Patrick said suddenly, 'It's better to have someone than no one at all, isn't it?'

'That's one of those propositions that become harder to sustain the further they're explored.' Graham almost gabbled in his relief that talk was on again. 'Someone, maybe. Anyone, havers, as we say north of the Border. And then again someone maybe not.' They turned into the walk at the top of the steps. 'Are your neighbours here reasonably well behaved?'

'Not too bad. As neighbours, that is.'

A light was on in 1A, though a dim one, and out of the open transom window there came the sound of a woman sobbing loudly. That would have been to please Stevie. He loved TV dramas, being more highbrow than Eric, who was partial to Westerns and crime series. No light showed in 1D, with Harold still presumably carousing at his do in the City and Wendy out on the prowl in Hampstead or Chelsea, hoping to find something a little bit special. 1E too was dark: no Tim.

Patrick was glad he was not coming back to 1B on his own. He brought out the Scotch.

'Oh no thank you, I'm just fine,' said Graham. Then he hesitated. 'It's still quite early, after all. I imagine if I well and truly drown it . . .' Having asked for and obtained leave to visit the lavatory, he hesitated again. 'Self-confidence and insecurity,' he said as he stood by the foot of the stairs. 'Overweening self-confidence and fathomless insecurity. You'd think they were poles apart, precluded by definition from co-existing in the same person unless one were to be a mere simulacrum, an artificial screen for the other. But no, there they are, side by side and autonomous, full-blown, in women.'

With that he went rushing upstairs, but was barely out of sight when the doorbell chimed. By all that was wonderful it could not be Jenny back after all, and it could not, it was Tim. If he had once dithered on this threshold there was none at all of that now, and he was in the sitting-room in two seconds.

'Jenny gone to bed?'

'She's away just till the morning. Where did you spring from? Your light wasn't on.'

'What? No, er, no I was next door. Fixing things up with Eric and Stevie.'

'Fixing things up?'

'We're going on an expedition one night this week.'

'An expedition? Sorry, what sort of exhibition? Fuck, I mean expedition?'

At this point the cistern upstairs began to flush, but Tim gave no sign of having heard. 'I say, do you think I could have a drink?' he asked.

Patrick was in the kitchen getting a glass when Graham reappeared and saw him but evidently remained unaware of Tim, having for his part not heard anyone ring the bell or be let in. 'From time to time,' said Graham weightily, 'my wife accuses me of thinking her boring. It doesn't seem to have occurred to her that this might be because she's boring.' Moving up to Patrick, he added man-to-man, 'To her mind, her being boring is a thing I do.'

Now he did notice Tim, who had looked on without the least apparent curiosity. Patrick introduced them in three and a half words apiece and rather wearily poured drinks. In silence, the two almost bowed almost stiffly to each other, behaving rather like two – well, two somethings-or-other, thought Patrick. Two climatological dendrologists or career torturers, pre-eminent in their respective domains but divided on some technical points. There seemed nothing to be done. Perhaps if he waited for a minute one or other of them would fall down dead.

'I just put my head in,' said Tim, settling himself comfortably with his glass in the best, most-newly-reupholstered armchair, 'to tell you I've managed to arrange that little outing with Eric and Stevie. Really just to thank you.'

'But you've already told me about the outing, and thank me for what?'

'Let's just say, for your good offices in making it possible,' said Tim, showing what he could do in the man-to-man line when it came to his turn.

No *don't* let's *just say* it or anything else, you raving lunatic, thought Patrick – what are you trying to do? 'Oh, that's all right. Well, Graham and I had quite a decent meal at – '

But Tim had already started to say to Graham, in a tone of

considerate explanation, 'These friends of Patrick's have very kindly promised to take me on a tour of, you know, some of these clubs you can go to in London now.' He was wearing a bright green polo sweater and did look fairly thoroughly disreputable in a tiresome, unilluminating way.

'You'll simply have to excuse me,' said Graham. 'I do not *know* or have the slightest acquaintance with any club of the kind I imagine you to refer to.'

To this urgent appeal for enlightenment Tim said, 'Well, between ourselves I've only a vague idea, but according to these friends of Patrick's you simply – '

'Nor have I the slightest desire to be instructed on the subject.'

'Caelum, non animum mutant qui trans mare currunt,' said Patrick firmly. 'Horace,' he added, and went on to add more. It was easy work for one who not so long before and just the other side of the party wall had damped down, at any rate for a time, the fiery Stevie with a comparable display of classical lore. That was how the old learning would end, he thought to himself while he talked about the problems of excessive leisure: like references to scripture, not understood but dimly recognised and venerated. 'Strenua nos exercet inertia – it might have been written yesterday,' he declared.

They seemed to be making some effort to follow him, but each in remarkably similar ways was using movements of his face to transmit urgent curiosity about who and what the hell the other might be. Patrick stopped for a moment in the hope of seeing them catch each other at it, but of course these two never would, so he started off again. He was on to dishwashers when Graham choked on a sudden gulp of whisky and water and went into a fit of coughing. Just as suddenly Patrick remembered that it was Graham's coughing-fits that used to bring on his renowned sneezing-fits, and sure enough at that very moment Tim's features began to pucker into the fretful mask that announced one of his own. Now they caught each other's eye.

A pang of dread and desperation ran through Patrick. He could not have borne, would himself have to die should it turn out to be the only certain way for him to miss, a sneezing-match between these two after all that had taken place that day and evening. His life hung in the balance for the time it took Graham's last searching cough to die away in grunts and Tim's features, as though sprayed with some relaxing agent, to return to normal, or normal for him. The moment of decision passed, never to return. But for a space there lingered in the air a sense of historic anti-climax, as if Christian and Turkish champions had sheathed their swords, turned their chargers about and cantered silently from the field.

The lowering of tension brought readiness to move. All three got up. Tim drained his drink, told Graham it had been fun to meet him, thanked Patrick again and was gone.

Graham stood for some moments looking at Patrick and breathing noisily. 'Who was that . . . person?'

'Lives in the end flat here. Well, he's going to.'

'Going to? What did he mean, it was fun to meet me?'

'Just an expression. Now, if you don't mind – '

'He's clearly some sort of homosexual.'

It crossed Patrick's mind that to have conveyed so much, and clearly too, to old Graham was something of a milestone in Tim's life, but he just said, 'Well, yes, he thinks he is. Some sort.'

'*Thinks* he is? Surely a man knows that about himself without taking *thought*.'

'You would suppose so, wouldn't you? It's, it's more complicated than that.'

'Oh is it now? You obviously have access to knowledge denied me.'

'Graham, it's not my fault,' said Patrick, hoping not to have to embark on a cosmic defence of sexual deviance. 'He isn't whatever he is for my benefit.'

'No,' said Graham, conceding the truth of that. 'Life just seems to have become very strange in London. Unrecognisable.' He sighed, contemplating it. 'What did that fellow think he was doing, going on in such terms to you and me?'

'I wondered too. He was probably warming up to demonstrating how thoroughly all right it is to be open about things like homosexuality. Not too convincingly, perhaps.'

'Things like . . . Oh well. They call them *queers* I believe. I remember there was a boy at my school who'd somehow heard of that, and we all thought . . . Excuse me.' Graham took out and unwrapped a couple of small squarish tablets and crunched them up and sluiced them down with water, looking very sorry for himself as he did so. 'All wine contains acid whether or not we would say it tasted acid,' he explained without rancour. 'You once said to me, no attractive woman can be unselfish. Maybe it was really attractive woman, I don't know. The distinction, if any, would be lost on the likes of me. Do you remember?'

Patrick nodded weightily. Of course he had no recollection whatsoever, but it seemed a bit mean to let all these flatteringly preserved items of table-talk go by without even a flicker. 'M'm,' he said.

'Well, first of all, any implication that it takes real attractiveness, or even mere attractiveness, to produce selfishness in a woman would be false. But, leaving that aside, the original statement in itself admits of one exception known to me. Jenny.'

Patrick had seen it coming, but only a second ahead. His mind was otherwise blank. He nodded again.

'I hope,' said Graham, spacing out his words, 'that you fully appreciate the fact,' and gave it a moment to sink in before going on to ask, 'Do you know what to me sums up, what epitomises, I can only call it the decline of our society?'

That was a tough one, but Patrick handled it. 'No,' he said.

'There's a little place in the High Street where I get my hair cut – so did you in those days.'

'I remember.' So he did this time: it was there that, about the time of the discovery of steam, Graham had solicited the attention of the long-nosed girl who had sold the razor-blades and took the money (often giving wrong change), and had once or twice lured her unavailingly out to the cinema.

'There's a plain but I should have thought perfectly decent woman assistant in the shop part I've known for years who the other day, without the slightest encouragement from me, quite out of the blue you understand, and altogether openly, we weren't even alone in the shop at the time, asked me if I would care to buy some *contraceptives*.'

Neither of them could find very much to say after that.

Patrick was used to spells of sudden extreme fear from no immediate or apparent source, used to them in the sense that he had experienced dozens of them in his life and yet was still there, still at large, not in the sense of being able to do anything with them, certainly not to assure himself at the onset of each one that, like all its predecessors, it would vanish completely in a few minutes. So, immediately on shutting behind him the door of the empty bedroom, he felt as if his mind was not his any more, no longer his – not somebody else's instead, just nobody's in particular, away on its own, leaving head and body and limbs to get on by themselves. Knowing he must not disturb Graham he made a continuous babble on a low note with his lips and tongue. A book, a novel, anyway a book was on the bedside table and he opened it and ran his eyes to and fro over the print while he felt for and found the little bottle of sleeping pills and put two in his mouth, then three. Still with the book held before him, still humming and mumbling, he went into the bathroom, got water, swallowed, went back to the bedroom and began to undress, mostly one-handed because it was not so good when he put the book down even though he never stopped looking hard at the words.

Dr Leacock had explained that they came on because some-thing perfectly real and substantial and meaningful had happened to him to frighten him, to raise the tension in him to the level where he was vulnerable to the form of panic he had become habituated to. Sometimes it might be two things, one to produce what was known as a state of high arousal, the other to build on that and make an attack almost inevitable as soon as external conditions were right. It would help, Dr Leacock had added, if he could manage to objectify the situation by identifying the real cause and allotting it its factual import-ance. Patrick tried to do that now, but found that the nearer he got to giving person-who-had-gone-away-and-left-him a name and nasty-thing-that-had-happened-earlier-on a description the worse it became, so that he had to hum on a higher note for a bit and bite his lips. A few inches at a time he settled himself so that he was half lying down on his side of the bed with the book held up in front of him, and it was not really very long before he felt his thoughts slipping away from him again but differently, marvellously, somewhere else, and he dropped the book and fell fast asleep with the light on.

Fourteen

When Jenny got back to 1B at a quarter past ten the next morning she was surprised to find Patrick still there. He called out to her gently as soon as her key turned in the lock to prevent her being alarmed, though in fact that sort of thing never bothered her. They held each other tight. He looked tired and a little jittery, she thought, with his hair not parted quite as straight as he liked it to be.

'You're usually gone at this time,' she said, and she had been expecting that today, counting on it.

'I told them at the office they mustn't be so slavishly dependent on me. Elsie's crisis under control?'

'It was more she just wanted a good moan.'

They moved into the sitting-room. Without turning her head to and fro too much Jenny saw that, far from harbouring even the most minor of overnight piggy messes, it was in almost good enough order for the eyes of Linda herself.

'Husband acting up, was he?' asked Patrick.

'Oh. No, er, evidently the husband's as nice as pie, never stops begging her to come back to him and all forgiven. The boy-friend's the one who acts up. Keeps saying she gets in the way of him being a writer.'

'He'll come to thank her in the end. The rest of us can get on with thanking her right away.' Patrick spoke with less than his usual animation.

'Are you all right, pet?'

'Yes, I'm fine. I had one of my frights last night. Not a bad one, I didn't let go. No, shut up, love, you must have a bit of freedom, I've got to learn to handle it by myself, can't go on

202

depending on you all the time. Anyway, Graham was here, stayed the night.'

He shut her up on that by telling her more than once that she would have had to read his thoughts to know the old bugger was coming. By the time he got on to the meal at Gioberti's he was beginning to look and sound more like his usual self. 'Can you imagine Graham on marriage? He said he'd been forced to settle for . . .'

Patrick stopped speaking so abruptly that Jenny said, 'What is the matter, sweet? Please tell me.'

'Inoperable hangover, would you like a coffee, I've got the whole shooting-match lined up, only instant if that's okay with you . . .'

She had been sure simply from his being there at all that something she knew nothing about was wrong, and now she was sure again. She hoped it was not in himself, none of that, just to do with him, money or work or the flat or one of those. It would have to come in its own time, though, or rather his: neither he nor she had any sympathy with the kind of woman who was always jumping guns and demanding to be told what was 'really' going on instead of letting it emerge in the way at least one grown-up person had thought was best.

Actually this particular bit of emerging, as she had sensed it would, came after only a couple of minutes, and by then she had as good as got there herself without realising it.

'Everything in order?' she asked when he left a space for it.

'No, love, everything isn't, I'm sorry to say. Frankie's gone missing. Since two nights ago – I haven't seen him since you went off.'

'Oh. Oh, I thought it was something terrible. Well, he's bound to come back.'

'I kept going out and calling him and beating his plate like you do. But . . . I'm afraid I forgot last night when Graham and I got in. We'd got a bit . . .'

'Of course, don't worry about it, pet.'

'Two nights is nothing in this weather.'

'He'll turn up when he's ready. Well, I think I'll just go for a lick and a promise.'

Putting her things away and freshening up, which took all of two minutes, still gave Jenny more time than she needed to weigh up how likely or unlikely in fact it was that Frankie would come back. There could be no figures that would help when all sorts of stuff like how intelligent he was, and how comfortable he was living with them, obviously had so much of a bearing, and no newspaper articles or wireless talks on the subject came to mind. True, they were always going on about a tremendous lot of UK cats (and dogs too) being reported lost every year, but they never seemed to say what percentage of them came back or after how long. She did think for a second of ringing up home, or rather her mother, but that would definitely have been just childish and pointless anyway. Either Frankie was going to come strolling in as cool as you please and looking round in amazement, wondering what all the fuss was about, or he was gone for good, simple as that, and after all, she might as well face it, what was so dreadful about losing a cat?

But the important thing now was not to let herself be upset to the point where her determination to go on behaving normally might start breaking down. The reason for rushing off to Elsie had not only been to help herself to a shoulder to cry on, or snivel on. She had always been rather a hard woman and had never really seen the good side of Patrick – not that it did any harm to listen to someone talking from that angle occasionally. No, the excursion had had at least as much to do with giving herself a cooling-off period away from him in which she could get over the shock she had had at those people's party. (To call it a shock was probably rather showy and grumpy, but it was hard to think of a proper word.) Anyway, whatever she did she was not going to have a huge row about it because in her experience they were just painful without doing any good, and because she hated the whole idea of being an accusing wife, and also slightly because to be quite honest with herself she was slightly afraid of Patrick. Not that he had ever raised his voice or raised his hand to her any more than her father had, and she had feared and loved him too. But there it was, she had never been clear why.

Well then, with rows ruled out, the only alternatives were working away at being a bloody misery round the place, taking it out of him so much at a time and when asked what was the matter putting on a special voice and face to say there was nothing, how could there be anything, forsooth, which in her opinion was even more objectionable than row-launching, and on the other hand gritting her teeth and trying to behave normally while waiting for Mrs Big-bottom Porter-King to slide off his agenda. Jenny inspected herself in her dressing-table mirror to see whether she looked to herself like the sort of woman who could manage that, and found to her disappointment that all she could in conscience say she looked was healthy, cautious and a bit stupid.

She had rather expected Patrick to be ready to leave when she came downstairs, but she found him hanging about waiting for her with a sort of hurt expression and manner she had seen before. Her heart sank. She was suddenly sure he was going to tell her what was really wrong and it would be worse than any cat.

'I just wanted to say,' he said, 'I am terribly sorry about Frankie. I blame myself. I should have called him for much longer and stayed out there and gone looking for him and not given up till I found him.'

'You couldn't have found him if he wasn't there, pet.'

'No, I know, but I do want you to see I really care and I really do know how much he means to you. I like him all right but it's more than that with you. It's more like a . . . I know I'm not a very good husband, I let you down in all sorts of ways . . .'

'Please stop,' she said, and tried to press her lips together.

' . . . but I am sorry about it and I want you to realise that if he has gone, no, whether he has or not I'll be better, I'll be like I was before . . .'

Even then it might have been all right if he had managed to keep his silly arms to himself and not leant his cheek against her forehead in the way he always had. As it was, all those fine resolutions of hers about carrying on normally went bust in a second, and before she knew where she was she had flopped down in an armchair and was trying to push the tears back into her eyes, furious with herself and not tickled pink with him either. There was a phrase for what he was doing, having it both ways or running with the hare and hunting with the hounds or something like that, but she was not going to work it out now and the sooner the blithering idiot left her to herself the better all round. At last, after enough telling for two he picked up his swanky brief-case and cleared off, still hurt, baffled, anxious, mystified and probably several more.

There would have been no point in trying to make out that what followed was anything but a pretty rotten day. It stretched before her like an Easter holiday with no outings or anyone coming, or like waiting to be seen at a hospital. To kick off with they were expecting her at a real hospital, the one with all those children waiting for her to teach them every perishing week-day morning. The previous morning she had had to ring it up from Elsie's, of course getting not the nice sister from Manchester but her nasty hairy-faced Irish assistant, and apologise and explain she felt too rotten to come to work, which was nearly absolutely true though not in the way she made it sound. This morning she felt not much less rotten quite honestly but she would have to go in regardless, would have to go in pretty fast too if she was not to be disgustingly late.

Then of course again she ran into the Irish SRN, who said, 'You're looking all worn to a frazzle.'

'Well, I – '

'Try and get a decent early night once in a way if you know what I'm talking about.'

Women like that always seemed to think Jenny spent every spare minute out on the tiles. It was something to do with being very dark, her sister had explained once, and admittedly she had sometimes wondered how different her life might have been if she had just been fair-skinned like Trixie.

Things were no better with six-year-old Brian who was taking a long time recovering from having his tonsils out. She started reading him a story, popular enough with others of his age, about a bad squirrel who stole the nuts a good squirrel had providently stored, simplifying the language as she went as a reaction to the chronic dullness of his gaze. Soon, after some moments of suspicious fiddling under the bedclothes, he pushed his forefinger up his nose hard enough to lift his head a couple of inches. No child of hers would have been allowed to do that, any more than he would have been landed with a haircut that made him look like a vicar's little girl, but neither was any business of hers. When the finger came down again she thought she saw a dim flicker in his eye.

'Yes, Brian?'

'Our teacher at school,' he said in his incredibly nasal voice, then at once dropped the whole matter, indefinitely to judge by his behaviour as he followed open-mouthed the flight of an invisible and very slow-flying bird round the ward.

'Your teacher at school . . . ?'

'Oh. Oh yes. Yes. Yes, our teacher at school . . .' – he nearly went off again, but scrambled back in the nick of time – ' . . . she read us a story about a boy called Sam who helped his . . . sister look after their . . . father when their . . . *mother* had to go to the hospital because she was ill.' He breathed heavily with the effort of this formulation.

'That sounds . . .' Jenny kept quiet about what she thought it sounded.

'Our teacher . . .' she says stories about animals and fairies and kings and queens and animals and witches are old-fashioned. She says they're old- . . . fashioned.'

With the last few words he focused on Jenny quite closely by his standards, managing to suggest that if he had known how to set about it he might have assured her in so many words that her choice of story for this or any other morning was altogether to be expected of her. On bidding him farewell, for longer than perhaps he counted on, she reflected that he finished ahead of the SRN, who at least had never tried to tell her she was old-fashioned at twenty-eight. Then lunch in the usually very good canteen featured macaroni cheese that was lots of thick tepid dry pipes of macaroni with a doll's portion of raw cheese at one end, and the only ones she knew there were the Jamaican nurse and the Canadian student nurse. And then at the library everything seemed to be out bar an enormous saga about Southern belles, but then she spotted a new Elizabeth Taylor on the returns shelf. So after all she settled down fairly happily in her chair in the sitting-room with those two and a milky coffee.

As it turned out the coffee was fine, but the new Elizabeth Taylor turned out to be an old Elizabeth Taylor in a new impression and with a different outside, and she must have been slipping not to have checked, always advisable with an author whose books were marvellous but rather the same. And then the Southern belles saga, though by another woman, was a terrible let down, with page after page in the historic present. This was probably meant to be poetical, but what it did for Jenny was keep reminding her of the style her father's less educated friends had told their anecdotes in.

Somehow, going round the plants, doing a pathetic bit of washing, messing about with the furniture, turning out the kitchen cupboard, she got through some of the rest of the afternoon. Picture of a thoroughly useful busy contented housewife, she thought to herself. Even when she had tidied every drawer in the flat, which they said made you feel on top of everything, it was still only half-past four. She made herself a pot of tea at working-to-rule speed and reckoned she would not exactly have to act her head off to droop and moon round Patrick depressingly enough to force him to take her out to dinner somewhere. But if she had wanted to rehearse the drooping and mooning she would not have had time, because before she had finished her second cup there was Patrick's key in the door. It was so unexpectedly early that she passed up a good chance of getting the act off the ground and just went out to meet him as usual.

'You're back early,' she told him, and then her heart sank again, because his face showed he was going to tell her something more. For a moment she thought she was in for one of his diversion tactics, when he made out he was bothered about something at work or was feeling sick after a bad bottle of wine at lunch to camouflage an attack of post-adultery guilt. She almost hoped it was that, in fact, because all she had to do then was let it happen. But no, there was none of the peevishness that was always there when he had been misbehaving. He kissed her about as passionately as a man might have kissed his auntie at a funeral and in a couple of minutes they had congregated in the sitting-room, by now more like two people who had turned up too early at a public meeting. She would have given a lot to have been able to stop the whole thing cold, but what with her nature and his nature and their lives together there was no chance of that.

'I've kept thinking about this morning,' he began. 'Haven't managed to get it out of my mind for two minutes together. Just tell me, love . . . now I know, I said so before, I know Frankie means a great deal to you and of course you were upset at the thought of him perhaps being lost, but what I couldn't help thinking, I couldn't get away from the thought that it was more than that. It was, wasn't it?'

'Oh, Patrick, don't let's go into all this,' she said in her hopeless way.

'We've got to.' He went into a swallowing routine, pushing his chin down and opening his lips. 'I want to say something.' He paused again and then hurried on. 'I've been having an affair with the Porter-King woman next door. There's all sorts of reasons why I shouldn't have done but I have. And you knew, I don't know how but you knew.'

She sat bent forward in her chair, waiting for him to get on to the next bit and thinking that at this stage a deaf person, one unable to lip-read, could easily have mistaken the scene for one where a man was telling a woman that he was very sorry and all that, but he would have no alternative but to fire her unless she returned the money she had stolen. Though the matter would go no further.

'I also told you I was going to be better, a better husband. Well, I am. I've never admitted having an affair before unless I've had to, have I?'

'No, but . . .'

'Yes? What were you going to say?'

'Go on.'

'It was just her being there really. Anyway I just want you to know we never, we've never done it in here. For what that's worth. There was a chance of that but I wouldn't take it. Anyway.'

'I see.' Now she actually knew it made no difference to her how near he was when he did it, short of there in front of her, and he would not have been far enough away if he did it on top of Mount Everest.

'In fact that was what put a stop to it really. Well, you don't want to hear about that. The point is it's been put a stop to. It's finished. As of yesterday.'

'Does she know it is? Or have you just decided?'

'Oh, she's in no doubt there.' He unwisely tried a laugh with that.

'And you're afraid she's going to blow her top and go on about it to me, so you want me to hear about it from you first. Well, I can quite – '

'No, it's not like that at all. She's not going to say anything.'

'You hope.'

'No. Because if Harold knew he'd give her a really serious going-over. Physically. She told me he beat her up once for being leered at in the golf club.'

She had to smile with him then but not for long. 'Oh,' she said, 'so he's not the puny little worm you'd taken him for after all.'

'There are worse things than worms.'

He had asked for a very nasty one back, and he knew he had, and he would have got it fair and square if she had not started to get cross. 'How do you know I'm not going to go straight off and tell Harold and hang about to watch the fun?'

He shook his head firmly. 'I know you wouldn't do that,' he said, reclaiming a point or two for being sure.

'I can't see . . . If it's over, and she's keeping her mouth shut, why do you want me to know about it?'

'Well . . .' He seemed to consider. 'So that you and I can make some kind of fresh start. Things out in the open. No secrets between us.'

'There weren't many before, really, were there? Me with none from you and you wrong about thinking you had one from me. Unless this is just a start and you've got a few more you want to get off your chest.'

'No, that's the lot, I assure you.'

'Oh, good.' Jenny felt her cheeks turning hot. 'When you've been like this before you've sometimes gone down on your knees and begged me not to leave you. When I wasn't saying I might. Well, if I ever do, it won't be because of your frightful sins, it'll be because you're a bloody fool. Here I was, I was just starting to get used to the idea, or trying to, hoping it would fade away eventually like always, and here you go like a bull in a china shop, pushing and shoving things out in the open. Can't you see things like that are better left not out in the open? Who's supposed to be better off?'

'I just thought – '

'Of course you're the one that's better off, showing me how much you care, and forget about how I might feel about it, being told, that's not the same as being sure in your own mind. You selfish pig. Selfish to do it in the first place, well yes, but bringing it up like this, that's worse because you'd time to think about it, hadn't you? Aren't you ever going to see – '

The telephone started ringing. Patrick swore and said let it ring, but Jenny had been brought up in a world where serious news, including bad news, was always liable to arrive by telephone. She hurried over, then paused to get her breath.

210

'Oh Jenny, it's Graham McClintoch speaking,' said a clear, fully articulated voice, one so distinctive that after a syllable or two its owner had no need to mention either of his names. At the moment it was full of affection too, which made it that much harder for Jenny to answer up.

'Hang on a moment Graham I'll just turn the wireless off,' she managed, and put her hand over the mouthpiece, taking it away again to flick it discouragingly at Patrick, who had followed her and was now hanging about in a concerned way and should have been thinking himself ruddy lucky not to have been treated to a hearty smack or two across the chops. After a few deep breaths she said into the telephone, 'I can hear you better now,' and stuttered maddeningly getting the second word out.

Graham seemed not to notice. First taking a little while to tell her how sorry he was to have missed her last night, he asked if by any chance Patrick was there.

'No,' said Jenny, looking at her husband for the first time for some minutes, staring him straight in the eye in fact. 'No, Patrick isn't here.'

'Oh. Perhaps you'd kindly mention to him that I wasn't offered the post I was going for. No no, it's nothing. A relief in a way. Well now, I mustn't keep you.' There was quite a long pause, then, 'Is all well with you?'

So she had unwillingly broken an old and important rule and let something show to an outsider, even though he was a family friend. She said everything was fine as normally as she could without thinking too hard about it. At the end of another, shorter pause he sent his love and rang off, leaving behind quite a strong impression of unsatisfactoriness and regret.

It soon faded. A lot seemed to have gone on in 1B in the few moments she had been speaking to Graham. She reached out to Patrick and they put their arms round each other, loosely and in an exhausted kind of way.

'He didn't get the job but he doesn't mind,' she said. 'I'm sorry I called you what I did. A selfish pig, I mean. You are getting worse, though. If you ever go off with someone, you know, it won't be because you're that smitten, it'll be because you're a bloody fool. Hey, listen to me saying that as if it was good afternoon. It must be living down south. Well now, I think I'd like a drink. More living down south.'

211

Patrick was delighted, triumphant. He set about making her a gin and tonic as if he had invented not merely that drink but all other drinks and specially for her, pouring himself a whisky by way of an afterthought. Jenny thought to herself that she had not been afraid of him much during that little lot. It must have been the getting cross that did it.

They settled down in their chairs. Jenny watched the pleased, relieved expression draining away from Patrick's face as he got himself ready for the last serious part that would round the whole business off.

'I'm sorry,' he said, shaking his head from time to time, 'I see it was selfish of me to go on like that as if I was the injured party, I just didn't think, what I said was quite true, I couldn't stop thinking how upset you were, I just wanted to sort of show you, I know I made a mess of it . . .'

'Poor little thing,' she said, having to go over to him, 'you did all that gearing-up to put yourself in the wrong and eat humble pie, it can't have been easy, and then I go for you like a pickpocket, don't I? Never mind . . .'

So now everything was all right, until next time of course, only it would have spoilt the party to say so, and after a bit what she had absolutely honestly not been expecting to happen happened, well all right, she supposed she might have done if she had actually been thinking about that side of life, anyway it did. And after that, ha ha, there was no question about them not going to go out for dinner somewhere. She gorgeously slept for a bit before getting into the bath and perhaps dropping off there too until the chime of the doorbell brought her round. As things had been going she would not have been surprised, in a manner of speaking, if the caller had been John Lennon or President de Gaulle, but as she first heard and then saw it was Tim.

'Just on impulse,' he kept saying, almost waving a glass of whisky about. He had perhaps had a couple of quick drinks already. This evening he was dressed and even to some extent had his hair done like a country gentleman in a play about the 1930s, with leather patches on his jacket. 'Little house-warming,' he said nearly as often.

It appeared he thought his set-up in 1E Lower Ground was now ready to be lived in, or at least inspected by those well disposed towards him. When Jenny got there, full to overflowing of curiosity, she was slightly cast down to find the place looking like a stage-set of nothing so definite as the 1930s, just hung with white and full of white-and-gold padded chairs and sofas with spiral bits at the tops of the legs and expensive-looking polished tables. There were pictures on the walls that would have done for anywhere at all where nobody lived.

'Yes,' said Tim, 'I thought it was time I made the move.' He was giving out drinks in glasses that were clean but not bright, almost milky, probably straight out of the packing, Jenny decided, and thought she could see a wisp of straw in one of them. 'You get on all right with Eric and Stevie, don't you?' he asked, blinking at a stuffed olive and pushing his mouth in and out at it before he put it into it. 'I thought I'd just . . .'

'Oh yes, very much so,' said Patrick in a way that reminded Jenny of how he used to say he was in favour of breaking down the British class system, enthusiastically but in a kind of general way as well. By moving his eyes he also signalled to her that he had something of interest to impart about those two.

'You like them, don't you, Jenny?'

'Yes.'

'You've seen that the bill's going through the House of Commons the day after tomorrow?'

'The bill?' Ancient Rome, thought Jenny, that was what the furniture reminded her of, or rather of a film of. The sort with emperors.

'To legalise homosexual acts between consenting adults in private.' Noticing perhaps that her expression stayed the same at this news, Tim went on, 'For this purpose an adult is a person over twenty-one.'

'Oh, I thought all that was all right already,' she said before he could start explaining anything else.

'Not in law.'

'Oh, of course I was forgetting you were to do with the law.'

And she had forgotten for a second longer that she had heard this from his sister, the blue-clad Mrs Wolstenholme, with other more basic bits she had not had time to pass on to Patrick. He took notice now of what she had let out, but not Tim, who swallowed largely from his glass, seemed to think for a bit and said,

'As you know, all this time I've felt very much constrained and . . . hemmed in . . . by the law as it stands at this moment.

213

It's had a great restraining effect on me and no doubt many others, as it was intended to.'

Jenny had no certain information about the many others, though she was still sceptical about their having been restrained by anything much. If the law had hemmed Tim in at all it was the first she had heard of it, Patrick too, evidently. But neither of them said.

'Patrick's probably told you I've fixed up with Eric and Stevie to be taken round one or two of the queer clubs the very night the bill goes through. A little tour of inspection and initiation. And celebration I suppose.'

When Jenny stopped somewhere in the middle of uttering the word 'initiation' Patrick said, 'No actually I haven't had a chance because she's been away only for a couple of nights seeing an old pal who . . .' and enough more to make Tim sit down on one of the white sofas quite possibly for the first time ever, and start juddering his leg. Not much later there was a pounding on the outer door, perhaps in token of a defective bell, and Eric and Stevie were let in.

One of Stevie's good points as seen by Jenny, and to be plain there were not all that many of them, was the way he made her feel less outnumbered when she was the only girl. This evening he was being extra like that, discussing the local grocer's shops with her and complaining chummily about the queueing in the Post Office and the smart-alecky little baggage at the cash-desk at the butcher's, where did she imagine she was, he would have liked to know, with her eye-shadow and her evening frock in the day with everything on top falling out. To have all this delivered in a Drake-is-going-West-lads accent made it better listening, but she hoped that that was as far as they were going to go for now along present lines. She happened not to be in the least interested in how much of a girl (or middle-aged lady) Stevie really thought he was and just why Eric always called him her.

Unwillingly but unstoppably, her thoughts flew to one of the innumerable small pieces of mild and not-so-mild awfulness about sex that Patrick was always dropping into the conversation without giving her a chance to dodge. Years ago, evidently, there had been a club in Wales which he had given a very rude name and which, at the time of a police raid, had been staging a cabaret turn by a chap dressed up as the Queen

214

of Sheba. What were you supposed to make of that? She looked at Stevie, who was now saying he was unhappy at the way the world seemed to be going, and asked herself what he would have made of the Queen of Sheba. Rather than answer herself she thought of another piece of awfulness, featuring a Mr Cornock. He was a commercial traveller who had allegedly done his travelling with his wife, a kitchen boiler and a lot of ropes and straps for her to fasten him to it with. Quite different in a way from the Queen of Sheba, and yet the same in being a huge way from anything she would ever understand. Perhaps there was not actually more of it; perhaps it was just you heard about it more.

Not before time, Patrick said something to Stevie. Tim appeared on Jenny's other side. 'So you've been talking to Ann.'

'You're very quick, Mr Vatcher.'

'In some things. You have to be, in the law. Which also teaches you to not necessarily show you've been quick at the time. Not a common name, Vatcher. Norman French. Means a cowherd. What else did she tell you?'

'Not much. Nothing to your discredit or that made you look silly. A bit about your wife, and you've had your difficulties the two of you like everyone else. Nothing serious.'

'She does talk, old Ann. I suppose you gave her a drink. Did you realise or suspect or anything that I was married?'

'No, I had no idea until she told me.'

'You're an amazing girl, Jenny. You're the only one I've ever met who wouldn't have said oh yes to that, you can't fool me, I wasn't born yesterday you know. Actually I suppose Gussie mightn't've. Gussie's my wife.'

'Yes, I know. Your sister wants you to get in touch with her, with your wife.'

'Oh, groan. All right. I mean consider your message delivered.'

'And it's no business of mine, but I gathered your wife wanted you to get in touch with her too.'

'Noted. Noted. You won't tell anybody about this little scheme of mine, will you?'

'If you mean your tour of inspection of those places you mentioned, certainly not, I promise you.'

Tim seemed not to notice the indignation with which she had spoken, or rather started to speak, because halfway through she suddenly thought there might be a Queen of Sheba turn at the club he was going to, perhaps always was at such places by tradition, sort of like the National Anthem, and her voice shook slightly. Anyway, he just said, 'Good girl,' and then, with a sharp look not typical of him, 'You don't think it's a very good idea, do you, my scheme? And please don't say it's no business of yours, because I'm asking you.'

This came out at his usual full volume. It was rude, her mother had impressed on her, to tell people to talk more quietly; what you did was set them an example without overdoing it. So Jenny said quietly, 'No, Tim, I don't think it's a good idea. I think it's a silly idea. It's a mad idea. I can't think why they agreed to take you, those two.'

'M'm, I see what you mean,' he said, not quietly. 'How it happened, I was just chatting away, and I suppose I must have said something about I'd never been anywhere like that but it sounded interesting, just for something to say really, and it was all fixed up in no time. It was Stevie's idea really, he was the one who was keen on it, I mean, Eric not so much.'

Jenny moved a couple of yards away and pretended to look at a picture of a boring-looking man without a hat on a horse as if it mattered. After wondering what she was up to for a bit, he came near enough for her to say without literally whispering, 'Of course Eric wasn't keen, he's got some sense, has Eric. Stevie's potty, surely you can see that.'

'Oh, I reckon I've got to know him a bit.'

'Not if you don't think he's potty you haven't. Look, it's not too late to call it off, you know. Just say you've had second thoughts.'

He shook his head resolutely. 'Ten to one you're right, but I've got to try it, I've got to see. Otherwise I'll always wonder.'

'Better that than know, if I'm any judge. And you didn't ask me this, but I think you're potty too.'

'Maybe I am. Don't look so worried, I'll be all right. I mean it's not as if I'm going to be actually risking my life. I'll tell you how it goes. Well, suitable bits of it anyway.'

Not more than a minute later Eric had just started to explain to Jenny that they would soon have to ban private cars in London when Patrick suddenly said in a loud voice, 'Do you know what time it is?'

'Hold on,' said Tim, carefully pushing back his cuff. 'Just

coming up to . . . half-past one.' He went on in a way that ruled out any possible humour, 'According to my watch.'

'Christ,' said Patrick to the world in general and then, grabbing Jenny's wrist, 'Come on.'

She just about thanked Tim over her shoulder and said good-bye. 'What was all that about?'

Patrick waited till they were in 1B with the door shut after them. Then he said, 'Tim just happened to mention he'd invited the people he called the other people to drop in too. On inquiry this proved to refer to Mr Harold Porter-King and his consort. Christ, that reminded me, I said, without specifying of what, and the rest you know. I thought in the circumstances we could do without them for a day or two or a lustre or two.'

'What's a lustre?' asked Jenny, preparing herself a glass of water on the rocks and feeling a spoil-sport for not finding what Patrick was saying completely as funny as he did.

'Five years. Hey . . . listen. Do you hear what I hear?'

What Jenny heard was the violent shutting of a nearby door, elaborate sound-effects with lock, keys and chain on a Bloody Tower scale, and two lots of footsteps moving away up the walk. Over it all there drifted the not very familiar but quite familiar enough sound of a high-pitched wailing male voice.

'Foof!' said Patrick. 'Talk about in the nick of knock. Well, that's the end of that. Right now madam, what do you say to the Caprice for din-dins?' He rolled his eyes boyishly on the last word to show he was not to be held responsible for it.

'Ooh, lovely, but isn't it terribly expensive?'

'I collected on my swindle-sheet today. Including a fair bit more than I laid out on my lunch with that Irishwoman. The seventy-seven-year-old one.'

217

Fifteen

Two nights later Jenny and Patrick went to a party given by a literary agent (not Trevor Fowler) at his house in Maida Vale. He was meant to give very good parties, though over all her years in London she had never quite fathomed what went to make a good party, except for costing a lot and going on a long time, especially that.

At the age of ten she had had to write an essay on the subject, 'What I Will Miss Most When I Am Grown Up', and she remembered taking up over half a page on the different excitements, like the ones you felt before Christmas and your birthday, the morning before you went off on holiday, especially anything like a camping holiday, and getting a new pair of shoes. She still thought it was a fair point, but you could hardly say you *missed* those times. Where she had been absolutely spot on was including in her list looking forward to and going to parties. Her reasoning had been off; she realised now she had been judging by the life she saw around her, and imagined parties just stopped when you were about fourteen; nevertheless she never went to one nowadays without wishing it was all over however many years it was ago.

And yet here she was going to another one, and not just because of Patrick. There was something in her that welcomed the idea, however faintly or briefly. It might be as she started to get ready, it might not be until they were going in the front door, but always she would have a moment of glad expectation that almost carried her away: perhaps *this* time ... This time what? She could think of no answer. Her father, on the other hand, would have had no difficulty there: he would have said a good deal about the triumph of hope over experience, something that had spread out as he grew older to the point where it accounted for pretty well everything people did and thought.

This evening it was late on, as she and Patrick were walking the last few yards, that Jenny felt her little thrill. Some of it was probably the gorgeous weather and the incredible display of foliage and flowers that seemed to be growing everywhere she looked. There were round specks of white and mauve blossom on the pavement, like confetti only more thickly strewn.

They moved up the broad path towards the front door past a yellow car that had been backed in off the road. A middle-aged couple waiting on the top step to be let in looked them over with the open, unsmiling curiosity and suspicion Jenny had noticed people down here going in for when they saw strangers. They were probably artistic, the man with a beard confined to his chin, the woman taller than he with a chimney-shaped fur hat on (in June?) and a military tunic that had metal buttons all over it. Between them they were exactly what Jenny was nervous of at do's like this, threatening not to make her curtsey, as at the Porter-Kings', but to ask her what stand she took on something unrecognisable to her or to address her in French.

Patrick cocked an eye at her and said, taking his time, 'Have you returned to rhymed metres in the new poem, or are you continuing your experiments with variable rhythms?' The couple joined in waiting for her reply.

'Excuse me, I'm terribly sorry to bother you, but would you please help me? I don't know this man and he's molesting me and using bad language.' It was no good: she did her best to say it, she knew it was what she ought to have been saying, but when it came to the point it was beyond her. She could not even say 'Bugger off' out loud, just went through the lip movements. He always got her like that.

The door in front of them opened at last, but whoever had opened it retreated so smartly as not to be seen by the time they were inside. Jenny muttered a question and Patrick told her the host's name again.

'And is he queer or drunk or anything?'

'Neither when I saw him last. There's a girl-friend but I don't know about her. She might be drunk, I suppose.'

'And did you say he's an agent?' She had still not managed to push quite out of her mind the belted raincoat and pulled-down felt hat under the street-lamp that agents had always had there until recently.

'Yes. This house is built on the bones of perished publishers. Ah, here, let me assist.'

Patrick considerately went back and reopened the front door to help two youngish men carry out of the house by his ankles and upper arms a third, apparently unconscious older one. Not liking to stare, Jenny turned away and at once caught sight of a tall fair-haired man standing some way off, beyond the room she was facing into, with a lot of greenery round him. It took only a second and she would probably not have noticed him at all if he had not seemed to be looking directly at her. Then Patrick was at her side again.

'What was the matter with that chap, is he dreadfully ill?' she asked solicitously, though not as solicitously as she would once have asked that sort of question.

'Not what I'd call ill, just pissed. Par for the course with him. He writes deeply sensitive and religious historical novels about the human heart as it was in the Middle Ages. You've got to work on putting back what that takes out of you, dammit.'

'Seems a shame.'

'Yes,' said Patrick, looking to and fro among the throng, 'life's full of little bits that aren't what we'd, well, you know, if it was up to us, et cetera, as many have remarked. Let's get a drink.'

If people had tended to hang back for the past half-minute they now all rushed up at once talking at once. Jenny identified that ex-girl-friend of Patrick's with the husband who was in television and knew David Frost slightly, the girl chum of theirs whose nose went too far down her face, the small bearded Australian poet from the last Gileses' party, the awful little girl poet with goggles called Vera Something who had also been there, though not the worrying Sebastian man who had wanted to drop in for a mug of char, but also Simon Giles himself, and that wife of his of course, and quite enough others once or twice or a dozen times dined with, gone to the pub with, been at the same do with, chatted to, met somewhere, seen before. Not dramatically, hardly noticeably, Jenny's hope began to trickle away and the evening to turn into just another dose of experience. But at that exact moment Patrick let out a kind of

220

controlled yell, flapped his whole arm in a wave and told her to come on.

With a sense that she knew what was going to happen without knowing or daring to say what it was, Jenny followed Patrick across the large and crowded drawing-room into a disproportionately large conservatory where a flourishing vine grew. There also grew other fruit-plants, flowers in earth-boxes and pots, cacti in a long grey metal tray at waist height, ferns, climbers, more than she could take in. On the black and white marble squares of the floor stood a bar-billiard table of the same three-hole, three-skittle pattern as the one at the British Legion at home on which, every Saturday night for years, her father had beaten the manager of the Luxor cinema in three straight games. But this too she took in only later, because for the moment her attention was entirely filled up by the tall fair-haired man she had glimpsed among the greenery a minute before.

'There you are, you old degenerate, you old *beast,*' Patrick called to him, grinning his head off. 'Love, this is the inexcusable Oswald Hart whom I've so often . . . Anyway – if I know you you'll already have discerned that this is Jenny – got it like a flash in that second. Ozzie's just back from Washington, leaving behind numerous inconsolable Congressional wives, of both parties let it be said, nothing narrowly partisan about Oz. Now I'm going to dump you on him, love, just for a couple of minutes while I find Peter and say about nine words to him before one of us gets pissed.'

Jenny remembered afterwards how Oswald Hart looked at her while this was going on, with pretended shock as part of the game, obviously, but also as if they were sort of in league, not against anybody at all, just making the two of them separate together, as a joke but seriously too. He was not as tall as she had thought though still tall, nor as fair, light brown hair really, straight, at a length that could have done with cutting but made you glad it had been left as it was. He had rather rosy cheeks, good for now, less good for a few years on perhaps.

'It's true I've been in Washington for a long time,' he said, speaking for the first time, in a completely ordinary voice without any accent whatsoever. 'Glad to be back though. Terrible weather there. Never just all right, always on the go.'

'Were you there for the politics?'

'Yes, I was writing on them. Actually we have met before. It must have been in 1963 when I was over for a bit. You hadn't been married very long. I can almost remember what you were wearing. Not quite, though, I'm afraid. Well, I say we met, we were at the same party in Staines, along with about a hundred other people. Something to do with flowers, I think it was. I had my wife with me then.'

'I just remember being at the party. They were friends of Patrick's.'

'I only saw you from a distance. It seems a pity to waste all this marvellous sunshine, doesn't it? We ought to be out in it while it's here.'

They went down a short iron staircase newly painted in a great many colours and into a garden Jenny realised she had seen the top parts of just now from the street. It was beautifully laid out with right-sized trees and shrubs and the lawn was really special, but she could somehow tell that it was all the work of someone brought in from outside, unlike the conservatory. A number of the other people from the party were strolling about in twos and threes and trying to look interested in what was growing.

'I'm sorry,' said Oswald Hart, 'I ought to have filled your glass up for you before we came out. How thoughtless of me.'

'No, don't worry, I'm quite all right with this.' If I can remember not to drink it.

'Are you sure?'

Here was a man doing what she would have betted was never seriously taken on, probably impossible, and showing interest in how someone answered that question. She tried not to overdo how very sure she was.

He nodded. 'I know it's a terrible thing to say, especially around here,' – he gave her another of his special looks and lowered his voice – 'but I've practically given it up. Drink, I mean. I've seen too many awful warnings in Washington. Of course it's a great scourge of journalists. Anyway, I still haven't learnt to like the taste, you know.'

'I do know. Or the effect either in my case.'

'Aren't people disappointing when they're drunk?

'Send you into a gloom if you let them.'

'You don't mind me taking you away from everyone like this, do you?'

222

'No, I don't mind.'

Near the top of the garden away from the house there was a place to sit, a circle paved like the conservatory with a painted metal framework forming a dome which a not very flourishing creeper might one day cover. Oswald Hart shifted two clumsy metal chairs into position. He had on a fawnish-coloured corduroy suit, worn and a bit elbowy and missing a cuff-button, a brown-and-white check shirt and sort of woven tie with one or two spots of gravy down it, and rather awful shoes that might have had a hole in the sole and certainly needed heeling. She went on telling him about the flat and the hospital and other miserably unavoidable stuff which he actually made sound less unfascinating than ever before by the way he listened. It was not at all that he never took his eyes off her, thank God, but he never seemed to look at anybody else or want to catch sight of anybody else. She said a bit about Patrick, going round the edges, naturally.

'I used to be married,' said Oswald. 'Technically I still am, but I'll never go back to her now. Or she'll never come back to me. No children, which I thought she was wrong about then. Whether she was or she wasn't it's more than just as well now.' No question followed about possible children of her own. He waited a moment and then said, 'The marriage was a great success at first. Nothing obvious wrong. Then about the same time we realised we had different temperaments. Or whatever you like to call them. The different ways we liked spending the time. I think that's a great difference between men and women and it breaks up more marriages than anything else. But then with my experience I would think so. Would you like to go back into the house?'

Jenny saw that they were the only ones left in the garden and felt the first cool breath of evening air, but she said, 'No. Not unless you want to.'

He hesitated again. 'Well, she liked company. She had to have company. I don't mean she wanted to go to parties all the time or anything grand, or give parties of her own. She just wanted company, chatting, people round. I must have a lot of time alone, to work but not just to work. Or I feel I must, which is the same thing. That was another reason why I left Washington. Am I the most hopeless boring prig you've ever met in your life?'

223

'Oh no,' said Jenny positively, taken by surprise.

'Are you sure?'

He said it in a way that showed he had seen her noticing how he had said it before. After holding that for a moment or two he laughed, something she had just started to think he perhaps never did. A man's first laugh was always a hurdle, especially if he kept putting it off, but this one looked all right and sounded fine, which was really more important. One of the handsomest boys she had ever known had sadly made people turn round in the street when he laughed and sometimes whisper to each other. Remembering that was what made her blush now.

'I'm sorry,' said Oswald, his eyes lowered. 'It's on my mind all of a sudden. It was that evening, the evening after that time I saw you in Staines, it was coming home afterwards we had our first awful row. After that the whole thing fell apart quite quickly. I might have tried harder if she'd been better-looking. No, that's a terrible thing to say.' He sighed deeply and looked helpless. She saw that he had good undainty chap's ears. 'I'm sorry,' he said again. 'You don't want to hear all this. Of course I dare say she got pretty fed up with me too. I didn't give her any trouble, you know,' which without anything you could have called a facial contortion conveyed jolly cleverly what sort of trouble he had not given her – the Patrick sort, 'but I don't think I paid her enough attention. Not even when I was there. I mean I neglected her by not being there and still didn't take enough notice of her when I was there.'

'Oh, I can't believe that.'

'It would probably have been quite hard for her to believe until we'd been married for about a year. By that time I'd got to the end of her. That's another terrible thing to say, but unfortunately it's true. By then she'd told me everything that had ever happened to her and I knew what she thought about everything. I'd used her up. I don't say she hadn't used me up. I don't think there's any way of seeing that coming until it very nearly has. Certainly not before one gets married. I suppose I really mean before we got married there wasn't. Oh well. I don't suppose you feel you're getting near the end of Patrick, do you?'

'Not in the way you mean, no.'

That was blurting it out rather, and she would probably not

224

have said it if she had not been concentrating her attention on what he was saying. But he let it go, in particular not suggesting anything gallant about there obviously being no question of Patrick having got to the end of *her*, which was right really, but she would not have turned up her nose at a hint pointing that way.

They got up and ambled back towards the house. It was beginning to get dark. There was a very quiet sound of what must have been traffic in the distance, then a great rising roar or yell of laughter and consternation from indoors, instantly cut off by the different kind of roar of a sports car gleefully tearing down the hill on the other side of the garden wall. The two of them stopped at the foot of the iron staircase. Oswald put his hand on the orange-painted rail, a rather large hand with a half-blackened nail where something had fallen on or hit it, a very slightly dirty hand too.

'I couldn't get married again,' he said. 'Could you? Patrick isn't going to fall over a precipice but imagine he did, or has. Could you marry someone else?'

'I haven't thought about it.'

'No of course you haven't. Think about it now for five seconds.'

'You can't.'

'It's probably just me. I live half and half these days, that's half alone and half not. I couldn't go through all that again, all that effort and emotion and deciding everything.' He moved aside to let her go up the stairs. 'No, I quite see you couldn't come to that conclusion in five seconds.'

They stopped for a moment on the little landing outside the conservatory, which looked from there as if it had an entirely new set of people in it, younger on the average and more brightly dressed and making quicker movements. Some seemed to be playing at the bar-billiard table. Lightly and abruptly, Oswald Hart touched Jenny on the shoulder.

'Just, there weren't really a lot of girls in Washington. There was one, and then another one. Saying there were lots, coming from Patrick that's just a polite compliment. A courtesy.' He smiled and gave her an in-league look that even so assumed nothing and asked no question. 'Now I'm going to get you a drink, just to quench your thirst that is, and leave you to look

225

after yourself.' They went through into the drawing-room and he very dully did as he had said.

Jenny sat down next to the girl with the stretched-out nose on a sofa near the conservatory door. The people in here, unlike the ones in there, had flopped into chairs, were letting their age show, though not by talking less or more quietly. Time went by. Now and then there would be a disturbance and a military historian or children's-classics editor would stumble from the room or have to be calmed down. By the fireplace, where a large basketful of glistening purple flowers bloomed, a bald man was trying to make another man and two women pay attention to what he was simultaneously doing and saying on the screen of a grand colour-television set, but they kept talking among themselves instead. Once or twice a sharp crack sounded as a billiard-ball came off the table and landed on the conservatory floor. Jenny spotted Patrick early in this section. He was part of a chatting group and waved to her without much enthusiasm, disappointed perhaps that she had not had a more prolonged view of him behaving himself.

More time went by, plenty of it, Jenny considered, but just when things looked like running satisfactorily down to a full stop there was a sudden awful renewal of activity. Food, everybody started saying. At least it was a more interesting idea than curtains, fur coats, mothers-in-law, or rather the girl with the nose's mother-in-law, who would have had to be an unusually understanding person, Dutch tiles, jewellery, and chance selections from what the girl herself had been up to since fairly recently. Jenny tried to think of cricket and stocks and shares.

The food was downstairs in a kitchen that was part of a hotel-sized complex of washrooms, laundries, larders, wine-cellars, linen stores and places set apart for home brewing and onion-pickling, marmalade-making too no doubt when the season came round. You queued up for the food with a plate and went past a very long stove and round a large square table. Simon Giles came past Jenny, his tongue showing in concentration as he tried to keep a couple of stone of hot and cold meat, vegetables, salads and buttered rolls intact on his plate and walk at the same time. He lost half a prize marrow in the doorway but continued otherwise undispossessed out of sight.

The husband of Patrick's ex-girl-friend, the man who knew

226

David Frost slightly, was immediately in front of Jenny in the queue with the ex-girl-friend herself in front of him. The pair of them helped themselves to food quite separately, neither dropping so much as a baby beetroot on to the other's plate, but when the wife, as she nowadays was, had disappeared after Simon, the husband's attitude to self-service changed out of all recognition. He took complete charge of Jenny's supper, picking out for her the pinkest, least fatty cold lamb cutlet, turning conscientiously through the leaves of lettuce till he came to the little crisp ones, seeing to it that she got a full unhindered choice of every condiment and relish in sight. It was a pity he had not done some of the last part on behalf of his wife, who was suddenly back on the scene because, she said, she had forgotten to give herself any Dijon mustard. Just as suddenly the husband left Jenny to fend for herself on the last stretch and stopped holding up the other people, who had been swearing to themselves and each other, some not at all quietly, while he had been looking after her.

Rather to her surprise Jenny found herself eating her supper in the company of the same two. They all settled down after a fashion in a corner with their plates on a big round brass tray on ebony legs. The tray clashed and boomed disconcertingly whenever any of them shifted anything on it. The husband, who must have been quite attractive before he got his paunch and lost so much hair, went off to fetch them glasses of wine. The wife kept quiet while he was away, but as soon as he came back she said to Jenny,

'Who was that gorgeous man you were keeping all to yourself in the garden?'

'He's called Oswald Hart. He's a journalist. He – '

'He was positively undressing you with his eyes, my dear. Didn't you find it the tiniest bit embarrassing?'

'Well, I didn't think he was really doing that, but – '

'Mind you, not that I blame you in the least. One doesn't come across something as dishy as that every day of the week, alas. Do tell me, did he say if he was married?'

'Yes, he said he had a wife, but they – '

'Not that that seems to make two pennyworth of difference in this day and age, does it? Of course, I think an awful lot of it's just bravado. I mean, you get these funny little men making plays for girls at parties and things, they're just cutting a dash,

227

that's all. They'd be horrified if the lady took them up on it. Don't you agree, darling?'

This was said to her husband, who at that exact moment had put a whole mushroom too far past his teeth to get it out again. Black juice appeared at the corners of his mouth as he dilated his eyes and chewed and nodded at top speed.

'On the other hand,' said the wife, 'I think your Mr Hart did you say, in my view he's made of sterner stuff. If I know anything about it, that guy means business. What would you say about that, how did he strike you?'

Jenny said, 'There wasn't actually much of a – '

'Over the years one gets to recognise the type. Oh dear, I believe I've said enough, I don't want to embarrass you or go spoiling anything. How, er, how's my fine feathered friend Patrick? Still the same old scapegrace?'

Jenny had not finished wondering what to say to that, or what to do about it, when a pale man with a pigtail, a complete stranger to her, came running into her view with his loaded plate held stretched out in front of him. She worked out afterwards that he could not have been really running, just trying to recover his lost balance, but however he was brought to it what he did was come down on more or less all fours an instant after depositing his plate on the brass tray, which resounded like a great gong. The sudden stop and bump sent bits of food and sauce flying over the edge on to the skirt of the wife's dress but entirely clear of the other two. The wife was on her feet in a wink going for the husband for not having foreseen an obvious thing like that and taken the necessary precautions. Jenny left them to it and, with some hazy intention of getting her money's worth, wandered into a smaller room off the hall.

Here her hand was seized and pulled hard downwards, forcing her to collapse abruptly but not all that ungracefully into a vacant place on a sofa next to, in fact very close to, the person who had done the pulling. As she saw soon enough, this was the small bearded Australian poet with the three names.

'I thought you'd got yourself stuck somewhere,' he said, looking her over in an attentive way. 'You're all right are you, girl? Enjoying the party? Are you feeling relaxed? It's important to feel relaxed.'

'I'm all right,' said Jenny.

'Does that mean you don't mind if I go on?'

228

Something told her she would if he did, and he was still looking her over, with an air of faint puzzlement now perhaps, and had not yet let go of her hand. All the same, it seemed a bit soon to be screaming for help, so she gave an encouraging nod.

'It's no good,' he said rather bitterly, 'I'm past it. Never mind the reasons and excuses – past it. I used to be a great hammer, you know? Anything that moved. Not any more. It's gone, and I can say that without fear of contradiction. You wouldn't believe, the really swell kids who've tried to bring it back to life, you know? Real little beauties, and with hearts of gold too. But . . .'

He gazed at her, again with that hint of uncertainty, but there was nothing anyone could have called a hint about his main line of thought, whatever trouble he might have had in turning thought into action. This failed to bother Jenny in the way his slightly different but no speedier approach at the Gileses' had bothered her. She had been confused then, though. 'That really is most distressing,' she said in a firm voice and snatched her hand away. 'Now if you'll excuse me . . .'

'What? You mean you don't take that as any kind of a challenge? After what you were saying earlier?'

Jenny made no reply. She had caught sight of a girl – well, a woman of thirty-five to forty – standing nearby and looking uncertainly about. This woman wore a dress that a very nearly blind man might have mistaken for Jenny's and had dark hair cut to about Jenny's length. She also had a hook nose, heavy eyebrows and hot greedy eyes. It was then that Jenny first fully understood what went through Patrick's mind when he shouted 'Christ!' But she went quite quietly up to the woman and said only, 'Excuse me, I'm afraid I'd taken your seat,' before going back into the main room.

Here Simon brushed past her, pale and slack-jawed, moving like a competitor in the London-to-Brighton walk towards the conservatory and the garden and peace and quiet at least. There was so little peace and quiet indoors that Jenny watched as if it had been in dumb-show an incident taking place by the inner doorway, where a man unbelievably different from everyone else in sight had appeared a moment before. He was there to take away some guest or guests; the host, lifting a hand, offered him a drink; he mimed a polite refusal; he looked where others

229

were looking, at an elderly woman trying to heave herself upright from a sofa by hauling at a curtain; after some seconds he turned back to the host and nodded vigorously. She was married to a novelist Jenny had seen described as one of the acutest and most caustic observers of the post-war scene.

Surely it was late enough for everybody to go home now. Jenny went to get what she hoped would be a last drink – of soda-water on the rocks. Oswald Hart was helping himself to something that looked like exactly that.

'One more party,' he said, handing her a clean glass. 'I can't wait to be old.'

'And all the time we could have been reading *Peyton Place*.'

An outburst of swearing in a female voice started up a few feet away. One or two of the words might have been unfamiliar to Jenny but she knew most of them. The one doing the swearing was the four-eyed little Vera, and the one being sworn at was a tubby man who was quite old, old enough for that not to happen to him, at any rate.

'I can't drop you in Fulham on my way to Muswell Hill,' he kept saying, mostly a bit at a time, 'because they're in opposite directions.'

'You' was the word Vera came back to most often, though she used a great many other ones in between, and she finished each paragraph by shouting, ' . . . you.'

After a time the tubby man moved off towards the street door with Vera following him and still shouting until her voice was lost in the general hubbub.

'Poets are the unacknowledged legislators of the world,' said Oswald to Jenny. 'Can I take you out to lunch one day?'

'That would be marvellous.'

Sixteen

'Coyote Books,' said Patrick. 'American based. He's in charge of the British end.'

'So he's quite important.'

'Well, if a publisher ever is important. No of course he's not *important* in the way Victor was or Jonathan or . . . But yes, he's got a lot of money to spend. Did he trip up or what?'

'I think he just went like one of those slapstick men, started staggering and couldn't stop. Without that plateful he'd probably have been all right.'

'I wish I'd seen it. Poor old Vanessa. Never one to react well to having grub thrown all over her dress. Bad luck though, some might reckon.'

'Yes, it was,' said Jenny in a far-away voice. 'If that chap had kept on his feet another second he might have managed to throw it all over her head.'

'Oh Christ, he might, might he? Sorry about that. M'm, nor one to react well to, you know, having something or somebody taken off her by somebody else, as she might see it. Quite flattering if looked at in the right spirit, I suppose.'

'You were pretty smitten with her, I remember you saying.'

'I'm not smitten any more, if that's what you mean.'

'I may be wrong, but I don't think she knows I know about you and her.'

'Oh really?'

'I'm not talking about just tonight, I'm going by the other times I've met her as well.'

'Oh. You mean I should have told her I'd told you?'

'Of course not.'

Jenny still spoke in a far-away voice. She could feel Patrick

231

looking carefully at her as the two of them stood in the kitchen, she at the stove heating up milk for her cocoa toddy, he keeping her company and being sober and responsible with a very weak drink in his hand. Actually, though she would have said she could feel him looking at her, what she meant was she could see him, see him quite clearly out of the corner of her eye, and the way he was looking at her was not only careful but a bit weary and a bit peevish and a bit patient, and none of it very subtle, and it was not only in his expression but in the set of his head and shoulders and his movements. Surely he knew she could see all that without trying. His eyes were wide enough set, about like hers, side eyes she had called them once to pull his leg, like a horse's or a dog's she had said, anyway in fact well placed to let him see just as much just as clearly himself if he wanted to. So perhaps he never bothered, or not any more. Of course it was a small point.

'I hope you didn't have too boring a time,' said Patrick when they were back in the sitting-room.

'No, there was quite a lot going on one way and another.'

'That female, the one they carried out at the end, apparently she's like that every night. Or worse. Started sparring with the butler at the Czech embassy for being a tool of Stalinism.'

'You'd think he'd leave her at home, wouldn't you?'

'Very much so, home in her case being Budapest.'

'Well, wherever it is.'

After a fresh set of careful looks, as it might perhaps have been like an assassin lining up his target, he said, 'How did you get on with old Oswald Hart?'

'Like a house on fire.'

'He's a, wooh, talk about – he's a one for the ladies if anybody ever was.'

'So you said when you introduced us. I thought he was a smashing chap.'

'He's a very nice bloke.' Patrick put a lot of deep feeling and force into that. 'I suppose he, well, he wouldn't be Ozzie Hart if he didn't – I mean he did – '

'He asked me out to lunch, which I suppose is the kind of thing you're getting at.'

'M'm yeah. What did you, er, what did you say?'

'I said it was a marvellous idea. It is, too.'

'M'm. Well, you'll be all right with old Oswald.'

232

'So you don't mind if I go.'

'Me? No. No, not if that's what you want to do. As I say, he's a very sound type of bloke.'

Jenny thought for a moment and said, 'Was there anybody smoking what do you call them, reefers at that party? Do I mean marijuana cigarettes?'

'Oh, them,' said Patrick, laughing affectionately at her mispronunciation. 'Not that I know of. I certainly wasn't, if that's what you're asking. Not my scene anyway, all that. The drink's quite enough to handle in my view.' He sounded quite British, almost gruff, when he said that, forgetting that a few evenings back he had said, well, anything for a lift out of the old encircling gloom and the stuff was no more harmful than booze. 'I'll stick to what I know.'

'And you're not all woozy or drowsy or anything?'

'No, not a bit of it, all merry and bright. Why, did you want to – '

'In that case I'd just like to make sure, you did mean it, did you, when you said you wouldn't mind if I went out to lunch with this Oswald Hart?'

'Why should I? According to you it's a splendid idea.'

'What about according to you? One for the ladies was how you described him, and our Vanessa just had time to say much the same before she was interrupted, and I even formed a similar opinion myself, and none of us means he's partial to their brand of common sense, so to save wasting anyone's time you also ultimately wouldn't mind if I went to bed with him. You might well go as far as thinking it was a splendid idea yourself, I mean the whole thing.'

Jenny felt quite amazed at having steered through this part keeping to a bright interested tone of voice, like somebody conscientiously describing the plot of a book or film. After hearing her out, Patrick said in a very reasonable tone,

'Well, I just wanted to make sure you knew what was on the cards, so to speak.'

'But I told you, I got there on my own without any trouble at all. So would anyone. Honestly.'

'I mean I didn't want you to think I was trying to con you about the situation.'

'But . . .' Now she felt amazed in a different way, but just said, 'I was asking you, at least I meant to ask you if I was

233

right and you actually wanted me to go to bed with your friend Oswald Hart. There.'

He twice seemed to be going to speak and never got there. Then he rubbed the back of his neck hard, frowning, and impatiently moved his chair round so as to be more straight in front of her. Then he gave an apologetic sort of schoolboyish smile and got down to business.

'Love, I never thought we'd go this far and I certainly never wanted us to, but we're none of us what we'd like to be and the best thing we can do is face up to it. I can't tell you how much I'd have given to be the kind of man you deserve, but very unfortunately I'm not. I told you once I didn't think perhaps there were any of that kind of man left these days, but anyhow I'm not one. As you know. Very sadly.' He looked very sad as he spoke.

'So . . .' he went on, 'that being so, my advice is, we make the best of it. Accept it. There's Oswald . . . a marvellous chap . . . you obviously think so . . . furthermore . . . a *civilised* chap . . . no snags . . . no emotionalising . . . no *mess* . . . everything open and above board. And when it's over, it's over. Like various things that have happened in my own life. But all the time . . .'

Jenny wanted to jump to her feet, but she stayed where she was and said, 'Patrick, please don't try and tell me that Oswalds may come and, what the hell's she called, Wendys may go but you and I go on for ever, because I might burst out laughing. Or is it bad form to laugh when somebody gets something as wrong as you have? You idiot.'

'You told me you fancied him,' he said stubbornly.

'I did. I do. Fancy him, like mad, he's marvellous, he's not the only fanciable one I've seen this year or any other year but he is marvellous. When he asked if he could take me out to lunch I said it would be a marvellous idea, but then I went straight on to tell him I couldn't come, I wouldn't come. Of course I did. I wouldn't go to bed with him however marvellous he was. I couldn't do that. I'd have to get so drunk to do that you wouldn't recognise me, because . . . I'm *your wife*, you bloody sodding . . . oh, I wish I could swear, I can't tell you how much I wish I could swear, Patrick Standish. Because if anybody ever . . .'

She stopped and turned away, but not to cry, not this time

234

– just she was afraid she would thump him if she saw any more of him staring at her all hurt and guilty and so terribly *sorry*, but fed up as well at having his lovely civilised discussion and civilised solution taken away from him. Although she had not actually raised her voice she realised she must have sounded something like half as furious as she felt, and that was too much. If she gave way to it she would most likely regret it. Remember a woman can never take back anything she says to a man, her mother had warned her one time when they had gone up to stay and she had seen easily enough that they had been having a difference about some forgotten big deal.

Not that thinking of her mother was that much of a good idea just at the moment. It reminded her of how Patrick always was with her, appreciating her so much – what had he called it? *Valuing* her – that your teeth went on edge, knowing her better 'in a way' than her own daughters did, being somebody the old girl felt really at home with and always wanted to see. That might have been mostly true, that last part, and full marks to him for trying, but more than once Jenny had found herself wishing he would get caught out swearing at her mother's dachshund or sneering at her overwaved hairdo. Anyway, by running off at a tangent like that in her mind Jenny had calmed herself down. 'I'm sorry I lost my temper,' she said, and meant something more than that because she could see he was actually quite funny without knowing it when he was being respectful to her mother.

'That's all right, darling.' He was by nature a good apologiser and accepter of apologies. 'We'll both feel different in the morning.'

'Maybe.' That could have sounded a bit grim, but never mind. 'There are one or two things I'd like to get settled if I could before we hit the hay. Unless . . .'

'No no, I'm in spanking form. But I think I will just treat myself to a small nightcap.'

'Would you get me a ginger beer while you're there?'

'Coming up.'

Alone for a second, Jenny shut her eyes and tried to think of nothing, because whatever she did think of was apt to be no help. But without choosing she thought of the Sunday morning years ago when Patrick had come to pick her up at her digs to drive to a country pub, most likely, and she had seen him from

235

the landing window making a little excited goblin's face to himself as he rang the bell. That was enough of that. She got up now and shifted his chair back to where it had been against the wall. When he came in again with their drinks he looked inquiringly and not at all happily at it but said nothing.

'Right, proceed,' he said as he sat down, rather on the grim side himself.

'I realise this is exactly the way husbands don't like wives to go on, but . . .'

'But there's also a way burglars don't like policemen to go on. Understood.'

'Sorry, pet. I know. But: you were expecting Oswald Hart to be there tonight?'

'Yes I was. No I wasn't, that's to say I only realised I'd *been* fully expecting it when I saw him. He was in town, would have had a book to flog. Why?'

'*Why?* You mean why did I ask you that question? *Obviously* because I was wondering whether you fixed it up with him for him to try and get off with me. That's *why*.'

'You think I'm capable of doing a thing like that?'

'Well of course I do. You are, aren't you?'

After one quick glance at her he turned his face away.

'At the back of my second drawer down upstairs,' she said, 'there's a packet of cigarettes. I've forgotten which brand but I don't suppose you mind much.'

He gave her another glance, not so very different from the first one, and went. When he reappeared he seemed to be already about three-quarters of the way through the cigarette he was smoking. After a break during a row, or a serious discussion as he sometimes called it, he usually started off with some fresh point he had thought up meanwhile, but not this time.

'What's it like?' she asked.

'It's more like a cigarette than anything that's ever happened to me,' he said, lighting another from the end of the first and putting the open packet down as close to him as it would go. Then he waited.

'So no, all right, perhaps you didn't fix it up with Oswald to get off with me, but you sure as hell thought of it the moment you saw him and did all you could to encourage it, didn't you, like shooting out of sight as fast as your little legs would carry you.'

236

'I suppose so, yes, but I didn't think it out quite like that.'

'You didn't have to, it came naturally to you. Of course I suppose you could have whispered in his ear to be on the safe side. But then you went on about he was this colossal ram. Fair play, you said just now, so I couldn't ever say you hadn't warned me. Or was it supposed to sex me up?'

'It doesn't make much difference, does it?'

'No, it doesn't. Probably just habit when it's a chap you like. Anyway, you thought the whole thing was a spiffing good idea, couldn't do any harm, could it, and at worst or at least it might cheer me up to have a pass thrown at me by somebody as attractive as him. Which would have appealed to you because you're quite fond of me in your way.'

'Christ.'

'Yes indeed.'

'I wish you'd be annoyed, it's harder to take like this,' he said, grinding out his cigarette in the way he had, making a great flourish of it.

'Oh, pity. And I'm annoyed all right, rest assured of that. Now, the scheme was for me to go to bed with Oswald so's you wouldn't feel so bad about going to bed with whoever's going to come after Wendy, or perhaps even Wendy again, I don't know. And seeing as how he's a civilised chap he wouldn't fall in love with me or persuade me to go and live with him, and we haven't covered me perhaps falling in love with him but let's cross that bridge when we come to it. And whatever happened it'd be that much easier next time because one of the things Oswald'd be doing is breaking the ice, isn't it?'

Patrick said nothing.

'And you thought I'd settle for that. Marriage 1960s style. I've been round the place for eight years as far as you're concerned and married to you for most of them and that's how well you know me.'

'I honestly didn't think it all the way through.'

'Oh, don't try and tell me the idea'd never crossed your mind before, I've seen it doing it. Actually I needn't really have bothered to bring love into it. That's rather gone out, hasn't it? This is going to be worse than just what husbands don't like wives to say, it's sort of square or whatever you call it, out of date, and I've tried it over in my mind and I'm going to sound selfish and ridiculous however I say it, but I'm going to say it

237

and *you listen*. If I think you're not listening I'll stop and start again at the beginning. Now . . .'

When he realised that it was to go over to the bookshelves that she had got up, his expression took another turn for the worse, not so much unhappier as properly scared for the first time. On his view of the matter, what people said could never be a hundred per cent serious – it might not be what they thought, not even roughly, and they would be saying something else the next moment, and the other person could say things back – but books were serious, permanent, not to be argued with. She was looking for two books now, found only one but the more important one, and took it back to her chair without going out of her way to let him see what it was. Quite dramatic of her really, and more power to her elbow, she thought to herself.

'I was after that omnibus of Somerset Maugham stories but never mind,' she said – 'you're sure to remember how he's always talking about love, how a fellow loved a woman for twenty years and never breathed a word, and another woman who was always loyal to her husband and a model wife to him even though she was in love with his best friend all the time – you know. All about people not doing things they very much wanted to do because they thought they had an obligation to someone else. And going on not doing what they wanted for years on end, not just a couple of weeks. Perhaps none of it counts really because he was queer, you told me, or perhaps it was just one of those literary conventions we used to hear about in the sixth form. Love without going to bed. What an idea.'

She opened the book she had brought from the shelves and turned through its early pages. 'You remember how much we enjoyed the film of *Tom Jones* two or three years ago, we went twice in the same week. So much so you got the paperback and chuckled over it a lot.' Now Jenny held it up for a moment. 'I read it after you, or some of it, skipping the parts with that awful girl. I found you'd marked a few passages.

'He began now – that's him, Tom Jones – he began now, at twenty, to have the name of a pretty fellow among all the women in the neighbourhood.

'I don't suppose the author meant quite what we mean by pretty, but even if he did, who cares? Better if he did, in a way.

238

Now here's a bit that gets things on the right lines. Definitely meant for Mr Pretty-Bum personally.

'Tom, though an idle, thoughtless, rattling rascal, was nobody's enemy but his own.

'Isn't that what you've always thought about yourself? In everything? But there's a . . . Hang on . . . Oh yes, this is marvellous.' She waggled the book to and fro to make it stay open better.

'Young men of open, generous dispositions are naturally inclined to gallantry, which, if they have good understandings, as was in reality Tom's case, exerts itself in an obliging complacent behaviour to all women in general.

'Uncanny, isn't it? Really gets you to a T. I particularly like gallantry, I bet you imagined old Henry Fielding winking when he said that. But now for the clincher. It looks as though you've underlined it heavier than the others, but there's probably nothing in that.

'Though he did not always act rightly, yet he never did otherwise without feeling and suffering for it.

'So that's all right, isn't it, Patrick?'

Patrick was dabbing the skin under his eyes at that moment, perhaps tears, more likely sweat because of the hot night. Either way the handkerchief did something to hide the enormous blush that was still all over his face. 'What am I to do?' he asked.

'Well, for a start you could try reading some different books.' Jenny went and stood replacing *Tom Jones* on the shelf. 'I doubt if that one means exactly what you'd like it to mean, but there's plenty these days that do and I don't think you're fit to be trusted with them. They encourage your bad instincts and make you ashamed of your good ones. Gosh, what do I sound like? Real goody-goody. M'm. Yes, well don't count on that lasting for ever, buster.'

'What does that mean?'

'It means I don't think I can go on loving you indefinitely, not like this. Of course, we might get on better that way. Then you could be a shit to your heart's content.'

'Is there any hope for us?'

'Not as we are. Not unless something happens. And I don't see anything happening.'

A door shut heavily nearby: the front door of 1A. Neither paid any attention. Jenny took her glass and cocoa mug out to

239

the kitchen, leaving Patrick to have another drink if he wanted one, and he was going to want one. He was going to want another cigarette too, in fact was in the middle of lighting one when she returned to the sitting-room. At the sight of her he stopped for a second in a guilty, inferior sort of way. He was all to pieces now and would be well brassed off and quiet, as though huffy, in the morning, but would start to chat non-committally soon after he got home from work. He always said it took a lot to get him down.

Seventeen

'I'm going to bed,' said Jenny a moment later.

'I'll stay on here for a bit if it's all right with you.' As Patrick spoke, a long loud laugh was heard through the wall, the door thudded shut again and almost at the same moment their own bell chimed. There was no one within a hundred miles Jenny wanted to see, but doors, like telephones, had to be answered every time.

At first she failed to recognise the person standing outside. The light was patchy and the general shape of whoever it was told her nothing. Then Tim's voice asked if he could come in. He seemed to be hunched up in a funny way, which must have been why she had not known him at once. When she could see his face properly it was quite a shock.

'Tim, what's the matter, what's happened?'

'Could I just come in and sit for a bit? Just for a few minutes. I realise it's late. Could I, just a couple of minutes. I don't want to be a nuisance.'

Telling him several times it was all right she more or less led him into the sitting-room. He looked round it as if he had never come across such a place before.

'Christ,' said Patrick after a glance at him, 'what have you been up to? Do you want a drink?'

'No thank you. I've had enough drinks. Can I have a glass of water?'

Jenny took him to a chair. 'You're not ill, are you? Say if you are.'

'No, I'm all right, just had a horrible time and been an idiot, worse than that. I must have been out of my mind, I didn't

241

know what I was getting into, I can't think what can ever have possessed me to . . . Thank you.'

Patrick had brought the water. 'Of course,' he said, 'I'd quite forgotten, this was the night of the great safari through the jungle of queerdom, hence your colourful attire. How was it?' One of his great characteristics had always been the ability to come round fast and completely from his own troubles and crises. Only a mean person would have suggested that perhaps he had not had all that far to come.

'How *was* it? Well, it was, what can I say, it was worse than anything you could possibly imagine if you sat up all night. Trying. To imagine something worse. I can't tell you.' He pinched the bridge of his nose violently, his eyes screwed shut. 'I had no idea. Nobody has any idea. They're not like ordinary people at all.'

'Tim,' began Patrick, 'you know I did try to – '

'I know you did, perhaps you did, but please don't start ticking me off for anything now, I don't think I could bear it.'

'Sorry. What sort of places were they?'

'Look, I want to forget them as fast as I can.' He appealed to Jenny. 'Don't I?'

'Of course you do, pet. Never bring them to mind again.'

'I only meant were they posh or – '

'Be quiet, Patrick,' said Jenny. 'Tim's said he doesn't want to go into that. Now please.'

'Not into any of it,' said Tim. 'Not into what they wore or what they said or what they drank or how they looked or . . . I say, could I change my mind and have that drink after all? Whisky or something. Anything.'

What they wore . . . Thoughts of the Queen of Sheba came unbidden as usual to Jenny's mind. Perhaps there had indeed been one on view this evening, not so much as a turn or an event, more to show what sort of place it was or what went on in it, like Father Christmas at the festive season in a way.

'Jenny,' said Tim, 'you don't mind me mentioning these things, do you? It doesn't shock you?'

'You can say what you like in here,' she said stoutly, and at once found herself hoping pretty hard.

'You're a very sweet girl. You see, what happened, I found out what it was like. Actually like. What happens, there are the two of you, and one of you – '

242

'I don't think Jenny wants to hear this,' said Patrick, but not in a very committed style.

They both looked at her. 'All right, carry on, Tim,' she said in a voice that sounded strange to her in some way, and curling up her toes as she spoke. It could not do her as much harm to hear it as it might do Tim good to tell it, or was she hoping again?

Tim said quite fast, 'One of you does something to the other one and then the other one does it to the first one. I can't think of anything more unpleasant than having it done. So it doesn't take a lot of working out, if you do it to somebody, either he finds it as unpleasant as you do, and just think of the sort of person that makes you, or, in some way I don't want to try to imagine, he finds it pleasant, and just think of the sort of person that makes him.'

There was a short silence. Jenny reached across and stroked the back of Tim's neck. Patrick cleared his throat and said, 'Yes, well, I quite see, er, that would rather tend to take the gilt off the old gingerbread in a manner of speaking.'

'Sorry to have bored you with all this,' said Tim.

'That is hardly the word. No, it's been most enlightening. Did you convey your feelings to Eric and Stevie?'

'I couldn't help it. But it was funny, Eric seemed not to care, quite indifferent, hostile perhaps, anyway he was hostile about something, or so I thought, and Stevie seemed to be blaming him for things going wrong and rather taking my side, I couldn't really follow it. But as soon as we got back, I was going to have a last drink with them but there was such an awful atmosphere I got out straight away and when I turned to go Eric gave a most horrible laugh, it was quite frightening.'

'Yes, we heard it,' said Jenny.

'There it is again,' said Patrick.

All three sat listening but heard nothing more. Tim had gabbled his last remarks even faster than before and was breathing heavily, appearing more upset than when he had first arrived. Patrick's face went through some surprising contortions as he battled with a great yawn.

After a minute Tim said more normally, 'Did you have the news on? I suppose that bill's gone through or is going through. Sorry, I mean the bill in the House of Commons. You know, the one legalising all that.'

243

'Oh yes,' said Patrick, lighting a cigarette as if he was already not noticing he was doing it. 'Well, chaps, better late than never, whatever anybody says.'

'One thing that did strike me quite forcibly,' said Tim, and left plenty of time for Jenny to wonder what it might be before continuing, 'was, well, you'd have expected them to be glad about that, wouldn't you? An end to persecution, as they'd call it. Celebrating, even. But they weren't. Well, some youngsters were . . .' Tim evidently decided that what the youngsters had been being or doing was better kept to himself even at this stage. 'Er, naturally I asked some of the others what they thought of it and they were very cool. Two of them even said they thought it would spoil things, of course it was great in a way but they were afraid it might spoil things. What things? Not being special any more, they said, but I couldn't follow that at all. There's no pleasing some people, is there? Now they can do exactly as they like and they still aren't satisfied.' He struck his thigh. 'Well . . .'

'You haven't got to go,' said Jenny. 'Stay as long as you like.'

'You are a sweet girl, but I can see you're both tired. That was all I wanted, just a little bit of company. I'll be getting along to my solitary couch. Isn't it ridiculous, I was thinking earlier . . . Good Lord, is that the time?'

Getting up from his chair Tim winced and grunted and cautiously hunched his shoulders. 'Just a twinge,' he said.

'They have put you through it,' said Patrick.

'No, it's just I've sort of cricked my neck because I was late at the prison.'

'Oh, of course.'

'No, you see, if you get there after tea, tea being at 3 o'clock if you please, the cells are shut, so in order to talk you have to lean over to talk through the grille in the door, which is quite a way down for a tall chap and a bit of a strain. It should be all right in the morning.'

'Well, what do you know about that?' Neither Jenny nor Patrick actually said the words to the other but they both looked them, and then looked away.

A loud altercation started up on the other side of the party wall, with Stevie's voice clearly distinguishable but the other one only to be labelled as Eric's because it could not have belonged to anybody else. The second voice worked up to a shout and then cut off and again nothing more was heard.

'I seem to have got out just in time,' said Tim. 'Or does it happen a lot?'

'Oh, once or twice a week,' said Patrick.

'Not like this,' said Jenny.

They waited. Just as they were starting to relax Eric gave another shout and, precisely as a few minutes before, the door of 1A slammed and the bell of 1B sounded.

Patrick turned abruptly but stayed where he was. Jenny began to move towards the door out of instinct but Tim put out a hand and told her it was his pigeon and went himself.

'Hallo, Stevie,' she heard him say at the open door – 'what can we – '

There was a sudden outburst of more shouting and some screaming too, and she saw violent confused movement on the far side of Tim and partly hidden by him. Two men seemed to be struggling there. In a second or so she realised that Eric must have followed Stevie out on to the walk, but more immediately she saw Stevie come lurching forward and fall into Tim's arms screaming now in a high-pitched way that was more of a squeal. Eric's voice, what could only have been Eric's voice, shouted something accusing and utterly wretched but impossible to make out.

Jenny hurried forward and she and Tim got Stevie on to the nearest chair, a demoted article with torn purple padding on which hats and scarves were thrown in the winter. Blood was pouring out of the side of his throat and soaking into his shirt but still flowing down. He looked thoroughly frightened and had started whimpering or crying. She had never seen so much blood.

'I'd better get that knife off him,' said Tim.

Jenny rushed out to the kitchen for something to staunch the bleeding. She was gone only a moment, but when she came back with two clean tea-towels Eric was over the threshold of the flat being pushed out again and struggled with by Tim. In another moment the two were out of sight and in another there was a loud cry of pain. She clenched her fists on the tea-towels and shut her eyes tight and prayed. When she opened her eyes again there was Tim sort of marching Eric in and sitting him

245

down in a very straightforward fashion. Neither seemed hurt, though Eric was squeezing at his wrist.

'Keep an eye on you in here,' said Tim. 'And don't you move,' but Eric was obviously not going to think of moving anywhere till he had to.

'What happened to the knife?' asked Jenny.

'Went over the wall.'

Stevie was not choking or anything, but there was still fresh blood coming through Jenny's tea-towel. He seemed to have blacked out. She and Tim carried him over and laid him out on the chesterfield, where his legs hung untidily over the end. Patrick, whom Jenny had not noticed for the minute or so since the first struggle, got on the telephone and rang an ambulance and the police. Tim took over from Jenny and pressed down as hard as he could on the wound in Stevie's throat without obstructing his breathing.

'I think that's all we can do,' he said.

In the short interval before the ambulance came Stevie went rather white and began breathing through his mouth in a scaring way. At no point did Eric show any interest in his condition or even glance across to where he was lying. Not that he, Eric, showed interest in anything or anyone else either.

The ambulance-men quickly got Stevie on to their stretcher.

'How badly is he hurt?' Tim asked them.

'Can't tell at this stage,' said the younger one, tucking in the blankets.

'He seems to have lost an awful lot of blood,' said Jenny.

'Yeah, you'll have a time getting it off that couch. You all right, miss, madam?'

'What? Of course I'm all right.'

'You never really get blood off,' said the older man. 'Not when it's ingrained. Good night all.'

The police, who were hairier than you still expected police to be, took a good deal longer over their business. Tim told them the story, or rather the parts of the story that mentioned a pleasant evening out with some neighbours, a sudden quarrel whose subject was obscure to him and an affray whose details could be confirmed by others present. At the start the police were unhappy about his appearance, and Jenny had to admit to herself that a lilac shirt with that collar would not have done much to reassure anyone, but they perked up a lot when they

246

heard his accent and seemed quite contented on being told that he was a member of the bar, especially after one or two questions and answers. Eric would say nothing, not a word, though he listened with close attention and nodded responsibly several times. He still said nothing, and looked no one in the eye, when at length the policemen removed him.

The door had hardly shut behind them and their charge before a kind of altercation broke out on the walk. It was soon recognisable as Harold Porter-King running into them on his way home and trying to hold them up until they had answered every one of his questions about what had been going on, and the policemen not letting him hold them up and getting away with telling him as little as possible. From the sound of it he followed them some distance towards the stairway, still baying requests for information, until he lost heart and broke off the pursuit. The three in 1B sat still as he paused outside its door.

'It's a bit late to bother them,' he said very audibly.

'Yes, they'll still be here tomorrow,' said Wendy Porter-King's voice, but in such an off-duty style that Jenny wondered who it was at first.

'I mean, they don't want people barging in at this hour.'

'No, of course they don't, they want to be left in peace.'

'What I'm saying is, they wouldn't thank us for disturbing them at whatever it is in the morning.'

'They're probably sound asleep by now.'

'The point being they've probably had quite enough for one night.'

After some delay, presumably while Harold screwed himself up to a final decision, and after the expected episode with the latch-key, the door of 1D shut and silence seemed to flow out from it. None of the three dared to stir for longer than that. Then Jenny said, 'You were terrifically brave, Tim.'

'Scared stiff actually. I was petrified silly old Eric was going to stab me, he was in rather a state, you know. He couldn't do much once I'd got hold of him, though, because I am quite large and strong.'

'I'm afraid I wasn't brave at all,' said Patrick. 'Of course I'm not very large or strong either.'

Jenny remembered an incident from years before, when they had been out for a country walk and a friend of Patrick's had fired a rifle over their heads – for a joke, and quite safely, but

247

they had not known that – and Patrick had dived for cover and Graham had gone marching over to the chap to protest. 'I suppose it was really your instinct to tackle Eric,' she said to Tim.

'If you mean I was too steamed up to think, yes, probably.'

'It wouldn't do if we all had the same instincts,' said Patrick.

After that nobody said anything for a while. Jenny rang the hospital number the ambulance-men had given her and made a vain inquiry about Stevie. Then she did milky coffees for them all and took them in to hear Patrick saying,

'All right, but just for your information, Tim, I watched those rozzers deciding in two seconds flat that all this 'ere was about one poof stabbing another, and then slowly and steadily discarding their further conviction that you were the third poof in a triangle and concluding instead that, appearances like that shirt notwithstanding, you yourself were about as queer as the Bank of England.'

'Ten out of ten,' said Jenny.

'What a bit of luck,' said Tim. 'Considering everything.'

'Call it fate.' Patrick was being serious now, even if perhaps drunk as well. 'The fate that decreed your inviolable heterosexuality. However burdensome it might be'.

If Tim heard that he digested it remarkably fast. 'Tell me, then,' he said – 'what do you say made Eric stab Stevie? Tonight rather than any other time, I mean.'

'Oh for Christ's sake, Tim. In that sense you *were* the third poof in a triangle. Stevie made up to you to make Eric jealous and it was once too often. You don't mean to tell me you didn't think of that?'

'Yes actually I did, but I thought it was too . . .'

'Argh! Too *what?*'

'Well, too conceited, I suppose.'

'Oh for Christ's *sake.* You don't suppose he actually fancied you, do you? Don't you see – try it like this: the more horrible you are from a queer's point of view, and I hope and believe that's very horrible, the worse it would be for Eric and so the better for Stevie. Conceited *my Aunt Fanny.*'

'I don't know, it seems too simple.'

'Shitty things are always simple. Same as great things. Patrick Standish, in conversation.'

'Patrick, your turn to try the hospital,' said Jenny. 'The number's there, on the thing.'

She felt mean doing it just then, but not very, and she considered she had a reason. As soon as Patrick was groaning and yawning and dialling, she said, 'I want to say this to you now, Tim. Get back to Gussie as soon as you can. She's waiting for you.'

He sighed, quite resigned to her knowing about Gussie, not bothering about what else she knew about. When he had sighed again he said, 'She's so terribly unexciting.'

'Oh, Tim. After tonight? How exciting do you want your life to be? Patrick could say it better than I can, but I suppose it might be exciting enough for you when you get your head blown off.'

'I see what you mean. Of course in your situation you would think married life was the best, I quite understand that.'

Jenny went straight on and said, 'A man belongs at home with his wife. Anyway that's where he *should be*. Especially you. I don't think you want to go on trying different ones, I think you want to go on trying the same one. One that likes you.'

'But she's so . . .'

'That's the whole point of her. Well, as far as this goes. I think your other ones get you too hot and bothered. Too tense. Huhm' – this noise, together with a tilt of the head, indicated Patrick – 'told me a bit about your trouble. What you have to realise . . . Tim . . . is that all men get that when they're over-excited.' Jenny made an impressive pause. 'Even . . . *huhm*.'

'What! No! Not . . . No.' Tim sat blinking and moving his mouth. 'I can't believe it.' But he was trying hard. It was another great upset, though admittedly not quite on the same scale as earlier ones that evening.

'Would I say it if it wasn't true? Didn't he say anything to you about it?'

'No. And now I come to think of it, Mr Perlmutter didn't look at it from that point of view at all.'

'*Screw* Mr Perlmutter,' said Jenny recklessly. 'Didn't he even mention it?'

'Well he *mentioned* it, but he seemed to think it was very boring.'

'He's lucky not to be behind bars, is that man. Now Tim,'

249

she said. 'Listen. Listen to me. You're to ring Gussie first thing in the morning.'

'Oh, hell,' he said, looking and sounding just like Patrick.

'You're to arrange things in such a way that when you look back you'll be able to say to yourself as follows. "What happened when I went out that time with Eric and Stevie showed me what a fool I'd been all along. It gave me such a shock I went back to Gussie straight away, just like that, no messing, and I've never had cause to regret it." Got that? What happened was the *shock* sent you *straight back* to *Gussie*.' She saw Patrick was on the point of ringing off and speeded herself up. 'Come on, Tim, have you got that? Quickly, now.'

'*Yes*,' he said quite peevishly and even more like Patrick.

'See you stick to it. Now this is just the first dose, just to set you off thinking on the right lines. You're to come back tomorrow and we'll go over it again. Say you will.'

'Oh, all right.'

That was as far as they went because Patrick was coming over and saying,

'He's comfortable. Comfortable's pretty shitty, I'm told. Like moderate in the Irish Sea.'

'At least he's not dead,' said Jenny.

'Yes, that's good. For Eric's sake, that is. Nobody else's.'

'Oh, come,' said Tim.

Eighteen

'What do you want?'

'I just want to see him for a few minutes, that's all. I'm a – '

'What do you want to see him about?'

'Just to have a chat. He's expecting me, didn't he say? I'm a friend of his. A neighbour.'

The woman facing Patrick from the open doorway, a middle-aged one with very tightly waved auburn hair and a face broader at the bottom than the top, started to relax at the last piece of information. Then, when he relaxed in his turn and smiled at her, she tightened up again.

'Are you that solicitor? Because if – '

'No, I'm the publisher. With the wife.'

She seemed to think about that, her downy upper lip bulging in concentration, her head nodding perhaps a millimetre each way. Meanwhile she continued to look him up and down with a diligence that breathed new life into the phrase. At one point she glanced over her shoulder along the passage behind her, perhaps making some physical calculation. Patrick waited, trying as often before to appear natural and thinking to himself that whoever said practice made perfect had kept his own counsel on the quantity of practice required. Finally, without saying what had tipped the scale in his favour, the woman backed off into the house, retreated with her face turned towards him, pointed grudgingly to a door that had on it a chipped and discoloured finger-plate of engraved glass.

'In there,' she said, keeping a close watch on him to the end.

Eric gave a first impression of being thinner and fitter, even younger, than when last seen, like somebody back from holiday, but when he got up with a smile of pleasure to greet Patrick he

251

had more of a convalescent air. The room was a fearful auntie's paradise, featuring pampas tops in columnar vases and, on a shelf apparently covered in mauve velvet, a cubiform teapot in pink and gold china with a half-inch spout in one corner, not to speak of other objects. There was a smell of expensive embrocation.

'Nice of you to look in, Patrick. Hell of a way for you to come.'

'Not really.' Patrick tried to settle in a discontinuously-padded chair where some unremembered Victorian poetess of tubercular disposition must often have perched. 'There's a defaulting printer just round the corner I had to go and ballock. I mean one of us had to, so I said I would, and here I am.'

'Nice of you all the same,' said Eric, who seemed to be speaking more quietly than usual. 'Jenny all right, is she?'

'She's fine. She sends her love. She went and saw Stevie yesterday.'

'Oh yes?'

'He's coming out tomorrow afternoon. He'll have a nasty scar on his neck for a bit but I gather that's all. But I expect you knew that.'

'How did he seem, did Jenny think?'

'Oh, all right. In fact very cheerful. Apparently the nurses have got the idea he grappled bravely with some sort of masked intruder and thereby saved the lives of who knows how many defenceless women and children and dogs.'

'That'll be the old TV and film image at work there,' said Eric informatively and still quietly.

'As will surprise nobody who knows him.' Patrick was glad he had not given the lead in any round of guffaws. 'Apparently he said he hoped he'd be able to go on living in old number 1A for a bit. But you've probably heard that too.'

'Yes, I have, Patrick.'

'Yes. Well. You seem well enough settled here. Did you say you were out on bail?'

'The police don't really mind the likes of me, you see, as long as we stick to stabbing people and that, nice uncontroversial stuff. No opposition to bail in my case. Old Armitage, remember him, my chief, he gave me a cracking write-up. Decent responsible cove like me, they should think themselves lucky I didn't do myself an injury. That magistrate, though, he doesn't like

252

me at all. In these mistakenly tolerant days we must be doubly vigilant against corrupting forces in our society. I'll be up before him again in a couple of weeks, charged with assault occasioning, as it's familiarly known, meaning occasioning ABH, that's actual bodily harm. Actual's better than grievous, but not by much it needn't be, and I was feeling quite downcast at my prospects until Tim came calling the other day. He'd been having a chat with the magistrate. Told him if he could be reasonably sure I wouldn't be sent to prison, then he reckoned he could give me strong advice to plead guilty. Hundred-nicker fine should do it. That's no joke for a man in my position, but Tim said he'd . . .'

Eric's voice died away and Patrick saw he was trying not to cry. After a moment he went on, 'In spite of everything I've nothing against Tim, never have had, never will have. Like tea, do you, Patrick?'

'What? Oh yes. Yes, I'm very fond of tea.'

'Good, because you'll be getting some brought in any moment. My sister likes to give my visitors tea and so they get tea, and sweet FA anybody can do about it.'

'You did tell her I was coming, did you?'

'Oh yeah. She'll have had the kettle on a low gas.'

'And who I was and everything?'

'Oh yeah. It's funny the way it's taken her. Before this she was fine. She didn't know much about my habits and she didn't want to know. Whatever they might be they were unpopular with the police, and she knows about that, she really appreciates that, Cedric, meaning her old man, Cedric having gone down for eighteen months one time just for hitting a copper, never mind what they called it. He got hard labour thrown in, this was back in '46 when inside really *was* inside. It was a lot, yeah, but he'd been leading them a dance something cruel for years with his forged petrol coupons, Cedric had.

'Sorry. What I was going to tell you, Patrick, me being concerned in an affray was water off a duck's back or better where Gertie was concerned, but I had to go and blab about all the other, didn't I, not forgetting the change in the law, and that was fatal. It sounds hard to credit, I realise that, but it's as if my habits didn't bother her whilst they were illegal, she could almost respect them, but now, well, I must be behaving like that on purpose, because I like it. It never does to blab,

253

does it? Ever. So he said he was sorry, it was nothing to do with him, if it was him making the rules I could put out my hand and he'd drop a refund straight into it, but unfortunately that was not the way of the world. Oh thank you very much, dear, that's really most thoughtful.'

Patrick had not seen the door open, and lacking a Bushman's ears had not heard it either, but sure enough Gertie as predicted was bringing in the tea, tea in a full sense, a pot not square but hemispherical on four stout feet, two polygonal cups and saucers in a butterfly pattern, spoons with a large olive-coloured bead at the top of the shank, hot-water jug, milk-jug with muslin cover incorporating more beads, two kinds of sugar, two kinds of biscuit, two kinds of *napkin*, or rather serviette . . . oh God, all laid out on the snowy linen of a two-tiered dinner-wagon. Somewhere in the house a clock struck the quarter. Past ten. In the bloody morning. In the long interval of unloading Patrick had seen all he wanted of this brother and sister with their coalition of intimacy and hostility, like a horrible little bit of marriage. Eric, trying feebly and vainly to be allowed to help with the tea-things, was uncomfortable in an unfamiliar way, and did look seedy, almost frail. There had been something repulsive and pitiful in the fluency with which he had said all that about the magistrate and Cedric and blabbing, as if the show had to go on.

'Milk and sugar?' he said now.

'Yes please. No, no sugar. Or milk actually. Is this standard or specially for me?'

'Oh, standard. Well, I say standard, Armitage come tea-time, four-thirty I mean, and he was lucky not to get chicken-and-ham pie and sweet Martini. It's partly doing the correct thing, you know, keeping up the style in a way it never was, and partly getting back at me for being here. After all, she is a woman.'

'Is Cedric around these days?'

'Nah, drove his Jag into a fire-engine on Brixton Hill eight years ago it is now. Him and me, we didn't get on so's you'd notice. I've never cared for blokes who lead that type of life. He didn't leave Gertie much, as you can see. Nine-tenths of it went to a bit of stuff in Kilburn. He was a good-looking fellow, I'll give him that. And he picked Gertie. Well, Patrick, you've seen my little bit of family. I was quite looking forward to

254

coming here after everything, but I'd hardly laid eyes on Gertie since we were at home together. The wedding, Cedric's funeral, and that was about the lot. And now, however much I might like to, I'm obviously not going to be able to stay here for ever.'

Patrick said nothing. Eric took off the discus-sized teapot-lid and poured hot water in. He had slowed down a good deal since Gertie had left them alone together.

'I think if you look ahead far enough,' he said, 'my life will be reverting to normal, if you'll excuse the expression. Not in every respect. Job's not that much of a worry, Armitage says I'll probably have to go in the end but I'll wind up somewhere not too painfully dissimilar. As for 1A Lower Ground, there's a clause in the contract where you promise them not to engage in unseemly behaviour. There always is. I'm afraid I've broken that one more often than I like to think, and got away with it in the past, but this time . . .' Eric went into one of his rare old-maidish grimaces and tut-tutted at himself.

'When you talk about things getting back to normal . . .' Patrick took another of the rather irritatingly good biscuits.

'With Stevie, yeah. Not there was much abnormal to speak of about that dust-up I had with him the other night. We've always had our squabbles, part of the way of life. Of course, the coppers having to be brought in, there was a novelty there. First time with a knife, too, there's that to be laughed off. But, you have to face it, nice little flat somewhere all ready to walk into and somebody earning regular, that's what wins Stevie's heart. Always has. Line of least resistance.'

This last part had been said quite indulgently, almost tenderly. Patrick concentrated on his biscuit for a moment or two. Then he said, 'That evening, before the dust-up as you call it. The part that led up to it. You didn't, did you, seriously think he was making a play for Tim, surely?'

'Oh no, that was what made me so hot under the collar. Mocking me with a thing like that, as silly and put-on as that,' said Eric, and adjusted his glasses. 'Now I know I went too far. Remember the Arcadia Club, Florrie and the major? They can read the papers there as well as anywhere else. I should have thought of that. That Maltese fellow, Colin Zurrico, you saw him, I wasn't going to go near the place anyway for a bit, like a quarter of a century, but just to be on the safe side he rung

255

me up and put me squarely in the picture. Very succinct, he was. Oh, I was lucky it lasted as long as it did.'

Eric was not boring him, but Patrick had begun to think about how soon he could get away. With his eye on an escape-route he had arranged to come here early so as to seem to have to proceed nearly as early to the negligent printer, who while fully real and adjacent and negligent could have been called on at any time within reason or even castigated down the telephone without much loss of effect. Now, when departure had crossed his mind, he tried to suppress the idea, to start lounging in the poetess's chair as if the whole day had suddenly become available to him, but Eric had seen.

'Nice of you to have come out, Patrick. It can't be very easy for you to understand, all this carry-on. But I'd like you to try.' Eric yawned savagely. 'You see, with all the differences, and if you and I were to add them up separately I know I'd score a lot more than you would, there's something I've been trying to define for years without really getting anywhere, but . . . The best I can do, you and I are by nature, by our respective natures, males who are irresistibly attracted by a non-male principle. In your case, straightforward, women; in my case not straightfor-ward, not women – *but*, non-male, except anatomically. And it's the clash between male and non-male that causes all the trouble. They're different from us. More like children. Crying when things go wrong. Making difficulties just so as to be a person.'

Eric had got up and taken a couple of paces towards the window. Now he whirled round and pushed a forefinger out at Patrick, like an old-school Shakespearean actor with half a monologue to go. '*And*, more important and practical, I'm as much tied up with Stevie as you are with Jenny. That doesn't mean I think Stevie's as nice and decent and as bright as Jenny. I couldn't, could I? That bag is indefensible, thinks of nobody but herself, not by choice, by her nature, she can't help it either. I know a lot of people in my position aren't in my position. Sorry, what I mean, a lot of pooves don't form these attach-ments. I can't help that. Perhaps most of them don't. So what, it makes no difference if I'm the only one in the world. Some-times I think I am. But I could no more leave that silly tart than fly in the air.'

Patrick tried to turn some of this over in his mind, but was distracted by wondering whether he was right in his impression that Eric had once or twice earlier referred to Stevie by the masculine pronoun, and what of it. He said, 'You mean there's no free will in sex?'

'Moths round a candle-flame, Patrick. That much say in the matter.'

'And there's only one candle-flame per moth?'

Without answering, Eric began moving gently towards the door. 'This law's going to make a lot of difference, you know. Not straight away, but when it's sunk in. I'd like us to stay in touch if you would. Because Patrick, I'm going to need blokes like you more then than I've ever needed you in the past. We all are. Yeah, you're not much but you're all we've got. Which way did you come?'

'Mile End Road.'

'This time of day you'd do better going up Bethnal Green and along City Road to the Angel.'

Patrick followed this advice. Behind the wheel he had an excellent opportunity to ponder on what Eric had said to him, but he did not take it. His visit to the printer had brought him face to face with four people one after the other, none possessing the slightest acquaintance with the matter that had taken him there. One of the four, however, did possess an apparently horizontal bosom. These days he was not supposed to look at bosoms at all, but he let this one weigh with him to the point of sparing its owner the display of menace and general implacability he put on for her colleagues. It was not much of a display, but he hoped vaguely that word of it would reach the guilty parties and felt that Hammond & Sutcliffe should get some return on their time.

The brother of the co-founder of the business no longer worried about things like that. When in its offices, which was not every day, Jack Sutcliffe went round them or held court in them simply being the publisher of the new Deirdre. He had not, as had been likely at one stage, moved to the rival house of Grimmett Bradman, but under Deirdre's influence had stayed with the old firm, where she said she felt more comfortable herself. So there he was in the hall as Patrick arrived, seeing off a couple of advertisers or broadcasters or some such journeymen with supercharged cordiality – 'Be back to you when I've put it to her' he said a couple of times. His new grey suit had a

257

fashionable sheen to it and he displayed not only an Old Something-Else-Again tie but a buttonhole, a rose you knew he would tell you had come out of his garden if he caught you looking anywhere near it. He inclined his head briefly but civilly to Patrick.

Upstairs, Simon sat with his feet on his desk telephoning and smoking a medium-sized cigar with an amber-coloured plastic holder. His outfit included an olive-drab infantry jacket and a Guevara beret pushed back on his head, its indoor position. Observing Patrick with his usual eye he made a skimming motion towards a chair. The elbow of his telephoning arm moved further and further out to the side as he struggled to wrench the instrument from his ear. He had barely achieved this and drawn in breath to address Patrick when there was a very quick knock-and-enter and Jack appeared. He came over with exaggerated delicacy, half on tiptoe. It could not have been said that he looked younger, especially after a glance at his eyes and the areas round them, but he was certainly showing more will to survive than he once had.

'Anything for me?' he mouthed in a sickroom undertone.

'Doesn't seem to be, Jack. You shouldn't have bothered to – '

'Just one little point *from* me if I may.' Jack switched his bloodshot gaze over to Patrick, who could have sworn that for once in his life the old buffer was glad to register him among those present. 'I've been meaning to say, but these last couple of weeks have been a bit hectic, in fact that's really it, just *I'm sorry* I seem to be dealing with all manner of things that are really *your* prerogative as head of the firm, er, Simon. It's just that, well, I am an old buddy of Deirdre's and you know what these old girls are like, they do tend to insist when they can on dealing with the fellow they're used to, even if he's a poor old antique like me, what? I've done my best to keep you informed about everything and I can only say I'm very sorry if anything's slipped through the mesh.'

'That's all right, Jack, I *quite* understand your feelings,' said Simon, doing his best to fight back with a humouring job. 'But I can't honestly – ' The telephone rang and he snatched it up with appalling speed. After some grunts and eye-exercises he handed it wordlessly to Jack.

There followed a double set of variations on 'Oh yes' and 'Oh really' while the poor old antique first contemplated and

258

then by degrees carried out the removal of an inadequate petal from his buttonhole without, so to speak, dropping anything. Much against his will Patrick followed the performance through to the end. Having hung up in a stagey, finicky way, Jack said, 'Sorry again, chaps. I keep trying to tell 'em if they can't get me on my extension to leave a message with my girl but you know what film people are, eh? Actually I can't imagine what the devil they want with me, I'm nobody and I keep telling 'em so, but there's Deirdre saying whatever it's about she wants me there to hold her hand. Quite ridiculous. Oh, I did tell you they're hoping to get Alec Guinness to play H.G.Wells, did I?'

He did, or had, but Patrick answered before he could stop himself, 'Oh, isn't that marvellous! That'll really lend it a touch of distinction if you know what I mean.'

'My very words as near as dammit.' Jack squinted momentarily at Simon. 'Not that they care a curse what I think, of course. Now I mustn't take up any more of your time. Oh, just one thing, Simon – glad I thought of it. Could you pass the word to whoever it is and ask them to get their skates on about my new room, you know, where the board-room was. They swore blind they'd put me in by the first of the month and the place is still festooned with step-ladders. If you would.'

With an unwonted flicker of restraint Jack left it at that. When he had gone, Patrick said something like, 'Well, I suppose we'll just have to put up with it, you know.' He felt a show of sympathy or support, in theory at any rate, was due to a man who had thought with fair reason that he was paying out a frightening sum for a supposedly sensational novel on the stipulation that he would be rid of a person he very much wanted to be rid of, and then found he was somehow paying the money and keeping the person after all.

Simon betrayed no appreciation of this fraternal gesture. 'Do you have anything for me? I don't for you,' he said guilelessly. Or it might just have been apathetically. He had a bad-news look about him today that Jack's demonstration could not fully account for.

'I couldn't get hold of Sargent-Stokes. Or his second-in-command.'

'Who? Where on earth have you been? What second-in-command?'

'That fellow, that printer in Stepney. The one who wanted more money for taking longer. And couldn't spell "priority".'

'Oh . . .' The trip had been entirely Simon's idea, but it was as if all memory of it had been erased from his mind. 'Well . . .'

'I'll try another time.'

'That business down your way, well it was in your place, wasn't it? You know, that chap who went for his pal with a knife. Nasty business that must have been.'

'Oh. Yes, it was rather.' Patrick wondered if the other had really forgotten the couple of times they had already discussed the matter. 'Could have been worse.'

'I suppose they won't be able to go on living there, those two, will they, after a business like that?'

'No, I gather not, actually I've just been – '

'Barbara never stops talking about what marvellous little flats those are. Well, she had more or less stopped until this thing came up and she was on at me straight away to check with you that the place will be vacant. She's still very keen, you see. And it just so happens that I think it's rather a good idea too. You don't happen to know if it's unoccupied at the moment?'

Patrick did his best to indicate that he was not to be depended on even in the smallest detail of the present and future status of 1A Lower Ground. He had forgotten to think up a fictitious rent-increase that might frighten Simon off without appearing grossly fanciful. With a deepening sense of alarm and helplessness he watched Simon drop his extinct cigar into a dismal pop-art basket or bin, claw the awful beret off his head and throw it backhanded across the room, and tell the switchboard he wanted no more calls, perhaps none in this life, for he added nothing about further notice. Nevertheless when he began to speak it was in a tone of leisurely explanation.

'It's only for a few months while we sort out our house in the country. We've got to get out of our place in Hampstead in a bit of a hurry. Great bore. We're really looking long-term for somewhere more substantial round here or in Bayswater.' Then, after only a short pause and at almost the same pitch, Simon went on, 'Barbara and I haven't been getting on too well recently. We've been having . . . difficulties.'

Oh, not another dose of those for Christ's sake, thought Patrick, not at this stage of the game. Consternation and apathy swept through him together. He felt like the man in the science-fiction story whose neighbours kept turning out one after the other to be androids. He said he was sorry to hear what he had been told.

'It's these books and articles she's always reading that tell her about her right to things like physical fulfilment. I happened to take home a copy of Anthea Schmutzige's *Trigger My Bomb* which we published last spring and I don't think it's been out of Barbara's sight since. Of course it's all fantasy really but she takes it literally. It puts me in an impossible position. And I mean impossible.'

'Well, it would put . . . King Kong in a *delicate* position,' faltered Patrick.

'Women shouldn't be encouraged to take the initiative in my experience.'

'Absolutely asking for trouble.'

'There were no difficulties to speak of till about a year ago, she seemed perfectly content with how we'd always been. Then quite suddenly she wouldn't leave me alone. I've thought about it a fair bit and the conclusion I've come to is she needs an outside interest. That's to say, she'll have to get what she wants from somewhere else. The question is where. I don't want things to get out of hand so it's got to be somewhere safe.' One of his eyes would have been quite enough to reinforce his message but he gave Patrick both for good measure. 'Somewhere I can stay close to. Somewhere . . .'

Not for this fellow the little informal lunches à deux (£15 a time), the avowals of friendship, the boys' night out (up to £30), the escalation of confidences, the sheer drinks (from 5s.) that a different type might have thought appropriate before offering his wife to another man, one he could hardly trust implicitly or even like much, but that was a different issue. After all, he had clinched many a momentous deal within these walls as briskly, at no more expense and with a similar avoidance of calling a spade a spade. Without much forethought Patrick said, 'I reckon one has to go carefully with anything like that. Approach it with great circumspection.'

'When you say carefully, you mean . . .'

'I mean very carefully. Very carefully indeed.' Patrick's thumbs were on the point of searching for the armholes of his gown. 'Best avoided in my view. Totally avoided.'

'You mean even if – '

261

'Whatever the circumstances.'

'You're probably right.'

After taking out another cigar and putting it back, Simon reached forward and told the switchboard he was now taking calls again. Patrick felt no lessening of the sharp desire to leave that had built up in him, but could not see how to for the moment. Then on the shelves behind Simon he caught sight of part of a book-jacket he thought he recognised.

'How's the poetry series coming along?' he asked with real interest.

'The *poetry* series?'

Simon had spoken not only as if he had no personal knowledge of any poetry series but as if even the term itself had no meaning for him, putting completely in the shade his nescience over the Stepney printer. In doing so he reminded Patrick with some force of the moment in the Powell novels when the narrator chap gets no change whatever out of his uncle on asking him if he has news of a former attachment of his who told fortunes with cards, Mrs Turdley or some such name. At the same moment a car-horn in the square below sounded a distinctively plangent yelling note that by accident or design was destined to continue without pause a little longer than the current conversation. Nevertheless Patrick said doggedly,

'Yes. Poets in Progress was the series title I think.'

It would have been asking too much for Simon to tell him at this point and in so many words that he could not understand what he was driving at, but he got as far as anybody could be expected to without recourse to speech. Not that he remained silent for long. Retrieving his beret, but deciding against wearing it for the moment, he said, 'Yes, when it comes to it I dare say I'll be quite sorry to go.'

'Go?' Patrick very nearly said. Faster than he would have believed possible, the notion of one man being unable to follow what another man was saying stopped being at all funny. He did manage to say, 'I think there must be something you haven't told me.'

'What? Oh, I wanted you to be the first to know. Yes, we're entering the age of the agglomerate without any question. Actually I find a merger with Grimmett Bradman rather an exciting idea as well as logical, I don't know about you. All right, they are quantitatively the larger establishment, but the main thing

262

is, I've got them to guarantee the total integrity of the H & S imprint. I needn't tell you you're on the list of key people here, so I shouldn't worry too much about your future if I were you.'

'I imagine you're doing quite nicely out of this yourself.'

'One mustn't complain,' said Simon philosophically.

'And you're off where?'

'Sorry?'

'You said you were going.'

'Oh. Oh yes, er, it's called Head of Lively Arts at LCM, that's LCM Television. Quite a challenge, don't you think? But there'll be a seat for me on the board of the new company, so it looks as if we shan't be losing touch. Anyway, nothing can happen before the end of the year.'

'Oh, that's all right, then.' Patrick thought for a brief moment of Deirdre, now translated to Grimmett Bradman after all with Jack attached, attached thereby to his job far more securely than any mere key person could hope to be. 'Is that the lot for now?'

'Yes, I think so. I hope to see you at the board-meeting – our next regular board-meeting that is.'

'Yes of course.'

'Oh, and on that thing, I underestimated the booksellers' inflexibility.'

'You what?'

'Sorry, I thought you were asking about that poetry series.'

Over the next half-hour or so things presented themselves to Patrick in a rather random order. They led off with a couple he would have said he had forgotten. The reason why he (and Jenny) had been invited up for that Saturday brunch was now clear. He even understood something he had considered for less than five seconds, what had been in Simon's mind when he so abruptly marched Jenny off to meet the Australian troubadour and left him advantageously alone with Barbara. But as to which of the two had conceived the masterplan and how far back . . . Surely not as far as that dinner-party in Herts?

In the hall of the building he was confronted by a broad-shouldered man in his forties who looked to him like a Spanish priest and was certainly wearing a sort of black suit and hat. The man had been sitting on a mahogany bench meant for visitors and his speed off it and into Patrick's path was impressive. When he spoke he sounded as if he was doing an imitation of something.

'Are you the managing director of this concern?'

He sounded as if he came from somewhere in Wales too, and the only relevant person who did was assuredly a man of the cloth, albeit one who had had it taken away from him. 'Good God no,' said Patrick – 'but you must be – '

'Pedrain-Williams of Betws-y-coed.' He shook Patrick's hand ferociously and two brisk remarks later was saying, 'Very demeaning indeed it is for a learned man to be told by a mere purveyor of books to send himself back to school and commence to master a fashion of composition more pleasing to English gentlemen and then to have an entire promise of publication broken in his face will you please consider. Also uncourteous to a scholar in truth to oblige him to kick his heels until such time as the managing director of a cluster of tradesmen shall not be too far distant in the realms of commerce to be recalled to his tasks of service do you see. A little shit tried to push me out of the door just now,' he went on without changing his delivery, 'but by damn I soon showed him who was top dog.'

'The managing director is available now,' said Patrick. 'In fact you're just in time. He's getting his things together ready to cut and run. In five minutes he'll be gone by the back stairs. First floor.'

The author of *Blood in the Tigris* gave an inarticulate cry and made for the stairs, swinging a heavy black briefcase in what even somebody moving fast in the opposite direction might have found a rather frightening way.

When not lunching at the expense of his own or another's firm, Patrick went home in order to save money or tell himself he was doing that. Today he spent the journey fending off thoughts of unemployment with thoughts of how he had turned down Simon's donation of his wife, how spontaneously, instinctively, irrevocably. At this all too safe stage he visualised Barbara's shape and fairly narrowly avoided driving into a (male) pedestrian on a zebra crossing. But he had unprompted turned her down. Perhaps he was growing up at last, a hope he tried to cling to when he found himself wondering how much difference, if any, he might have made to his prospects of continuing with Hammond & Sutcliffe by accepting Simon's offer instead. He would never know, any more than he would

264

ever know what he would have done if Tim had not been present when Eric went for Stevie with the knife.

He parked the Mini in the alley and crossed the road, where now he was on foot himself the traffic seemed to him to be speeding to and fro with a new savagery. He was having quite a good time despising a man resolved to lease his wife to another when it occurred to him that he had tried something not so dissimilar on his own account not so long before. No, actually pretty dissimilar. Different reason, for one thing. And anyway . . .

By now Patrick was pretty well used to the new interior of the Princess Beatrice. It had been furnished, admittedly a new thing for a pub to be in his experience, and was now a long continuous room got up rather in the style of the model lounge to be seen in the department store window opposite the flat. But it looked more expensive and was more comfortable, or would be until the pastel-blue upholstery went knobbly. Up a couple of carpeted steps that had not been there before a juke-box slumbered for the moment, but showed its readiness by being lit from within and humming sonorously. The snob-screens and ornamental corks and stoppers had of course vanished, along with the alcove under the window where Patrick and Jenny had taken their drinks once or twice.

Well, he was more used to the look of the place than to that of its landlord. On Cyril's formerly naked skull a saucer-sized tonsure was now surrounded by a thick belt of mouse-coloured stubble, and a similar operation seemed to have been launched on all the hair-producing parts of his face. He wore a tan suede jacket with a central zip and knotted round his neck a green silk scarf covered with little pink caricatures of people on skis.

'Want me to give you one, do you?' he asked Patrick with conscious humour.

'Make it two while you're about it.'

First looking this way and that with pretended furtiveness, Cyril reached below the counter-top, brought out an opened paper packet of Gauloises and passed two over. He shook his head slower and slower as Patrick lit one and put the other ready.

'What do you want to go on mucking about like this for? Why can't you either give it up or come out and bloody smoke?

265

It can't do your system any good, you know, this neither one thing nor the other.'

'No, I do know. It's just a thing about me.'

'I mean how can it? White Shield?'

'Please.' When it had come and Patrick had paid the right price for it and double for the cigarettes, he said, 'Ta. Quiet today. People got something better to do, have they?' This was meant half-humorously too, in feeble satire on pub ritual and not far off a ritual of his own by now.

'They'll be in tonight, mate. When *Coronation Street*'s over. Some of 'em before, I shouldn't wonder.' He gestured with his half-grown head at the juke-box. 'Yeah, it brings the youngsters in, you see. I'll tell you something now. You know my motto? 'Plus ça change.'

'Right,' said Patrick after a pause.

'There's those as'll break and those as'll bend. I'm bending, mate. I'll go along with all this' – he moved his head more largely, bringing in the new décor and more abstract spheres beyond it – 'as long as I consider it expedient. Survival, that's the name of the game. As long as all these glorious new ideas are in the ascendant I'll stick with 'em. But no longer than that, Peter, not a teeny-weeny moment longer.'

It had been 'Patrick' for weeks, to all appearance irreversibly, but over just the last couple of days the text had become corrupted. The timing of this one was not good for Patrick, whose vision had turned greyish and was pulsating slightly as the nicotine surged into his bloodstream.

'I remember a poem at school. "We are the secret people of England, and we have not spoken yet," and when we do, look out, a few of you. Because we won't just be speaking. Chester-field, that was it.'

When Cyril moved away, Patrick was surprised to find himself soon wishing he would come back. The interval was overcast by unwelcome thoughts, one in particular being that arriving home had ceased to be the unconditionally pleasant prospect it had always been. So, on being served with a large Scotch, Patrick hardly minded at all for the moment when Cyril said to him,

'I see that next-door neighbour of yours got taken for a hundred quid.'

'Yes, I think he was quite lucky.'

266

'He'd have gone inside if he hadn't been deserving of special sympathy as a member of a persecuted social group. You want to know how long I give all that?'

'All what?'

'All what?' Cyril spoke in light clear tones, as to a child. 'All the filth in the papers and on TV and the bad language and the living in sin and going round half-naked and letting the kids do as they like and all the abortions and the sex education and the . . .' His voice strengthened. '*And* encouraging very disgusting people indeed to behave exactly as they like with who they like *where* they like. I give it five years, same as till they bring back the rope. Ten at the outside, before the people speak out.' Cyril stretched out his hand behind the counter where Patrick remembered or guessed he kept the pointed iron bar he had once shown him. 'Know what I mean?'

'I think so, yes.' Now, Patrick could see every reason for going home. He drained his whisky.

Cyril watched him. 'You seem like an educated man,' he said.

'Well, that's good to hear. What about it?'

'Nothing. How's that, er, very beautiful young wife of yours?'

'Fine, thank you.'

A what-about-it went with that too, a silent one, and Cyril again declined to answer, but moved his mouth and eyes in a way that suggested grave doubt of Patrick's fitness to be a husband to that wife, or perhaps any wife, anyway that was how Patrick took it at that moment. Then the landlord shifted himself along to the little old girl with the shawls and jewellery who had come up to the bar.

The sky had turned dark with thunder in the last half-hour, darker than slate over 1 Lower Ground. A narrow sunbeam rather theatrically lit up part of the front of the building, missing by some yards the figure of Jenny at the sitting-room window. One of her pot-plants was near her on the sill and she might have been attending to it just before, but she now stood looking fixedly downwards through the glass, perhaps not seeing much. Soon she dropped her head further, paused and slowly turned away in a movement that expressed for Patrick all he had ever imagined of resignation, disappointment and loneliness. He tried to swallow, and said 'Like the base Indian' in a voice that

267

made an old bag in a green check trouser-suit swing round and stare at him in an affronted way.

Nineteen

'If you stick your finger up your nose in front of me again,' said Jenny, 'I'll bite it off.'

'You . . . couldn't do that.'

'Care to try me?'

Six-year-old Brian looked dazed, a bit more than he did all the time, and too much so in any case to hold on to what Jenny had said, but then when his finger was halfway back to his nose some twitch of insect-level instinct made him lower it once more. He wriggled against his pillows. 'I'm going home on Friday,' he said, keeping his jaws open after he had spoken.

'Don't count on it.'

'. . . What?'

'I'll see you tomorrow. When I do, I'll expect you to have gone over this page and drawn a little circle round any of the words you find you can't read. The pencil's on there.' With a nice long point so you can get through marking all the real stinkers like *cup* and *bat* and *leg*.

He came back to her fast on that one, about low-IQ-pensioner speed. 'Our teacher at school . . . she says it's old-fashioned to spell words all the time. She says – '

'Maybe she does, but she won't be here tomorrow. I shall.'

'I think you're marvellous with that Brian,' said the Manchester sister as Jenny was leaving. 'We can't wait to see the back of him here. Nasty little bit of work.'

'Bad luck on him picking up that virus, wasn't it?'

'Bad luck on us too. No, it goes deeper than that. Mind you, what can you expect? Mother living with a coloured gentleman. I mean it's not really fair on a youngster, is it?'

Before Jenny could think what to say they had reached the door of the sister's cubby-hole.

'You are looking well, Jenny dear, much better than a few weeks ago. Like a ruddy advert for vitamin pills or something. You're a fair treat to see.'

That was as nice as anybody could wish for, and it seemed carping to wish Sister had not said it exactly when she had, but there it was. But then again anything like that soon disappeared in the marvellous sunshine outside and in various thoughts. With Patrick coming home for lunch, as he mostly did now, Jenny skipped the hospital canteen, which if the truth were known was no great loss these days. By 1 o'clock she had reached No 1 Lower Ground, where for the first time in her life she saw the door of 1C standing open and heard voices from inside. Curiosity fought a brief, familiar battle in her with the irksome duty of keeping oneself to oneself, and as usual irksome duty won, but it was less than a minute before someone rang her doorbell.

A young girl stood there. She was quite pretty in a pale, rather shiny way and well enough turned out and she seemed a bit shy and was very friendly and was not one of Patrick's types, but it was the young part that struck Jenny, that and a sort of unused look.

'Mrs Standish? I'm called Mrs Fellows, Diana Fellows. Me and my husband are just – '

'Oh, you must be the couple who've been living abroad.'

Over the next two or three minutes it was established at top speed that that was true up to a point and so was a good deal else besides, until Mrs Fellows mentioned the name of Mr Bigger, who had very kindly come down with them to show them how to turn on the –

'Mr Bigger?' said Jenny. 'You mean the superintendent man?'

'Yes, he's been ever so – '

'Where is he now?'

'Well, he's just been showing my husband the – '

In a flash and without trouble, Jenny put aside her cultural conflict about whether to offer Mrs Fellows a drink or put the kettle on. After making a remark or two that she forgot before she had finished speaking she hurried out on to the walk literally just as Mr Bigger was leaving. She recognised him straight away even though he was about forty years younger and a foot shorter

270

than she remembered from their one encounter those months before. The master-skiver was a thin, freckled, sandy-haired type who, she saw just as fast, could stay ahead of the game as easy as winking while he was on the telephone, or rather not on the telephone, but soon caved in when faced by a determined person in the flesh. 'If you'd like to come up with me now I'll just show you the stain on my bedroom ceiling.'

'I'm afraid I must be – '

'It won't take you a minute.'

At the end of that minute he was saying with spineless hatred that he would do something about it on Monday.

'Where can I ring you?'

'My number's in the – '

'I mean really ring you, Mr Bigger.'

From the way he looked at Jenny now it was not at all hard to guess that he had seen some of this coming from the moment he had heard her arrive at 1B, certainly from when Mrs Fellows had popped along to drop in on her new neighbour and left him just five seconds too few to disentangle himself from Mr Fellows and run for it. He took a card from his wallet, quailed under Jenny's eye, crossed something out with a ballpoint, wrote something in and passed the amended card to her like a mayor handing over the keys of a captured town in the Hundred Years' War.

'There's something you can do for me right away if you would,' said Jenny.

He waited with his arms dangling.

'Perhaps you'd tell that Linda not to come to me again. She's untrustworthy, idle, incompetent and dishonest. And cheeky with it. So please could you send me someone else.'

'I'll see what I can do. I mean I'll send you someone else.'

'Thank you very much indeed, Mr Bigger.'

'My pleasure, Mrs Standish.'

For five minutes or so after that, in and out of 1B and 1C, Mr and Mrs Fellows asked Jenny questions and told her things. He wore his hair really short and brushed flat and straight across his head and looked even more as if he had turned up here straight from school than his wife did. At one point they revealed they had been married nearly a year and seemed to consider this an impressively long time. Jenny had the feeling now that she was talking to two newly arrived replacement

271

pilots in a film about the Royal Flying Corps in the Great War. How many hours' solo have you had? Six, sir (eagerly). And you? Eight, sir (proudly). And the major, no more than a youngster himself of course, turned away sick at heart, thinking it was criminal to send poor little schoolchildren like this against the ruthless Red Devils. This got so vivid just in a couple of seconds that Jenny found herself wishing Mr and Mrs Fellows good luck in a voice that quivered with suppressed emotion, but they took no notice and thanked her nicely.

This part took place at the open door of 1B, whose telephone instantly started ringing. The Fellowses scampered off hand in hand.

Jenny lifted the receiver to hear the sound of a medium-grade mental deficient reacting to having his favourite pudding being snatched off him, with a touch of an ordinary man having a nightmare. Two falsetto yelps followed.

'Hallo, Tim.'

'Is that Jenny? Tim here.'

'Yes, I recognised your voice.'

'That noise you may have heard was me sneezing. Gussie's got a cat – well, it's our cat now. She got it while I was away. Rather a nice little thing, I suppose, but I have got this allergy that makes me sneeze whenever there's a cat about. Something in their fur.'

'Yes, I remember.'

'Of course I could have put my hand over the mouthpiece, but I thought if I did you might wonder what the hell was going on. And anyway I had a drink in that hand.'

'Shame on you at this time of day.'

'It's only a glass of beer. Jenny, I thought you'd like to know Eric was very cheerful when I saw him yesterday.'

'Oh, I am glad. Where is he now?'

'Somewhere in Hackney I believe it's called. He told me I'd understand if he didn't have me along to where he was staying. He took me to a pub, a rather peculiar place, I thought. There was a . . . Hallo?'

'I'm still here.'

'He said he was having a very difficult job finding a flat to suit Stevie, who apparently wants his own sitting-room. And he did say one thing that puzzled me a good deal.' On previous form Tim would have paused here to let Jenny wonder, but this

272

time he went straight on. 'He said he hadn't been expecting it, but he found he was quite sorry not to be sent to prison after all, because it would have been such a good way of getting away from Stevie. I mean I thought they were like a married couple in spite of their differences, those two.'

'Yes, after all he did go for Stevie with a knife.'

'He said it would have been such a relief not having to worry about what he might be up to.'

'Well, there you are, then.'

'How do you mean?'

'Oh, that's a very big question. What about you, Tim? How are things with you?'

Anybody else Jenny knew would have taken this as a thoroughly unpersonal question in the circumstances, but after making a series of wordless sounds with an obvious fade where he looked over his shoulder, Tim said in a lowered voice, 'We, er, yes, we have tried it a couple of times. Three, actually.'

'And was it all right?' There was not much hope of making that sound unpersonal, but she did her best.

'Oh no, absolute disaster. No improvement at all.'

'Oh, I am sorry.'

'Except . . . I don't sort of seem to mind in the way I used to. Gussie noticed straight away. In fact she said, "You don't seem to mind in the way you used to." I think that might be a good sign, don't you?'

'Oh, most certainly it is.'

'The other thing I rang up for was to ask you and Patrick to dinner. Gussie wants to meet you. And I want to see you, of course. My sister wants to see you too. She says we all have a lot to thank you for. Got your diary?'

When they had fixed up he said, 'You know looking back, I think I must have been a bit off my rocker to leave home like that, and I don't just mean silly or misguided. What it must have been, I thought I could see a way out of what had been getting me down all those years. Well no, actually it wasn't all those years. It must have been sort of saving itself up all those years, and then it all boiled over and came bursting out when I was having a chat with a friend. He said it was shocking and wrong of me, iniquitous of me, all manner of things of me to go on putting up with what I'd got. Bloody silly way to talk. Thank God I came to my senses in time. Phew. Is Patrick there?'

273

'No, but I'm expecting him back any minute.'

'It was funny, the only time Eric looked at all fed up was when he said he knew all along he'd be back with Stevie. I just can't understand that, from Stevie's point of view. Would you calmly go back and live with someone who'd tried to kill you?'

'Not calmly, no. But people are doing that kind of thing all the time, aren't they?'

'Good Lord, are they really? I've obviously a lot to learn still. But then women always know more than men, don't they? Look forward to seeing you on the . . . Oh, Jenny, by the way . . .'

'Yes?' This must be it, what he had most wanted to say coming up.

'That night at your place, you know, when it all happened, there was just one very minor point that I found interesting, though it wouldn't mean much to anyone else. I doubt if you noticed it yourself. It's quite simple. I didn't sneeze . . . Hallo?'

'I'm still here.'

'I didn't sneeze because there was no cat in the place – one of you said your cat had gone missing, didn't you? So – no cat, no fur, no sneeze. Confirms my theory, you see. Has he turned up, by the way, your cat?'

'Yes, he came ambling in a couple of days ago.'

'Oh, good, well, they usually do, don't they?'

After Tim had rung off Jenny sat by the telephone for a minute or two and thought to herself that Tim's last few remarks had been more peculiar, or shown him to be more peculiar, than anything else she had heard him say. But then perhaps that was just her. Nothing divided people more deeply than how they felt about cats. Surely that must be her, that bit. And anyway was she sure how she felt about cats? Frankie had been reading her mind as usual and came along just then and gave her shin a dose of the head-butt treatment. She had missed him so terribly and kept imagining how she would feel if he ever came back, and then when he did she had merely gone half out of her mind with relief and delight. There must be a connection somewhere: she must have already been sure of what she had only known for a fact since this morning.

'Not until you've eaten every single one of those biscuits,' she said severely in the kitchen when Frankie made his famine-victim face at her. When that had sunk in she got out the tomatoes and set to work taking the skins off them, and was

274

ready to start the dressing by the time Patrick's key rasped in the door.

'Hallo, love.'

'Hallo, sweetheart.'

When they kissed, it might have been her fancy but she could have sworn he had guessed straight away there was something. But neither of them said anything, or anything about that. He poured himself a pretty small whisky and filled it up with water. She went on with the salad dressing.

'I heard from those academic publishing people this morning,' he said. 'They want me to go for an interview next week – well, they don't call it an interview but that's what it'll be. Er, I did mention I'd probably have to take a dip in money, didn't I?'

'Yes, and we said we'd probably survive that.'

'Yes, well, it rather looks – from the way they were talking I'd be dropping a little more than I was counting on. It would mean giving up the car and perhaps leaving here.'

'It wouldn't break my heart to do *that*.'

'No,' he said, and looked away. Then he looked back and said, grinning himself, 'What are you grinning at?'

'Oh, just, I happened to pass Mrs Porter-King Esquire OBE on the corner this morning and she had the most tremendous black eye I think I've ever seen in my life. It was so huge, she was wearing an eye-patch thing but it came out outside that all the way round. It had sort of red and mauve edges.'

'Well, anyone can walk into a door.'

'She must have been going like a bat out of hell, uh-boy.'

Jenny thought of going on to say that if Mrs Posherina Barbara Giles still felt like taking one of those dear little funny little maisonette places she would soon have three to choose from, and then of more vaguely and crudely asking Patrick to bring old-girl-friend Vanessa round one afternoon in her Yves Saint-Laurent dress to have an entire Devonshire tea with clotted cream and home-made strawberry jam poured over her, but no, it was not the day for that. So she got on with chopping the parsley for the omelette very small and started to tell him about the Fellowses and Mr Bigger.

She was still not halfway through when he said, 'Yes, but hang on a minute. What's happened? Something's happened, hasn't it?'

'Yes,' she said, and turned and faced him. She had imagined

275

herself looking stern at this point for a joke, but now she came to it she could not have stopped smiling for anything in the world.

'Please don't ask me to guess, I couldn't bear to get it wrong.'

'Oh, I'd never do that. What it is, I'm going to have a baby.'

He put his glass down on the kitchen table.

'I got the result of the conclusive test just this morning but I think I'd known some time before then. I asked the doctor if he thought it would stay, you know, after what happened before, and he said there was nothing to show I was any more likely to lose it than any other mother. But don't go falling down any stairs, he said.'

Patrick's face was covered with tears. He came over and put his arms round her and just squeezed, and they stayed like that for some time.

'How wonderful,' he said. 'For us both. I'd stopped hoping or imagining. You clever little thing.' He kissed her hands. 'You've done it. Changed everything. You've saved us.'

Jenny was happy. She was going to have him all to herself for at least three years, probably more like five, and a part of him for ever, and now she could put it all out of her mind.